MW01701173

The Shape of Time

Merlin in Moab, Book Three

CARYL SAY

Copyright © 2020 by Caryl E. Say.

All rights reserved. No part of this publication may be reproduced, distributed, or transmitted in any form or by any means, including photocopying, recording, or other electronic or mechanical methods, without the prior written permission of the written permission of the author and publisher, except in the case of brief quotations embodied in critical reviews and certain other noncommercial uses permitted by United States of America copyright law. For permissions requests, please contact the author at Caryl@carylsay.com.

This book is a work of fiction. Any references to historical events, real people, and real places are used fictitiously. Names, characters, and places are the product of the author's imagination.

Front Cover Design by Ginger Aaron.
Front Cover Image: Park Avenue, Arches National Park (Source: US Gov.).
Interior Layout by StandOut Books.

Contact the author via email at carylsay.author@gmail.com or on her website www.carylsay.com.

Printed in the United States of America

ISBN (paperback): 978-1-7348537-0-4
ISBN (ebook): 978-1-7348537-1-1

Caryl Say's MERLIN IN MOAB series

The Heart of Magic

God of Magic, Child of Light

The Shape of Time

ACKNOWLEDGEMENTS

There are many people who I would like to thank for their ongoing support of my literary efforts.

Lisa Albert, Jean Carson, Carol Martin and Amy Loren—I can't thank you enough for taking the time to read through the manuscript, make corrections and provide constructive criticism. Publishing this book would not have been possible without you.

Also, I would like to thank Miriam Graham for helping me with editing, Brad Weis at Moab Internet for website design, Barbara Grassey for marketing advice, and Ginger Aaron for designing the cover.

I would also like to express my appreciation to Chief Bret Edge of the Moab City Police Department for his assistance in pointing out some procedural errors I'd made.

And, of course, I want to thank everyone for buying my books! I'm so glad that you enjoy my stories.

Last, but not least, thanks to Peggy Di Mauro, my sister and traveling companion, for our wonderful trip to the Republic of Ireland in September, 2019.

CHAPTER 1

Caledonia, Early Fifth Century

As the last of the light faded from the sky, whatever warmth there had been during the day also faded, leaving the two of us shivering in the dark.

"Well, now what shall we do?" I muttered crossly, as hunger and thirst assailed me.

My taciturn companion merely grunted and turned away, walking purposefully back up the slight incline to the spot where we had both regained consciousness. At least I hoped that was where he was going, since I was following him and could not see my hand in front of my face. Although the sky was thick with stars, there was no moon this night and it was as black as pitch beneath the trees.

I could hear the man rustling around and wondered what he was doing. Suddenly, a length of cloth was shoved into my hands and I realized it was a cloak. Not questioning what could only be a gift from the gods, I immediately drew the thick, slightly damp wool around me, adjusting it until I found the cloak pin and fastened it snugly at my neck.

I sighed with relief as I started to warm up, and whispered a brief prayer of thanks to whatever god had taken pity on us.

"The cloaks were here, on the ground, where we first awakened. Perhaps it was Elves who left them." The man's voice was rough and unfamiliar, even though I was sure I knew him from a past encounter.

"I wonder if they have also left us food or drink," I said, hopefully, but not really expecting that to be the case.

The man handed me a skin containing some sort of liquid, and I wasted no time pulling the stopper and drinking. Despite the fact that it was stale and tasted slightly gamey, the water nevertheless seemed like ambrosia, and I had to stop myself from draining the skin dry. I hastily replaced the stopper and handed it back.

"Many thanks, my friend."

"Not your friend," the man muttered.

"Whatever you say." I felt so fatigued that all I could think about was curling up on the ground and going to sleep. I was hungry as well, but satisfying that bodily requirement would have to wait until daylight, when I could forage for berries and edible plants. I hoped that I would be able to remember which plants were edible or we would surely starve, unless my companion had a plan for obtaining food.

As if he had perceived my thoughts, my reluctant companion muttered, "I will hunt at first light, so we will have meat…Emrys."

I had given him my name shortly after we had awakened here on the hillside, but he had not yet returned the favor. I eyed him speculatively. His accent was so unusual that I could not determine from whence he came, and my curiosity finally overwhelmed my sense of caution. "Who *are* you?"

He hesitated for so long that I felt certain he would not answer. But then he said quietly, "I…do not remember..."

I lay awake for some time, exhausted but unable to sleep. The sound of my companion's stertorous breathing was a constant reminder that we were strangers to each other, thrown together for some unknown reason. I could not help but wonder how he proposed to hunt game the next morning, as neither of us had any sort of weapon in our possession.

As I finally succumbed to a restless slumber, I knew that the other man was not the only one concerned by his lack of memory.

CHAPTER 2

Moab, Christmas Eve, 2015, 11:45pm

THE CHRISTMAS TREE WAS ON fire. Bright tongues of orange and yellow flame speared upward from every branch.

Lumina blinked and the image came back into focus. The seven-foot-tall fir tree stood serenely in front of the picture window, delicate ornaments and tinsel gently reflecting the twinkling lights winding around the evergreen boughs. It was an enduring symbol of peace and goodwill that should have made her heart sing with joy, but she just couldn't get past the melancholy caused by her father's absence.

It was late now, and she knew she should have been in bed hours ago, but she'd had to wait until her mom and grandmother were fully asleep before she could put her plan in motion. She'd been waiting for weeks for a chance to read the journal, but her mother had been reluctant to let the book out of her sight until she'd thoroughly read every word the others had written and entered her own contribution.

Lumina gazed down at the leather cover of the journal in her lap, and ran her fingers over the Celtic design, appropriately called a Myrddin's Knot, tooled on the front of it. The cabochon amethyst in the center richly accented the ancient symbol.

The journal had been started sometime back when Jim Singleton, her nephew Morry's friend and roommate, had decided that everyone in their group should document their thoughts and experiences since her father had disappeared more than a year and a half ago. The intent was to try and find a common thread that might help them figure out where he was, and to bring him home. So far, it hadn't worked.

She had planned to return the journal to her mother's bedroom as quickly as possible, lest Emily wake up and realize it was gone, but she found she wasn't ready to let go of it yet. She'd read all the entries and written her own at the end, but her mind was in turmoil trying to make sense of the whole situation. Because she and her father were connected on a level so profound that only the two of them understood it, she knew that Myrddin Emrys, the god of magic—or Merlin Ambrosius as he was also known in this human realm—still existed, somewhere, in another time or dimension. She hoped that he would eventually remember his true identity and come home to them; she missed him terribly, and she was worried about her mother's state of mind. Emily's sadness grew day by day and, immortal or not, Lumina wasn't sure her mom could truly survive without her husband.

Lumina suspected that the one God, who ruled over all the gods and goddesses, had created this situation as a lesson for her father and Beli, the god of death. When they had both learned what they needed to learn, Merlin would come home. It seemed logical to her, but then, she was young, so maybe she was wrong. Maybe she should make an effort to find him.

Sis, why're ya still up? Derek's concerned voice with its slight southern accent sounded clearly in her mind. Her brother lived across the street with his fiancée, Sarah Gordon, and ever since their father had disappeared, Derek had stepped in to make sure she, Emily and Grammy Rae had everything they needed. Lumina couldn't help but grin affectionately. With a few exceptions, the whole family was immortal and had the gift of magic, so they really didn't need his protection, as such. But because he blamed himself for what happened that day, Derek felt responsible for them.

I'm not sleepy yet. I'll go to bed in a little while, don't worry. See you in the morning, 'kay? I love you, Der.

Yeah, see ya in the mornin'. I love ya, too, munchkin.

He had started calling her that about six months ago, and she wasn't sure whether she liked it or not. They had been watching *The Wizard of Oz*, and despite the fact that she wasn't anything like the characters in the movie, the endearment had stuck.

She made a face and stuck her tongue out at her brother—a futile gesture since he wasn't there to see it—then thumbed through the last few pages again.

"What's going on?" Sarah mumbled as she sensed that her lover was awake and communicating with someone telepathically.

"Everythin's okay, darlin', I was just chattin' with my sister. She's still up, readin' and writin' in the journal." Derek yawned and rubbed his eyes.

Sarah reached out and turned the light on, glancing at the clock on the bedside table. "It's almost midnight. Shouldn't she be in bed by now?"

Derek kissed her cheek and chuckled. "Ya sound like her mother. Lumina's a teenager now, so I guess she can stay up late if she wants to. Did ya think she was waitin' for Santa Claus?"

She gave him a wry look. "Hardly. But I keep forgetting that she's not a child anymore. It doesn't seem very long ago that she was just a little girl."

"That's 'cause it wasn't. Technically she's not even two yet." Derek yawned again. "God, I'm tired. Let's go back to sleep; we're supposed to be over there early for Christmas breakfast. Everyone's gonna be there, includin' Chris." He flicked a hand at the lamp and the bedroom went dark. *I love bein' able to do that*, he thought to himself as he drifted back to sleep.

Sarah turned over and took a few measured breaths as she tried to clear her mind and sleep again, but she started thinking about Derek's ex-wife and the fact that she'd become part of the group in the past year and a half. Chris was actually a very nice woman and they had formed a friendship of sorts, but it bothered Sarah that Derek still had feelings for her. And she was curious to know if Morry had really slept with Chris and… oh, hell, she'd think about it tomorrow. She finally scooted over so that her back was against Derek's. Only then was she able to fall asleep.

Lumina leaned against her bedroom door with a sigh. She was grateful that her mother hadn't stirred when she returned the journal to its original spot on the dresser, then teleported back to her own room. She crossed the thickly carpeted floor and climbed into bed, pulling the covers up to her pointy little Elf ears. She scratched the tip of first the left ear and then the right—sometimes the darned things just *itched.*

She remembered when her ears had completely changed shape to reflect her Fae heritage on her mother's side. She had experienced a major growth spurt when Merlin had reset time after the cataclysmic destruction of Moab by his nemesis Nimue. Lumina had come back to life with everyone else the morning of May 13, 2014, but she recalled very clearly being incorporeal again in the realm of the gods. And she was aware that the growth spurts she had experienced in her young life were the price she paid for the privilege of coming to this realm as the daughter of Myrddin Emrys.

She smiled to herself. Actually, she thought her pointed ears were really cool, but it was difficult to hide them effectively. It was a good thing she liked her hair long, because it covered those ears that would reveal she wasn't completely human.

Lumina was just drifting off when she heard her grandmother mumble something unintelligible in her sleep. She smiled to herself, and thought about how deeply she loved her grandmother. She wondered why Grammy's ears weren't pointed, since it was *her* grandfather who was Fae. Lumina started to doze off again, and then realized she could hear the disjointed thoughts in the older woman's dreaming mind. She felt vaguely guilty for listening in, but it was really entertaining to know that Grammy was dreaming about pledging herself to Merlin's quest.

Then her grin faded as she remembered the entries she had read in the journal. How they had all failed to locate her missing father. It was ridiculous that not one of them had succeeded in finding and bringing him home in the past year and a half. And her persistent feeling of helplessness made her even more determined to actively pursue the search for him. She *wasn't* helpless, darn it. She was powerful, she was a goddess! She just hadn't figured out yet how to fully access her powers. She did have magic, of course, and she had utilized it several times in the past to bring her father back from not only the god realm, but from Hell. But her skills as a sorcerer had so far been ineffective in locating and bringing him back from wherever he was now. She sighed sadly, decided to turn over, plumping her pillow as she did so, and finally relaxed into sleep.

CHAPTER 3

Moab, Christmas Day, 2015

CHRISTMAS MORNING DAWNED CLEAR AND cold. Emily, already dressed in a warm red sweatshirt and designer jeans, stood sipping her coffee and looking out the window at the Rim, a jagged, thousand-foot-high cliff of sandstone running the length of the Moab valley. She never tired of watching for the first rays of sun to light up the red rock cliffs, and this morning was no exception. She loved the colors and textures of the wall of rock she saw every day from the house, the boulder-strewn base of which was no more than six or seven hundred feet away. When she gazed up at the snow-covered profile of the jagged ridge so far above the rooftops of the houses across the street, she was awed by the magnificence of the ancient geological formation.

As she brought her attention back to the lambent glow of the Christmas tree next to her, Emily remembered the morning two years ago today when she had stood with Merlin in the same exact spot, admiring the view of the Rim, his arm around her shoulders as she rested her own atop a massively pregnant belly.

She gritted her teeth. *How could he* not *have known what was going to happen*? The god of magic and healing should have been able to see into the future and perhaps arranged to fix this situation ahead of time. He had told her that he couldn't always see what would happen to his own family members—including himself—so she knew she was being unreasonable, but damn it, she was so angry. She knew that her anger stemmed from her loneliness, and from the fear that she would never see her husband again, but that didn't really change anything. She closed her eyes against the tears that threatened to fall.

"Emily, honey, have some faith."

She blinked and turned towards her mother, who was standing in the hallway wrapped in a fuzzy pink bathrobe, red hair tousled and eyes still heavy with sleep.

"I'm sorry I woke you, Mom. I thought I was being quiet."

"You were quiet, darling. I sensed your emotions, which are very intense." Rae Crandall padded out to the kitchen and helped herself to a cup of coffee. She stirred in a small amount of sugar, and then joined her daughter at the living room window. "Ever since Merlin unblocked my powers I've known just how you were feeling, which in the past few months has been very sad. Oh, Em, he's a god—he'll be back, you know that. Besides, you're immortal now, so you have nothing but time." *Which is more than I have*, Rae thought, wondering when her husband would come after her. She turned her attention back to her daughter, hoping she hadn't noticed her momentary distraction.

"Don't remind me," Emily murmured, taking another swallow of her now tepid coffee. She planted a kiss on Rae's cheek. "Merry Christmas, Mom. Sorry I'm so moody."

"It's alright, darling, you know I love you, and I'll be here for you as long as you want me to be."

"I'm glad," she said softly. "Thanks, Mom." Em paused for a moment as she thought of something she'd forgotten to do. "You know, maybe I'll put on some Christmas music."

Rae smiled. "Good idea."

Around seven forty-five, Derek and Sarah decided to do the mundane thing and actually walk across the street to Emily's rather than teleport, since Sarah hadn't yet been able to adjust to the magical form of transportation Derek preferred—her stomach felt queasy every time. He couldn't figure out why this was so and sincerely hoped that in time she would become accustomed to it.

It was still early, but it was obvious from the telepathic buzz in Derek's mind that the women were already up, including Lumina, despite her late night.

"Merry Christmas!" Cheerful greetings abounded as the two of them stomped their booted feet briskly on the mat, hung their coats up on the coat tree by the door, and entered the cozy warm living room. The heavy cloud cover of the day before had released a good three inches of snow in the middle of the night and then moved on. Now, with the sun peeking over the La Sal Mountains, that layer of pure white in the yard glittered like diamonds: exquisitely beautiful, but icy cold.

After removing his outdoor footwear and conjuring a pair of fleece-lined slippers, Derek headed for the kitchen and poured himself a mug of coffee, considerately topping off Em's and Rae's cups. Lumina was sipping her usual hot chocolate, apparently enjoying the camaraderie of the family get-together. He leaned over and kissed her cheek as she acknowledged him silently with an enigmatic look.

"When is everyone else supposed to show up?" Sarah asked Emily as she walked into the kitchen and started making herself a cup of Earl Grey tea. She'd recently been experimenting with other drinks besides coffee, which had been upsetting her stomach, and she particularly enjoyed the flavor of the Earl Grey. Of course, she had to endure the inevitable teasing about being pregnant, which she wasn't.

Emily glanced at her watch. "I suspect the knights will be punctual. We planned breakfast for eight thirty, and it's barely eight now, so they have time." She turned to Derek. "Have you talked to Morry yet this morning?"

"Nope, I haven't. I'll check and see what his and Jim's plans are." His eyes became unfocused for a moment as he communicated telepathically with his son, and then he refocused on his stepmother.

"Morry and Jim'll be here in about fifteen or twenty minutes. They had a hard time climbin' outta the sack this mornin'. What do ya wanna bet Morry was out carousin' last night? He's become a real party animal lately." He grinned at the intentional pun. "And I suspect Jim was waitin' up for him. Ever since Morry decided to shift into cat form and got picked up by that good-lookin' neighbor of his, Jim's been worried that he'll give himself away and blow our cover."

"Oh, I can't believe Morry would be that irresponsible, do you? I just think that Jim's more emotional than he used to be ever since he found out he was Guinevere in a past life." Em looked at her watch again and grimaced. "I hope Chris gets here soon—she's supposed to bring the sweet rolls." She started organizing the ingredients and cooking utensils for the rest of the holiday meal.

Derek had no comment about Chris's intentions. He kind of wished she'd decided to visit her sister for Christmas. But she'd been afraid—and rightly so as it turned out—that the highway to Denver, particularly the pass at the Eisenhower Tunnel, would be closed in this weather. He still cared about his ex-wife and probably always would, but it was obvious that Sarah was inordinately jealous of her. He didn't really understand why, since he and Chris had divorced years ago and had no intention of getting back together. And besides, Sarah had his engagement ring on her finger and they were living together. Could her insecurity be the result of his refusal to get married until Merlin returned? Well, he was sorry for that, but he was adamant—no wedding without his father's presence. Then, he started thinking about Chris and Morry being here at the family gathering, and he couldn't help remembering when the two of them had had a brief affair, and how awkward it was, knowing that his ex-wife and his son were having sex. They'd actually looked kinda cute together, but it was just…weird.

He closed his eyes and sighed. The truth was that *nothing* had really been right since the day Merlin had been sucked into that wormhole in the sky.

"Sweetheart, remember we decided to try and enjoy the holidays?" Sarah had sensed his moodiness and had slipped her arms around his waist from behind, leaning against his muscular back.

"You're right, I'll try," he murmured, as he covered her small hands with his large calloused ones. That subtle tingle as they touched, reminding them of their magical connection, always pleased them both.

They stood quietly listening to the London Philharmonic Orchestra's rendition of "We Wish You a Merry Christmas," enjoying the music and each other's company. Abruptly, Sarah tightened her hold on Derek as Chris came in the door and rushed past them, heading for the kitchen with the anticipated sweet rolls. Ironically, it was now his turn to remind Sarah, gently and silently, to not let Chris's presence ruin Christmas for her.

When Morry and Jim showed up around eight fifteen, they made a big production of stamping their feet outside to dislodge most of the snow, then throwing off their heavy outerwear and hanging it on the already overloaded coat tree. The warm house smelled deliciously of sizzling bacon, scrambled eggs and cinnamon sweet rolls, and the lovely Christmas music played in the background as the sounds of laughter and conversation filled the air.

Rae had managed to sneak off and get dressed in black jeans, a flashy holiday sweater and black flats right after Derek and Sarah had arrived, and now, as she set the table, she marveled again at the interaction of this group of magical individuals. She was continually amazed that her granddaughter was almost grown, despite the fact that she had been born less than two years ago. In fact, it was extremely hard to reconcile the entire family dynamic. Besides the fact that her daughter was married to an immortal sorcerer whose son Derek also possessed magical powers, Derek's own son Morry was a shapeshifter, and Morry's friend Jim Singleton possessed the soul of Guinevere Pendragon. On top of that, the three men who had been King Arthur's knights in the fifth century walked through the front door, chatting in the ancient and long-dead British language—at least she assumed that's what it was since she couldn't understand a word of it. She knew it wasn't French; she'd studied that in school. The language the knights spoke sounded nothing like it. As she was contemplating ancient languages, she noticed the thirty-something, rough-looking blond knight stealing glances at Jim. She wondered at the emotion in those looks until she remembered that Sir Lancelot had loved Guinevere in Arthur's time, and— Rae released the breath she had been holding in one long sigh. Sometimes it was all just too overwhelming to take in. You'd think she would be used to it by now.

"Grammy, it's alright, everything is the way it's supposed to be," Lumina whispered softly in Rae's ear as she hugged her and kissed her cheek.

"I'll take your word for it, dear," Rae answered quietly, putting her arms around the tall, slim, self-assured young woman.

"Come on, let's help Mom get the food on the table." Lumina pulled away from her grandmother and grabbed her hand, and the two of them headed into the kitchen.

CHAPTER 4

Moab, Christmas Day, 2015

MORDRED COLBURN LEANED AGAINST THE wall and watched his family and friends interacting. The meal had turned out to be a happily boisterous affair; everyone enjoyed not only the food, but each other's company as well. And he was impressed that all of them cooperated so readily in getting the kitchen cleaned up after the meal, so that everyone could congregate in the living room. It had been decided that instead of presents, each person would recite a story or treasured memory of Merlin. He thought it would be a nice gesture, since many of the people attending this morning didn't have the ability to share those memories telepathically. He glanced surreptitiously at Chris, curious to know if she ever regretted breaking up with him. It was just as well that she had, though, since their affair had made his father uncomfortable.

Rae broke the ice as she began relating how Merlin had released her Elven powers almost two years ago, and what a blessed relief it had been to reconnect with her innate talents—and her daughter.

Morry soon lost track of Rae's voice, as his mind wandered back to the time shortly after his grandfather had disappeared…

Early August, 2014

He had been at work at the newspaper for a couple of hours already, but he was feeling restless and bored. When he heard a few of his colleagues raise their voices in a heated discussion about a new account, he looked up hoping something earthshaking would happen in which he could participate. His slightly long, multicolored hair gleamed in the mundane light from the fluorescent bulbs overhead, and his slanted gray eyes lent a fey aspect to his appearance. He brushed a lock of hair back from his face and thought about making an appointment for a trim. It grew so fast these days that he could hardly keep up with it. And the colors—it still gave him a jolt when he saw himself in the mirror and noted the gray, blond, black and even a few red strands, mixed in with his original medium brown.

Morry sighed as he shuffled the papers on his desk for the umpteenth time that morning. What good was it to be a supernatural being if he couldn't use his powers half the time? He closed his eyes briefly, as if resting them, and pushed his senses out past his cubicle into the room. Instantly, he knew that there were half a dozen people working, some sitting as he was, at a computer workstation, one person heading into the hallway leading to the restrooms, and one pouring coffee from a carafe in the break room.

He grinned and blinked his eyes. He'd never have to wear glasses again—yet another benefit to being a sorcerer. He cautiously opened one of his desk drawers with his mind and levitated a pad of sticky notes onto the desktop. God, he really enjoyed having magical abilities.

Suddenly, strong fingers gripped his shoulder and he nearly jumped out of his skin. The note pad flew into the air and ended up out in the middle of the aisle.

"Caught you," the male voice said quietly in his ear.

Morry quickly turned and saw his supervisor—who was also his friend—standing behind him, grinning from ear to ear.

"You bastard," he breathed, keeping his voice low.

"Is that any way to speak to your great-aunt Guinevere?" Jim Singleton took an immense amount of pleasure in reminding Morry that in his first life he had been the wife of the legendary King Arthur.

"Well, you're not Guinevere anymore, are you? Besides, I was born before you married Arthur, and by the time you came to Camelot, I'd been in the twenty-first century for years." It still seemed unreal to Morry to talk about his past so casually.

And he had a hard time relating to the fact that although he looked like a normal human being, he was only a quarter human. He was the grandson of Merlin Ambrosius, the Sorcerer of Camelot and the Welsh god of magic and healing, and his father, Merlin's son Derek, was a demigod. Unbelievable.

Morry looked up at Jim and said playfully, "Isn't it time to go home yet? I need to go out to Arches and talk to my dad about something, and also I'm dying to shift and go for a run." He knew that Jim would understand about his magical nature, as the man had been present at his transformation, when the black magic imbedded in his cells had been forcibly removed by Merlin, with assistance from the entire family.

Many times since then, Jim had asked if he could witness Morry's transition from human form to animal shape, but Morry had just replied that he wasn't ready to share that experience with anyone but his immediate family. Jim knew that his favored shape was that of a wolf, so he teased him unmercifully about being a werewolf.

Morry snorted. He wasn't a werewolf; he was a sorcerer first and foremost, and his primary magical ability was shapeshifting.

He was forced back to the present from his ruminations as Jim answered his question.

"It's only eleven o'clock, my friend. Get your articles done and checked, and the time will just fly by."

Morry gave him a dirty look, but then thought about the possibility that he might be able to use magic to his advantage.

As if he knew what his friend was thinking, Jim said quietly, "And no cheating by using magic. One of these days you're going to end up giving yourself away, and I can't imagine that you-know-who would be too pleased about that."

Unfortunately, Jim was right. Morry's entire family used their magic sparingly in order to keep a low profile—at least for the present—so he shuddered to think what his grandfather would do if he inadvertently revealed their secrets. Some day, when the time was right, Merlin planned to reveal his presence here on earth, but first he intended to follow through on his quest to bring Arthur back from Avalon.

In the fifth century, Arthur Pendragon had wanted to unite all of the separate kingdoms of Britain into one peaceful and prosperous "united kingdom." His death in AD 474 had put those plans on hold until such time as the world was ready for Arthur's return.

Eventually, of course, many centuries later, Great Britain had been molded into a very different United Kingdom, but the ideal state of Albion that King Arthur had envisioned had never really come to pass. Merlin planned to resurrect Arthur Pendragon and help him to unite all of the people of the world into a global Albion.

Morry still had difficulty believing that he was a part of that whole scenario. The task itself seemed daunting, impossible, even for someone as powerful as his grandfather was. And, of course, Merlin was still missing after his confrontation with the god of death in mid-May. Morry hoped he'd return soon—he really missed him.

Morry glanced at Jim, who was still quietly and patiently standing there watching him, his arms folded comfortably across his chest. At a wiry five feet six, he was not a large man. And with his soft mop of curly brown hair, it was easy to visualize the woman he had been in a past life. In fact, Jim had an almost regal bearing which belied his slight stature, reflecting the monarch he had been so many centuries ago.

Morry shook his head and grinned. "You're persistent, I'll give you that. Now, why don't you just go back to your desk so I can work in peace?"

Jim rolled his eyes. "God, you're arrogant." He turned on his heel and started to walk out of Morry's cubicle, but then he paused thoughtfully, and glanced back at Morry. "I'll tell you what. Buy my lunch today, and get your work done, and I'll let you go early, maybe around three, three thirty." He raised his eyebrows questioningly and Morry shrugged and nodded. He'd take whatever he could get.

An hour later, they were heading out the door for lunch when Jim asked Morry what his plans were for the evening. In the past, they had spent considerable time after work playing pool and drinking beer at Moody's Tavern, but ever since Morry's transformation their evenings had been a little strained.

Morry had no interest in going to Moody's, especially tonight. He was eager to meet with his dad, and then shift to his wolf form.

"As I already mentioned, I've got plans," Morry said irritably.

"Let me watch you shift, Morry, what do you say? You know I won't tell anyone." As a reporter earlier in his career, Jim had had

the reputation for pursuing his prey until they literally gave up in exhaustion.

Morry gritted his teeth, then sighed and nodded his head slowly. "Okay."

"Oh, come on, man, I—wait, what did you say?"

"I said, 'okay.'" Morry stood on the sidewalk outside of the newspaper office and looked amused.

Jim's eyes lit up with pleasure. "You won't regret this, kid."

"I sincerely hope not." Morry stared seriously into his friend's brown eyes. "Meet me at my house around five thirty—I should be back by then. I'm driving out to Arches to talk to my dad in person. I'm really concerned about him; he seems so depressed lately. When I get back, I'll shift and we can take your car out to Sand Flats."

"Sounds good! I'll be at your place around five thirty," Jim said excitedly, as they took off across the street to the Moab Information Center parking lot where he'd parked that morning. They decided to eat lunch at Moab Brews and it was too far to walk. Morry figured it was fair that Jim should drive since he'd finagled his way into watching him shift to wolf form.

Later that afternoon as he showed his pass at the fee booth, the man informed him that Derek had gone off shift at least thirty minutes ago. As he drove past the visitor center and headed up the hill and out into the park, Morry thought about where he might find his father. Derek had been blocking him telepathically for days for some reason, so Morry didn't actually know his exact location, but he headed out towards Balanced Rock since that was one of his dad's favorite spots to levitate.

Morry was envious of his father's ability to levitate and teleport, but then again, he was the only one in the family who could shapeshift, besides Merlin, and he was undeniably proud of that. He couldn't fly in his human form, as Merlin could, but as soon as he shifted to bird form he could soar alongside his famous grandfather.

All of a sudden, the irrefutable reality of his transformation hit him anew and he threw back his head and laughed out loud for the joy of it. All those miserable years as an orphan, convinced that he was a failure as a human being, were over. When he'd found out he really wasn't entirely human, it was a relief.

He grinned when he spied Derek's truck in the Balanced Rock parking lot and swung in beside it. Still feeling euphoric, Morry walked jauntily down the wide concrete sidewalk. He hadn't gone far before his preternaturally sharp hearing picked up a man's muffled sobs coming from the far side of Balanced Rock. He paused, his elevated mood abruptly shattered, and Derek's mental anguish resonated through his own being. Worried about his dad's state of mind, he headed in the direction of the emotional storm.

The sun was still fairly high in the sky above the mountains to the west of Arches National Park, and the light had that particularly vivid quality unique to a summer's late afternoon in red rock country. There was a fresh breeze bringing a slight respite from midday's scorching heat, but he barely noticed, so focused was he on reaching the source of those heart-wrenching cries.

His face now set in grim lines and his own emotions in turmoil, Morry left the walkway and clambered up the rough path around to the back side of the huge sandstone structure, where he found his father sitting in the shadows, his head in his hands. Still dressed in the Park Service uniform he had worn during his shift earlier in the day, Law Enforcement Ranger Derek Colburn was the picture of abject misery, his longish sandy-brown hair hanging, lank and uncombed, around his face.

"Hey, Dad, it's me." Morry announced himself quietly, afraid that he would startle the unhappy man.

"I know. I sensed it when ya pulled into the parkin' lot." Derek glanced up at his son with red, streaming eyes, and then paused for a moment before he hung his head and groaned, "It's all my fault."

Morry frowned. "What are you talking about?"

"It's my fault that he's gone! If he hadn't had to rescue me from Nimue, this whole fuckin' disaster wouldn't have happened." Derek impatiently wiped his eyes on the sleeve of his uniform, and then blew his nose violently into the crumpled tissue he found in his pocket. It had been almost three months since Merlin's old

adversary Nimue, in the form of Derek's half sister Adrestia, had abducted him in order to draw the ancient sorcerer into a trap. After defeating Nimue and delivering Derek to safety, Merlin had gone on to battle Beli, the god of death, in the skies above Moab, and then they both had disappeared into a huge dark funnel in the sky. It felt like it had happened only yesterday.

"That's ridiculous! It's not your—" Morry started to respond heatedly, when Derek held his hand up to stop him, and spoke to him telepathically for the first time in days. There's a couple of hikers comin' 'round from the front. Wait 'til they're gone. *He swiftly cloaked them with an invisibility spell.*

The two sorcerers watched the progress of the park visitors as they walked by, totally oblivious to the drama unfolding right next to them.

As soon as the couple was out of sight, Morry started talking. He wanted to reassure his father that he had done nothing wrong. "Dad, really, it's not your fau—"

"Crap, I thought I was alone out here," Derek muttered, interrupting Morry again as he hauled himself to his feet and slapped the dust off the seat of his pants. He barked a word in Latin, removing the invisibility spell, then turned, and without another word started back to the parking lot.

Morry followed on Derek's heels, anger simmering beneath the surface of his deceptively mild countenance. He was losing patience with his father's one-man pity party. "Well, it's tourist season—what the hell did you expect?" A group of tourists stared at the two men as they passed by them.

Mindful not to be overheard, Derek didn't speak again until they were back in the parking lot. "Do ya realize that I've only known about my abilities, and about Merlin bein' my father, for a little over a year? Now he's gone and I might never see him again!"

"Yeah, as a matter of fact, I did know that. Don't you remember when you and I Saw each other? Merged our minds? How can you have forgotten already? And you aren't the only one grieving, you selfish bastard! Emily's lost him, Lumina's lost him—and I've

lost him too! All of us have lost him and may never see him again," Morry shouted, almost as furious with Derek as he'd been the day his dad had stolen Sarah away from him.

At that time, Morry hadn't known about any of it: that he had magic, that Derek was his father or that Merlin was his grandfather. All he knew was that Derek had taken from him the only woman he had ever loved. But in contrast to that day when he had felt nothing but loathing for Derek, now there was a profound sense of caring, of love, in his heart, which took the rough edge off of his initial furious emotional outburst. The love he felt for his father, and for the grandfather he might never have the chance to know better, flowed through him so strongly that he was nearly overwhelmed by it.

Morry abruptly decided that he'd had enough drama. He strode quickly to his own vehicle, a compact little Jeep Patriot, and yanked the door open. He practically threw himself into the driver's seat and thrust the key into the ignition. He felt an acute, almost painful, pressure in his chest and knew his magic was about to erupt. He gritted his teeth and tried to ignore the sensation.

As he revved the engine he heard Derek shout, "Morry, wait!" He ignored him as he jammed the transmission into reverse, then into drive, and sped out of the parking lot, back down the hill towards the park entrance. Sightseers driving at a leisurely pace through the spectacular scenery quickly pulled over to let him pass.

In his mind, Morry saw Derek watch his hasty departure, and felt his dad's concern that his son was driving under the influence of raging magical energy. The vehicle was practically glowing with the power he was emanating, but Morry was too pissed off to think about the consequences of losing control.

He knew that the state he was in could be dangerous, not only to himself, but to everyone around him. Morry didn't fucking care. His phone chirped the tone he'd assigned to Derek, but he ignored it. He figured Derek was worried and wanted to warn him to calm down, but he managed to make it back to his small house in downtown Moab in one piece—miraculously without getting a speeding ticket. Morry hastily parked in the short graveled driveway, then continued to sit in the car until his heartbeat slowed and the pulsating energy inside him started to taper off. He kind of wished he'd stuck around to discuss the tragedy of Merlin's disappearance with his dad, commiserating with him instead of reacting like an undisciplined adolescent. He shook his head, realizing that hindsight really was 20/20. He should return Derek's call, but still he sat in the car, doing nothing. What the hell was wrong with him?

Finally, he had to admit to himself that at this point, his reticence had little to do with his run-in with Derek. He was afraid to go inside because he was reluctant to see Sarah, his roommate and best friend, who was busy planning her new life with his father. The past few months had been full of major, life-changing events and Morry wasn't sure he could handle it. His magic was still making his chest feel tight, so he closed his eyes and focused on the Light inside of himself as Merlin had taught him the night after his transformation. He hoped it would calm his nerves and subdue the pulsating power still raging within.

A short time later, when his magic had retreated into whatever place inside him it lived, he reluctantly opened his eyes, looked at his watch and noted that it was only five twenty-five. And he remembered with a wave of relief that Sarah would still be working at The Moab Herbalist. His soon-to-be ex-roommate wouldn't be home until six o'clock or so. He could worry about her later.

Then, he remembered that his buddy Jim was stopping by after work in about five minutes. Against his better judgment, Morry was finally going to allow someone watch him shift.

"Damn it," Morry breathed. It couldn't be worse timing, with Derek's meltdown fresh in his mind. And he had to admit that he was apprehensive about letting anyone outside of his immediate family witness him changing shape; it seemed way too personal. But he had promised Jim and hated to go back on his word. He finally got out of the car, walked across the parched patch of grass they optimistically called a lawn, and approached his front door. He fumbled through his pockets, searching in vain for his house key.

"Crap," he muttered. He must have left it sitting on his dresser this morning. Then, it dawned on him that he never had

to be locked out again; he could use a spell to unlock the door. He'd had the use of his magic for such a short time, and he was inexperienced, to say the least, but he could feel the magic waiting inside of him, and the feeling of pressure was building up again in his chest. He glanced around surreptitiously to make sure he wasn't being observed, focused on his goal and self-consciously muttered a simple spell. The lock clicked and the knob turned, and Morry laughed out loud.

At that moment, Jim Singleton pulled in beside Morry's Jeep. As he leaped out of his vehicle and jogged up to the door, Morry turned to greet him with a big, shit-eating grin on his face and told him what he'd just accomplished.

"Good work, man." Jim clapped him enthusiastically on the back. "I'm really proud of you. But now it's time for the main event." His face shone with anticipation.

Morry rolled his eyes at Jim's exuberance as they both entered the house, which was only marginally cooler than the outside air. He turned the overhead evaporative cooler to high, then headed into the kitchen and grabbed the pitcher of cold water out of the refrigerator.

"You thirsty?" As Jim shook his head impatiently, Morry poured himself a tall glass of water and downed it slowly, savoring every drop. Then he rinsed his glass, which was completely unnecessary, and carefully put it in the dish drainer. He realized he was procrastinating and motioned to Jim to follow him to his bedroom at the end of the hall. As soon as Jim entered, Morry closed the door behind him and started to undress.

"Whoa, what're you doing?" Jim asked with a nervous laugh, glancing away in apparent embarrassment as his friend stood before him in the buff. However, curiosity got the best of him and he looked back at his friend in surprise; he couldn't help but notice how Morry's body had changed. The younger man was now sleek, slender and muscular. Impressed, Jim gave a low whistle. "Damn, you're looking good, kid. When did you lose the weight?"

"Believe it or not, it happened the first time I shifted," Morry said, bemused at Jim's discomfort with his nudity. After all, they

were both men, and presumably, Jim had seen men's private parts before, other than his own. "Alright, bud, you wanted to watch, so pay attention."

Jim still felt a bit embarrassed about Morry's lack of clothing, especially when he noticed his friend's more than adequate masculine attributes.

Morry eyed him impatiently. Jim was acting as if he'd never seen a dick before. "Look, if I shift with my clothes on, they'll end up shredded. Maybe when I've had a lot more practice I can incorporate the clothing into the shift, but at this point, I'd rather not destroy my wardrobe, okay?" He decided not to say anything else, but he suspected Jim might be channeling Guinevere's personality again—it would certainly explain his apparent shyness.

He swallowed his annoyance and decided just to get down to business. He closed his eyes and focused inside of himself, picturing his wolf shape, acknowledging the wild spirit of the animal and allowing the beast within him to take over. He felt a stirring in his body and a strange sensation as if the entire universe moved under him. He could actually feel the cells of his body rearranging themselves.

Jim watched in fascination as his friend changed from man to beast. It was extremely disconcerting to see Morry's feet and hands turn into paws, his arms and legs lengthen, change shape and grow long, coarse hair. And when Morry's cock disappeared into a sheath covered with fur and his testicles shrank in size, Jim had to stop himself from clutching his own package in horror.

Morry slowly opened his eyes and looked up at the man who was staring at him with unutterable disbelief.

He opened his mouth to laugh at Jim's reaction and out came a very canine-like bark. His tongue lolled over sharp teeth as he panted, suddenly too warm, even though the swamp cooler was making a valiant effort to bring the temperature down inside the little house. He stretched and shook himself. It felt good to be a wolf.

CHAPTER 5

Moab, Christmas Day, 2015

MORRY BLINKED, AND REALIZED HE'D totally zoned out during Rae's commentary. She was still talking, so he guessed he hadn't missed a great deal. He was glad—he liked Rae and didn't want to seem like he was deliberately ignoring her.

But he couldn't help that his thoughts kept returning to that day in August of 2014. He enjoyed the memory of Jim witnessing his transformation, and glanced at his friend, a half smile on his lips. He really cared for the man, and he wondered if part of that feeling stemmed from the recognition that in Jim's previous life, he was family. Having been an orphan as he was growing up, Morry valued family more than most people did.

Jim grinned back at him, suspecting that Morry had been remembering the day he'd first shifted to his wolf form in front of him…

August, 2014

My God, he'd done it! Jim Singleton couldn't take his eyes off of the animal in front of him, who was actually Merlin's grandson. Despite the earthshaking events of the past few months, he wasn't used to the magic flowing unchecked around him anymore. He had a sudden flashback to his life—that is, Guinevere's life—when Arthur had been alive and the Round Table had been a smoothly operating military and political machine. Merlin had always been there at Arthur's side, loyal and trustworthy. He was sometimes a dark, protective shadow, and other times a raging magical force helping Arthur ensure that justice prevailed in the kingdom.

So where in the hell was Merlin now? *Jim asked himself. His thoughts again turned to Arthur, who had been a forceful, charismatic leader, and at the same time, a gentle, loving husband. An unexpected jolt of loss and grief caused tears to well in Jim's eyes. He wasn't the queen anymore, hadn't been for more than a thousand years, and he hadn't even been female in the last few lifetimes, so why was he feeling this way? As if all he wanted was to be held against Arthur's slender yet powerful body again, protected and loved.*

Jim blinked the moisture away self-consciously and shook off the feeling of melancholy, deliberately bringing his mind back to the present. The wolf was no longer at his feet, but was waiting impatiently for him to open the door and let him out. He was panting, obviously too warm, his pelt thick and heavy. Of course, it was hotter still outdoors, but at least there was a breeze.

"Are you sure that's a good idea, Morry?" Jim frowned as he thought about what could happen if anyone found out that his friend was a shapeshifter.

I had a disagreement with my dad earlier and I really need to work it out of my system. Sand Flats is perfect for a run—no one will think twice about someone taking his dog out for a little exercise.

Jim blinked as he heard Morry's voice in his mind, and then exclaimed, "Dog? Are you kidding me? You're huge—no one in his right mind is going to mistake a timber wolf for a dog!"

And in reality, the animal standing before him was even larger and broader than a mere timber wolf. He was formidable. He had unusual streaks of blond, red, gray and black liberally interspersed throughout his glossy brown coat. Just like Morry's hair.

You'd be surprised. Human beings can be extremely unconscious. They only see what they expect to see. I should know—I used to be one of them.

Jim sighed and reluctantly opened the front door, whereupon the wolf bounded down the steps and pranced excitedly next to Jim's vehicle.

"Morry, come on, you're overdoing it, man!" Jim complained as he locked the door behind him and walked over to his car.

Oh, I don't know, I think I make a convincing dog. *Morry whined and pushed his cold wet nose against Jim's crotch as the man reached to unlock the car.*

"Hey, cut that out, dog-breath, or you can forget about your

run," Jim grumbled. He heard a masculine chuckle in his mind as he opened the vehicle door and Morry jumped into the back seat.

Jim had been correct about the way people would react to the wolf. Despite Morry's dog-like antics as he ran and played among the sand dunes and rock formations, he drew the attention of a group of hikers, and despite Jim's efforts to try and control the situation, it got out of hand anyway.

"Hey, fella, is that your wolf?" One man, at least six feet tall and burly, approached him in belligerent manner and got right up into his face, towering over him.

Jim was taken aback by the fellow's attitude and imposing physical presence. "Uh, yeah, he's mine. What about it?" He suspected that there could be trouble, so he called silently to Morry, hoping he actually heard him, and then made a big production out of whistling for him. The wolf came and sat next to him obediently, staring up into his face.

"It seems to me that it's illegal to keep a wild animal as a pet," the hiker stated pompously.

Jim thought frantically then replied, "That might be true, but as you can see, he's not wild. He's actually half German Shepard, but looks like his sire, who is pure wolf." He winced inside, as he knew that his comment wouldn't go over well with Morry.

Hey, thanks for insulting me, Bro! I'm no fucking German Shepard!

"Just shut up, will you?"

"What did you say to me, asshole?" The man scowled and made a threatening move towards Jim, who hadn't realized that he'd spoken aloud.

Jim was uneasy, and more than ready to be done with the confrontation at this point, and he sensed Morry tensing up protectively beside him. When the wolf bared his teeth, growling fiercely at the stranger, Jim heard Morry in his mind, saying, What the hell is his problem? If the bastard doesn't back off, I'll bite him.

"I'm calling the sheriff—this animal's dangerous and needs to be put down!" The man swiftly pulled his phone out of his pocket and started entering the number.

"Come on, Morry, let's get out of here!" Jim turned and threw open the car door, beckoning to him to get in.

He'll just get your license plate number and the cops will end up following us. I have a better idea. *Jim looked at him in puzzlement, and then in horror, as Morry reared up and at the same time morphed back into his human form. There was a collective gasp of astonishment and fear from the assembled hikers as they beheld the impossible—an animal changing into a naked man right before their eyes.*

Beside him, Jim heard Morry take a deep breath, and watched him as he threw his arms out, as if to embrace the crowd, then bellowed a single word as white Light burst from his splayed fingers: "OBLITUS!*"*

On the way back to the house, Morry sat quietly brooding in the passenger seat with his arms crossed in front of him and an old shirt of Jim's wrapped around his hips. "Overkill."

"What?" Jim glanced at him as they stopped at the traffic light at the intersection of Center and Main Streets.

"I expended way too much energy out there trying to make everyone forget they saw us. I think I could have accomplished the same thing with half, or maybe even a quarter of the power."

"Well, I'm impressed—you sure got the job done. I was scared to death that someone would realize what you are, but there's no possible way any of them would remember it after what you did. You'll learn to fine-tune your spells in time, I'm sure." Jim grinned, remembering the blank looks on the hikers' faces as he and Morry jumped in the vehicle and made their escape.

Morry looked contemplatively out the window. "I wonder if I might be able to use my magic to help bring Merlin back from...wherever he is." He sighed. "I'd better give my dad a call tonight. Maybe we can put our heads together and come up with a plan."

Jim pulled up in front of Morry's little house and waited until his friend had stepped out of the car. "Hey, thanks for letting me watch you shift. It was unbelievable!"

Distractedly, Morry said, "You're welcome. See you at work tomorrow." Then he hurried into the house, presumably to get dressed.

Jim was glad Morry hadn't noticed that he'd been staring at his half-naked body.

At home that evening, Jim sat alone in his small, neat living room in his comfortable overstuffed recliner, with a bottle of his favorite beer from the local microbrewery, and sighed unhappily. Only a few hours ago, he had watched Morry change into a large wolf, and had spent time with him in that form. He should be feeling pumped, excited that he'd witnessed such an outstanding feat of magic. Instead, he felt curiously empty, lonesome and unexplainably sad.

He closed his eyes and thought about it, realizing that he'd felt that way more and more frequently since Merlin had shown him his past lives, shown him that his soul was actually that of a woman. He didn't really understand it, and he wasn't sure he wanted it. But sometimes he felt that feminine sensibility taking over his current masculine state to the point that he often yearned to be Guinevere again, back in Camelot where it had all begun. He'd agonized over it, pondered it and approached it intellectually. Nothing helped. Damn it! He had a penis in this life, not a vagina, and physically, at least, desired to have sex with women. And yet, every night he dreamed about having sex with a man who had died in battle more than 1500 years ago.

No wonder he'd never been very successful with women. He didn't think he was gay—but he was a male with the soul of a female. And he hated to admit it, but sometimes, he just wanted his woman's body back.

He reached down and adjusted himself in his pants. The damned thing never cooperated. Every time he tried to have sex with a woman, it was a chore keeping an erection. Now, imagining himself having sex with Arthur gave him a raging hard-on. He scowled at his crotch. Fucking thing.

Watching Morry undress this afternoon had made him extremely uncomfortable—the guy was hung like a horse and Jim was afraid he'd give himself away. He'd never been physically attracted to Morry before, but good God, watching him practically do a striptease in front of him was just too tantalizing, and he had felt his cock begin to stir. What would he have done if Morry had noticed? How embarrassing would that *have been, for God's sake?*

He wished he could just shapeshift into a woman's form and stay that way if he wanted. He grinned at the thought as he finished his beer and then reached for his phone to order a pizza.

CHAPTER 6

Moab, Christmas Day, 2015

JIM TWITCHED AND OPENED HIS eyes, his cheeks hot as he blushed. He glanced around carefully, hoping nobody had noticed his inattention as he remembered that past experience. He managed to avoid the questioning gaze of Ryan Jones, who had been Guinevere's lover, Sir Lancelot, in his past life. No way was he going to open *that* can of worms. He had never really examined his, or rather Guinevere's, feelings for the man.

Across the room, Ryan couldn't take his eyes off of Jim Singleton. While Jim shared certain characteristics with Guinevere—his height, his coloring and his curly hair—he didn't look particularly feminine. But there was something about him. The fact that Ryan was not gay didn't seem to matter; he was becoming aroused. And he remembered everything from his life in Camelot, particularly the shameful fact that Arthur had trusted him even while he was betraying his king. Ryan remembered the flowery scent of Guinevere's long, curly brown hair and the feel of her slim body beneath him as he thrust into her. He'd loved her so completely that even now, sixteen centuries later, Ryan's heart ached with the pain of his memories. He almost groaned out loud, barely catching himself from exposing his feelings to the entire group gathered here in Merlin's name.

Then, Ryan realized Derek was staring at him curiously, and wasn't that awkward, considering that Derek was Arthur's nephew and closely resembled Camelot's ruler. Derek was the same height as Arthur and had the same muscular build. And his hair was same color, although a shade darker. Ryan decided that it would be wise to concentrate on the stories being related here today—other people's stories—and keep quiet about his own.

Jim, still holding the throw pillow on his lap to cover up his body's reactions to his own memories, didn't notice when Ryan turned his gaze away.

Morry was puzzled when he felt Ryan's distress, and he sensed that it had something to do with Jim. However, the source of Jim's discomfort was clear when he realized what his friend was hiding beneath that plush throw pillow. Morry carefully didn't give any outward sign that he noticed, but he wanted to know what was going on, especially since Ryan had been gazing at Jim with his heart in his eyes.

Emily was now happily reminiscing about meeting Merlin for the first time. Morry listened for a while, but his thoughts kept returning to the night after he'd enchanted that group of people out at Sand Flats…

August, 2014

Morry lay in bed, staring up at the ceiling with its little reflective stars scattered across the width of the small bedroom. He figured it had been a kid's room at one time, and while it might be childish, he thoroughly enjoyed the effect.

What would happen if he enhanced it with magic? He whispered a word in Latin and the stars on the ceiling began to twinkle. He grinned in satisfaction.

Then he recalled what had occurred this afternoon and reality intruded like a bucket of ice-cold water thrown in his face. He'd called Derek, but the conversation had been supremely unsatisfying, as his father hadn't been in a very communicative mood. True, he'd apologized to Morry for his behavior earlier in the day, but Derek seemed stuck in a depression from which he would have to extricate himself.

Morry sighed, then abruptly threw off the sheet and sat up on the edge of the bed, too warm and restless to sleep. He decided to shift and roam around town in animal form for awhile to take his mind off of his father's dilemma.

He walked quietly through the kitchen and unlocked the back door. He couldn't remember the last time he'd oiled the hinges and hoped the noise wouldn't wake up Sarah, as he hadn't bothered to get dressed. He was rather surprised she wasn't at Derek's house tonight. Maybe she was as fed up with his attitude as Morry was.

He stood in the back yard, naked, listening to the night noises around him. Music and laughter emanated from the place at the corner and crickets chirped in the overgrown hedge that grew along the property line. He wondered what it would be like to experience the night through a cat's senses. He focused briefly inside himself, and then easily shifted into the form of a good-sized tomcat. It felt electrifying, magic shimmering through his body, changing him at the cellular level almost instantaneously.

He stretched luxuriously and then lifted one brown paw and started licking it. He seemed to be able to think clearly, just as he had in wolf form, with his animal mind less crowded with extraneous thoughts than it was in human form.

When he was done cleaning his front paws, he sat and gazed around the yard, noting how his perspective had changed. His sight and hearing were many times more acute in this feline form than in his human body. Cool. His cat's body felt limber, flexible; he stretched again, enjoying the sensation. He liked having a long tail, and whipped it back and forth in mock fury. It was weird though, to realize that his genitals were strangely placed compared to a human male's—his penis was hidden and his balls were in little furry sacs a good inch below his anus. He experimentally lifted his leg in the traditional pose and started washing himself. His rough tongue ended up with a few hairs caught in it, as well as something else he wasn't sure he wanted to identify. Okay, that was kind of gross. He did his best to rid himself of what was stuck to his tongue.

He decided it was time to explore, and squeezed through the hedge, trotting arrogantly around the corner of the house and heading down the street towards the bar.

A car pulled out of the neighbor's driveway unexpectedly and he narrowly missed being run over. He screeched in fear and cowered beneath a bush at the side of the road.

Crap, that was a close one, *he thought. Maybe this wasn't such a good idea after all. Cars were awfully large compared to a small animal like a cat.*

The driver of the car slammed on the brakes, threw the door open and jumped out.

"Oh, no, damn it! Here kitty, kitty—oh, God, where are you? I'm so sorry, are you okay?" The young woman got down on her hands and knees and peered under the bush where he was hiding.

He saw the tears in her eyes and wished that he could tell her that he was all right, just shaken up. Instead, he let out an undignified little mew and crawled out from under the bush.

"Aw, poor kitty, come here, baby," she said softly, picking him up and cuddling him against her ample breast.

He started to purr as she scratched his chin and then gently stroked his head. Oh, it felt so good to be held and—whoa, what the hell was he doing? How embarrassing! His whole perspective was warped in this small animal brain, and it was obvious that certain actions were almost instinctive.

"Aren't you a sweet boy? And what an unusual color you are—brown with gray streaks. Oh, you're just gorgeous! I'd better take you home with me, just in case. I'll keep an eye on you tonight, and we'll see how you're doing in the morning, okay?"

No, no, no! This is absolutely not okay, *he thought. But what was he going to do? If he jumped out of her arms now he might scratch her, and he really didn't want to do that.*

She left her car parked at the side of the road and carried him back to her house, which was only a few doors down from his own place, Morry realized. She held him close to her as she unlocked her front door and took him inside. She set him down gently and he followed her as she made her nightly trek through the house, making sure all doors and windows were secured. He ended up sitting on her bed watching her undress and brush her long shiny dark hair the requisite one hundred strokes. He thoroughly enjoyed himself, especially when she crawled into bed naked and pulled his furry cat self up against her voluptuous body, stroking him until he purred in pleasure. He knew he should try to get out and go home, but it was so nice snuggled against her that he relaxed and went to sleep.

The next thing Morry knew, someone was beating on him and screaming, trying to push him out of bed. His eyes flew open and he remembered being in cat form. Apparently, he had spontaneously reverted to his human form during the night. He hadn't expected that.

"Who are *you? How the hell did you get in here?" the woman shrieked, still pummeling his head and shoulders.*

He couldn't respond as he realized it was morning and he was in a stranger's home, naked as the day he was born. He leaped out of bed and backed towards the door, unsuccessfully trying to cover his crotch with his hands.

"God, I'm so sorry, I, uh...oh, shit," he stuttered.

They stared at each other. He was horrified to be standing buck-naked in her bedroom, with his normal morning hard-on a little difficult to hide. Shit, he could get thrown in jail for this!

The young woman glanced down at his crotch and scowled at him, quickly retrieving a container of pepper spray from the top drawer of her bedside table, her full breasts swaying as she moved.

She pointed the nozzle at him. "I said, who are you and how did you get in here?"

Forgetting for a moment that he could use magic to resolve the situation, he croaked, "My name is Morry, and you brought me home with you last night."

"What? I brought a cat home with me last night! What kind of bullshit are you trying to pull? I'm calling the cops!"

"Wait, let me explain! I...I'm a shapeshifter, and I'm really new at this. You almost ran over me. It scared me, so when you picked me up, it felt so good that I let you bring me here. I'm sorry!"

"That's ridiculous!" she snapped, her eyes narrowed in fury. "I almost ran over a young tomcat."

"Yeah, I know. That was me," he squeeked, his dignity having evaporated.

"You are so full of it, Morry, or whatever your real name is." She was seething, she was so angry, and he really couldn't blame her. He pulled himself together and thought about shifting and getting the hell out of there. But he was locked in the house. God, he wished he was able to teleport. Well, he guessed he had no choice. He would have to use the same spell he'd used yesterday to make

the hikers forget. As she raised the canister of pepper spray, he accessed his magic and looked her in the eye.

"Oblitus,*" he whispered, using considerably less power than he'd used the first time he'd tried the spell. Her eyes glazed over and her face lost its angry expression.*

Thank God. He quickly walked out of her bedroom and headed for the front door. He unlocked and opened it and was about to step outside when he remembered that he had no clothes on. He had never attempted to conjure clothing, but what the hell—there was a first time for everything. He pictured himself clad in his normal at-home attire of shorts and T-shirt and willed them to appear on his body. Aaand...nothing happened. Shit.

He tried again, picturing just the shorts, how they hugged his body; the soft texture of the worn denim, the way he moved in them. And finally, he felt the shorts on his body and looked down. Not perfect, but at least they covered him.

Morry heard the woman starting to stir in the bedroom and left the house, carefully locking the door behind him. As he trotted gingerly through several of his neighbors' flower beds over to his own yard, he hoped she would think she dreamed the whole thing.

CHAPTER 7

Moab, Christmas Day, 2015

As Emily finished her story, Morry refocused on the present, and cautiously glanced around at everyone gathered in the warm, cozy living room with the Christmas tree lights twinkling cheerily at the front window. He locked eyes with Derek, who grinned wryly, and Morry realized his father had shared that last reminiscence with him. He lifted his eyebrows in acknowledgement, and let out a sigh.

Can't a guy have a private moment now and then?

Ha. Not in this family. I thought ya appreciated the connection.

I usually do, Dad, but once in a while I'd just like a little alone time in my own head.

Uh, huh. Good luck with that, Son.

In the comfortable silence after Emily had stopped talking, she picked up on the silent conversation between Morry and Derek.

"Hey, you two, come to the party! Morry, why don't you go next? I know that you had some extraordinary experiences with Merlin. We'd like to hear about at least one of them." Emily hoped she wasn't too hard on him, but he would have to toughen up to be part of this family.

Morry thought about all the strange yet wonderful things that had occurred since he became part of this unusual group of people, and finally decided to describe the first time his grandfather had taken him flying. Once he got into the swing of it, he was pleased to find that he was enjoying himself. As he spoke, he noticed when Derek's eyes closed, and he realized his father was indulging in his own remembrances…

October, 2014

The day Sarah moved in with him, his ex-wife, Chris Colburn, showed up. Derek was thrown for a loop, as Chris hadn't displayed any interest in continuing their friendship after she sold the herb shop to Michael Reese (who unbeknownst to her was actually Merlin) a year and a half ago and moved to Colorado. Derek knew that her twin sister Cathy had some kind of chronic illness and had temporarily needed live-in assistance, so he'd understood Chris's preoccupation. But his feelings had been hurt, nevertheless. The two of them had at one time been more than spouses, they had been each other's best friend. In truth, they had realized years ago that their friendship was more important than their marriage and had amicably divorced. They had once shared everything, but he'd never had the chance to tell her about the life-altering events he'd experienced.

In the afternoon of that bright autumn day, Sarah had returned to her old place to retrieve the last of her belongings, while Derek unloaded the only piece of furniture she owned from the bed of his silver Chevy pickup truck. The antique cedar chest was awfully heavy even empty, and Derek saw no reason to heft it the entire way, as he would have done when he thought he was a normal human being. But he decided to wait to use magic until he reached his front step. He didn't want to put on a show for the neighbors, so he'd unloaded and carried the awkward sucker that far. He'd set it down carefully, using his legs to spare his back, even though he wasn't really concerned about injuring himself.

Merlin can heal me instantly, *he thought absently. Then, his face fell as he remembered once again that his father wasn't around, and hadn't been for several months. Perhaps Emily or Lumina or even Morry could heal a strained back. He wasn't sure his own regenerative abilities were entirely developed—since he wasn't a god like his father, he might never be able to heal himself instantaneously; although he* had *come back from the dead after that dragon attack out at Arches in March.*

Maybe I'd better not injure myself to begin with, *he thought grimly, his good mood disappearing just as quickly and completely as his father had.*

He sighed, then stepped back to consider the proper wording of his spell. Ready to begin, he centered himself and then muttered the incantation, channeling a brief surge of power through his hands and lifting them at the same time. He knew that someday he wouldn't need spells—he would be able to use his magic instinctively—but it might be decades, if not centuries, for him to acquire that kind of expertise.

The chest rose effortlessly and started moving forward through the doorway at his direction, and he grinned in satisfaction. Man, he loved being a sorcerer!

"Ooh!" A shrill cry in a feminine voice instantly diverted his attention, and the chest dropped to the concrete step with a splintering crash, straddling the door sill.

He turned sharply and saw a petite blond figure staring up at him in disbelief.

"Chris!? What are ya doin' here?" He reached out to give her a hug, but she pulled back.

"Never mind that—who are you and what have you done with my ex-husband?" Chris demanded sharply, her eyes narrowed and her hands on her slender hips. Derek watched her as she scrutinized the way his jeans hugged his toned physique. His sandy-brown hair was longer than he used to wear it and a bit shaggy, but he felt that it fit his new aura of confidence. He saw the look on her face as she noticed the light brown stubble on his chin and upper lip, and he heard her thought that it made him look sexy as hell, besides enhancing his look of maturity. Derek almost grinned—he figured she'd never admit it.

"Okay, 'fess up. How did you do that? And don't bother lying to me, 'cause I saw you."

Derek stared back at her briefly, then looked away, debating whether he should divulge his true nature to Chris. He wasn't at all certain that she should be included in their rapidly growing ranks. She had no magic of her own, at least that he was aware of.

What would Merlin say if he were to appear in front of them at this moment? And God, how he wished he would. Derek could imagine the ensuing conversation.

Uh, hi, Dad. I seem to have a problem, *he might say.*

And his dad might respond, I can see that. But I just dropped in to let you know it's alright to tell her our secret.

Then, Derek would look skeptical and say, Really? Well, okay. But she doesn't have magic, does she? I've never felt it before, anyway.

And Merlin would raise one dark eyebrow and look expectantly at him.

Way to put me on the spot, Dad. Thanks a lot*! Derek would say sarcastically.*

You are most welcome, Son. Seriously, I think it's essential that you bring her into the group. Believe me, I have my reasons.

The imaginary conversation came to a halt at that point, as Derek was unsure how to proceed. However, after a few moments of indecision, it was obvious that he needed to man up, so he cleared his throat and laid it all on the line.

"Somethin' happened to me last year that changed my life, Chris. I found out I have magic. That's how I moved the chest."

*"You have...*what*?" Taken aback by the unexpected admission, she glanced at him suspiciously, thinking he would laugh at her gullibility. Instead, she saw that he was totally serious, a new poise and sense of accomplishment obvious in his demeanor.*

Derek smiled mysteriously and turned away. She wondered what he intended to do.

Chris watched him as he reached one hand towards the damaged chest, fingers splayed out. She thought she was hallucinating when she heard him recite a short phrase in Latin (Derek, who'd had a difficult time with high school Spanish, had learned Latin *in the relatively short time she'd been gone?). She glanced curiously at the chest and gasped. It was completely repaired, restored to its original, unblemished state in a manner of seconds.*

Chris quickly turned back to Derek to question him about it, only to hear him recite yet another phrase that did sound suspiciously like a spell. My God, what was he, a wizard or something, like Harry Potter? Could this be real? Her question was answered as the chest rose smoothly into the air and made its way through the doorway and down the hall.

Her jaw dropped and she glanced uneasily at this man she thought she knew. He let his outstretched hand drop to his side, then turned to her and shrugged. "Things have changed for me since the last time I saw ya, Chris. Found out I'm a sorcerer. Hard to believe, huh?"

"How about impossible?"

"Oh, it's possible, believe me," Derek said, amused at her adamant refusal to see what was right in front of her.

Chris frowned in confusion as she pondered how to answer. "I don't understand. How did you find out you can, uh, work magic*?"*

Derek looked at her speculatively. "Do ya remember Michael Reese, the guy who bought your shop?"

"Well, of course, I remember him. He had just come here from Great Britain and seemed to have a difficult time figuring out how to use all the electronic devices."

Derek chuckled. "That's because he was born in the fifth century. Not too many phones, calculators or computers in Camelot."

She sat on the couch with her head in her hands, while Derek told the tale as Merlin had related it to him, introducing Chris to the man who, even in his absence, meant the world to him.

When Derek had finished he waited for her to comment. She raised her head and tried to make eye contact, whereupon he neatly avoided her gaze.

"What haven't *you told me? Seems like you're holding something back," she said, resigned to hear one last unbelievable detail.*

"Actually, there's two somethin's. And both are gonna blow your mind."

"Oh, because everything you've told me so far has been so mundane and boring?" she said sarcastically.

Derek grinned, and she thought she saw, for just a second, a glow of light around him. She shivered and waited for him to speak.

"Merlin's my real father." Derek's voice deepened and his countenance shone with pride.

Chris paled and stared at him in silent amazement, wondering what could possibly top that pronouncement.

Suddenly, an enormous gray and brown dog trotted in the open front door. And then the animal was gone, and a tall, good-looking and very naked man in his early twenties stood not more than three feet in front of her.

"Hey, Dad, since Sarah's not back yet I thought I'd...oops, uh sorry, I..." Morry looked guiltily between Derek and Chris as he realized that he had just revealed his magic—and his naked assets—to a total stranger, and a woman at that.

"It's okay, she's my ex-wife," Derek said nonchalantly, as he handed the young man his flannel outer shirt to wrap around his waist. He turned to Chris with an engaging grin. "I'd like ya to meet my son, Morry. He's the other somethin', or I guess I should say someone, I was gonna tell ya about."

"Your...your son?" Disbelief oozed from her voice. Quickly, she tried to mask her reaction. "Uh, it's nice to meet you, but I'd appreciate it if you'd put some clothes on," Chris said, dismayed to find that even with his groin area covered up she was intensely attracted to him. His muscular chest had a nice amount of silky brown hair that surrounded his nipples, narrowed across his washboard abs, and finally disappeared beneath the shirt barely covering his outstanding male assets. He was breathtaking.

Morry's face reddened for a moment in embarrassment as he saw the look on her face, and he headed towards the master bedroom right away, intent upon borrowing some of Derek's clothing. Luckily, they were the same height and both weighed in at around a hundred and ninety, so the jeans and T-shirt that he pulled on fit him pretty well. He didn't bother with underwear; he'd be home in a matter of minutes and could change into his own clothing then.

As the young man left the room, Chris stared up at her ex-husband in confusion. The person he'd introduced as his son had changed from a large dog (or had it been a wolf?) into a man. A man that was way too old to be Derek's son. How the hell did that work? He was only a few years younger than Derek. And come to think of it, Derek was only a few years younger than Michael—or rather, Merlin.

Now fully clothed, Morry walked back into the living room, and he and Derek looked at each other and grinned. Then, he turned to his father's ex and spoke to her as if he had just been introduced.

"It's nice to meet you, Chris. I'm Mordred Colburn, and yes, I'm Derek's son. And Derek really is Merlin's son. I'm not a hundred percent certain I understand how it works, either—I think time must be relatively flexible. Both Dad and Grandpa have tried to explain it to me, but I still don't really get it. All of us were born in the fifth century: Merlin was born in 420, Dad was born in 442, and I was born in 460, and yet here we all are in the twenty-first century, and we all appear to be close to the same age." From the amused look on his face, he seemed to be enjoying the circumstances.

Chris felt as if she was about to faint when she realized Derek's son had heard her thoughts. So had Derek, apparently. They were both telepathic and Morry was a shapeshifter. She groaned out loud and covered her face with her hands. She hoped that Morry hadn't noticed her attraction to him. But how could he not? She had been eye-level with his junk.

Both men hovered solicitously around the distraught woman as she struggled to grasp the situation, which was far beyond her mundane frame of reference.

"What's going on here?" Sarah asked suspiciously as she walked in the front door, her arms loaded with clothing, and saw her men being entirely too chummy with a woman didn't recognize. She realized that she was jumping the gun to call them "her men" since she and Derek weren't married yet, but she felt very possessive about both of them.

Derek hurried to take the bundle of clothes from her and to give her a kiss. "Hey, sweetheart, I'm glad you're here. I'd like ya to meet my ex-wife, Chris Colburn, who just came back from Denver. Chris, this is my fiancée, Sarah Gordon." He glanced nervously between the two women.

"Hi, Chris. I don't mean to be rude, but this is the first I've heard about you, so forgive me if I'm a little confused. I never even knew he'd been married before." She glanced accusingly first at

Derek, who looked back at her sheepishly, and then at Morry, who put up his hands as if to ward her off. He muttered, "I'm staying out of this," and slipped quietly out the still-open front door.

Chris stared at Morry's retreating figure. His backside was tight and flexed intriguingly in his borrowed jeans. She blinked and forced her attention back to the striking strawberry-blond woman who looked like she was sizing her up for a made-to-measure coffin. Chris decided she might want to face this woman on her feet and stood up, although it didn't seem to make any difference. She was only five two, and Sarah had to be at least five seven in her high-heeled boots.

"I'm really sorry to just show up like this. I had no idea so much had changed in Derek's life since I've been gone. The whole magic thing—not to mention that Michael Reese is Merlin—has me totally overwhelmed and I—" Chris was at a loss for words.

Sarah, who'd had a long, busy day and was worn-out, struggled to let go of her pique and sighed. "No, I'm the one who's sorry; I haven't been very understanding. And since the 'magic thing,' as you put it, is fairly new to me too, I know how you feel. The only difference is I've been working closely with everyone at The Moab Herbalist for the last six months, so I'm somewhat used to it by now."

Chris smiled tentatively. "I heard that Emily had gotten married, but I didn't realize it was to Michael. I mean Merlin." She cleared her throat, and then swallowed with difficulty. "Do you think I could have some water? I'm really thirsty."

*"Sure." Sarah glanced at Derek, who nodded. She then held out her right hand, palm up, and concentrated. "*Aquae speculo,*" she whispered.*

Chris's eyes widened as a glass of water appeared in Sarah's hand. "Oh, my God, you have it too!"

Sarah handed her the glass. "You make it sound like we all have some kind of communicable disease."

Chris flushed with embarrassment. "Sorry, I'm not usually so rude." She lifted the glass to her lips with an unsteady hand and drank several swallows, hoping that she could get herself under control.

"Don't worry about it, Chris." Sarah glanced at her watch. "I think I'm going to start dinner. Would you like to stay and eat with us? I'll call Morry and see if he'll pick up some wine." Then she remembered that he had left quite precipitously. "If he still intends to come to dinner, that is."

"I...sure, okay. Thanks." She looked back and forth from Sarah to Derek, hoping that she wasn't creating a problem between them.

"No, Chris, you're not creatin' a problem," Derek said with a crooked grin.

She winced, knowing she'd never get used to the fact that he could hear her thoughts. What if he'd heard her when she was thinking about Morry's, uh, attributes?

"Why don't you two take a walk and have a conversation. Maybe you can even, you know, give her a little sample of your powers." Sarah wiggled her eyebrows at Derek. She felt bad that she'd been so surly with Chris and was trying to make up for her unwelcoming behavior.

He frowned at her uncomprehendingly for a minute, trying to process her sudden change of heart. "Well, okay, if you're sure." He muttered something unintelligible and the clothing in his arms disappeared.

"Come on, Chris." He took the glass from her and set it on the coffee table, then grabbed her hand and pulled her out the door. They walked quietly along the sidewalk until Chris finally said, "This is real, isn't it?"

Derek glanced at her. "Yeah, it sure is."

"I'm glad you're happy, I really am," she said emphatically. "You were always fascinated by the legend of King Arthur and Merlin, and all that sword and sorcery stuff. I noticed you still have that poster of Merlin standing on a hill above Camelot with his sorcerer's staff in his hand."

He nodded. "I know now that it's not very accurate—I mean,

Merlin doesn't really look like that—but I keep it as a reminder of how lucky I am to be a part of the whole legend."

Chris looked at Derek quizzically. "What do you mean?"

"Merlin and I were actually in Camelot earlier this year. We were somehow transported back in time to the year 460, and I met my uncle, King Arthur." His handsome face glowed with pleasure as he remembered that once-in-a-lifetime experience.

Chris stopped walking and just stared doubtfully up at the man she thought she knew.

Derek met her eyes for a moment and then swiftly glanced away. "I look enough like Arthur that we could be brothers. That's why I've been wearin' my hair like this—it's exactly the same style as his. My birth mother was human; she was Arthur's older half sister, Cara."

"Uh, what do you mean, your mother was human? You say that like you're not," Chris said faintly.

He just winked at her and casually kept strolling along the sidewalk ahead of her.

"Oh, God, this can't be happening," she groaned and walked a little faster to catch up with him.

Derek chuckled quietly. Chris had had a shocking introduction to a world she didn't understand and had previously thought existed only within the pages of fantasy novels. He thought for a moment, then reached out and firmly grasped her forearm, teleporting them to the spot on the Rim above Moab that he and Merlin favored, where the old chairlift used to terminate. It had been removed in 2005 by The Nature Conservancy to protect an endangered species of plant found only in that location. Derek experienced a brief pang of regret when he thought about the chairlift—he'd really enjoyed riding it, especially on warm summer evenings.

Chris let out a little shriek of fear as they materialized almost a thousand feet above the valley floor and she threw her arms around him. He held her against him, feeling bad that he had frightened her. Her trembling, originally caused by her fear, became a physical reaction to the hard masculine body molded seamlessly to hers.

Before his own response could escalate, he pushed her gently away from him. But as he gazed at her, her thoughts and feelings surged into his mind and he saw himself through her eyes.

He looks like a god standing there, so tall and handsome. When we were married he was a self-conscious boy, and now he's a confident, powerful man. God, I wish I'd never divorced him; he's sex on a stick and I'd love to lick his—

Embarrassed, Derek slammed the door shut on those thoughts. The look on his face must have given him away, though, because Chris looked outraged.

"You bastard, you were reading my mind, weren't you?" She was furious—and dismayed—that he had caught her thinking about him that way.

"Sorry," he muttered. He could feel his face flaming.

Chris scowled fiercely for a moment and then relented with a sigh. "I'm sorry, too. I shouldn't be thinking those things about you. I lost you a long time ago and I have to live with it. Sarah's a lucky woman, and I'm jealous. But, the truth is, I'd never be a good match for you now anyway." She peered fearfully over the edge of the cliff and shivered. "I don't know how you got us up here."

"It's called teleporting. Don't you remember some of the stories I used to read?"

She nodded, but still looked so miserable that he decided to cheer her up. He held out his hand to her.

Chris glanced at him suspiciously.

"I know ya love the La Sal Mountains when the aspens turn color. The leaves started turnin' a few days ago, and there hasn't been a lot of wind, so there should still be plenty left on the trees. Why don't we go to Warner Lake and check it out?"

"What, now? How are we going to get back in time for dinner?"

"Really? Chris, ya were just now thinkin' of me as a god. Well, in a sense, I am. Merlin is the god of magic and healin', so that makes me a demigod. Trust me; I can get us there in seconds." Derek again held his hand out to her, his palm glowing.

"Come on, let's go," he said softly.

She swallowed worriedly and hesitated for a moment, then placed her small hand trustingly in his large calloused one.

Suddenly, she felt as if her entire body was being wrenched apart, and then she was standing in a grove of aspens at the edge of a campground, not far from a body of water she hadn't seen in years—Warner Lake.

"God, that was really uncomfortable." She took a few shallow breaths, hoping her stomach would settle down. "But that's an astounding ability. Can Sarah or your son teleport?"

"Nope, just Merlin, my sister Lumina and me. Sarah's a wizard, so she only has basic magical powers, and Morry, although he's a sorcerer, is mainly a shapeshifter and can't teleport or levitate. Emily's part Elf, and her magic apparently doesn't include teleportation either."

Chris nodded wisely, as he detailed everyone's magical attributes, though none of it made sense to her. Then she looked up through the white branches and quivering leaves of yellow-gold to the clear blue sky above them and sighed with pleasure. "Oh, it's so beautiful!"

"It sure is. Here, let's lay down for a moment and just look up. Remember how we always used to do that when we first started datin'?" Derek quickly conjured a thick, double-sized patchwork quilt and spread it out on the ground between several large, old aspen trees.

She blinked at the quilt and then at her old friend. He silently indicated that she should sit, so she did, and he followed suit. Then they both reclined as plump pillows appeared under their heads, and they gaped at the glorious colors above and all around them.

"You're right, Derek, I've missed this. Thank you." Chris turned her head and admired his striking profile.

"No problem. I know ya always enjoyed our trips up here."

They reclined quietly for a few more minutes and then decided to walk down to the water's edge. As soon as they were on their feet again, Derek snapped his fingers and the quilt and pillows disappeared. Chris jerked a little in surprise.

"I don't think I'll ever get used to you having magic powers,"

she murmured, as they made their way through the tall grass, kept green by the constant presence of water.

"To tell ya the truth, I'm still not used to it. But since I'm immortal, I guess I have plenty of time to adjust," he said with a straight face, knowing that she would be speechless at his announcement.

She didn't disappoint him. She was standing still, and when he looked back at her, her mouth was hanging open and her eyes were huge.

He laughed. "Sorry, I couldn't resist."

She laughed too, convinced that he had to be playing her. "You're such an ass!"

He just smiled and continued walking to the edge of the small lake, and she followed a short distance behind him.

Oh, God, he's not kidding. Christ, he's immortal? She couldn't imagine it, and didn't have a clue what to say, so she just stood quietly next to him as they took in the peaceful scene.

Derek saw the disbelief on her lovely face and heard her thoughts as she tried to accept this new reality. He was grateful for the calming influence of the spectacular setting, and suggested that they sit down on the grass near the water's edge as it lapped rhythmically against the shore.

The lake was clean and full of fish, and the area had always been popular with the Moab residents as a destination for camping and picnicking, especially during the summer, when the heat in the valley soared into the triple digits during the day.

However, this time of year, at an elevation of nearly 8,000 feet, the air was crisp and cool, and the clear water glistened in the late afternoon sunlight. The shadows under the trees in the nearby campground were deep and mysterious, and there was only one trailer present, evidence of someone's reluctance to admit that fall would soon give way to winter. The sun still shone brightly on the rocky slopes above them, and the azure of the sky seemed unreal. The golden leaves on the aspen trees glowed in a last burst of autumn color, and a light but chill breeze lifted Chris's hair, blowing it gently around her face. Derek sensed that she was getting cold and conjured a light jacket for her. She put the pink jacket on gratefully, and then continued to appreciate the scenery.

"It's gorgeous, and so peaceful. Thank you." Chris breathed in slowly and allowed herself to relax. Then, she turned to him and gasped. "My God, you're glowing just like the leaves." She gazed wide-eyed at her ex, and thought, He's so incredibly handsome.

Derek sat still, hearing her but not answering, his eyes closed and his aura pulsing brightly around him. He finally blinked as if coming back from far away and looked over at her, his eyes a startling gold. "Sorry, my grandfather was communicatin' with me. He's joinin' us for dinner, which is really unusual. He normally just drops in once in a while, so I'm hopin' he's heard from Merlin."

"Does your grandfather live far from here?" Chris asked curiously.

Derek paused before answering, wondering how she would react. "Ya could say that. He lives in the realm of the gods."

"Ah, okaaay, I'm sorry I asked."

"Chris, I'm not kiddin'. Llyr is Merlin's father; he's the Welsh god of the sea. He's incorporeal unless he comes to this realm, and then he takes human form."

She smoothed the errant locks of wispy blond hair away from her face and looked directly into his eyes, which had returned to their normal warm brown color, trying hard to believe him.

He allowed it for a moment then glanced away, unable to meet her gaze for any longer than that.

"That's at least the third time you've done that! Why won't you look me in the eyes, Derek?" she asked, hurt.

He sighed, afraid she wouldn't understand. "It's not what ya think. If we looked too deeply into each other's eyes, we'd trigger what's called the Seein', and that's not a good idea between the two of us."

He decided to be frank with her. "Look, Chris, we've been friends a long time, but I'm with Sarah now, and if she knew I'd allowed ya to See my inner self, it would make her really unhappy.

It's a very special experience between two people; even more intimate than havin' sex."

Chris frowned and pursed her lips. "I already know you pretty damn well and—"

"No. Sorry, but ya don't, not anymore," he interrupted. "Believe me. You may know Derek Colburn, but ya don't know Emrys Ambrosius."

"Who?"

"Me. That's my birth name. Merlin's last name is Ambrosius. His maternal grandfather was a Roman centurion named Flavius Ambrosius." Derek stopped talking, as it was apparent that Chris wouldn't be able to absorb any more. Then, he realized that Sarah was trying to reach him. She still hadn't perfected her telepathic skills, but was able to get through to him most of the time.

Is everything okay, honey? I thought you'd be back by now. Morry showed up and brought the wine and Llyr just got here.

Yeah, everythin' is alright. We're up at Warner Lake and we'll be back in a few minutes.

See you soon, babe. I love you.

Love ya, too, Sarah. *Derek focused on Chris again. "Time to go. Everyone's waitin' on us." He stood up and pulled her to her feet. They took a moment to gaze one more time at the scenery around them, and to savor the pure mountain air.*

"Ready?" he asked with a smile.

She nodded, and with just a second of gut-wrenching movement, they were again standing in Derek's living room.

CHAPTER 8

Moab, Christmas Day, 2015

DEREK BLINKED AND REALIZED THAT Lumina was recounting her memories about helping their father come back from Hell. He felt vaguely guilty for letting his mind wander again when he should be listening to everyone's stories.

Lumina paused for a moment to take a sip from the mug of lukewarm chocolate on the coffee table in front of her and glanced questioningly at her brother.

Don't mind me, sis, I just zoned out for a few minutes—I'll tell ya about it later, okay? Derek directed his thought to her alone.

Lumina frowned briefly at Derek in response and then continued with her story. "And I walked into the kitchen with my blue and yellow blanket wrapped around me and said, 'Daddy, I helped.' I'd grown to the size of a three-year-old from using my powers to help Mom bring Dad back, and then…"

The sound of Lumina's voice faded into the background as Chris stared at her ex-husband. Even though she sensed Sarah glaring at her, she found that she couldn't take her eyes off of him. He had obviously been thinking about something else as Lumina was talking, his eyes closed and his aura flaring brightly around him. That reminded her of how shocked she'd been to discover the unbelievable changes Derek had experienced.

And she remembered that unforgettable meal when she'd met Derek's grandfather, the god Llyr, and what had occurred after that…

October, 2014

Chris stepped away from Derek self-consciously when she saw everyone looking at her. Her breath caught as she noticed an extremely tall, well-built man standing next to Morry, dressed as informally as the rest of them in jeans and a T-shirt. He looked rather like Merlin, with the same green, slanted cat's eyes that she remembered from her introduction to the sorcerer in 2013, but the man's hair was neither as dark nor as straight as Merlin's and his physique was more muscular. He appeared to be as young as all the men in Derek's family were. But he couldn't be, she realized. If his normal state was incorporeal—a god existing in another dimension—he could very well be many thousands of years old. Unable to imagine such an immense span of time, she just gaped at him helplessly.

At once, Derek kneeled in front of the 'man,' bowed his head, and said with the utmost respect, "Grandfather, I'm glad to see ya. Thanks for comin'."

Chris was caught off guard by this spontaneous display of reverence, and wondered if she should follow Derek's lead and bow to the god of the sea.

Apparently hearing her thoughts, Llyr gazed down at her from his prodigious height and chuckled. "No need for that, young woman, as I have constantly reminded my grandson. And my great-grandson." He winked at Morry, and Chris noticed that Derek's son looked even more ill at ease than he had earlier in his nakedness.

She just nodded and smiled timidly at the god, silently agreeing with Morry that this being could undeniably give one a reason to be nervous.

"Dinner's ready, everyone, so let's eat. Please go ahead and serve yourselves," Sarah announced, motioning to the food and dinnerware assembled on the counter between the kitchen and the dining room.

It was a veritable feast. There was spaghetti with meat sauce, garlic bread, steamed broccoli, green salad with Italian dressing and a hearty Chianti, the bottom of the bottle wrapped in traditional raffia. It all looked and smelled delectable and Chris realized that she was starving.

Everyone, including Llyr, helped themselves to the various dishes and then carried their plates to the dining room table. It was apparent that Derek wasn't sure what to expect from his grandfather's presence, so perhaps Llyr didn't socialize with them very often.

"You're actually gonna eat, Grandfather?" Derek asked with a note of astonishment in his voice.

Llyr turned, looked into his eyes and grinned boyishly. "It's my prerogative after all, Grandson. I don't need to eat, of course, but I decided to do so this time to honor your woman's efforts—it's as simple as that." And then he winked at Sarah, who blushed with pleasure.

Derek nodded, and then dug into his meal. He paused with a forkful of salad halfway to his mouth as he thought of something.

"Grandfather, is it possible that Merlin is in the Other World right now?"

Llyr swallowed a bite of bread and shrugged nonchalantly. "I don't know. Perhaps."

Derek frowned, wondering if Llyr was being entirely truthful. "Okay, what if we wait until Samhain, when the barrier between the two worlds is thin, and try to find him there?"

"Sowen? What's that?" Morry and Chris shared a bewildered look, then he quickly looked away from her. She figured he didn't want her to See him.

"Samhain means 'summer's end' in Gaelic," Llyr explained. "It marks the beginning of the dark half of the year, and it is a time to honor the dead."

Llyr glanced at Derek. "But as you mentioned, the barrier between the worlds is thin at Samhain, and therefore it could be a dangerous time to search for him in the Other World. You wouldn't want to inadvertently release any spirits, as they do not belong in this realm; nor would you want to become trapped there yourself." He paused to take a sip of his wine and then blotted his lips with a napkin.

"Well, maybe that's not such a good idea, then. What would you suggest?"

Llyr eyed his grandson with barely concealed impatience. "Derek, did it ever occur to you that Merlin's absence isn't just about you or Emily or Lumina?" He turned to Morry with a tight grin. "Or you Morry, even though all of you miss him and think your lives cannot go on without him? The Creator of this universe has determined that the situation is necessary for many reasons, including lessons to be learned and experiences to be had by all of you. Time, as you may have noticed by now, is flexible, particularly for those of us who have access to realms unseen by the beings who reside on this plane of existence." He took another swallow of the Chianti, as if he wasn't used to talking so much and his throat was dry.

Chris noticed the astonished looks on everyone's faces, and surmised that Llyr's long speech was indeed a rather unusual occurrence.

Then the god turned his green gaze on her and she was overwhelmed by the power and control that radiated from him. Chris shivered and looked down at her plate, hoping he would turn his attention elsewhere, which thankfully he did when Morry asked him a question.

"Uh, Great-Grandfather Llyr, I'm curious about something." It was obvious that Morry was a little tense. "Why is it, if you are the Welsh god of the sea, you don't seem to spend any time in Wales, near the ocean?"

Llyr calmly finished his dinner before answering. "And how do you know that I don't?" He raised one eyebrow and looked directly into Morry's eyes, holding his gaze until Morry finally blinked and replied hoarsely, "I, I...uh, well..."

Everyone just stared back and forth between the two of them, and then quietly finished their own plates of food. No one noticed when Llyr grinned to himself while his great-grandson sweated bullets.

Then Llyr decided to let them in on a secret. In a way, he was surprised at himself, for he really wasn't one to reveal every little detail about the god realm. But, what the heck, he liked these relatives of his and their friends and enjoyed keeping them off-balance.

He cleared his throat, and there was complete silence in the room.

"Perhaps you were not aware of the fact that the Irish god of the sea is called Lir as well." He smirked in satisfaction as he saw the stunned looks exchanged, as everyone realized that the god

sitting with them had been revered in ancient times in both Wales and Ireland.

Derek and Morry glanced covertly at each other, wondering what had brought on Llyr's decision to share that information. It was unlike him to be so forthcoming.

After dinner, Sarah offered coffee and biscotti for dessert, but everyone was so full that they all politely declined. Llyr thanked Sarah and Derek for inviting him, and then disappeared into thin air, which would have totally freaked Chris out if not for her other unusual experiences earlier that day. As soon as the god was gone, Morry took a deep, cleansing breath and relaxed.

"I wish I would have just kept my mouth shut," Morry muttered as his father said at the same time, "Well, wasn't that fun."

After a pause, Morry asked quietly, "Did you know he was the god of the sea for both countries?"

Derek shook his head. "Nope. Shocked the hell outta me."

"Wow, that was intense." Chris laughed nervously, as she helped Sarah clear the table and load the dishwasher.

"Yes, it was." Sarah glanced towards the living room, where Derek and Morry were talking quietly together. "Why did he confront Llyr like that?"

"I can't imagine."

Chris had had all the excitement she needed—and then some—for the day, so as soon as the kitchen was cleaned up, she thanked Sarah for the delicious meal, said good night to Derek and Morry, and left the house.

She wished she'd had a chance to speak privately to Morry, but she was almost too tired to care at that point.

Earlier in the day, she had walked over from her friend's place a couple of blocks away and hadn't thought about bringing a flashlight. Luckily, the moon was so bright this evening that she didn't really need one. It was chilly, though, so she was grateful for the warmth of the cute pink jacket Derek had conjured for her up at Warner Lake. She shook her head in disbelief that she was now taking his magic for granted.

Suddenly, she heard footsteps and realized someone was following her, and she started walking faster, her heart pounding in fear.

"Hey, Chris, wait up," said a familiar male voice behind her.

She stopped and turned around, waiting for Morry to catch up with her. And now her heart was pounding for a different reason.

"Can I walk you home?"

He sounded eager for her company, and it was apparent that this handsome man wanted her. There was no reason he wouldn't be attracted to her, but she almost felt guilty for her own attraction to her ex-husband's son.

"Sure, I'd like that," she said, her heart in her mouth. She wanted Morry so badly that she could hardly stand it, and he apparently sensed her interest—or had read her thoughts and her body language loud and clear.

Without thinking, she blurted out, "I'm actually staying with a friend until I can find my own apartment, but she's not home tonight." God, she might as well have announced she wanted to have sex with him.

He grinned at her and she smiled at him tremulously when he put his arm around her shoulders. Oh, boy, he obviously heard that *thought.*

When they reached the apartment complex on Kane Creek, she guided him to her door and unlocked it. "Would you like to come in for awhile?" She held her breath, hoping he'd say yes.

"I'd like that." Morry glanced at her suggestively.

As soon as they were inside the dimly lit front room, Chris turned to face him and looked into his eyes, and Morry pulled her close to him. He held her face as he plundered her sweet mouth, both of them moaning in anticipation. She was such a little thing that he had to bend over a ways.

Chris felt the undeniable evidence of his desire, and kissed him back almost frantically. Finally, she took a breath and said, shyly, "I need a shower—would you take one with me?"

"I guess I can do that," he murmured, running his fingers through her soft blond hair and nipping lightly at her neck.

She led the way into the bathroom, and while she got towels for them, Morry stripped. Still clothed, she turned around and inhaled sharply. Before her stood Derek's son, in nothing but his skin, and with such a look of desire on his face that she couldn't believe it was for her. She was aware that men considered her attractive, but, well, she was just a regular mortal and Morry was probably a demigod. She winced, hoping she hadn't said that out loud.

"Yes, actually I am," he said in a matter-of-fact tone of voice. "No, you didn't say it out loud, Chris. I heard your thoughts."

She just stood there, staring at his face and then at his erection, which looked huge to her. She felt embarrassed, overwhelmed and just a little afraid.

"Chris, it's okay," Morry said reassuringly, holding out his hand to her. "Come with me..."

She walked slowly towards him, feeling like he'd mesmerized her. He took the towels from her and left them on the counter, then led her back into the bedroom that his heightened sense of smell told him was hers and began undressing her, kissing each part of her thus revealed. He was sure that Chris's need for a shower was just a reaction to being anxious. She smelled like fresh flowers and tasted as sweet as he expected she would.

Chris was breathing hard, and became greatly aroused as he gently suckled her breasts, then stroked her intimately, slowly pushing several fingers inside her, preparing her for him. He eased her against his naked form and she groaned with pleasure, reaching between them to grip his hardness. He thrust against her hand, his desire unmistakable.

Then, she smiled as she knelt in front of him and took him into her mouth. He sucked in a breath as she ran her tongue down the swollen length of his penis while she cupped his testicles.

Morry moaned. "Oh, God, Chris, I can't wait any longer!" He gestured with one hand and the covers rolled back. Carefully lifting her onto the sheets so she was flat on her back, he joined her, stroking her belly and thighs and between her legs. She gasped and arched her back, pulling him closer, until he was on top of her. She was so small that he completely covered her.

Then, he positioned himself and gazed raptly into her eyes as he slowly impaled her. He was very large and she gasped as he filled her. Automatically, she tilted her pelvis, allowing him to penetrate even further into her body.

And then, their limbs entwined, they began to move slowly, rhythmically, in a dance as old as time. The feeling of him inside of her was exquisite, hot and tight, filling her completely, and as he thrust into her repeatedly, the pleasure was almost more than she could bear. Chris moaned as he brought her ever closer to the highest pinnacle of sensation.

"Morry," she whispered, her fantasies all fulfilled in that moment as her body literally erupted into the most overpowering orgasm she'd ever had.

He achieved his own climax and lay heavily on top of her for a few moments, reveling in the feeling of their joined bodies. Carefully, he pulled out and rolled to the side. He rose up on one elbow and reached out to tuck a strand of hair behind her ear, then kissed her again.

"Chris," he breathed, "I think I love you."

Unprepared for his confession, she didn't respond, and had a hard time meeting his gaze. She didn't know why she felt so embarrassed. They hadn't done anything wrong—it was a case of mutual attraction between consenting adults.

Morry knew he'd made a mistake by declaring his feelings so soon, and it was plain that she felt guilty for 'seducing' him.

"I know you're feeling kind of weird about this, but please, just give us a chance. I think we could do pretty well together, don't you?" He hoped he could salvage the feeling of closeness and pleasure they'd experienced. It was everything he'd ever wanted.

"It was fantastic." Chris admitted. "And I...care about you, too."

She thought about it for a moment, and then continued with a shy smile, "Okay, I'll give it a chance."

"Awesome!" He felt a profound sense of relief and wished they could spend the night together, but he suspected that she really wasn't ready for that.

"Well, I guess I'd better go, so you can get some sleep." She nodded, and he turned to get dressed.

Reluctantly, he headed down the hallway. She got up and put her robe on, following him into the living room.

He opened the front door and stepped outside, then paused and turned back to smile at her reassuringly. "Everything will be alright, you'll see. Good night, Chris. I'll call you soon." He looked into her wide hazel eyes, gave her one last kiss and walked away into the darkness.

Chris watched him go, almost regretting that she hadn't asked him to stay. She thought about calling him back, but she didn't. She decided to just let things ride. She'd already had an incredibly confusing day and didn't need to add to it.

And she couldn't believe that he'd said he loved her. They hardly knew each other.

After showering and brushing her teeth, she studied her reflection in the mirror above the sink. Was she looking for a sign that she'd lost her mind? How ridiculous, *she thought. She used the toilet then padded back into her bedroom, smiling as she noticed how neatly Morry had pulled the covers off the bed with his magic. She tugged them back up and then got in bed, trying to compose herself for sleep, but the sheets smelled like him and all she could think of was Morry making love to her.*

Finally, the long stressful day took its toll and she fell asleep. She dreamed that she was with Morry again, and the sex was amazing. The feel of his smooth naked skin inflamed her senses and he took her to one satisfying climax after another.

But then, as is the way of dreams, it wasn't Morry making love to her, it was Derek. She awoke from her dream wondering what her subconscious was trying to tell her—that she had never really wanted Morry, but it was the only way to be closer to his father? She drifted back to sleep before she could figure it out and slept soundly and dreamlessly for the remainder of the night.

When she woke up the next morning, she stretched, feeling rested and physically satisfied. She got up and washed her face, dressed for the day, and headed into the kitchen to make coffee.

She was feeling optimistic and thought that maybe she and Morry could make it work. If not, she could still enjoy the fantastic sex while it lasted, right? She grinned and started thinking about their next rendezvous.

Her future planning came to a screeching halt when she realized they hadn't used a condom. Oh, no, what if she was pregnant? Well, at least the baby would have a demigod for a father, she rationalized. Then she took a breath and relaxed when she remembered what time of the month it was.

CHAPTER 9

Moab, Christmas Day, 2015

CHRIS STIRRED AND REALIZED THAT Emily was looking expectantly at her. "I'm sorry, what did you say?" She knew she was blushing, but nobody mentioned it, so she tried to act nonchalant. Hopefully, neither Morry nor Derek had been reading her mind as she daydreamed about them.

"I asked if you could tell us how you originally met Merlin and sold him The Moab Herbalist."

"Oh, sure, I'd be happy to," she replied, and proceeded to describe her first encounter with the sorcerer. "Only I didn't know about the magic then!"

Everyone laughed, each person remembering his or her own first-time experiences with Merlin's abilities.

Around eleven thirty, Emily poured herself a last cup of coffee. She sank down into her favorite armchair in the living room, took a calming breath and relaxed. "Well, that was fun, but I'm glad everyone's gone."

"How are you doing, Em?" Rae asked from her seat on the couch.

"Oh, I'm okay. It was nice having everyone here, but it was awfully hard to keep being reminded of my husband. I just feel so helpless—I wish I could use my own magic to bring him home, but I know I'm not that powerful."

"Mom, I don't think our powers have anything to do with getting Dad back, or at least not entirely," Lumina said as she joined them, carrying another mug of hot chocolate. She knew her mother would have no objection if she wanted to drink coffee, but she just didn't like it.

Lumina sat down next to her grandmother and took a sip of her drink. "I spent a lot of time thinking about it last night before I went to sleep, and I'm convinced that when Dad is ready to come back, he'll *allow* us to help him come home. Does that make sense?"

"It does. Nothing else has worked, so far," Emily said, wryly. "However, you'll have to convince everyone else of that fact."

"Actually, I'm going to suggest to Derek that he try a different approach at our next meeting. Maybe he can use that special ability of his. Can't hurt."

"When is the next meeting?" Rae asked.

"I'll confirm the date so the three of us can be there."

"That sounds like a plan. At least it will help us to feel that we've made a little progress." Emily sighed.

"Mom, don't worry, everything's going to be okay."

CHAPTER 10

Old Inverness, Caledonia, Early Fifth Century

WE HAD BEEN CAMPING ON the banks of the swiftly flowing river for many weeks, not far from the hill I had originally identified as Tomnahurich, when the feeling washed over me once again that there was something wrong about this adventure. Neither one of us was supposed to be here. Exactly where we were supposed to be, I still had no idea, but it seemed to me that we were both fish out of water, in an environment that was not natural for either of us.

We had been here for several weeks when my companion blurted out in that accented voice of his, "Bel. My name is Bel." I could not get him to say anything else for some time, since we rarely spoke to one another. Our daily interaction was more like a silent truce—perhaps a temporary cease-fire between longtime mortal enemies.

I had spent long hours over the previous weeks pondering how the two of us had ended up together. We seemed unlikely companions at best, and I could not help but wonder about our obviously fractious history.

This night, with our evening meal long over, Bel had acted even more reclusive than usual. He retreated to our shelter of rough hides, which housed our beds: pallets on the ground consisting of the furs of the animals Bel had slaughtered for our food and warmth. The hides had been quickly and inadequately scraped and cured, and smelled more than a little rank, but I scarcely noticed once the penetrating cold of the night came upon us.

I sat on a flat rock with my back turned to the warmth of our campfire, staring out into a darkness that was unbroken except for the pale reflection of the crescent moon on the swiftly moving water. I pulled my cloak closer around me to ward off a sudden chill breeze. Expecting a wash of pain from my right hand, I felt only a slight tautness from the recently healed flesh. I rubbed it tentatively with my left hand, wondering yet again how I could have burned myself so severely, and yet the blistered skin had healed up before my eyes. I had made light of the incident when Bel looked at me askance, but it worried me mightily. I was merely an itinerant healer, no one special, and certainly not what that incident would lead someone to believe—that I was an individual who practiced the dark arts. But even if it were true, I knew that I had not initiated the healing—it had occurred without any conscious effort on my part.

For just a moment, I stilled as the river seemed to speak to me and I was cognizant of an ancient truth, which then slipped away even as I tried to hold onto it. I drew the scent of damp peat into my lungs, forcing myself to focus, but it was no use. The knowledge I had glimpsed so briefly was gone.

I sighed in frustration and scrubbed my smooth hands—which should have been calloused and rough from work and the cold—over my face, once again feeling the lack of facial hair and wondering about it. I knew that I was not a young man. The reflections that I could see in still water indicated that I was at least a score and ten in years—far beyond the age at which the beard of a man should have grown. Bel certainly had no problem growing hair on his face, but his body was as hairless as a child's, prompting me to conjecture that he and I were perhaps related. Gods help us if we were, since we usually felt a vehement dislike for each other, although neither he nor I understood why.

Without warning, I had a brief flash of memory. I saw myself in a cave lined with crystals, with a full, luxuriant beard and moustache as black as the hair on my head, flowing down across my robed chest. When and where that moment in time had occurred was a complete mystery to me. I shivered involuntarily.

It was now very late and I knew I should retire, as dawn would come too soon and we would have to resume the unending tasks associated with our daily survival. Bel, of course, did the hunting, as he seemed to relish killing animals. It turned out that he had a dagger, which he had used to bring down a young deer the first day. I shuddered when I remembered the bloody results of that hunt, although I had to admit I had eagerly consumed the meat once it had been cooked.

He had then skillfully created a bow and a few arrows, using the tendons from the animal for the bowstring and sharpened stones for the arrowheads, secured with thin strips of hide. The arrows were fletched with the split tail feathers of birds he had killed, and he had contrived a quiver from the deer hide. He still used his dagger for skinning and butchering the animals he hunted.

I knew that we needed the meat and hides to keep ourselves alive, and I did value his skill, but his unabashed enjoyment of the slaughter disgusted me.

It was my job to gather firewood, and at the same time, I spent hours harvesting as many medicinal herbs as I could find, along with edible plants to augment our meals. Although I had no memory of learning about herbs and their various uses, I thanked the gods for my invaluable knowledge. I bartered for other goods that we needed by successfully treating the sick and the wounded among the local clans, much to the chagrin of the men who styled themselves physicians. Butchers would be a more appropriate term.

Often, I had been fortunate to have treated members of the wealthier families who lived across the river and been paid for my services in coin. Eventually, I hoped to be able to purchase a horse or two. It had never occurred to me until now to wonder how these primitive people had possession of such coins. And why did I think they were primitive? Compared to what?

I drew out the soft leather pouch that hung on a narrow strip of hide around my neck underneath my tunic, loosened the opening and shook the contents out into my lap. My treasures consisted mainly of healing stones—bloodstone, soapstone and quartz—and a few coins.

The first coin I examined appeared to be Celtic, depicting the horse goddess, Epona. I set that one aside and reached for another. I selected a large coin and turned the disc over, trying to decipher a date or identifying mark, but most of the markings had been worn off. The only thing I could make out in the feeble glow from the dying fire was a man's visage. It appeared to be a Roman coin, which meant the current year could be anywhere between AD 43 and the early fifth century; in other words, during the Roman occupation of Britain. Considering that I had seen very few centurions in the vicinity since we arrived, I surmised it was probably around AD 400, or even as late as AD 415. But if my memory served me correctly, the Romans had never established a permanent outpost this far north in Caledonia, merely a small, temporary fort at Cawdor, several miles east of Inverness.

I stopped that train of thought abruptly and frowned. How strange. Why would I think of the time period in those terms, as if I belonged in some future era, looking back at a long ago past? And why would I be aware of the details of Roman occupation in this area?

I sighed in frustration. Again, my efforts at trying to determine who I was and how I came to be here proved fruitless, so I decided to mentally create a list of the things I did remember. The first and most important thing was that my name was Emrys, a Welsh name to be sure, and that felt right. But it seemed somehow incomplete and may not have been the name I used on a daily basis.

Secondly, I was an accomplished herbalist and healer. The extent of my skills had been revealed recently, when I had stitched up the leg of a man whose ax had slipped as he chopped firewood. Then, later on that same day, I had delivered a babe who had been turned wrong in the mother's womb. I had saved all three—woodsman, mother and child—to the astonishment of the local "physician," who had apparently lost more patients than he had saved.

I now added to those valuable memories the vision of a cave in which I had apparently dwelled and prospered, if the quality of the robe I had been wearing was any indication. But trying to re-create the glimpse I had had into the meaning of my life caused a severe pain to flare in my head.

I finally gave up and decided to turn in. Carefully, I replaced the stones and coins in the kidskin pouch, for which I had gladly bartered an herbal tonic. I banked the fire carefully, then entered the cramped enclosure and crawled fully clothed under our meager blankets and assorted deer hides, next to Bel. I hated the rank smell of the man, but conserving body heat was a necessity these cold nights. As I tucked my cloak in around me under the hides, I was grateful it wasn't raining—being damp as well as cold held no appeal for me. It was fortunate that we had not arrived here in the dead of winter during a time of snow and ice, for we would surely have been in dire straits.

As I started to succumb to exhaustion, it crossed my mind that I probably smelled no better than Bel. Not to mention the fact we both were crawling with lice again and would need another herbal treatment soon. I sighed, scratched my head and then my groin, and reached for the solace of sleep.

Bel shifted restlessly as he felt Emrys settling in next to him. He was glad his companion had finally come to bed—he disliked the cold and the darkness even more than he disliked Emrys, so he was relieved to have the man's warmth and presence near him.

He had been thinking about the unusual circumstances the two of them had experienced since they had awakened on the hilltop. It bothered him more than he ever let on that he could not remember anything except his name, and even that did not seem altogether correct. He realized that he was not a particularly intelligent man, but still his missing memories disturbed him. However, he did have the physical skills it took to help the two of them survive; for one thing, he was an accomplished hunter. If it were up to Emrys, who was so squeamish about killing, they would be eating nothing but roots, berries and herbs. He, on the other hand, excelled in hunting and killing things, especially those creatures that challenged his skill and courage.

Sometimes Bel did not understand why he disliked Emrys so intensely. He often felt a close kinship with the man and kept trying to find similarities between them. They both had the blackest hair he had ever seen and both of them had a lack of hair on certain parts of their bodies. But their other physical differences told him that they most likely were not related. His own skin was swarthy and his eyes were black as coal, like many of the dwellers in the nearby village. Emrys had pale skin and strangely luminous green eyes—almost like a cat he had seen once—so he most likely came from the south, from the kingdom of Gwynedd, perhaps. True, they were both tall and well-built, but Bel knew he was somewhat taller and more muscular and…Bah! He was disgusted with himself and his pathetic attempts to feel closer to Emrys; in reality, the man often made him feel ill at ease and fearful.

Just this morning, Emrys had burned his hand severely, and yet it had healed up in front of his very eyes. Shocked, he had watched the man try to hide the fact, and this made him feel most perturbed. It occurred to him that Emrys must possess some sort of magic.

Unreasonable feelings of anger, resentment and even hatred of the other man arose in him. How could he feel that way about someone he had just met? Did Emrys feel the same way about him? Sometimes he felt almost as if they were brothers, or cousins. None of it made sense.

Bel sighed, shivering despite the thick hides covering them, and closed his eyes once more, waiting for sleep to take him.

CHAPTER 11

Moab, Christmas Day, 2015, Early Afternoon

After discussing it with her mom and grandmother, Lumina decided she should talk to Derek right away about her idea. She knew he would be home—he was on furlough, after all—but thought she'd better not barge in without announcing herself, just in case he and Sarah were engaged in unmentionable activities.

Hey, Derek, are you busy? Can I come over and talk to you?

Yeah, sure. We're not doin' anythin' important anyway, just watchin' TV. What do ya need?

She didn't bother answering and teleported directly into Derek's living room.

"Hi, Sarah. I hope I'm not interrupting anything." Lumina said with a saucy grin.

"No, honey, you're not. I think I'm going to take a walk and work off all that food I ate this morning." Sarah got up off the couch and retrieved her coat, scarf and hat, then grabbed her snow boots, pulling them on hastily before she went out the front door.

"Brr, it's cold out there." Lumina shivered as a cold draft wafted across the room after Sarah's departure. She plopped down on the other end of the couch and tucked her sock-clad feet under her.

Derek turned towards her and crossed his arms over his chest. "Okay, what's goin' on?"

"How would you feel about me helping you develop your secret ability?"

Derek just stared at his little sister. Sometimes he completely forgot that she wasn't just a teenager—she was an ancient goddess. Maybe not on the same level as Merlin, but a powerful entity, nevertheless. She had a different kind of connection to their father—one that he could never have. In fact, she had tried to utilize that specific connection, the god Light inside of her, to guide Merlin home, but she couldn't determine exactly how to do that.

"Remember how you and Dad traveled through time coming back from Camelot? And then you merged with Dad's essence to keep his soul from being ripped out of his body?"

"Of course I remember, probably better'n you since you were a tiny baby when it happened. But I have no idea *how* he brought us through time—I only know he used his god powers. And I never actually figured out how I did what I did to save him after we got back to Moab, either."

The two of them had been immersed in a vision, during which a dark force had attempted to extract Merlin's soul from his body to sever his connection with the mortal realm. Merlin had taken the only action available to him at the time; he had transformed himself into the god of magic and healing, leaving his human body an empty shell. It turned out that the vision had been generated to disguise the theft of Merlin's soul, but Derek had prevented the dark force from completing that wicked deed.

"It's okay, Derek." Lumina reached out and smoothed his hair back with a loving hand. "I'm not totally sure this is going to work, but we need to start somewhere. So here's what I think you should do first…"

And she projected an idea into his mind, a concept that made sense to him as a step in figuring out and utilizing his "secret" ability.

"That seems doable, munchkin."

She flicked her finger against his ear.

"Ow! What was that for?"

"Just to let you know I really don't like it when you call me that!"

"Jeez, Sis, sorry. Way to put me in my place," Derek complained as he rubbed his ear to ease the stinging sensation.

"Let's get back on track. Did Dad ever show you how to open up a portal? No? Well, here's what you might want to try…"

CHAPTER 12

Old Inverness, Caledonia, Early Fifth Century

I WAS DREAMING OF KISSING a lovely maiden with long, golden-brown hair and sparkling hazel eyes, when I awoke with a start in the chill predawn hours. The feeling of wrongness that I had felt the previous evening was magnified tenfold. I quickly crawled out from under the skins and leaped to my feet, my heart pounding in excitement or fear, or a combination of the two. I eased my dagger out of its sheath and stood at the edge of our encampment peering into the gloom.

Bel sensed my movement and jerked awake, levering himself up onto one elbow. "Is something amiss, then?" he asked in a sleep-roughened voice.

"I know not," I answered quietly. I heard rustling as Bel also got up and ducked out from the hide tent, preparing to fight if someone attacked us.

Abruptly, I was beset by the feeling that I was being watched. I glanced over my shoulder as if that someone was standing behind and to the right of me, and for just a moment I could have sworn that I saw the outline of a man that I recognized. I even thought I heard him call to me in a language that I did not understand, yet which sounded strangely familiar. As the apparition faded, I shivered and turned away, trying to convince myself that I had been dreaming, yet considerably disturbed by this occurrence.

I slipped my dagger back into the stiff leather sheath, and turned uneasily to Bel.

"Did you see him?"

"See who, Emrys?"

I stared at him, wondering if he truly had not seen the apparition. "Never mind, it was nothing, just my imagination," I said quietly, and then turned to the task of rekindling the fire.

I could feel Bel's eyes boring into my back as I prepared the morning meal.

CHAPTER 13

Moab, December 30, 2015, Meeting at the Knights' Residence

DEREK STUMBLED AS HE STEPPED back through the fold in time just as the portal closed up with an almost audible pop. Hands reached out to steady him and many excited voices demanded to know what he'd witnessed.

"Well, I think I found him. I'm pretty sure it was Merlin, but the light was so dim, I could hardly make out his features," Derek exclaimed. "And he seemed to sense that I was there. I think he heard me, but he acted like he couldn't understand what I was sayin'."

"Could you see anything else, any landmarks, or the type of clothing he was wearing? Anything at all that would help us to pinpoint the year, the location?" Emily demanded irritably. She looked careworn and exhausted, as if she hadn't slept since Christmas. Rae Crandall stood quietly next to her daughter, offering moral support.

Derek blinked wearily, then closed his eyes and concentrated. "He had a long, rough cloak of some kind wrapped around him, and I could see his breath, so it was cold. I think there was someone else behind him, a big man who could have been Beli. They seemed to be campin' in a forest, 'cause I saw what looked like a lean-to made outta animal skins under some huge trees. It must have been really early in the mornin' 'cause the sun wasn't up yet. I thought I heard the sound of runnin' water, like there was a stream or river nearby.

"Damn it all to hell! I just can't keep the portal open long enough! So close, so close…" He gritted his teeth and clenched his fists in frustration.

"Derek, get a grip, my friend, you did the best you could, and at least we know he's alive." Ryan Jones threw his arm across the distraught man's shoulders in a gesture of support. The not-so-friendly rivalry that had marked the beginning of their relationship several years prior had mellowed into a true friendship since Merlin had been gone from their midst.

"Yeah, Dad, at least you found him. That's more than the rest of us have accomplished since he disappeared," Morry said, trying to offer some comfort. The younger man no longer found it strange that his father was only a few years older than he was. That didn't matter anymore and he loved Derek unconditionally.

Morry glanced at his future stepmother, Sarah, who returned the look gratefully. The two of them had been best friends until they came to Moab and had found that their destinies were considerably different than they could ever have imagined. She had fallen in love with Derek Colburn at first sight, to Morry's sorrow.

The young shapeshifter paused as he thought of something that might be important. His own senses had become immeasurably sharper since he'd been spending a significant amount of time in his wolf form.

"Hey, could you tell what the air smelled like?"

Derek thought for a moment, and then said, "It was kind of a damp, earthy smell."

"You mean like peat?"

"Yeah, I'll bet that's what it was."

"Maybe he's in Scotland;" Emily suggested, hopefully.

"Maybe…" Derek sighed. "Ya know, I think we've done all we can for the night. Let's wrap it up so I can go home and do some meditation. Maybe I'll figure out somethin' that'll help me keep the portal open so we can actually communicate with him." Exhausted, he reached out to Sarah and she took his hand.

"'Night, Dad, Sarah, see you tomorrow. I've got to run, I'm supposed to meet someone and I'm already late." Morry waved as he hurried out the front door of the knights' home.

"'Night, Son," Derek managed to say just before the door slammed behind his offspring.

"Another date? How many does that make this week?" Gary Gardner, who had been known long ago as King Arthur's knight Sir Gawain, shook his head. He'd love to date someone, but apparently, his allure ranked a lot lower than that of a demigod who exuded the pheromones of a healthy, young male animal. Tonight, Gary felt every one of his thirty-odd years, as well as the weight of all the centuries that had passed since he had fought at the young

Pendragon's side. Normally, people didn't remember all their past lives, but for some reason, he did. Not that it helped to remedy his current lack of female admirers.

"There's someone out there for you, Gawain, I just know it," Emily said kindly, emerging from her self-involvement for a moment to give the attractive former knight a quick hug.

"I'm alright, Em, but thanks. Honestly, I live to serve Lord Merlin, even in his absence. I knew that I would most likely be keeping only the companionship of my fellow knights once I pledged myself to the quest."

"Speak for yourself, sirrah," Percival muttered darkly, as he deftly pulled his new phone out of his pocket and started texting his girlfriend.

Gary just glanced at Emily and shrugged, as if to say, what can you do?

Everyone departed for his or her respective homes, except for Sarah who waited for Derek in his truck, while he and his sister stood outside on the knights' porch for a few more minutes. It was very cold and it had started to snow, but they felt the need to discuss what they had accomplished that evening.

Lumina gave her brother a hug. "Derek, you're really getting the hang of it, and I'm so proud of you."

Derek rolled his eyes and sighed. "I don't know about that, Sis. Yeah, we seem to have found Dad, but we're really no closer to bringin' him home."

"How can you say that? We seem to have pinpointed his location—ancient Scotland!"

"I just want the waitin' to be over with, don't you?"

"Of course, but being too impatient won't solve anything or bring him home any faster, will it?"

"I suppose not," Derek muttered, still annoyed that he hadn't been able to keep the portal open longer.

"Hey, we'll just keep trying, Der." Lumina patted his shoulder. "Next time I'll see if I can't help amp up the power for you, okay?"

"Okay, thanks, Sis. I love ya," he said, then kissed her cold cheek. "I'll talk to you soon."

That night, Derek lay in bed, watching Sarah brush her hair. The reddish-blond strands shone in the lamplight, and while he appreciated the sight, his mind was elsewhere.

"Okay, what's wrong? You haven't heard a word I've said in the past few minutes." She put her hairbrush down on the dresser and reached for her gardenia-scented hand lotion, squirting a small amount into her palm and smoothing it over her hands and elbows. She waited patiently for Derek to answer her.

He glanced at her and smiled wanly. "I've been thinking about what happens when I travel through time." He shuddered as he remembered that rushing, screaming darkness trying to pull him apart. He had tried to describe to Sarah how it felt, but had a difficult time putting the experience into words.

"I must be doin' somethin' wrong, 'cause I don't remember that happenin' when Dad brought us back from Camelot. I mean, I'm a demigod, so there should be some way to bypass the actual time travel altogether…" Derek frowned as something occurred to him. "I wonder if I can step through directly into the time period on the other side of the portal?"

Sarah took her robe off and slid into bed, then turned off the lamp using magic, something she had been practicing for awhile.

She cuddled up to him and kissed his cheek. "Maybe you should wait until tomorrow to figure it out."

"I know, but—" Warm, soft lips covered his and a small hand reached down to caress his thigh, and he decided she was right.

CHAPTER 14

Moab, January 31, 2016

DEREK STOOD ATOP BALANCED ROCK in Arches National Park and gazed appreciatively at the spectacular geological formations before him: Petrified Dunes, The Windows, and in the distance, the La Sal Mountains. It was early—the sun hadn't yet shown itself above the horizon—and the temperature was typical for late January, in the teens. His blue down jacket and watch cap kept him warm, but he couldn't help wondering if his status as a demigod would eventually allow him to regulate his own body temperature. He looked inside himself, wherein the source of his powers lay, and thought that it was possible he could learn to do so in time. After all, he was still young, for an immortal being. It could take decades, or even centuries to sort out what he could do—and what he couldn't.

Case in point: his so-called "secret" ability that his sister was helping him to develop. So far, he could "fold" time, affect its shape, and step over that fold and through a portal into the past, but he still had a hard time keeping the portal open in conjunction with the fold. And of course, keeping the portal open depended upon the strength of the connection he had with Merlin's essence. If he had no sense of his father's presence in a particular time, neither the fold nor the portal manifested at all.

At least he had determined how to avoid that horrifying sensation of being torn apart that he'd had to endure the first few times he'd traveled through time after stepping through a portal.

Derek sighed and sat down, dangling his feet over the edge of the immense sandstone structure. God, he missed his father so damn much. His grandfather had assured him some time ago—in fact, it was the night Llyr and Chris had had dinner with them last fall—that Merlin would return when the time was right. But Derek couldn't just sit back and do nothing. That's why he'd been training so hard with Lumina every day since Christmas, more than a month ago.

Of course, from Llyr's perspective in the realm of the gods, a thousand years was a mere blip in the timeline of the universe. And while Derek would live forever, well, he didn't want to wait that long. Merlin needed to resurrect Arthur Pendragon as soon as possible. The state of the world had become critically unbalanced, desperately in need of some common sense and guidance. The politicians were continually being influenced by lobbyists financed by the pharmaceutical companies, the oil companies, the Russians and God only knew what else, and no matter what—or who—people voted for, it didn't seem to make any difference. It was damned scary.

The other thing on Derek's agenda was entirely personal. His fiancée was growing more and more anxious as time went by, and he still refused to finalize their wedding plans. Not because he didn't love her, he did, and he recognized that the two of them were soul mates. But he wanted his dad to be present at the wedding. That was nonnegotiable. And Merlin was still missing, lost in time, or at the very least, existing in another dimension. He thought about what he had experienced recently, and knew that he still didn't have enough information to determine *exactly* where Merlin was, or how to bring him back. He'd come so close at the end of last month, but hadn't had much luck since then.

Merlin had always contended that time was flexible, and Derek had accepted that, but now that he himself could manipulate the *shape* of time, he understood the concept better. But it appeared he still had a lot to learn and a long way to go before he achieved his goal of bringing Merlin home.

He inhaled the pure, cold air, held onto that breath for a moment, and then slowly exhaled. He felt good—calm and relaxed. He might as well go home; Sarah probably had breakfast ready. They shared the cooking, and this morning it was her turn. Neither one of them wanted to be stuck in traditional roles, so they were careful to avoid that. Both had jobs and both had magic, so it just seemed fair that they share the household chores.

Abruptly, he got to his feet and then stepped forward into space from his rocky perch, at the same time teleporting back home, materializing in the middle of his living room almost instantaneously. He had been aware of and using his sorcerer's abilities for several years now, and he admitted to himself that he had become rather nonchalant regarding his powers. He had almost perfected the timing from the "step-off"—when gravity tugged inexorably on him—until he teleported to a different physical location.

As he steadied himself and started into the kitchen, he paused as a thought filtered into his consciousness. *What if he combined his ability to teleport with his ability to fold time and open portals?* He'd been having problems *staying* in the past after he stepped through the portal, so maybe that would help. He actually felt lighthearted for the first time in weeks, maybe months.

"Breakfast is ready, Der." Sarah turned and smiled as she finished transferring the pancakes from griddle to plates. She was relieved to see that he had apparently made a decision regarding his next step.

He smiled back as he took his place at the table and accepted the plate of food she handed to him. He grabbed the butter and the syrup and applied them liberally to the golden-brown discs, then dug in, hungry for the first time in days.

CHAPTER 15

Caledonia, Early Fifth Century

SEVERAL WEEKS AFTER I HAD experienced that strange vision (and I still was not entirely convinced that it had really happened), I had been awakened by a messenger, who bade me make haste to a farm east of the village to attend a child who was gravely ill. I assured the boy that I would indeed be there as soon as I was able, and sent him back to his master with that message. I dressed quickly and did not bother starting a fire, grabbing a cold oatcake left over from last night's meal. It was hard and unappetizing but I gnawed on it anyway.

Bel, having also been awakened, decided to accompany me and pay an early morning visit to a woman he had been seeing recently. He didn't bother to eat anything before leaving camp, so he probably anticipated she would feed him breakfast after taking care of his carnal needs.

I glanced at him as we strode through the early morning fog along the path next to the river. "You had better pray that this woman is not diseased. How do you know that other men are not also bedding her?" Many men had found to their horror that they had contracted the pox from contact with women who routinely sold their bodies. Bel didn't answer, but he didn't seem overly worried.

Finally, Bel glanced at me as we walked towards town. "I know that you do not think very highly of me, Emrys, but I am actually quite particular about the women I bed. In fact, I normally see only the one, and she is cleaner than most." With this statement ringing in my ears and the knowledge that he himself had not recently bathed, I barely contained the mirth that arose inside me.

He looked at me with eyes narrowed. "When was the last time *you* had a woman?"

I was surprised at his outburst, as he was normally not very talkative. "Uh, I have not been with a woman since we arrived here. I am a married man and do not wish to break my vows."

Bel snorted. "You do not even remember her, or who *you* are! You might as well find your ease within a warm female body—a real woman—instead of the unsatisfying thought of a fantasy wife."

I frowned and walked on silently, thinking on his words and not wanting to admit that perhaps he was correct.

When we reached the village, Bel left me to pursue his private business and I continued on east into the rising sun. The family who had summoned me had a decent-sized farm several miles outside the village of Inverness, about halfway to the fort at the abandoned Roman settlement of Cawdor.

The moment I arrived at the thatch-roofed dwelling, I was shown into the room in which the boy's pallet lay next to the cooking fire. The peat smoldered hotly and the resultant smoke filled the poorly ventilated room. I coughed several times and wondered how the family could tolerate breathing the pungent, thick air.

The child's mother stood back, wringing her hands, her brow furrowed with worry. I knelt beside the makeshift bed and felt his forehead. The boy was burning with fever, but as I checked him further, I was relieved to note that there was no sign of swelling or pustules, which might have been indicative of plague. I silently thanked the gods for their benevolence. After I had done all I could to facilitate the child's recovery, using herbal potions of rue and milfoil, and by the judicious application of healing crystals, I finally left the family's dwelling with payment in hand, pleased that the boy was awake and his fever significantly reduced.

I walked back towards the village lost in thought, once again feeling uneasy about our strange situation. The land and the people, the language and culture, all seemed somewhat familiar to me, as if I had been here before, but it was patently obvious to me that I was not native to the land that we currently called home. Nor was I used to living rough as we had been doing since we had arrived some weeks ago. I was now convinced that I had been a prosperous merchant or physician, a family man. I had no calluses on my hands from doing manual labor, and moreover, I had an inadequate knowledge of living off the land. And I had a costly and oddly-designed ring upon my finger that I knew without a doubt was a wedding ring.

It was obvious to me that I had been used to having marital relations frequently. I found myself most nights missing the comfort of a woman's body, as if I was used to sharing a bed with a mate. I chose not to consort with the women in town who regularly sold their bodies, as Bel so frequently did; I refused to be unfaithful, even if I could not remember my wife's name. And finding relief by taking matters into my own hands did not appeal to me at all. I grimaced as I remembered our conversation this morning, and again conceded that he might be right—perhaps I needed to bed a woman.

I had just about convinced myself when I remembered the dream in which a lovely maiden had come to me, just before the appearance of the man in my vision. A shapely young woman with long golden-brown hair and a smile that warmed my heart, I could almost see her reaching for me and—

"'Ware the horse, healer!" A masculine voice shouted urgently. I opened my eyes, realizing that I had stopped in the middle of the stone bridge that spanned the River Ness at the west side of the village. Although the narrow bridge was normally for foot traffic, occasionally messengers on horseback would use it as well.

And now a rider was bearing down on me, heedless of my presence directly in front of him. In imminent danger of being trampled, I instinctively moved out of the horse's path. Immediately, I heard cries of fear, and I wondered what had happened to cause such a response. Then, I realized that I was now standing several feet away from where I had been just a second ago, and I had no idea how I had gotten there.

A man shouted fearfully, "Witch! He is a witch! Did ye see how he disappeared and reappeared at the side of the bridge? 'Tis magic, I say!"

"Stand away from him—he will curse your house and family!" Another man added his voice to the increasing furor.

A large crowd had gathered and the tension was palpable. The shouts and imprecations continued until everyone's voices were raised in terror at what I might do to them.

I stood rigid with a horrified awareness that they were speaking the truth—I had not walked out of the path of the oncoming animal, I had used some kind of magical talent to transport myself. And then I recalled the day not so long ago when I had healed unnaturally fast from a severe burn. Oh, gods, what was happening to me?

I knew that having displayed such an arcane talent, I very well could be in danger from this group of simple folk unless I acted swiftly. Perhaps I could convince them that I was an emissary of the gods, walking amongst them. I knew that most of the townsfolk still honored the gods of their forefathers, but the audacity of my plan amazed me—how could I possibly do such a thing since I was not really a god?

As the crowd's hysteria grew and several men became more and more threatening, I knew I had to act, so I abruptly threw my arms out to the sides, hands splayed, in a gesture that I hoped was somehow godlike.

I heard an intake of breath and there was suddenly complete silence.

"'Tis true," I said loudly and forcefully. "I have magical powers, but I am not a witch. I have been sent here as an emissary of the gods to help you. How think you I have healed so many folk when your own physicians have failed?" I held my breath as these people with whom I had been interacting for weeks suddenly saw my actions and me in a different light. Many of them promptly got down on their knees and bowed to me, taking my statement to heart. Strangely enough, I did not feel as if I had told them a blatant falsehood—the words I had spoken had a ring of truth. But how could that be? I frowned, sorely perplexed.

Bel, who had apparently finished his morning's visit to his woman, appeared at my side. "What is this, Emrys? What have you done?"

"I fear I have made a terrible mistake," I said quietly, then briefly described to him what had happened.

In the meantime, the crowd had grown in size but also in such a disorganized fashion that I was no longer the center of attention.

"Yes, it appears that you have. But let us take advantage of their inattention and depart this place before they realize we have gone," Bel muttered, grabbing my arm and tugging me away from the seething crowd.

Running as swiftly as we were able through the trees, avoiding the main path along the river, we finally paused to rest for a moment about halfway back to our camp. The forest was dense here, with towering old oak, pine and birch trees practically blocking the sun.

"We must leave this place, Bel." I was so winded I could barely speak. It was obvious that I was a man who did not physically exert himself often.

He nodded as he labored to catch his own breath. "But where are we to go?" He acted bewildered, as a small child would when faced with making a decision that required cognitive skills beyond his years. He seemed to have lost all the confidence he had exuded earlier in the day.

"Come, I have an idea," I said, and started out once again. The way through the forest was strewn with fallen branches and thick with patches of low-growing vegetation which slowed our progress, but we persisted, aware that we were probably being pursued. It was gloomy and chill beneath the ancient trees and I shivered at a momentary sense of foreboding.

Once we arrived back at our camp, we made short work of gathering only the most essential of our belongings, which were sparse in any case, as we had not been here long enough to put down permanent roots. For just a moment, I felt a brief pang of loss. This camp, as rough and uncomfortable as it had been, was the only home I could remember.

"Where are we headed?" Bel asked, shouldering the burden that I handed him.

"Back to Tomnahurich Hill. If the tales told by the villagers are true, there are Faeries, Elves and the like living beneath it. Perhaps they would be willing to help us."

"Or perhaps they will eat us," Bel said uneasily, his fear obvious as the rank odor of his sweat filled my nostrils.

"The Fae do not eat people," I reassured him. "But, on the other hand, they are not necessarily trustworthy." Somehow, I knew that I had dealt with them in the past, although I could not remember specifically when I had acquired that bit of lore. I knew that the Fae were an ancient race of beings purported to have untold powers and the gift of immortality, and for a brief moment I questioned the wisdom of depending upon them for our salvation. But what choice did we have?

We trudged along in a westerly direction, hoping that we would reach our goal before the villagers caught up with us. We had begun hearing sounds a ways off, and I knew that they were in hot pursuit. If they caught us, the gods only knew what the outcome would be. Witches, or any person suspected of practicing the dark arts, had been killed for less than I had done. I shivered. How *had* I done it?

I forced myself to think about what had occurred at the bridge, and wondered if I could duplicate that feat of magic. I had been entrenched in my thoughts at the time and had reacted instinctively.

I stopped so abruptly that Bel almost ran into me. "I have to relieve myself."

"Now?" He looked around fearfully. "If you must, but do not tarry, Emrys, they are not far behind us."

I nodded and stepped behind a large oak tree. I urinated, then, closing my eyes, I exhaled slowly and cleared my mind. I embraced the energy I felt inside of me, and imagined myself standing next to my companion. I felt a strange heaviness in my chest and a slight wrench.

I heard a gasp and opened my eyes to see Bel staring at me, his eyes wide and frightened. By the gods, it had worked. I *was* a witch.

I had no time to dwell upon this alarming discovery, as a group of angry men brandishing clubs and scythes burst out of the trees behind us. Without further thought, I gripped Bel's muscular forearm and pictured in my mind moving both of us to the base of the hill where we had found ourselves stranded weeks ago.

A moment later, I recognized the dense brush and trees through which we had come that day as we descended the steep path from the top of the hill, and I knew I had succeeded. I glanced at my companion, who had turned a ghastly shade of gray and gave every indication that he was about to be sick.

"Pull yourself together, Bel, there is no time to indulge a weak stomach. We must both mentally call to the Fae who dwell beneath the hill."

Bel nodded weakly. We did our best, but nothing happened. Undoubtedly, there was a hidden door by which to enter. However, we faced a solid expanse of vegetation at the base of the slope and for a moment, I panicked. The mob of townsfolk, now furious that I had eluded them not only by magic, but also by sheer speed and determination, was approaching quickly, caught up in the fear and panic generated by ignorance.

How were we to enter the supposed haven in the Faery realm when we couldn't even locate the entrance?

Bel and I stared into each other's eyes and for once, we felt the same way. I was as fearful as he was.

But then it occurred to me that if I indeed possessed magical talents, I ought to be able to utilize my senses in locating and opening the door to a magical realm. *If such a place truly existed,* I thought to myself as a sudden wave of self-doubt washed over me. And if it did not, if it was just child's fable, where did that leave us?

No, I could not allow myself to be overcome with doubt at this point. So I closed my eyes once again, reaching for the information I needed. Then, I opened my eyes and blinked as a bright light glowed in front of me. And I realized that the entrance had been there all along, hidden by the illusion of a brush-covered hillside.

I glanced back, noting that the mob was much too close.

"Emrys, look."

I turned around and saw someone gesturing from a doorway in the hill, now ajar, a bright, warm light pouring out and inviting us to enter.

As we stepped forward into the light, I could not help but wonder what would become of us.

CHAPTER 16
Beneath Tomnahurich Hill

As soon as the door shut behind us and we were safely ensconced in the enchanted world beneath the mountain, I sensed, but could not see, the presence of many different types of beings surrounding us. For a moment, I thought that the sense of safety might be an illusion, and I was afraid. There was always a price to be paid when asking for help from beings such as these, and I hoped that we would not be paying it anytime soon.

Then I realized that our belongings, including our bone-handled iron daggers had disappeared. Cold iron was most deadly to the Fae, so I could understand why they would not want us to have it in our possession. But I felt bereft, for everything else was gone as well: my carefully garnered medicinal herbs, our extra clothing, Bel's painstakingly crafted bow and arrows, our blankets. I particularly mourned the loss of my leather pouch full of coins and healing stones, so hard-won. But it could not be helped; at least we had escaped the irate townsfolk.

With a sudden flash of fear, I held up my hand. My ornate wedding ring was still in place. It encircled my finger even more tightly than before, as if it wanted to reassure me that it would not leave me. The relief I felt was overwhelming; it was my only connection to my wife.

Now that my concern for my ring had been allayed, I was curious about my surroundings. I looked around, trying to make out the details of this place, but bright lights and dark shadows seemed to coexist here and it took some time for my eyes, and perhaps my other senses as well, to adjust.

"Emrysss." The disembodied voice caressed my name and conveyed a sense of respect, reverence and something else that I could not comprehend.

"How do you know my name?" I asked uncertainly, unable to see who addressed me. "Please show yourself so that I might…uh, express my admiration for your timely intervention on our behalf."

I had almost come out and said "thank you," which would have been a dangerous mistake, putting myself in debt to the Fae for some future favor.

A being with long, rainbow-hued hair glided sinuously out of the shadows. He was taller than I was by several hand spans, slender, and so beautiful that I might have taken him for female but for the lack of breasts and the timbre of his voice. Even knowing his gender, he exuded such a potent sexuality that I found myself attracted to him. I fought to retain my objectivity, as one could easily lose a sense of self here.

The Fae male approached me with what appeared to be a pleased expression and I forced myself to focus on what he was saying. He was speaking an unknown language, but I understood him nevertheless.

"Assistance was freely given to you and your companion, with no implied obligation. You do not recognize us, but we know you, Emrys. If you truly wish to grant a boon, however, you may entertain us with a song and a tale during our banquet. As always, a harp stands ready for your hands, and your audience awaits you with great anticipation."

"You…you knew I was coming?" I was baffled.

"Of course, Emrys," he replied, his voice soothing and pleasant. He exuded a calmness and certainty that I did not understand, but I was in no position to question his motives or his actions. And while his intent seemed benign and I sensed no immediate threat, I intuitively knew that unless we cooperated, we might never escape from this place. I hoped that my doubts did not show on my face, and I gravely nodded my assent.

"I would be happy to provide entertainment, though it has been some years since I have played the harp." In fact, I had no memory of having played the instrument at all, but I had to trust that I would be able to do so.

It was now obvious to me that this, as well as the singing and storytelling that were expected of a harpist, would be payment for our rescue. I sincerely hoped that my contribution would suffice for both of us, as I was certain that Bel had no skills that would be acceptable here in this underground Faery kingdom. His skill in bedding a woman would hardly afford him leniency and possibly just the opposite.

"We are pleased that you will play for us, Emrys, and we are not concerned with your technique."

"Very well, then, I shall be happy to do so," I said politely, sketching a slight bow.

"You and your companion are most welcome to rest and avail yourselves of our bathing chambers. Robes will be provided for your use while your own garments are being cleansed."

Bel and I exchanged a look. I should have known, at that point, to decline such a gracious offer. I was awfully suspicious of accepting favors from these beings, considering what the consequences might ultimately be.

But, on the other hand, both of us were desperately in need of baths, clean clothes, rest and food, in that order, and I realized that we had very little choice in the matter.

We were escorted to a bathing chamber, impossibly large and ornate, the ceiling so high above us that the details were obscured. The walls appeared to be sheets of gold, and along each wall at eye level was embossed writing that seemed familiar to me, although I could not decipher it. The azure water in the immense sunken pool steamed seductively, and I was eager to relax in its warmth and welcome. The pool itself was lined with brightly colored tiles in the style of a Roman bath house. Female attendants of spectacular beauty came forward to assist us in undressing, and although I felt uneasy to be unclothed in their presence, the allure of being clean overcame my reluctance and I immersed myself gratefully into the clear, warm water.

Ah, gods, to be clean again, and warm, I thought, *what a luxury*. I ducked my head in the water and ran my fingers through the long wet strands of my hair.

The air was perfumed with an intoxicating scent that relaxed both the body and the mind, and I found myself half asleep, my thoughts drifting. It could have been a few minutes or several hours later when I observed several of the Fae females hovering over Bel, cleansing and caressing his willing body, and then realized that I was also being attended to in like fashion. One female washed my hair with some type of foaming soap and massaged my scalp with sweet smelling herbs, while another washed my body. Being pampered by these handmaidens was incredibly seductive, and before long, we had both exited the pool and were reclining on padded benches, engaging in carnal pleasures. The Fae female beneath me was exquisite. She had long dark hair, lavender eyes, plump, luscious lips and high, round breasts, and she exuded the scent that I had noticed earlier. I was literally enthralled by her and had no thought but to pursue the heights of pleasure that she offered.

After I had climaxed, I promptly sank into the bottomless pit of an unnatural sleep.

I dreamed of impossible stone structures, which loomed in a stark landscape of red rocks, with the sky overhead a vivid shade of blue. People that I felt I should know surrounded me, clothed in odd garments in a foreign style. Although I could not hear any sounds, these individuals apparently knew me and were calling my name, and I sensed that they were mine—both friends and relatives—under my care. Then, they were all gone but one, the tall young woman with the long, wavy, golden-brown tresses, and she was weeping brokenheartedly. Somehow, I knew that this woman was my wife, and even in my dream state realized that I had just broken my marital vows by bedding another woman.

I awoke suddenly, my mind clear and sharp, completely aware of what had transpired since we had entered this underground kingdom, and utterly convinced that we needed to leave at the first possible opportunity.

CHAPTER 17

The Realm of the Fae

"EMRYS, OUR BANQUET COMMENCES, AND we would be honored by your presence in the Great Hall." Worded as a request, it was clearly a command.

I turned my head and beheld a Fae male dressed in somber robes that seemed fitting for a servant or a messenger, standing at attention next to the chaise upon which I reclined. I did not recognize him as being the male who had originally brought us here, but he was equally beautiful and just as eerily seductive. If I was physically attracted to these Fae males, how could I have possibly resisted the sexual allure of the female Fae? I was devastated that I had broken the sacred vows of marriage, but what was done was done. I would be most vigilant for the remainder of our time here so that it did not happen again.

I sat up, ready to be dressed and out of this chamber of seduction. "Yes, of course, I will happily attend as soon as I am properly clothed."

At once, the male beckoned to a handmaiden. She came forward with her head bowed subserviently and helped me don the garments she had brought. The tunic was of an indescribable hue and texture, and as I drew it over my head and settled it over matching loose trousers, the fabric seemed to move and shimmer with all the colors of the rainbow, constantly changing. Soft-soled slippers that molded themselves to my feet completed my attire.

I finger-combed my hair, which felt luxuriously clean and was still damp from bathing. Several inches past shoulder length, it seemed longer than I remembered and that fact seemed somehow significant. How long had we actually been here? But I did not have time to contemplate this mystery, and followed the male out of the bathing area.

As we traversed corridors sparkling with crystals embedded in the walls and ceilings that gave off a soft, diffuse glow, we were joined by Bel, who was accompanied by his own Fae servant. I hardly recognized him. His hair, beard and moustache were clean and neatly trimmed, and his powerfully muscled body was clothed in garments similar to mine. He glanced at me intently, as if trying to convey information to me silently.

Emrys...

I frowned as I thought I heard him say my name, and then shrugged, certain that I had imagined it.

As we approached the Great Hall, the enticing scents of the sumptuous banquet made my stomach rumble with hunger. I assumed that I would be asked to play and sing before we could eat, and I felt a certain amount of trepidation about performing. Playing the harp and singing hardly seemed a logical pastime for a healer.

I was led to a platform in front of a vast hall filled with low tables. Both males and females sat on plump cushions, quietly waiting, all of them focused on me. I surveyed the crowd and realized that for some reason, I could not make out the features on any of the upturned faces. It was as if I beheld a painting in which all the colors were blurred. I hastily looked away, shaken to the core of my being.

I took a seat on a fancy upholstered stool and pulled the instrument into position in front of me with a confident professionalism that amazed me. I fingered the strings in a preliminary fashion, testing the tuning, and after making several minor adjustments, I began to play. The sweet notes reverberated through my soul, and I sighed happily. I began to sing the story of an ancient god who wanted to become human, in the end being born to a human mother, and walking the earth among men. The words flowed effortlessly, my voice pure and true, and I never questioned how I had known such a story. I was certain that what I sang about had actually come to pass, or would occur in the near future.

When the final lyrics had been sung and the harp was quiet, there was a moment of silence, and then the Great Hall erupted in a roar of satisfaction and approval. I arose and bowed from the waist, acknowledging their appreciation, and then left the platform. A Fae male silently guided me to a table with an enormous and elaborate centerpiece of flowers that I could have sworn did not occur in nature. As I seated myself on a cushion next to Bel, I sat for a moment in a daze, and he turned to me with a perplexed look on his face.

"Emrys, I do not understand. How do you come to play the harp? To sing a ballad? What know you of gods being born to human women? And the other, what you did before we entered this realm. Emrys, you have *magic*. You are obviously more than a healer and an herbalist; you are a witch."

"I cannot refute your logic, Bel. Believe me, I am as mystified as you are, and sore afraid as well," I murmured quietly. I was stunned by the implications of my performance, and of my actions in Inverness.

Our dinner finally arrived. Served in a huge tureen of silver, the first course was soup, exquisitely flavored with herbs and unfamiliar spices, and thick with all manner of tasty vegetables, many of which I did not recognize. As I ladled out a bowl for each of us, our stomachs both growled, and we wasted no time in beginning the meal. As we finished the soup course, a platter of various meats, cheeses and breads was placed on the table in front of us. We filled our plates and began to eat ravenously, the soup having only whetted our appetites. I identified thin slices of venison and wild boar, wedges of goat cheese and freshly baked loaves of bread, but the other foods, though delicious, I did not recognize. Exotic fruits and crunchy nutmeats followed the main course and we both ate our fill.

Finally replete, I settled back in my chair, sipping my wine, and felt satisfied for the first time in many weeks. Bel finished his meal as well, a slight frown adding to his already solemn expression. It was obvious that he was worried, and his concern spurred my own doubts about our hosts' intentions. I glanced surreptitiously around the vast hall; gold, jewels and colorful semi-precious stones adorned every surface. Their facets reflected the surroundings, multiplied many times, making me wonder what this cavernous room really looked like without all the trappings. I had a very bad feeling that even though the Fae had helped us, welcoming us unreservedly, they had an ulterior motive for doing so. Perhaps our seduction by the alluring females next to the bathing pool was such a motive. For all I knew, the banquet hall and all the guests were an elaborate illusion, and we were actually asleep and dreaming, under some kind of spell, being used for some unimaginable purpose.

I was utterly convinced that it was time to leave—in fact, the sooner, the better. We had been in this Fae realm too long. As I casually wiped my hands on the damp linen cloth provided, I motioned to Bel to follow my lead. He nodded imperceptibly to indicate he understood me, his dark eyes hooded.

I glanced around one more time and realized that we were no longer the center of attention, which would indisputably work in our favor. We both stood up and started walking in the direction that my senses told me would yield an exit through which we could escape. As soon as we left the main hall, we hastened down a narrowing corridor, leaving the jeweled reflections behind. The sound of our footsteps was very loud to my ears, and I peered worriedly over my shoulder a time or two.

The occasional torch provided inadequate illumination, as if there were no point in lighting that area; the further we went, the darker it became. I knew that Bel detested the dark, and I could feel his tension mount. Bel's fear and agitation increased until suddenly, a piercing white light sprang from his splayed fingers, reaching the ceiling above and banishing the darkness. I was utterly amazed at this turn of events—Bel had magic as well! I knew we had to leave without delay. There was no way to determine where we would come out, but at this point, I truly did not care. I just wanted to depart this realm. Instinctively, I gathered my power, but as we approached the end of the tunnel, a Fae male appeared and intercepted us.

"Emrys, Bel, where are you going? Do you not think it rude to leave so precipitously, without a 'by your leave,' or at least some small gesture of gratitude?" It was the same being that had greeted us initially, and had at the time assured us there was no need to offer thanks. His voice chided us in the way an adult would speak to disobedient children, but it held an underlying threat. As I gazed at him, I realized that something was different about his features. It was as if he had decided that there was no longer any need to hide his true appearance. Gone was the too-perfect beauty that I had seen when we first arrived in the Fae realm. He now seemed more sinister, his features more angular and his eyes strangely shaped, with vertical pupils that reminded me of a lizard.

He seemed aware that my perception of him had changed. He turned away from me with a sneer and waved his arm negligently. Bel's white light was extinguished, leaving us once more in the dark.

It was obvious that our time had run out. Despite the fact that I had seen no doors or exits of any kind, I grabbed Bel's arm and focused with my entire being on moving us outside of what had become our prison. I felt a massive jolt and a sense of movement and we were catapulted from the cave's suffocating darkness into blinding sunlight.

CHAPTER 18

Edinburgh, Scotland, Sixteenth Century

WE STUMBLED ONTO A ROCKY promontory, the uneven surface beneath our feet throwing us off balance even as a powerful, cold wind stole our breath away and did its best to knock us to the ground. I dragged myself upright and stared. We were atop a mountain which afforded a view in all directions. To the north, a glittering body of water stretched as far as the eye could see. Northwesterly of our position, barely visible in the valley below us, was a large settlement, with an imposing fortress standing guard on a cliff above the town. Turning to the southeast, I noticed the scattered ruins of what might have been a keep in a vale just below us, and a peculiar feeling stirred in me. I knew this place. I had been here in another life, another time, when the area had been known as Eidyn. For a moment, I saw the place in the vale as it had been, a solidly built structure flying a banner with a blood red dragon upon it, juxtaposed with the current reality of ruins. A shiver coursed down my spine. I remembered the story I had told the people of Inverness—that I was the servant of a god, and how oddly appropriate that declaration had felt. I had magic and used it as naturally as if I had been born with it, so I was clearly not a normal man. Was I even human?

And what of Bel? I turned to the man I had spent so much time with recently and realized we were more alike than I could have imagined. That incident in the dark corridor of the Fae realm, when he demonstrated his own powerful magic, confirmed my suspicions that while we might not be related by blood, we were somehow connected by the magical abilities we had both displayed.

As if he sensed my thoughts, Bel stared at his hands and then back at me. "How did I do that? What are we, Emrys?"

I could not speak as I turned my gaze to what could only be the town of Edinburgh below. The answer that came to mind was inconceivable.

I finally decided that we were accomplishing nothing by standing in this savage wind, particularly as we were again garbed in our original threadbare clothing and worn-out boots. Our cloaks were gone, so I was feeling decidedly chilled and assumed Bel felt the same. And then I remembered my treasures. Quickly, I reached for the soft leather pouch that I had worn prior to entering the domain of the Fae, and to my vast relief, it was back around my neck. I knew not where it had gone during our time beneath Tomnahurich Hill, but I was very thankful that it had returned to me after leaving that underground realm. I just wished that our cloaks had been returned to us as well. And then it occurred to me that the cloaks had most likely been provided by the Fae originally. I certainly had no intention of returning to Faery to retrieve them. I had had my fill of their machinations.

We needed to find shelter, which required us to descend from our perch on this mountain. But before that, I desperately wanted to get closer to the ruins I had glimpsed. I was drawn to them, and as the remains of the old structure were close to the path that presumably led down into the valley below, I felt that I could rationalize taking the time to explore. Perhaps I could connect somehow with emanations from the past, which might help us to identify where—and when—we actually belonged.

“Well, what do you sense here, Emrys?” Bel asked impatiently, for the third time. He was pacing back and forth, apparently to keep warm in the increasingly cold wind. I was standing in the midst of the ruins, trying to concentrate, and neither my own chilled body nor Bel’s queries were helping me in the slightest.

“Why do you not start down the mountain and I will catch up with you. I require a few moments of solitude.” I remained still, with my eyes closed, hoping that my companion would take the hint.

Bel muttered something in the affirmative and I could hear the scuff of his boots in the precarious scree as he clambered back to the path and started down the mountain.

I drew a quiet breath of relief and was finally able to focus on my innermost thoughts and feelings. Immediately, the banner of the red dragon which had appeared to me when we first arrived on this mountaintop passed once again through my consciousness, along with that sense of recognition. I could almost see the silhouette of a young man underneath that banner, and the yearning I experienced brought tears to my eyes. I had served that man in the distant past, but I could not remember who he was or in what capacity I had served him. The vision soon faded, but I remained on that spot far longer than I should have, hoping for more revelations.

As Bel trod the narrow path down the slope towards the town in the valley, he muttered angrily regarding the selfishness of his companion. After a time, he reluctantly admitted to himself that he was becoming too dependent on Emrys. Perhaps when he reached the town proper he would just fend for himself and forget about the other man. He was perfectly capable of finding food and shelter—he did not need anyone else in his life.

But when he came to a fork in the path, he found himself wondering if Emrys would know to choose the left-hand trail. It seemed the appropriate direction in which to proceed, but Emrys had never displayed a lot of common sense when it came to basic survival lore. Bel paused, then decided to build a cairn of rocks to show which way he traveled so that Emrys would not become lost, a distinct possibility as the light of day rapidly faded. He shook his head and sighed, resigned to wait for Emrys at the bottom of the hill, come what may.

It was long past full dark when I started down the steep trail towards the valley floor. In my attempt to stimulate my memory by somehow connecting with the past, I had waited overlong to follow Bel. I was disappointed that my efforts had mostly been in vain, and now I was in danger of losing my way. A crescent moon provided only a small amount of illumination, and I found myself stumbling dangerously close to the edge of the rocky path. Once, I had to pitch myself backward onto the trail to avoid plunging down the slope, which disappeared into Stygian blackness. I paused several times, trying to determine if I was headed in the right direction, but all I was sure of was that I was going downhill. In frustration, I thought about the light that Bel had called upon in the hall of the Fae. If he could do that, perhaps I could do so as well.

I held my left hand out and pictured a round globe of light resting there. Summarily, a surge of power originating in my chest and traveling swiftly down my arm erupted into a flare of white light in the palm of my hand. The light glowed brilliantly, illuminating my surroundings. I was able to see a cairn of rocks at a fork in the trail ahead and I intuited that the marker had been left for me by my surly companion. Once I had traveled some distance beyond the fork, I could see a multitude of torches off in the distance to my right, several hundred feet below me. I was curious what they signified. I continued to descend, taking care not to slip on the loose pebbles under my feet.

Finally, as the path leveled out, I found Bel sitting disconsolately on a large boulder, staring at the frenetic activity surrounding what appeared to be an enormous manor house about a quarter mile to the west of us.

"What news, Bel?" I asked, out of breath from hurrying down the trail. I had extinguished my globe of light some distance back, not in the mood to explain how I had created it.

"Something terrible has happened, Emrys. I know not what, but I sense that an evil deed has transpired this night." Bel gestured towards the group of men congregating near the castle of stone.

As I turned to gaze towards the courtyard of the imposing structure, I frowned as I recognized the place, and knew instinctively that we should not linger here.

Without warning, information flooded into my consciousness. The date was March 9, 1566, the structure was actually the Palace of Holyroodhouse, and we were observing the aftermath of the murder of David Rizzio, the private secretary of Mary Stuart, Queen of Scots.

The fact that we were witnessing the confusion following that dreadful event could put us in grave danger. Queen Mary's estranged husband, Henry Stuart, Lord Darnley, had perpetrated this foul deed through a political conspiracy to become the lawful King of Scots. He had not been alone, but his co-conspirators had vanished soon afterwards, and if we were caught in the vicinity, we could very well be accused of complicity in the crime.

I felt an escalating sense of urgency and blurted out, "We must depart now, and find some place in which to conceal ourselves." We needed food and shelter this night in any case, but it was imperative that we make ourselves scarce until this event had reached its natural conclusion. I shivered, fear and the cold evening breeze combining to leach the warmth from my inadequately clad body.

"I do not understand, Emrys." Bel's voice reflected both his confusion and his exhaustion.

I was tired as well, but as I closed my eyes, information poured out of my mouth effortlessly. "There has been a murder this night committed by the husband of the queen and his associates, and the repercussions of this dire act shall reverberate down through history. Lord Darnley will die in a mysterious explosion within the next year, and the actions of the queen herself will cause her infant son, James, to be placed on the throne in her stead. In 1587, Mary Stuart will be executed at Fotheringhay Castle by her cousin, Queen Elizabeth of England."

My eyes fluttered open and realized that I had been speaking as an oracle might, prophesying the future, one detail after another. I winced as a vicious pain exploded behind my eyes and I groaned aloud, holding my head in my hands.

"Emrys, what in the god's name is wrong with you?" Bel exclaimed, becoming increasingly agitated until he finally leapt to his feet and gripped my arms in his powerful hands. Then he stiffened, a look of alarm transforming his normally stoic features as he stared over my shoulder. "*Bollocks*! We must go!"

Despite the cover of darkness, we had attracted the attention of the guards at the palace and they were approaching rapidly, torches held high.

Thankfully, the pain in my head had subsided to a manageable level, and I grabbed Bel's arm, intending to transport us out of harm's way to the west side of Edinburgh in hopes of finding shelter there. However, before I could do so, I remembered there were no streets or buildings in that area yet. In the future, it would be called "New Town," as opposed to "Old Town," the section of Edinburgh in which we presently stood. But those details did nothing to help us at this moment. Annoyed, I pushed the information aside and we took the logical next step—we ran.

As we rushed past closed shops, we stumbled and slid over the uneven cobbles, slimy with disgusting substances that had most likely been discarded out of the second story windows of the living quarters. We observed a flicker of soft candlelight emanating through gaps in wooden shutters here and there along the way, and occasionally the stronger light of lanterns shining from the inner chambers of otherwise dark establishments, the only evidence that the city was truly inhabited. Except for the distant clamor of troops at the palace, it was unnaturally quiet. No dogs barked, no night insects whirred, and no sounds of human habitation came from any of the living quarters above. We continued up a steep lane, our labored exhalations visible in the chill night air. Finally, ahead of us on the right we spotted a sign illuminated by a single torch, revealing a roughly carved outline of a boar's head. I recognized it for an inn and turned to Bel.

"There…" I gasped, and gratefully stepped inside as Bel pulled the heavy wooden door open. Loud, overlapping conversations halted abruptly as a crowd of men, all dressed in the simple, rough clothing of workingmen, turned their attention to us.

The main room of the public house had a low ceiling of rough, smoke-blackened beams, and the inadequate lighting made it seem as if we stood in a cave. The warmth from the enormous fireplace at the far end of the room emphasized the odors of food, ale, smoke and unwashed bodies. It was obvious that these men were well aware of the commotion taking place at Holyroodhouse, and our precipitous entrance was regarded with suspicion.

I have to admit, I did not think twice before using the same deception I had used on the bridge in Inverness: I announced that we were the exalted servants of a god. I called up a bright light around the two of us, hoping that it would enhance my claim.

I heard gasps of astonishment and fear as I continued in a pompous voice I barely recognized as my own. "We are here by the direction of Jesus Christ himself and under his protection, and we require your understanding and cooperation. We ask that you do not interfere with our mission, which is to bring the clarification and resolution of recent events at the palace."

Every person in the room, including the innkeeper and a young, red-haired serving wench, remained silent, glancing at one another as if for reassurance or moral support. Or perhaps, in the worst case, they did not understand my words or my accent. Fortunately, no one moved to detain us, apparently interpreting my announcement as intention to investigate the murder.

Thankfully, we were able to proceed up the stairs to the rooms above unchallenged, and we chose one at random. Without hesitation, I created a small light orb to find and light the candle on the low table near the window. It never occurred to me to forego the candle and keep the light orb.

Bel closed the door and collapsed against it, releasing a sound that could have been a sigh of relief or a moan of exasperation. "Emrys, why would you say that we are the servants of the Christian deity?"

"Honestly, I had no intention of doing so, but it occurred to me that in this time and place, people do not worship the old gods, nor do they follow the old ways. You and I would appear to be pagans or magicians, and therefore more likely to be persecuted."

"That may be true, but it would behoove us to leave this place as soon as possible anyway. What say you?"

"I agree, but we are in no position to leave right away—we are tired and hungry and in need of rest. We will depart at first light." I looked around and noted that we had chosen a room with two narrow beds, the one small table holding a pewter candlestick, and a commode on which rested a chipped pitcher of water, a lump of harsh yellow soap and a single thin length of dingy linen. The window on the far side of the room contained small panes of glass, so dirty that it was impossible to see through them, and it was shut tight against the evening air. The accommodations were meager, but still seemed a welcome change from roughing it in the woods on the banks of the River Ness.

"I shall go back downstairs and procure food and drink for us, and try to convince the proprietor that we need not pay for either the victuals or the room," I said in a wry tone. Bel closed his eyes and nodded wearily as he stretched out on one of the beds to await my return. His immediate capitulation was so out of character that for a moment I just stood and gaped at him. Then my stomach growled loudly, reminding me that I should be on my way downstairs.

Surprisingly, without any coercion on my part, the innkeeper provided golden- brown-crusted meat pies and two pints of ale, which the serving wench arranged on a large tray. Not a word was uttered regarding payment, and as I followed the girl's broad backside up the narrow, creaking wooden stairs to our room, I gave silent thanks to the gods.

The girl, who turned out to be the innkeeper's daughter, set the tray down on the rickety table and then posed provocatively, her breasts close to spilling out of her bodice. It was apparent that she intended to service our carnal needs as well, presumably in exchange for a goodly amount of compensation. I wondered fleetingly if her father realized she was selling herself to his patrons. I swiftly but politely declined her unspoken offer, at the same time ushering her out of the room as quickly as possible. I had no desire to witness Bel's sexual proclivities should he decide to respond to her invitation.

For once, Bel made no comment regarding my decision. We proceeded to eat our supper without further delay, too hungry to waste time discussing it. Our hunger struck me as strange, considering that we had eaten a large meal in the Fae realm not so very long ago. Perhaps for us, Fae food did not—or could not—satisfy our needs. More likely, though, our meal had actually been a very long time in the past.

After we finished eating and had each made a brief trip outside to the privy, we retired for the night. As I started to fall asleep, I suddenly realized what had been bothering me ever since we entered the pub, other than the obvious situation in which we had found ourselves involved. We had been hearing, and speaking, an entirely different language than we had used in old Inverness. I recognized it as Middle English, the form of the language that was spoken in the sixteenth century. I sat up in bed, eager to discuss this bizarre discovery with Bel. As I turned to speak to him, his breathing evened out and I knew he was asleep, so I decided to wait until morning. I tried to get comfortable, eventually finding a position that suited me. Then, despite the occasional burst of raucous laughter from below, I finally descended into a restless slumber, full of disturbing dreams.

CHAPTER 19

Edinburgh, Scotland, March 10, 1566

I AWOKE WITH A START just before dawn and for a moment did not know where I was. Then, the events of the previous day came rushing back to me and I felt restless and uneasy. There was no light, the stub of the candle having gone out some time ago. The unfamiliar scents and sounds of the old building, along with the impenetrable darkness in the room, made me long for the fresh air and faint light of the stars and moon that I had taken for granted in our makeshift camp. The splash of the river as it flowed past, the pungent scents of the peat in the water and the burning wood of the fire as we cooked our food—I had no idea that I would miss those things. And surprisingly, I missed Bel's warmth next to me as we slept on the hard ground under those evil-smelling animal pelts.

The covers on my bed were thin and I was cold, despite having slept in my clothes. The room had no hearth, and therefore we had no way to heat it. Perhaps the owner was afraid of fire. While the exterior walls of the inn were smooth gray stone, the interior was primarily wood and the roof was thatched, and with the cooking grease from the kitchen and the alcohol in the pub, the place could easily go up in flames with very little provocation.

I shifted slightly on the lumpy, straw-filled mattress, scratching my head and then my groin area. I sighed. It was obvious that *one* thing was the same, whether we were camping beneath the stars or under a roof. The ever-present fleas and lice had to be some of the most annoying of all the creatures on earth. Their very existence was a mystery to me. I picked a particularly large louse out of the hair on my chest and crushed it between my fingernails. I shuddered in disgust.

I heard Bel turn over in the narrow bed next to mine and start scratching as well.

"Emrys, are you awake?"

"Unfortunately, yes."

"I have been thinking. Why would Queen Mary's husband kill her secretary?"

I turned my head towards him despite the fact that I could not see his face. "I do not know for certain. Perhaps he was jealous of the time Rizzio spent with her."

"Do you think Rizzio was bedding her?"

I thought for a moment. "I do not know. Perhaps. Most marriages in royal families are by arrangement, so it is common practice to take lovers, but Lord Darnley is her cousin as well as her husband. And there are rumors that Rizzio had previously been *Henry's* lover. An awkward and complicated situation, to be sure."

Bel was silent for a few minutes and then replied, "But murder seems a bit extreme."

"I agree," I murmured. Abruptly, I could no longer ignore my restlessness, nor could I tolerate the stale air in the room. I sprang out of bed and attempted to open the window, but it was stuck fast, and no matter how much force I applied it refused to budge. I gritted my teeth in frustration and strained harder.

Suddenly, my chest felt tight and the now familiar feeling of power rushed down through my arms and hands, until it erupted through my fingertips. Blue fire engulfed the window, blowing out the brittle glass, which fell onto the deserted lane below. A gust of wind blew in through the broken panes and brought a chilling rain which instantly drenched me.

White light flared briefly from Bel's hands as he sat up in bed and stared at the demolished window. "Gods, Emrys, what have you done now?"

I looked at my handiwork and swallowed convulsively, outwardly calm, but with my heart pounding wildly in my chest. "We must depart posthaste."

Bel leapt silently from his bed without further comment and donned his boots. I quickly pulled mine on as well, and we hastened down the stairs as quietly as possible, stumbling in the dark. Gaining the ground floor, we made our way towards the front of the main room and found the door, fumbled with the latch, and finally opened it. Frigid air rushed in as we rushed out, into the unwelcome embrace of a dozen armed men.

Cruel hands roughly restrained and gagged both of us, and we were hustled through the cold, wet, predawn gloom uphill towards the hulking darkness of Edinburgh Castle. It was ironic that we had chosen as a sanctuary an inn so close to the imposing gates of our soon-to-be prison, but at the time, we only had one thing on our minds—finding food and refuge for the night. Now, rain-soaked and miserable, we regretted that we had not left the Royal Mile in search of a safer haven.

Our captors were silent for the most part and I could not help but wonder how they had known where we were. The answer came swiftly to mind—any one of the occupants of the pub could have slipped out last night and informed the Holyroodhouse guards of our location. While that conclusion could be accurate, I realized that an additional aspect to this whole fiasco was that our captors, only a few of whom were in uniform, probably included Darnley's associates, looking for someone else to take the blame for their actions.

It was painfully obvious that I had been too complacent and indeed arrogant, convinced that our ruse as messengers of Christ would be sufficient to keep us from discovery. The noise caused by my unfortunate destruction of the window most likely did not help our case, either, but perhaps it would have made no difference.

I glanced at my companion and he returned my gaze, his eyes hooded. Then, I thought I heard his voice in my mind.

Now what shall we do, Emrys?

I stared at him, wondering if I was losing my wits. *Bel?*

Who else? Can you transport us away from here? I have no desire to be imprisoned in some filthy dungeon and then executed, which is undoubtedly to be our fate.

I overcame my amazement at our ability to communicate silently and nodded slightly in agreement. I focused my attention within, searching for that unusual talent I had displayed so recently. Where in the world would such an attribute be found? Was it in my mind, or in one of my bodily organs? Or perhaps it could be found in that nebulous, undefined but highly prized place in the heart that the Christians called the soul?

Finally, I found my ability to transport us away, but for some reason, I could not control the use of it, perhaps due to the anxiety I felt as we were forced ahead of our captors towards certain doom. Between the restraints, which kept my hands secured behind my back and did not allow me to touch my companion, and the fear engulfing me, the use of my "talent" eluded me. Regret felt like a lead weight on my chest and I wished that I did not have to inform Bel of my failure.

Unfortunately, I am unable to use that ability now. He did not respond, but I could feel his hopelessness as he realized we were doomed.

I wished I could figure out a solution to our predicament. Obviously, I did not want either of us to die, particularly for a crime we had not committed. The injustice of it infuriated me. In the meantime, we were fast approaching the place of our imprisonment—tall, stone towers rising like ghostly sentinels ahead of us in the gloom.

The portcullis at the entrance to the forbidding castle slowly rose in response to a shouted command from the captain of the guard, and we were pushed forcefully forward, under that heavy iron grating and into the courtyard. The rain had finally stopped and there was a hint of color in the eastern sky, and I prayed that this would not be our final morning upon this earth.

We passed by a stone wall stained dark with what could only be old blood. Metal cuffs on chains were embedded in the wall, waiting for the next hapless victims. We glanced at each other, and no words or even thoughts were necessary to express our relief that at least we were not to be executed on the spot. But that relief was short-lived as our captors took us directly to the dungeon, where we would be held until it was determined what grisly fate awaited us.

We entered the bowels of Edinburgh Castle on rough stone steps that were narrow, steep and slippery with mold. Cold, dank, stale air slapped us in the face as we descended. When we finally reached the cell we were to occupy, our restraints were transferred to iron rings attached to the stone wall above our heads. Fortunately, our gags were removed. The filthy rag had wicked the moisture from my mouth, and I requested some drinking water, to which one of our captors replied, “Ye willna live long enough tae die o’ thirst, lad.” Evil-sounding laughter erupted from the men in response to his remark. After securing the cell door, they took their leave, taking the torch with them. As they ascended the steps I heard one of them say that we had been the perfect scapegoats. The fact that I had predicted this very scenario did nothing to alleviate the horror of our situation.

Unrelieved darkness descended upon us as the last man exited our prison.

Despite the anger, indignation and fear that I felt regarding our treatment, at some point I must have passed out. As I slowly regained consciousness, I became aware of a tingling, aching discomfort in my arms and hands. I stood up as straight as I could to take some of my weight off of my arms and it seemed to help. I had no idea exactly how much time had passed, but it could have been quite a few hours, considering how stiff and sore I was.

Then I sensed Bel’s extreme agitation and remembered his abhorrence of the dark.

Emrys, I have tried to create light and cannot. His inner voice vibrated with frustration and anxiety.

I will see what I can do. I was not certain that I could do anything without my hands free, but I had to try. I forced myself to concentrate, to reach into that powerful place inside me that could create light.

Suddenly, I felt a burst of energy rush through me, and the cell was filled with the brilliance of a spring day, even though we were far below the earth’s surface and surrounded by solid rock. The light banished all shadows and lifted my flagging spirits.

Bel’s entire body relaxed as much as it was feasible to do so, considering his awkward position against the wall. “Thank you,” he whispered, “my…friend.”

I looked over at him inquiringly—he had never referred to me as his friend before. His dark eyes expressed his appreciation and I smiled in response.

We enjoyed the light for only a few minutes before we heard booted footsteps, and my heart sank when I realized that our time was up. Despite the fact that I understood how we had been manipulated into this position, I truly could not conceive of anyone condemning innocent men to death. In my dismay, my focus lapsed and the light was extinguished, just as our captors came through the door, the flames from their torches casting sinister shadows on the walls.

Numb with shock and disbelief, we trudged slowly up the steep narrow steps that led back up to the courtyard. I practically wept with sorrow and at the same time seethed with frustration at my helplessness. Ahead of me, Bel was silent, his shoulders drooping as he stumbled awkwardly through the doorway and out into the courtyard

We both came to an abrupt halt when we saw that blood-stained wall ahead of us and realized we only had a few minutes left to live.

"Move along!" A tall, muscular man barked as he shoved Bel across the uneven cobbles. Another man grabbed my left arm in a bruising grip and hustled me along behind him.

As our wrists were manacled above our heads, we voiced frantic pleas regarding our innocence, but our demands for the opportunity to defend ourselves in a court of law were met with laughter and jeers.

In desperation, I tried once more to find any trace of whatever so-called power I might have, but I failed. Would I have been successful if I had been less agitated? Perhaps, but I was never given the chance to find out.

Before we were ready—and certainly no one could truly be reconciled to dying, especially so ignominiously—the signal was given to the soldiers to prepare their weapons for our execution. My horrified mind perceived the process in slow motion, as powder, ball and wadding was inserted in the barrels of the muskets and then rammed home. The pans were primed, the weapons brought up to their shoulders and sighted on us, and triggers pressed, which swung the mechanical arms forward so that the glowing end of the matches contacted the primer powder.

I barely had time to close my eyes and whisper to my wife, whoever she was, "I love you," before the weapons discharged their deadly ammunition in a violent burst of sound. My body jerked as lead balls slammed into me. I felt excruciating pain as my lungs collapsed and my heart exploded in my chest.

And the ultimate darkness took me.

CHAPTER 20

Moab, February 25, 2016

LUMINA GLANCED AROUND AND NOTED that the small shop was practically bursting at the seams, every seat taken. Normally, meetings were held at the spacious house on 400 East that the knights had rented some time ago with the intention that everyone attending would be comfortable. But she'd insisted that this meeting, which could possibly be their last, should be held at The Moab Herbalist. She was proud of the success they had experienced with the business Merlin had purchased back in the spring of 2013. They had painted and redecorated the interior of the place in the past year, and the soft green walls and off-white trim were perfectly suited to an herb shop. All of the signs and price tags had been reprinted meticulously in an old Celtic-style lettering that enhanced the already old-fashioned atmosphere. They had replaced the original industrial vinyl flooring with real oak wood planks, sanded, varnished and polished to a natural shine. After all, they wanted her father to be pleased with what they had accomplished when he came home. She deliberately didn't add what others might be thinking: *If he came home*.

She brought her full attention back to the front of the room as Ryan Jones put his fingers to his lips and whistled shrilly. "Let's call this meeting to order, people."

The buzz of conversation finally died down, and all eyes turned towards the burly blond knight.

"Okay, here's the deal. Lumina has a suggestion that makes of lot of sense, and even though you may not agree with her, at least give her a chance to explain, alright?" He motioned to the tall young woman with the long dark brown hair sitting in the front row.

Lumina Rae Ambrosius arose gracefully from her seat and stood next to the man she had known all her life. She gave him a brief smile and he nodded to her in return.

"Thanks, Ryan," she said quietly to him as he sat down in a folding chair at the side of the room. She turned to face her family and friends, all of whom watched her with varying degrees of concern, compassion and curiosity on their faces.

"First, I want to say that I appreciate everyone's efforts. It's been almost two years since Merlin disappeared, and despite all we've done recently, we still haven't been able to bring him home."

She gazed at her brother, who looked depressed and embarrassed. "Derek, don't you dare feel bad about that! It was an extraordinary accomplishment to locate him a few months ago in Inverness, Scotland—oh, I guess that Scotland would have been called Caledonia in the early fifth century, right? Unfortunately, as you all know, we weren't able to continue to hold onto his location. Derek has to sense Merlin's essence to be able to even open a portal, and that just hasn't happened lately."

Everyone glanced at Derek, whose body posture reflected shame and defeat. "God, I've been trying so hard," he muttered.

Jim Singleton spoke up. "Yeah, you have, man, don't let it get to you!"

"You're doing a great job, Dad." Morry slung a comforting arm over his father's hunched shoulders.

"Don't be so hard on yourself," Gary Gardner, alias Sir Gawain, growled.

Lots of throat-clearing and a few distinctly feminine sobs later, Rae Crandall spoke up. "Lumina, honey, go ahead and finish what you have to say."

"Okay, thanks, Grammy. Anyway, the bottom line is, I've spoken to Llyr recently, and he insists that we stop searching for Merlin, as of right now. This doesn't mean—"

A general roar of protest arose from the entire assemblage interrupting her before she could finish. Tears overflowed as she witnessed the love, loyalty and frustration being expressed by all of them. She closed her eyes, slowly raised her arms, and with her palms up sent out a wordless message of love and peace, along with a burst of white Light.

Silence and a sense of awe pervaded the room, as everyone was reminded that Lumina was a goddess in her own right.

She opened her eyes and began again. "You all know me, and I would never suggest that we give up on our desire to see Merlin come home to us. But remember, Llyr has mentioned this several times in the past and we have not heeded him. Now we must. I'm as anxious as all of you are for Merlin to return—maybe more! After all, I have been by his side for millennia. He is not only my father, he is my *god*, Myrddin Emrys." As she looked around the room her eyes shone with power, and her voice rang out, "Please believe that he will return when he is ready and not before."

She knew there was nothing more to say. They either believed her or they didn't. As she returned to her seat, the room was silent.

Derek slowly stood up and turned to his friends and family, making eye contact with each individual. He took a breath and released it in a long sigh. "I hate to admit it, but Lumina's right. We all need to have some faith that Merlin will be home soon. And I'm goin' to keep my eyes and ears open for any sign of supernatural activity in town, in case it might have somethin' to do with his situation. I hope y'all will do the same."

As Derek sat down, everyone began talking at once.

When the heated discussion finally wound down, Ryan stood up and addressed the crowd. "Well, I guess that's it, folks. If you need to talk, I'm available. Just give me a call. Meeting adjourned." His mouth turned up in a forced smile. After all, these people were temporarily in his charge and he wanted to come across as confident and helpful. But in reality, he was as clueless and worried as the rest of them.

He watched as Derek, Sarah and Morry converged on Lumina from one side, and Emily and Rae put their arms around her on the other, each reassuring the other that they could survive until Merlin came home.

Ryan motioned to the other knights to join Jim Singleton and Chris Colburn as they started to file respectfully out the door, intending to give the family some space.

Then Emily's voice rose abruptly in a shrill wail of grief, and one by one, the devotees of Myrddin Emrys dropped to the floor, unconscious.

Derek blinked and sat up. What the hell happened? Cradling his aching head, he realized that Emily was sobbing helplessly next to him. And then he remembered the sensation of his father's presence, which he'd always taken for granted, suddenly wink out, leaving an ominous feeling of emptiness that he'd hoped never to experience again.

"Dad, oh, God, *no*!" It was bad enough when Merlin had died after killing Nimue. Now, that emptiness felt as infinite as a black hole in space.

Horrified, he glanced over at Emily, who was rocking herself as a river of tears cascaded down her cheeks. And then, he noted that the six of them—all in varying degrees of shock—were on the floor surrounded by their friends, whose sad, sympathetic looks revealed an understanding of what must have happened.

Lumina finally stood up, her expression serious yet peaceful and calm and more mature than it had been only minutes ago. The voice that issued from her mouth was not that of a teenage girl. "Hush, my friends. Be at peace in your hearts. Have faith, and remember that Myrddin Emrys is truly immortal. He cannot continue in this state of ignorance—once he comes back to life and realizes that he cannot die, he will remember the truth and return to us."

Then, she blinked and looked around, noticing the awe on everyone's faces. She must have been channeling her goddess and didn't remember what she'd said. She only knew that the anguish she'd experienced as her father died had been replaced with a feeling of hope and renewal.

"Mom, it's okay, please stop crying, he's not really gone." Lumina reached out to Emily and gathered her against her smaller body. "Come on, let's go home."

Ryan silently assisted Morry, and Chris, Jim and Percival helped Rae and Sarah up off the floor. Derek, with a hand from Gary, slowly got up like an old man, and then went out to bring

Em's Xterra around to the back of the shop. He figured that she wouldn't be able to drive home. He wasn't sure *he* could.

Sensing Derek's distress as he came back into the room, Sarah gently touched his arm. "Are you okay?"

"Yeah, I'll be alright, darlin', but I'll need you to drive the truck home so I can take Em, Lumina and Rae in the Xterra." He could hardly focus, he felt so drained. "Please?"

"Why don't I just squeeze in with the four of you, and you can come back and get your truck tomorrow. Would that be okay? I think it would simplify things."

"'Course, Sarah, sorry, I'm not thinkin' straight." As he faced her, she noticed that the lines of grief and fatigue on his face made Derek look ten years older. He was hunched over as if the weight of the world rested on his muscular shoulders.

"I'm here for you, Der. Always," Sarah said softly, cupping his cheek, rough with beard stubble, in her small hand.

He straightened, her loving declaration giving him the strength to keep going. He nodded, kissed her hand, then gathered up his family and ushered them out the back door. "Let's go."

CHAPTER 21

Moab, February 26, 2016

Colin Campbell sat at the battered old oak desk with his arms folded across his ample belly, staring at the computer screen in front of him without seeing it. He was a man in his early forties, more than a little out of shape, wondering what the hell he wanted to do with the rest of his life. Until now, police work and family life had been his only focus, but now he wanted more.

He was lost in thought, his normal behavior when trying to figure out a thorny problem. He had been a detective with the Moab City Police Department for many years, and since the summer of 2013 he had been suspicious of the guy that owned The Moab Herbalist. Although there had never been any overt criminal activity at the modest little shop, or associated with its owner Michael Reese, the escalation in odd behavior surrounding the herbalist and his business continued to trigger Colin's inner sense that something was off. Especially since the man had mysteriously disappeared several years ago. And the big meeting at Reese's shop the previous night put the icing on the proverbial cake, in his estimation.

Colin had initially become a regular customer of The Moab Herbalist in an attempt to ferret out the truth, but he personally had never ventured into the store. Instead, he'd sent his teenaged son, Josh, to purchase various potions and herbal soaps without revealing exactly why he wanted them. His son was accustomed to requests like this since Colin was always so busy working that he never had time to run his own errands. At least that's what he told Josh.

Detective Campbell routinely had the products he purchased tested—at his own expense—for illegal or harmful substances before he used them, but to his everlasting chagrin and frustration, he had never discovered anything remotely suspect. To the contrary, the products always contained the purest of ingredients, without even a hint of adulteration.

In fact, the potions were so effective that if he hadn't already tested them, he'd *swear* that they contained some kind of psychotropic drug; he felt such a sense of happiness and well-being after using them. His favorite was a product for sore joints and gout, from which he had suffered for years. The active ingredient was an herb called squirting cucumber, also known by its botanical name, *Cucumeris siluatica*, which was listed on the label. He thought that was the Latin name for it, but couldn't be sure; he had never studied the language in school. Whatever the stuff was, it worked. The salve contained some kind of sweet oil plus the herb, and he had never experienced such complete cessation of joint pain in his life. Pure bliss. Of course, this had originally made him suspicious, but after he had used it for several months, the relief was so profound that he knew he should stop questioning it and just be grateful. Easier said than done.

If he didn't know better, he'd swear that Michael Reese was a magician, his concoctions worked so well. Colin laughed to himself at his foolishness, because there was no such thing as magic; the man was just a talented tradesman. But to be on the safe side, he'd pursue his investigation.

Campbell had never confided in his family about his suspicions. And he'd certainly never told his co-workers. He figured that he'd tell them only if he found something harmful in the products. He had always been a cautious man, believing wholeheartedly in the old adage, better safe than sorry. In that way, he followed in the footsteps of his Celtic forebears, who never let anyone pull the wool over their eyes, according to the family history that had been handed down for generations. His Campbell ancestors had left Scotland early in the eighteenth century and found a home in Ireland, staying there for several generations before traveling to America.

Thinking about his ancestors and their dogged determination to prosper even under difficult circumstances, he remembered that he was descended from Robert the Bruce, a man who knew his path and stuck to it until he reached his goal, which was to become the King of Scotland. Colin decided to stick to his guns as well, and to pursue this quest of his come hell or high water. His desire for justice to prevail was one of the reasons he'd gone into law enforcement.

His mind swung back to the issue at hand and he took a swig of his rapidly cooling coffee. He stroked his dark moustache absent-mindedly, contemplating the times he had observed Mr. Reese and an attractive woman with long, golden-brown hair (presumably his wife, Emily) walking together downtown. He had been impressed with—and suspicious of—the glow of health and happiness surrounding the couple. The man was slender and only moderately tall by today's standards, around six feet two, and while obviously muscular, not overly so. He carried himself with absolute confidence, moving with the ease and agility of a professional athlete or dancer. Josh had made the comment once that with his shiny, pitch-black hair and brilliant green slanted eyes, Michael Reese kind of looked like a panther. Colin had scoffed at that fanciful notion initially, but after seeing Reese striding along the sidewalk one day just before he'd disappeared, he reluctantly had to agree that the man had a feline grace and presence about him that was almost preternatural. To cover his unease, Colin had commented to his son sarcastically that the herbalist had probably been a ballet dancer or something. In the privacy of his own thoughts, he wondered if the man might be from another planet.

The events that began in the spring of 2014 cemented his conviction regarding the oddness of the Reese family when more and more off-beat people kept showing up at the herb shop. Josh reported that the couple had had a baby in January of that year, but by March, the baby had disappeared and a three-year-old child with the same coloring and features had taken its place.

One day his son had called him at work, excited about the three men who had started hanging around the shop, ostensibly to watch the little girl. He had described the men as soldiers. No, that wasn't it, Colin thought, Josh had called them "knights." What the hell that meant, he didn't know, except his son described them as tough-looking, as if they were prepared to pull a gun—or a sword—at the slightest provocation.

Apparently, the men loved to sit in the reading area and tell particularly detailed stories about ancient times. They talked about Camelot and the life of King Arthur and the Knights of the Round Table. Josh, who had always been captivated by stories of that nature, was very impressed. Because of the way the men spoke, the stories seemed real, as if they had lived in those times. Campbell was very suspicious of them. Why would such men be hanging around in an herb shop to babysit Michael Reese's child? He snorted derisively. If indeed, it was his child, since of course it was impossible for a baby to grow to the size of a three-year-old in a few months.

But even that conundrum wasn't sufficient to overlook the glaring fact that Reese was still missing. The situation more than intrigued Colin—he was obsessed with it. He encouraged his son to find out for him what the hell was going on in that shop. The force of his curiosity burned hotly inside of him.

Since Josh was interested in Reese's niece, he was more than willing to spy on the family for him.

And wasn't it a coincidence that the teenaged girl showed up when she did. *The child vanishes into thin air and suddenly the niece shows up? That's suspicious as hell*, Colin thought.

One day last winter, Josh had called Colin at work and reported a conversation he'd overheard between Michael's wife Emily and their employee Sarah.

"Pop, it was so strange. I'm sure they didn't mean for me to hear them, but you know how good my hearing is, right?"

"Yeah."

"Well, Emily—Mrs. Reese, I mean—said that at their next meeting she was going to accuse everyone of losing hope, and that he must be stuck in the past."

Colin frowned. What the hell that was supposed to mean? "Oh, yeah? What else did she say?"

"She hates that people think her husband's a deadbeat dad, abandoning his family, 'cause he'd never willingly do that."

Colin could understand that, as he was acutely aware of the increasing issue of men abandoning their families and responsibilities, something that he could never imagine Michael Reese would do. A man who was as devoted to his wife as Reese seemed to be, would never just up and disappear.

Something was terribly wrong in that family, he had concluded.

He sighed and glanced at his watch. Five o'clock. Huh, he could actually go home. He'd think about last night's unusual happenings at The Moab Herbalist later, over a beer.

CHAPTER 22

Edinburgh, Scotland, March 10, 1566

PAIN. MY ENTIRE BODY BLAZED with agony, particularly my chest. I opened my eyes reluctantly, drew in a shallow breath and groaned. Then, I tried to move and realized that there was a heavy weight on my legs and a number of sharp objects poking into my back.

I heard a disgruntled male voice growling his discomfort, and I did not recognize it. My muddled mind finally came up with a name to match the voice, and I opened my mouth to speak. It seemed to take forever before I could produce any coherent sound at all, and when I did, it had a rough, rasping quality.

"Bel..." I coughed and the pain took my breath away.

A voice whispered, "Oh, gods above, what happened? Where am I?"

"At the moment you are on top of me, and you are quite heavy."

"So I am," he muttered. He struggled to get to his feet, and in the process put unwanted pressure on my abdomen.

"Bel, you are crushing me! Get off!"

"My apologies...here, give me your hand." He reached down and helped me up, and we both stood awkwardly on the uneven ground, looking around for some recognizable landmark. A thick layer of mist swirled around us, obscuring our sight, and despite the fact that we had no way to determine what time it was, it felt very late.

I had no idea where we were, but wherever it was, the stench was overpowering.

Both of us called up orbs of light which cut through the mist and enabled us to see that we were in the middle of a midden, a vast refuse pit just beyond the weathered stone walls of the castle, which reared up high above us. There was a small door set into the base of the wall, with no visible handles. Apparently, it could only be opened from the inside when it was necessary to dispose of something. The contents of the midden (at least what we could see and smell) seemed to consist of human waste, household garbage, carcasses of dead animals, scraps of lumber and broken furnishings, spread across a steep rocky slope.

Our ragged, bloody selves were perched precariously right in the midst of the filth.

We glanced at each other, both of us seething with indignation.

"They killed us and threw our bodies out like garbage!" Bel spat out.

As our glowing balls of light hovered over us, we finally dragged our bruised and battered, but very much alive, selves up and across the rough boulders lining the pit. We collapsed onto a small strip of grass and weeds, which smelled clean and fresh compared to our noxious place of rebirth.

I decided to expand my light orb in order to get a better idea of our location. As I peered through the tall bushes just beyond our grassy space, I saw that the ground dropped away abruptly into darkness. I surmised that we were on the south side of the castle. We'd be safe here, temporarily, as long as we did not move past the bushes that were clinging to the edge of the cliff.

I inhaled carefully and noticed that I no longer experienced any pain. I stretched like a cat and sat up with a sigh, running my fingers through my hair to dislodge some unidentified refuse. Whatever it was, at least it did not smell too bad.

After pulling up my filthy shirt to look at my now-unblemished chest, I decided to extinguish my light, having satisfied my curiosity. Bel's provided ample illumination. He directed his orb of light towards his own chest and began to examine the holes in his tunic. Blood covered the entire front of the garment, but it had been so many hours since our execution that the fabric was dry and stiff. He looked into my eyes and broached the subject we had both been avoiding.

"How can we be alive again, Emrys? Not that I am complaining, mind you, but it makes no sense."

"I have no idea, but somehow the gods have given us another chance at life. I, for one, would like to leave this place while we can." I was anxious to depart this country that had ended up being so ill-fated for us. I had no particular destination in mind, but a vision of a land across the sea with rolling hills in myriad shades of green entered my mind, and although I did not know its name, it called to me.

Bel nodded in agreement, and as he extinguished his own light, I grabbed hold of his forearm and we disappeared, leaving our horrendous experience in Edinburgh behind us.

CHAPTER 23

Republic of Ireland, 2007

ONE STRAY BEAM OF LIGHT partially illuminated the cramped space in which we found ourselves. I looked around cautiously, having learned the hard way not to trust my surroundings. There were large rocks stacked around and above us in an organized fashion, creating a room. The air was stale and flat, the space smelling of the earth yet devoid of life. I felt as if we were being watched, but it was obvious that there was no one there. I was normally not a superstitious man, nor was I subject to flights of fancy, but for a moment, I felt the spirits of people who had died thousands of years ago hovering over the two of us. This was a place of ritual, ancient and enduring. I sensed that, more recently, untold numbers of living human beings had occupied this space, a few at a time, and then departed. A slight trace of body odor and a few other scents that I did not recognize permeated the chamber, certainly not more than a few hours old.

Perhaps they had come to pay homage to those who had gone before.

Bel tipped his face up and his nostrils flared as he drew in a breath, almost as if he was tasting the air. "Emrys, it smells very strongly of death in here. Is this a tomb?"

"Yes, it appears to be a burial chamber, but I have no idea why we ended up here."

Bel chuckled. "You obviously transported us here, so you must have had a purpose in doing so. You found a portal of some kind to accomplish the task"

"Well, of course I brought us here. I envisioned a land of green hills prior to transporting us out of Edinburgh, and I focused on that. But I swear to you that I do not remember having been *here* before," I said, spreading my arms wide to indicate the structure in which we were now standing. "As for *how* I find and utilize the portals? When we arrived on that hilltop in Edinburgh in the year 1566, I realized I had been there before, so it seems logical that I would choose, even subconsciously, a place I had visited in the past."

Then I frowned as something occurred to me. "Is it possible the gods are guiding our journey?"

Receiving no comment from my companion, I glanced at Bel, who still seemed to be sampling the air. "How can you smell the deaths of people who died so long ago?"

"That appears to be one of the major differences between us, Emrys. Perhaps I am more attuned to death than you are. For me, this place reeks of it." He paused and looked around. "Do you see yon beam of sunlight coming from an opening on the far wall? It appears that we can leave the tomb over there, although the passage seems much too narrow for either of us to fit through."

"Perhaps we can squeeze through if we turn sideways. In any case, I must get out of here." I was feeling more and more uncomfortable, for the atmosphere was oppressive and however unlikely it was, I felt as if some entity would try and take over my body and soul if I were to stay here any longer. I was a healer and, it seemed, a witch or a magician, and obviously sensitive to the essences of those who had passed on. Or perhaps psychic residue was a more appropriate way to refer to what was left after the death of the body. I paused in my ruminations for a moment, wondering how and where I had learned such terminology. Then I shuddered and simply wanted to be out in the fresh air. I had been subjected to way too many confined spaces recently.

Bel nodded in agreement when he realized how distressed I was. "Let us go then, my friend." He gestured towards the far wall.

I led the way, bent almost double in some places to avoid hitting my head on the vertical rocks that protruded into the passageway. The people who had built this structure must have been smaller and shorter to have created such a low and narrow passage into the tomb.

Once I was past the worst of it, I turned to note Bel's progress. I was afraid he would not be able to get through the passage at all, being a good deal bulkier than I was. With some effort, he squeezed through, albeit somewhat painfully. His arms were full of bloody scratches where sharp rocks had ripped through his sleeves.

Seeing my concern, Bel assured me that compared to dying, the scratches were insignificant. I had to agree with him.

Just as we were ready to step through the opening and into the light of day, we heard the murmur of a number of voices. I peered outside carefully. There was a large group of people facing one tall man who seemed to be in charge. He made a shrill whistling sound and once everyone's attention was upon him, he began to speak clearly and concisely.

"Welcome to Newgrange, one of the majestic stone tombs of the UNESCO World Heritage Site at Brú na Bóinne. My name is Thomas, and I will be your guide today."

Initially, I could not comprehend exactly what the man was saying. But then something occurred that I could not explain—the more I listened, the more I understood, until I recognized the language. I looked at Bel askance and his eyebrows shot up in surprise.

"I can understand what he is saying, Emrys! How can this be? What language is he speaking?"

"It is English," I whispered, realizing that I hadn't yet discussed the language issue with him.

Bel scowled and started to say something, but I motioned to him to stay quiet. I wanted to hear what else this charismatic man had to say.

The guide continued with a flourish, "Newgrange is one of the finest examples of Stone Age passage tombs in Europe. It was built in approximately 3300 BC as a part of a huge cemetery on this ridge above a bend in the Boyne River. It is actually older than Stonehenge and the Giza Pyramids. Isn't that remarkable? At one time, it was assumed that a tomb such as Newgrange would have been the final resting place of royalty. However, that is purely speculation." He went on to describe the excavations and research that had been done from 1962 to 1975 to determine the original shape and appearance of the mound.

Bel and I turned to stare at each other when we realized that we had traveled into the future more than fifteen hundred years since we awakened atop Tomnahurich Hill.

Meanwhile, Thomas completed his introduction. "Now, we are going to split up into small groups, since only a few of us can fit inside the tomb at one time. After each group has been inside, please make your way to the waiting area next to the road, and you will be taken by shuttle to a lot near the visitor center. You will then take the path across the bridge to the visitor center itself, where you may purchase souvenirs and use the toilet facilities. Then, you will need to walk quickly to the main parking area and find your tour bus." He continued to speak in his lilting, accented voice, designating the boundaries of each group.

I frowned in concentration, not understanding many of the terms he had uttered. By the gods, what was a "shuttle?" "Visitor center" made no sense to me, and neither did the term "tour bus." And what in the world was a "souvenir?"

"How are we going to get past them without being seen?" Bel muttered.

"Hmm, I wonder if we can make ourselves invisible?" I was joking, but my companion took me seriously.

He glanced at me doubtfully. "Invisible? Well, we can try. We have done other things we did not know we could do."

What did we have to lose? After being resurrected from a grisly death, becoming invisible seemed like child's play. "Then we need to attempt it soon. The first group appears to be ready to approach the opening."

We exchanged a look and both of us closed our eyes, concentrating on being unseen. I felt pressure in my chest, similar to the sensation I experienced when I moved us from one place to another, accompanied by a slight tingling throughout my entire body. I cautiously opened my eyes, hoping that we had succeeded. I grinned with satisfaction. "Bel, you did it, I cannot see you!"

"Nor can I see you. This is unbelievable!"

A small group was approaching the tomb and I realized we needed to take advantage of our unseen state and depart without further ado. There were large boulders with detailed carvings upon them just ahead of us that impeded our progress, and there were rough wooden stairs on each side of those boulders leading down to ground level.

Cognizant of the first group climbing the stairs on our left, Bel spoke to me through our mental bond. *We must leave posthaste, Emrys. We do not know how long this condition will last.*

I agree, Bel. And I have a feeling that if those people saw us suddenly appear in their midst, with blood on our clothing, it could cause a panic.

Most definitely. Let us go, then...

We hurried down the stairs on the right and moved toward an open area away from the remaining throng.

When we had reached what we thought was an adequate distance away from the entrance to the tomb and the milling crowd, we looked around to get a feel for the surrounding land.

I inhaled the clean, warm air, fragrant with the scent of flowers and grass growing around the perimeter of the tomb, and took in the glorious view. The massive, ancient mound faced with white quartz was perched atop a hill, and a gentle, grassy slope swept gradually to a river below—apparently the River Boyne. It was not a wide river, but it sparkled in the sunlight and flowed lazily between banks that were covered in thick vegetation. The land on either side of the river was a vivid shade of green, lush and dotted with trees, and thick hedges created pastures in which herds of sheep and cattle grazed. The sky was a vast expanse of cerulean blue with a few fluffy white clouds scattered about. I had seldom experienced anything so pleasant. Bel's face reflected the serenity I felt. We were so caught up in the scenery, however, that we did just what we had said we would not do—we allowed ourselves to become visible again. And when I heard the muttering of voices, I knew we had been spotted.

I turned around, forgetting that I was covered with blood and filth. Bel turned as well, wondering what I was looking at.

People were staring at us with expressions ranging from mild interest to horror, as they saw the blood on our garments. But since they seemed reluctant to approach, I was not as concerned and alert as I should have been. In fact, I was distracted by their clothing, so different from what I was accustomed to. At first, I thought the entire group consisted of men, but I gradually realized that both genders were wearing trousers and shirts. No dresses or long skirts were in evidence. In what year had we ended up, that women felt comfortable dressing in such a masculine fashion?

I was jolted out of my observations of modern garments when several of the men in the same uniform as the guide started towards us. It was clear that we should leave this place or face some unintended consequences. And having recently suffered through death and rebirth, I was sure that neither of us wanted any further confrontations this day. We took off across the gentle slope, heading in a southeasterly direction from the huge mound behind us. Our only goal at that point was to put some distance between our pursuers and us. We came to a narrow road strangely covered in some sort of hard, smooth black material, and deciding to take advantage of it, we began running. Without a specific destination in mind, I prayed that the gods would provide inspiration when we came to a crossroads.

CHAPTER 24

Moab, January 16, 2017

DEREK HAD SENSED FOR SOME time now that someone had been surveilling his father's shop. It had started in late summer of 2013 as a slight, jarring feeling of being watched, but he had dismissed it as his imagination. Over the past few years, as his confidence in his magical abilities had grown, that feeling had coalesced into absolute certainty—someone was definitely spying on them. Ever since Merlin had disappeared from their lives, the frustration of not being able to do anything about his father's continued absence had become a nagging ache in his gut. He hoped that solving the mystery of the watcher's constant, irritating presence would help alleviate some of that frustration. And apparently today was the day. He was fed up with it and decided to act.

That morning at breakfast, he had been complaining and, according to his fiancée, generally being a real pain in the ass. He and Sarah had been living together for several years, but were still getting used to each others' idiosyncrasies.

"Sweetheart, instead of getting all worked up about this situation, can't you, I don't know, do something telepathically? Try to get a fix on whoever's spying on us at the shop?"

Derek rolled his eyes. "Sarah, my mental abilities don't work quite like that. You have some telepathic ability. Can *you* do that?

"Well, no," she replied. "But you're considerably more powerful than I am, so I figured it would be worth a try."

Derek sighed and rubbed a hand over his eyes. "Maybe you're right. I don't have to work today, so I'll stop in at the herb shop this mornin' and sit in the readin' area and meditate. Maybe I'll be able to sense somethin' since I always seem to have some peculiar feelin's when I'm there. I'll use some of the techniques Llyr's been teachin' me lately."

"Okay, honey, that sounds like a good plan." Sarah kissed her lover, left the kitchen, and then hurried down the hall and into the bathroom to finish getting ready for work. She'd been employed at

The Moab Herbalist for almost three years now and loved her job. She enjoyed utilizing her modest magical skills to create many of the potions, herbal soaps and salves that they sold in the shop, and it was satisfying to be able to use the botanical knowledge she'd acquired in college. She finished brushing her wavy, reddish-blond hair, examined herself in the mirror, and decided she needed a little extra makeup today. She was pale from having been inside most of the winter. She brushed on a small amount of powdered blush and carefully applied her new shell pink lipstick. Then she added a quick swipe of dark brown mascara to her lashes and was pleased with the result. She checked the time on the whimsical cat clock on the wall and realized she'd better get going or she'd be late. Emily depended on her to open the shop most mornings and Sarah didn't want to let her down.

As she was heading out the front door a few minutes later, she happened to glance into the kitchen and noticed Derek still sitting at the table, with a coffee mug clutched tightly in his hands. He had been more frustrated than usual since Llyr had directed them to stop trying to retrieve Merlin from the past.

"See you soon, babe," Sarah called out, and thought she heard an echoing reply in her mind.

An hour later, Derek pushed open the door of The Moab Herbalist, letting in a gust of cold air, and was confronted with an unusually large number of people waiting at the counter to purchase their selections. Emily and Lumina were taking turns at the cash register ringing up sales while Sarah bagged the merchandise. Rae was busy restocking the rapidly dwindling inventory.

He shook his head in wonder. What the hell was causing such a run on herbal products, especially now? Winter had always been a slow time, but so far this month they were swamped. Maybe people were still curious about the missing proprietor?

He sat down in one of the newest overstuffed chairs in the reading area and closed his eyes, relaxing his body and focusing his mind, then tuned in to the thoughts of the customers.

Instantly, he was inundated by an overabundance of turbulent thoughts and feelings emanating from the people milling about the shop. He forced himself to use the techniques shown to him by his grandfather, who occasionally visited and helped him hone his skills. It still surprised Derek when the normally reclusive being consented to spend the time outside of the god realm to guide him, and he appreciated the gesture. He knew it took a considerable amount of energy for Llyr to maintain a human appearance in this realm. He loved his grandfather, and was in awe of the god's powers, but Llyr's resemblance to Merlin made it difficult to be around him. Fortunately, his personality was so different from Merlin's that it kept Derek's mind off the painful subject of his father's continued absence.

Derek took a breath and let it out slowly, finally able to sort through all the extraneous thoughts entering his mind. As he ran the information through the mental filtering system he had created (with a lot of help from his sister), he observed that there was a telltale glow coming from a young man in the crowd. Derek narrowed his focus, shutting out everything but the teenager's thoughts.

I hope Lumina has time to talk to me today...gosh, she's so pretty...I wish she'd go out with me...I wonder how old she is... why doesn't Dad ever come in here and buy his own shit...I think it's kinda fun being a spy...I wonder where Mr. Reese is...maybe he's a drug dealer and Dad wants to crack down on this place...I hope not, 'cause I'd hate to never see Lumina again...God, what a body she has...I'd love to suck on those sweet tits...

At that point, Derek had heard enough. He leaped out of his chair and grabbed the teenage boy in the crowd who was thinking such inappropriate thoughts, propelling him into the back room where he pushed him roughly up against the table. He was so focused on what he was doing and feeling so self-righteous that he never saw the outraged expressions on the customers' faces—or on Emily's face.He abruptly shut the door between the rooms.

The boy was furious. "Hey, what the hell, man? Get your hands off me, asshat! My dad's a police officer and—"

"And I'm a law enforcement ranger at Arches, as well as the older brother of that young girl out there who you're mentally undressin'," Derek growled, wishing he could give in to his urge to beat the livin' shit out of the boy. "What's your name, you little pervert? Who's your dad?"

"I'm Josh Campbell, and my dad is Detective Colin Campbell with the Moab City PD," he said proudly. Then, he realized what the man had said, accusing him of *mentally* undressing Lumina. He frowned. How in hell did he know that?

It was crystal clear that the kid's father was the one who had been spying on the business by purchasing herbal products with the intent of testing them for illegal drugs. The boy's mind was an open book. Derek laughed to himself as he thought of the look on Detective Campbell's face when all his fancy tests came back negative.

"What's so funny?" Josh asked, spoiling for a fight.

When Derek realized that he had actually laughed out loud, he knew he had screwed up, but he would definitely go see Campbell about reining in his son. Lumina's appearance was misleading, as she was actually less than three years old, having aged magically back in 2014. Not that he intended to reveal *that* information to anyone.

"Nothin'. Now get the hell out of here and stay away from my sister," Derek growled angrily. He opened the connecting door and gave the belligerent teenager a shove. Furious, the boy slammed out, knocking the little bell off the front door with a chiming clatter.

"Hey, what in the world is going on? Why are you accosting a paying customer?" Emily stomped over and stood in front of him with her arms crossed, a frown of annoyance marring the smooth perfection of her forehead. She and Sarah had hustled the customers out of the shop as soon as they were able, not wanting them to hear the confrontation in the back room.

"Detective Campbell with the Moab PD is the one who's been spyin' on us—through his son. He takes the products and has 'em tested for drugs."

Emily gritted her teeth. "So what? You know he'll never be able to prove anything since it's magic that makes everything so effective. He probably spends close to $100 a month in here,

Derek, and we can't afford to lose his business. Since we spent a huge amount of money on renovating the shop, and I haven't been able to get in touch with the Reese family to obtain more funds, our bank account is seriously depleted. The income from this shop is all we've got right now, and you can't afford to keep paying the bills out of your own pocket." Her gazed softened as she looked into his warm brown eyes. "Not that I don't appreciate it," she said quietly.

"Don't ya think I know that?" Derek started pacing back and forth across the back room, furious not only with himself but with the whole flippin' family, and most of all, with his father for abandoning them. It wasn't fair to Merlin that he felt that way, but he couldn't help himself. Derek's skin fairly crackled with energy and he knew he had to calm down before his magic exploded—literally. He stopped, closed his eyes for a moment, and turned his attention inward. He forced himself to remember everything Merlin had taught him the year he first started exhibiting his advanced sorcerer's abilities as well as a ferocious temper. The two made a dangerous combination.

Emily kept quiet while Derek worked through his anger, aware that he was dangerously close to the breaking point. They all were. Now, she could feel his volatile emotions subsiding as he regained control of himself, and she breathed a sigh of relief. She remembered all too well the consequences of uncontrolled sorcery, and it frightened her. Losing her husband was the worst, but if she lost her old friend and stepson as well, she really couldn't handle it.

When Derek opened his eyes and looked at her calmly, she walked up to him and put her arms around him. They held each other close for a few moments before stepping back.

"I'm sorry for losin' my temper with the Campbell kid, Em. I'm havin' trouble keepin' it all together since Dad's been gone."

"I know, Der. I'm just glad that you, Mom and Sarah are here. I don't know how I'd cope if I had to deal with this alone."

Derek sighed. "I know what ya mean." He leaned forward and kissed her cheek. "I think I'll go to the pool and swim some laps. Hopefully, I can work off some of my excess energy and get my head back on straight." He disappeared in a flurry of glittering particles.

"Everything okay?" Rae looked at Emily askance as she came out of the back room with a box of inventory to be stocked.

Bemused at the unusual sight of those glittering colors that had winked out soon after Derek had gone, Emily missed her mother's question. "I'm sorry, what did you say?"

"I said, is everything alright?"

Emily smiled wanly. "Oh, it will be, Mom, sooner or later."

Late that night, Em sat alone in the living room with a mug of hot peppermint tea, listening to an old CD of Derek's that he'd given her. It was called *Lonestar, From There to Here: Greatest Hits*. She was not necessarily a fan of country western music, but she liked this particular band. The song Derek had specifically asked her to listen to was called "I'm Already There," and she had to admit it was very special. It lifted her spirits, so she played it again, pretending that it was Merlin singing to her.

"...And I'll gently kiss your lips, touch you with my fingertips, so turn out the light and close your eyes.

"I'm already there, don't make a sound, I'm the beat in your heart, I'm the moonlight shining down, I'm the whisper in the wind, and I'll be there until the end.

"Can you feel the love that we share? Oh, I'm already there..."

Derek felt an ache in his heart as he heard Emily's thoughts and sensed her emotions. He knew the song and loved it, and it was so appropriate to her and Merlin's situation that he was glad she'd decided to listen to it.

He hoped that wherever his dad was, he was feeling Emily's love beckoning to him.

CHAPTER 25

Dublin, Republic of Ireland, July, 2007

"CAN'T READ MY, CAN'T READ *my, he can't read my poker face...*"

I chuckled as I danced to Lady Gaga's recent hit, "Poker Face," and the redhead with whom I was dancing looked startled. I was normally reserved, spoke very little and never laughed while we were on the dance floor. She and I had danced together every evening at this pub in the Temple Bar District of Dublin for the past week, and we seemed to be physically compatible, at least for dancing. She was tall—within a handspan of my own height—and slender, with blue eyes and a kind smile, and we moved well together. I truly enjoyed her company.

Siobhán was a lovely, desirable woman and I was attracted to her, but I just couldn't take that attraction to its natural conclusion, despite the fact that she was more than willing for me to bed her. She apparently thought she knew me well and wished to take our "relationship" to the next level.

I still didn't know myself, so how could anyone else? And I certainly had no desire to bed her after that disastrous experience in the realm of the Fae.

Even though I didn't remember exactly who I was, I was starting to remember *what* I was, and rediscovering what I could do. I was a practitioner of magic, and among other things, I could read minds and transport Bel and myself to different locations, both in time and space.

And I was adept at keeping a "poker face," never letting my thoughts or intentions show. I hadn't actually played the card game mentioned in Lady Gaga's song—the game of poker—but I was aware that it was quite popular in American culture and had been for over a century, and to be successful at it, one couldn't give away any indication of what one's cards were.

I wasn't a gambler as such, but I sensed that I was used to taking enormous risks. I had come to the conclusion that I was basically a good man, not an evil one, although with powerful magic at my beck and call it was an ongoing battle to remember that. The temptation to cross the line came close to overpowering me on a daily basis. I had already slipped into the gray areas several times. First, when I used magic to obtain what we needed when we arrived in Dublin with only the filthy, blood-stained clothes on our backs, clothes from the wrong time period at that. We had initially landed inside the tomb at Newgrange after fleeing Edinburgh Castle. Then we had slowly made our way through the Irish countryside south to Dublin. We had stolen the garments we needed, including finely woven trousers (or "slacks" as the signs in the store called them), fitted silk shirts and elegant footwear. When I could magically transport myself into a clothing store after hours, and then depart, decently clad with no one the wiser, it was tempting to help myself to any merchandise I wanted. Second, when we had discovered that this time period had no opportunities for hunting or bartering for other necessities, namely food and shelter, we had used magic to obtain money from a machine outside a banking establishment. While this was the act that I felt the most ashamed of, I was also sorely tempted to repeat it.

"Emrys, take care. We mustn't fall prey to the dark desires in this world. They will surely eat us alive," Bel said quietly, sensing the direction of my thoughts.

I realized that the song had ended and I was standing next to our table staring pensively into space.

I sat down next to him and took a sip of my whiskey, the condensation from the ice-filled glass leaving a ring of moisture on the table. It didn't taste right mixed with water and ice and I wondered why I had ordered it that way.

I made sure that my lady friend and Bel's were on their way to the toilet—*leithreas*, as the sign above the door indicated—before I glanced at Bel and smiled. I certainly didn't want the women to hear our conversation.

"You are most assuredly correct, my friend," I replied. Bel and I had both changed drastically in the months since we'd fled Inverness, letting go of our long-standing feud, the details of which neither of us could recall anyway. It seemed like only yesterday that I had guided him through the door into the world of Faery beneath Tomnahurich Hill in Old Inverness, the stench of his fear sharp in my nostrils. And I remembered my amazement when he had revealed his own magical abilities as we attempted to depart the Fae realm unnoticed. We had finally gotten out through what we'd later understood was a portal connecting to the ancient ruins atop the mountain peak called Arthur's Seat, which loomed above Holyroodhouse Palace in sixteenth-century Edinburgh. Then, after our deaths at the hands of Henry Stuart's henchmen and our subsequent resurrection, we had hastily departed Scotland.

And now we were here in Ireland, in the city of Dublin in the summer of 2007, nearly overwhelmed by culture shock. However, the ability to absorb a new language was one of the many feats that convinced me of my unusual nature. I found that I was already familiar with the English language, and although in this modern Ireland there was no need to use the Gaeilge, or Irish Gaelic, I found that I knew the basics of that language as well. During our sojourn in Caledonia in the fifth century, we had learned a dialect of Old British, a Celtic language that had long-since disappeared. Recently, I had discovered that I knew Latin and Old Welsh as well. This propensity for languages—especially long dead languages—was somewhat disturbing, since I couldn't imagine a reason I should be multilingual to that extent.

There was no doubt whatsoever in my mind that Bel and I were, at the very least, witches, perhaps even sorcerers, and at most something that I hesitated to name for fear of incurring the wrath of a higher power…dare I say it…*gods*? No, that just couldn't be, it was too outrageous to even contemplate, although I had done so frequently in the past few months as we traveled from one time period to another.

We had actually spent more time in the Republic of Ireland than anywhere else. We were used to it and felt safe and comfortable here in the city of Dublin.

It was obvious to me that the two of us had a connection that defied logic. We both had missing memories we needed to regain if we were to explain the purpose of this journey of ours through time and space, and to come to some sort of resolution.

As I studied Bel's features, I noted the stubborn jaw, the dark eyes that I now recognized as being full of intelligence and understanding, and hair as dark as my own. Suddenly I was overcome by what could only be termed a vision, or perhaps a vivid memory. In this vision we were incorporeal beings, and I experienced images of a time and place that made no sense whatsoever to the human mind. And then, just like that, I suddenly realized the truth—neither of us *was* human. For a moment, I saw that our guise of human men was an illusion. Our real selves were beings of light and energy, not flesh.

I was rendered speechless, and Bel frowned as he saw the look on my face. "Emrys, what's the matter?"

"Does it not seem odd to you to be doing what we're doing right now? This isn't our world! We do not belong here any more than we belonged in fifth-century Inverness or sixteenth-century Edinburgh. We're not even *human*, for God's sake!" I was glad that the noise level was high in this place as I blurted out that last sentence.

"You have remembered something?" Bel spoke with an intensity that made me think he had his own suspicions. "Why would you think that?"

I glanced around the pub to make sure no one was paying attention to us. "I remember being immersed in light, light and energy. I think that is my true form, and yours." I sat back, curious to see what his reaction would be to my pronouncement.

Bel blinked, looked down at the considerable bulge in the crotch of his form-fitting trousers, and then cupped himself as if to assure that his genitals were still there. He grinned at me and said, "At the moment, my friend, I can assure you that I am a man. However, I understand what you're saying. I, too, remember light and energy, formlessness, and being in the presence of a supreme being. I believe it was another realm than this physical one."

"Yes, that's exactly it!"

As I hesitated to reveal my previous thought, Bel said it for me, in a voice that was barely audible. "Emrys...are we... *gods*?"

We stared into each others' eyes with uncertainty for a moment and then looked away, neither of us willing to pursue such a controversial train of thought.

Deciding to focus on more mundane matters, I gestured to our server to bring us another round of drinks, and Bel and I chatted about the delicious Italian food we'd had for dinner that evening.

The drinks arrived—without ice this time—and I peeled a few bills off the roll of euros in my pocket to pay for them. "*Go raibh maith agat,*" I said, with a smile, thanking the server in Irish. I hoped that she understood the language, for not many people did in this modern age, even though Irish children were still taught the basics in school.

"Keep the change," I added. It was easy to be generous when the procurement of funds only required a moment of focus and a wave of a hand.

"*Tá fáilte romhat*! You're welcome, sir!" The server walked away with a pleased expression on her face, tucking the exorbitant tip in her pocket. I felt her immense relief as she realized she now had enough money to pay her rent. I was happy to know that I had helped her.

"*Sláinte!*" We raised our glasses in a toast to our health, and then drank deeply of what the Irish called *uisce beatha,* water of life.

"*An bhfuil tú ar meisce go fóill?*" I asked Bel slyly, testing him.

"Seriously, Emrys? Am I drunk yet? No, and I doubt that you are either. Why are you speaking Irish all of a sudden?"

"Because I like it. It has an interesting cadence. And I feel as if I've been to Ireland before." I didn't bother to tell him that I also saw a banner of a red dragon in my mind, which seemed connected somehow to my visit to Ireland in the distant past. "Don't you wonder how we know these languages? Especially when we came through the portal inside the tomb at Newgrange and understood what the guide was saying to that group of tourists?"

Bel had just opened his mouth to reply when our lady friends returned to the table, excited about the change in the tempo of the music and ready to dance again. He glanced at me and shook his head slightly, which I took to mean that we would talk about it later. I nodded back in agreement and then smiled at Siobhán, getting up from my seat with the intention of heading out onto the dance floor. I was reaching for her hand when a vision suddenly blinded me.

I flew high above the earth, oblivious to the cold or the lack of oxygen. I saw the land below me, recognized the continents, knew where I belonged and who was waiting for me. And then there was only darkness...

"Emrys, are you alright?"

The concern in that rough male voice brought me back and I opened my eyes. I was lying on the banquette, with Bel hovering over me, worry apparent on his swarthy face. The ladies were nowhere in sight, having abandoned us, I assumed, for much more normal partners. I can't say that I blamed them, although I was a little insulted that the woman who had been so eager to bed me had given up with nary a qualm.

I struggled to sit up, trying to recall the names and faces that I had seen in my vision, but the information eluded me.

"What happened?" I whispered, my head pounding so hard that I couldn't stand the sound of my own voice.

At least half a dozen patrons of the pub had gathered around curiously, several offering assistance, which we ignored.

"Come, we need to leave this place. We're attracting too much attention," Bel said quietly as he pulled me up and braced me against his powerful body. I was weak and limp in his arms, no help at all.

He muttered, "Oh, to hell with it," and threw me over his shoulder. He was massively built, tall and muscular, but I was tall as well and heavier than I looked. As he staggered towards an exit sign glowing brightly in the corner, everyone that had been hovering around us reluctantly dispersed, disgruntled that they had been deprived of a moment's entertainment. As Bel opened the door, I heard the bartender make a rude comment regarding my state of inebriation.

Once we were out on the sidewalk, I insisted that Bel put me down, as being carried like a sack of potatoes was exacerbating my headache.

It was still dark, a few hours before dawn, and it was past time to return to our hotel. Bel wanted to hail a cab, but I felt somewhat better and we decided to walk, the cool moist air helping to clear my mind.

I breathed in the myriad scents of the sleeping city. The salty tang of the sea to the east and the slightly stagnant smell of the River Liffey only a few feet to my left, the odor of old beer and the smell of overflowing garbage bins, and the lingering acrid odor of car exhaust and construction machinery all wafted on the light breeze.

We were walking along Aston Quay and could see the O'Connell Bridge up ahead when we were accosted. Two men stepped out of the pitch black where a streetlight was out, pointing guns at our chests.

"Give us your money, lads, and no one has to get hurt. Come on, hurry it up, now." The lilting accent was a temporary distraction to the deadly intent of the confrontation.

Bel and I looked at each other and started laughing. This confused the robbers no end, and then sparked their anger.

"Well, lads, you're not awfully smart now, are ya? Quit feckin' around and hand it over. Now." Both men were almost as tall and burly as Bel, but they had no idea who—or what—they were dealing with. Bel was thinking about conjuring a large fireball, but I had a better solution. I stretched out my right hand, palm splayed open, and quietly uttered a word in Latin.

"*Desino.*"

The men were caught motionless as insects in amber, their eyes wide in stunned disbelief.

I sent a telepathic message to them with a warning, *Gentlemen, as soon as I let you go, you had better run for your lives, and never attempt to rob anyone again, or we will find you. And believe me when I say that you* will *be sorry.* Then I released them.

"Holy Mother of God! Forget the money, Sean, and let's get the feck out o' here!" the other man yelled, and they both started running. At the last minute, Bel decided to lob an invisible energy ball at each of them, which produced a few high-pitched screams. We didn't kill them, but it was evident that they were injured even as they got away. Anger surged through me, and I could sense it in Bel also. I knew that we both undeniably had the capacity to kill if such an action proved necessary.

We came to the conclusion simultaneously that at this point we would be better off curtailing our walk and transporting ourselves back to the hotel. I gripped Bel's forearm, closed my eyes and took us directly to our rooms.

CHAPTER 26

Dublin, Republic of Ireland, July, 2007

"DID YOU SEE THE LOOKS on their faces when you froze them in their tracks?" Bel chuckled.

"And when you bombarded them with those balls of energy after I released them? Yes, it was most satisfying, wasn't it?" I grinned widely. A part of me thought that I shouldn't be making light of injuring human beings, but I shrugged it off. Those two ruffians didn't deserve my concern.

Bel looked thoughtful for a moment. "By the way, how did you know what spell to use?"

I shrugged. "It just popped into my head and I knew it would work."

"Perhaps you'll remember other spells. For instance, if you could create money out of thin air, we won't have to keep 'borrowing' from the banks."

"I promise I'll work on that," I said with a wry look.

We were settled comfortably in our suite at the Riley Court Hotel, cut crystal tumblers of Irish whiskey in our hands, as we continued to discuss the night's unexpected adventures.

Our sitting room was aesthetically appealing, with a high ceiling and a Waterford crystal chandelier of which I was particularly fond. The walls were painted dark gold and the trim was cream, creating an atmosphere of richness and luxury. The chairs were large and comfortable, upholstered in a paisley print of royal blue, red and gold, and had matching ottomans so we could put our feet up. It was ironic that the hotel appeared to be built in Victorian times but was actually only a few decades old.

I took a final pull on my drink and made a face. "I've decided I prefer Scotch."

"You're joking. That stuff tastes like cleaning solvent."

"And you're in the habit of drinking cleaning solvent, are you?"

"Well, no, but that's what comes to mind." Bel grimaced. "Emrys, I'm beginning to feel extremely dissatisfied, for some reason. Like I'm supposed to be doing something vital, but I can't remember what it is."

I glanced at my friend. I could sense his unhappiness and knew exactly how he felt.

"As if we were just wasting time?" I thought for a moment, and then continued, "I wake up in the morning feeling like the answers are right there, if I could only break through this blockage in my memory." I set my empty glass down on the table next to my chair, careful to place it on a coaster.

"Let's try right now. What do we have to lose?" Bel closed his eyes and gave every indication that he was concentrating hard.

"Okay, I'm willing." I put a throw pillow behind my back for support, so I could sit up straight. I rested my hands on my thighs, palms up, then closed my eyes and cleared my mind, hoping that this time I would succeed in penetrating the barrier that prevented me from connecting to my past. I was feeling focused and relaxed when I sensed Bel staring at me, but I didn't say a word, and just kept sinking deeper.

For an instant, I glimpsed a lush, green hillside with a grove of ancient oak trees, thick bushes, sheep grazing, and what appeared to be the opening of a cave. And then the scene was gone. The only thing I retained was the certainty that the hillside was located in the south of Wales, and that I knew it well.

"It's frustrating to see something, just a small segment of a memory, but have no idea what it means." I sighed and scrubbed my hands over my face. "You know, I'm tired of living in a hotel. I thought I would be content once we were able to live in comfort such as this, not having to survive outdoors. Being able to bathe regularly, *eat* regularly, and sleep in a comfortable bed in a warm room.

"And being able to work magic is certainly extraordinary. But I really just want to go home—wherever, whenever, that happens to be. I may not remember my wife, but I miss her. I have a connection with her in my heart, so I know she's alive—somewhere—and I am certain that I have children, too. Perhaps even a grandchild."

Bel jerked and gave me a serious look, as if he was remembering something important.

"What?"

"I had a daughter, but I think she is…dead…or something. It's not really clear. I may have a granddaughter." He frowned and closed his eyes, fighting to keep the elusive memory in the forefront of his mind.

"Damn it!" He exploded off the couch and started pacing.

"Bel, it's alright, my friend, calm down." I was more than a little alarmed at his reaction since he had been relatively calm and good-natured for weeks.

"*No*, by the gods, it's *not* alright! Something is very wrong and we are at the center of it! You and I have *always* been…uh…" As his understanding faded again, his voice tapered off as well and he looked tired and confused, then completely disgusted.

"Oh, fuck it!" He stomped into his bedroom and slammed the door, and a few minutes later, I heard the water running in his shower.

I continued to sit stiffly erect, staring at his closed door as a memory ripped through me. When Bel had lost his temper, his dark face and angry countenance had brought forth a picture in my mind of the two of us facing off on the top of a mountain, red rock dusted with snow under a sullen winter sky, Bel flying backwards into a field of low spiny plants. What in the world? And just before that, I had fallen at least a thousand feet off a cliff but hadn't died…

Long after the images had faded, I sat there, shaken, wondering what they meant. Finally, my body aching, I realized that further rumination was useless, and I decided to go to bed. As I trudged into my room and shut the door carefully behind me, I felt very old, as if I had the weight of more than a thousand years of history pressing down on my shoulders. And how likely was that?

As I slowly undressed and carefully hung my clothing in the closet, I wondered if I could direct my dreaming mind to resolve our dilemma. The thought drifted away as I stepped into the bathroom and focused on my reflection in the mirror. I looked the same as I had when we checked into the hotel—tall and slender with green eyes, black hair, and a long, straight nose. And then, just for a moment, my perspective shifted and I heard someone say, "You already know how handsome you are, so quit staring at yourself in the mirror." My wife's voice, it must be, and I was suddenly so homesick I wanted to cry.

Depressed and exhausted, I stepped into the luxurious marble shower stall and turned on the faucets. I stood motionless under the cascade of hot water for a few minutes, then soaped up and rinsed. I knew that I had done something similar many times in my own home, in a modern bathroom such as this one—well, maybe not as opulent, but still well-appointed. I stepped out, then held out my hand and levitated the large, thick white towel from the rack, distractedly drying myself off. My mind elsewhere, I grabbed the toothpaste and did a cursory job of brushing my teeth, then dragged my weary self back into the other room and fell into bed. As I rapidly succumbed to slumber, my last coherent thought was that I was more than ready for this journey to end.

I drifted in the fog and rain for an eternity, finally drawn to a remote hill upon which a stone pillar stood, glowing with a light of its own. Storm clouds billowed and lightning illuminated the top of the hill. Abruptly, I was among a group of silent beings, tall and fair, who radiated power, and I knew they were the Tuatha Dé Danann, the Tribe of Danu, a magical race who had inhabited Ireland in pre-Celtic times. They greeted me silently, acknowledging my god status, and then they were gone, lost in the mists of time. I watched as burial mounds were created and forts were built, many of them subsiding into the ground as the centuries passed in a whirlwind of colors and sounds. Then, a king stood next to me, his banner a red dragon, and he was asking me how we could transport the monstrous stone sentinel to Britain. He intended to bring the barbarian inhabitants of Ireland under his rule by capturing the Lia Fáil, their Stone of Destiny. I told him that while we could engineer the feat, the gods would frown upon such an action. Eventually, he and his troops marched away under lightning-threaded skies and disappeared, and I once again stood alone next to the enduring stone structure, while the world changed.

Then, I was in front of a cave, on top of a hill in the old

Kingdom of Dyfed in southern Wales. Staring out across the rolling, green hills, I mourned the loss of my king and contemplated a sleep that would last for centuries—

"Emrys? Emrys!" I heard Bel's strident voice calling me, but it didn't seem relevant so I just kept sleeping. But when he started pounding on the door, each successive knock escalating in intensity, I finally opened my eyes, struggling to keep the dream images from fading.

What in the god's name is wrong with him? I thought groggily, as the insistent barrage continued on my bedroom door.

I groaned and hauled myself out of bed, casually glancing at the clock, expecting it to be around eleven in the morning. Instead, it was five o'clock. The shadows in the room indicated late afternoon, and I had apparently slept the entire day away. No wonder Bel was concerned.

"Emrys! Open the fucking door, damn it!" Before I could respond, the door was ripped off its hinges and Bel stomped into the room behaving like an angry god.

I stared at him, wondering how he was going to rationalize such blatant destruction of hotel property.

"You've been sleeping since early yesterday morning! I couldn't wake you up, Emrys! What the hell is wrong with you?" Beneath his dark, frowning countenance and furious speech I could sense his concern.

I couldn't believe it—I had slept thirty-six hours straight. It seemed impossible, but it began to make sense when the images I had seen in my dreams poured through my consciousness, and I remembered everything.

CHAPTER 27

The Irish Sea, July, 2007

IT WASN'T UNTIL WE WERE standing at the rail on the top deck of the Swift Ferry the next day on the way to Holyhead, Wales, that I finally revealed the truth to Bel, or should I say, Beli, the god of death, for that was who he really was. While I wished he had remembered his true identity on his own, I couldn't justify allowing my friend to suffer in ignorance any longer.

The day before, it was so late when I finally got out of bed that I'd insisted on going to dinner straight away at my favorite pub. The service was good, the food was exceptional and the atmosphere quaint, always resulting in an enjoyable dining experience. On that particular occasion, however, the only thing that really mattered to me was assuaging my raging hunger.

While I consumed a platter of sliced beef, roasted potatoes and peas, Beli sat fuming, hardly touching his own meal, because I wouldn't tell him what I had remembered. I eyed him over the rim of my pint of ale as I drank, and briefly considered revealing my information right then. But I refrained, because I felt very strongly that a strategic time and place was needed for such earthshaking revelations. And that's exactly what they were. In fact, I could hardly contain the elation I felt, having finally broken through the barriers to my lost self-knowledge. I hoped what I had to share with Beli would trigger his own memories; I suspected he would have a very hard time accepting the truth from my lips. And I also prayed to the one God, that all of our experiences together in the past few months would allow us to let go of the negative feelings for each other that we'd harbored for thousands of years, and would help us resolve the major issues that had originally made us enemies.

We stood watching as the city of Dublin receded from the stern of the ferry, and Beli waited impatiently for me to speak. I finally turned toward him and cleared my throat, wondering where

I should begin. For just a moment, I was distracted by the motion of the ferry and glanced seaward. I remembered how seasick I had been in the distant past the few times I had been on the water. I was grateful I no longer had that problem and could appreciate the way the spume blew back from the tops of the waves and the gulls flew over us, hoping for a handout. The breeze was refreshingly cool and the sky uncharacteristically free of rain clouds.

I reined in my wandering thoughts and admonished myself for getting sidetracked when I needed to focus on the information I was about to impart. I looked at Beli as he turned to me, his dark face suffused with fury.

"I'm through with waiting, Emrys! You have obviously figured out, or remembered, who you really are—I can see it in your eyes, so don't bother denying it. I sincerely hope you also know who I am, because I am sick and tired of this adventure and want an end to it." Beli scowled ferociously and crossed his muscular arms over his broad chest. A young family standing a few feet away looked startled at his outburst, and his visage was so intimidating that the man grabbed his wife and small son and hustled them as far away from us as he could get.

"Relax, my friend, you're scaring people," I murmured, and then looked directly into his eyes, hoping for the best. "Yes, I have remembered who I am and I know exactly who you are as well. It's ironic that we have both looked for similarities between us, because we really are brothers of a sort. We are both gods, created by the one God eons ago, at the beginning of time, to serve him. I am Myrddin Emrys, the god of magic and healing, and you are Beli, the god of death, worshipped by the ancient Welsh people millennia ago." I waited for him to comment, and when he did not, I continued, "Rather mind-boggling, isn't it?"

He stared at me as if I was totally demented, until it was obvious that his own memories had finally started to return. His expression changed to one of astonishment, then in quick succession, disbelief and recognition took turns flowing across the harsh planes of his dark face. Finally, acceptance dawned, overriding the evidence of all his other emotions. Unfortunately, he also remembered why we had been so antagonistic towards each other.

And as Beli's memories assaulted him, I recalled the events that precipitated our quarrel.

When I was fifteen years old, I had been seduced by an older woman, a sorceress named Nimue. At the time, I was unaware that I was a god and that Nimue was the daughter of the god Beli. All I knew was that she was beautiful and I was overwhelmed by adolescent passion. But she and I had not remained lovers for long. I discovered she was using her magic for evil and I could not condone that, so I left her. Months later, unbeknownst to me, she had borne my child, a daughter she had named Adrestia. Nimue had hated me for leaving her and had been my nemesis for centuries, seeking retribution for what she perceived as my ill-treatment of her. Our enmity had finally come to a head in 2013 during the battle at the Matheson Wetlands Preserve west of Moab. I had killed her, but in the process, I had also died. Fortunately, I was able to return to my body; she was not since she had been decapitated. Nimue's spirit had then inhabited our daughter's body, taking over Adrestia's life and using it for her own purposes. She had engineered an elaborate plan to destroy me through my grandson Morry, and when that hadn't worked, she had abducted my son Derek. What she hadn't planned on, was that I was able to overpower her and put her in a state of suspended animation until I could deal with her once and for all. She remains in that suspended state in a cavern below Balanced Rock to this day.

I surfaced from my grim thoughts as Beli's voice deepened to a furious growl.

"You killed my *daughter*, Myrddin Emrys! How can you expect me to continue our friendship after remembering that?"

I had been afraid of just such a reaction from him. But the knowledge of my own losses triggered a wave of burning emotion in response.

"Beli, you allowed Nimue to use *my* daughter—your granddaughter—to further her centuries-long persecution of me! And

Nimue isn't actually dead, as you are quite aware. Her essence took possession of Adrestia's mind and body years ago, so that it may not be possible to save Adrestia's soul. Your daughter was—*is*—pure evil; though I know now that she did not get that from you, despite the fact that you are the god of death." I took a quick breath to calm myself, then continued, "Our adventure together allowed us to really get to know each other, to connect on a personal level, and I for one am most grateful for that." My throat tightened as my feelings for the man threatened to overwhelm me.

Beli's rage and indignation gradually faded and an emotion I had never expected to see—sadness—twisted his features into a mask of pain and regret.

"I truly did not realize just how deep Nimue's obsession was, Emrys, and I do not now, nor did I ever, condone my daughter's treatment of you. I suspect my feelings for her blinded me to her true nature. No one wants to believe that his child is evil."

Beli looked into my eyes searchingly, seeming to ask for absolution. Apparently, what he saw on my face reassured him that I bore him no ill will. Then he expressed aloud the conclusion I had come to as soon as my memories returned.

"God must have set this whole thing in motion, as a lesson for both of us." Beli leaned forward, resting his arms on the railing. He took a long, calming breath of the pure salt air, then exhaled slowly, letting go of his pent-up frustration. His long, dark, wavy hair blew back in the breeze and his eyes were closed.

"Yes, I believe he did just that, my old friend." I marveled to myself that it really was true. After all, the gods—myself, Beli, Llyr and all the rest—had been created at the beginning of time to follow the will of God, in whatever shape or form it might take. Therefore, we were all essentially brothers and sisters, the very first children of the Creator.

I emerged from my ruminations and saw Beli watching me, so I held out my hand. He hesitated for only a second before he extended his, clasping mine warmly.

"Friends," we pledged.

CHAPTER 28

Wales, July, 2007

As we approached the coastline of Wales, I felt a yearning for my homeland that I had not anticipated. Of course, the land of my birth as it was in the fifth century no longer existed. I smiled sadly as the memories of my life faded away until they were firmly entrenched in the past where they belonged. I felt a warm hand on my shoulder as Beli gave me a bit of comfort, having sensed my deep welling of nostalgia.

We disembarked at the Holyhead ferry terminal and waited until everyone else had dispersed before we became invisible. It was the only way that we could get through customs, as we had no passports or other identification.

Once we had passed the customs agents, we made sure we would not be observed and allowed ourselves to become visible again. Then we only had to walk a short distance to the train station ticket office.

Beli glanced at me. "Why are we bothering with this, Myrddin Emrys? I can understand your desire to take the ferry from Dublin; it was really quite enjoyable, and it provided a backdrop for stimulating my memory. But why not simply teleport to your Crystal Cave from here? I presume that is our ultimate destination?"

"It is, but I wanted to stop at Segontium first, even though there is probably little evidence of its occupation extant." I had been immersed in memories of my travels in the fifth century and needed to see the place again.

Beli looked at me askance, then stepped up to the window and spoke briefly to the ticket agent. Turning back to me, he said, "If you insist on using mundane transportation, we can take the train to Bangor and then a bus to Caernarfon. It would be easy to conjure a few tickets. We can walk to the site of old Segontium from the bus stop if you wish, so you can look at the *ruins*—you'll note that I'm emphasizing the word 'ruins'—but personally, I think it's a waste of time."

He had a point. I was holding onto our recent habit of using human transportation methods. I came to my senses and recognized that it *was* a monumental waste of our time, now that we were both aware of our true natures and abilities.

I gave him a wry look. "You're right, let's just teleport to Segontium, and then on to the Crystal Cave." It was true that I was longing to return to my family, and I missed Moab. I had been gone for many months and I suspected that more time had elapsed there than I was aware of, in which case my family would be frantic, trying to ascertain my whereabouts and find a way to bring me home. Of course, I could utilize my god powers to discover exactly what had transpired in my absence, but I was reluctant to know every aspect of past, present and future. I was afraid it would destroy the last remaining semblance I had of a normal life.

We materialized at Segontium, and though I had been forewarned, I was still inordinately disappointed. I gazed at the low section of foundation wall that was the only surface trace left of the old Roman fort, which dated back to AD 77 and had been active up until AD 394, twenty-six years before I was born.

Segontium had been the westernmost legionary fort of the Roman Empire, constructed when Julius Agricola had completed the conquest of Wales by capturing the Isle of Anglesey. It was an active garrison so large that a thousand infantrymen could be housed within its perimeter. Later, after the Romans were long gone and the original structure had fallen into ruin, Arthur Pendragon had reestablished the fort and put it to good use as one of his outposts.

This, of course, was the main reason I had wanted to see it again, because it reminded me of those halcyon days when King Arthur ruled Britain.

Then, I remembered the truth. That time had actually been anything but calm and peaceful while Arthur battled lesser kings of the realm to bring order to his kingdom. Why had I thought I could resurrect the place in my mind, for what good would it do? It would certainly not bring Arthur back.

I sighed and accepted the fact that some things were gone forever, unless I intended to go back in time and change those things, and that was clearly not an option.

Oh, I unquestionably had the power to do that, but that didn't mean I *should* do it. I had deliberately ignored that fact in 2014, when my son Derek and his friend Ken had been killed by a dragon in Arches National Park. Derek, who is immortal, came back to life without my help. And since I couldn't bear to witness my son's grief, I had returned Ken's departed soul to his body. Although Derek had been grateful to have his lover back, it had turned out badly for Ken in the long run. I'd had to erase his memory and substitute a fabricated backstory in order for him to live without the severe depression and anxiety he'd experienced, knowing he had been denied his original destiny.

I glanced at Beli, who was waiting impatiently for me to finish my ruminations so we could leave for my cave, which was situated near the top of a hill outside of the modern town of Carmarthen. In the days of my youth, Carmarthen had been called Maridunum, a bustling settlement complete with fort and amphitheater established by the Romans.

I was more than ready to see my cave again. Any other destination now seemed irrelevant.

"Let's teleport to the Crystal Cave, Beli. It's time."

CHAPTER 29

Moab, May 15, 2018

IT WAS A SPECTACULAR LATE spring day, and Derek Colburn was patrolling in Arches National Park feeling vaguely dissatisfied with his life. Really, he had nothing to complain about—he was married to his soul mate, had a comfortable home and a job he enjoyed, and best of all, he was an immortal sorcerer and a demigod. He was thirty-three years old and still looked twenty-eight, the age he was when he'd inherited his powers. How could he possibly want anything more?

Except his father had been missing since 2014, four long years ago this month. They had never found a way to bring him back, and his grandfather, Llyr, who claimed that Merlin would return when he was ready, had insisted that they cease recovery efforts. Derek's sister Lumina, with her ancient connection to the realm of the gods, had announced Llyr's mandate at their last official group meeting in February of 2016, and everyone who had previously expended considerable effort and time trying to find Merlin had reluctantly given up the search. Of course, they still gathered together at least two or three times a month, ostensibly to touch base and to socialize, but hoping that Llyr would relent and show up, bringing news of Merlin's whereabouts. He never did.

Needless to say, the knights were restless and at loose ends. Their main purpose in life, serving Merlin in lieu of King Arthur, was on hold indefinitely.

Although Derek had vehemently objected to getting married until Merlin could be present, Sarah finally convinced him they should go ahead with their plans anyway. So they had settled for a quiet ceremony on August 22, 2017, in Swanny Park, with just family and close friends present, and swore that they would have another, larger celebration when Merlin returned.

As neither one of them were churchgoers, they had arranged for a local pastor, the husband of one of Sarah's friends, to officiate. Derek smiled as he remembered looking into the pastor's eyes as the man spoke of the sacred bonds of matrimony, wondering what he would say if Derek told him that his father had known God since the beginning of time.

Derek had invited his adoptive mother, Lisa Colburn, to the ceremony, and she had accepted with alacrity. He regretted that he hadn't been in regular contact with her for some time and wanted to share the happiness of his wedding day with her. She was thrilled to be included in Derek's life once again.

Sarah's foster parents, Helen and Roger Thompson, had driven all the way to Moab from Bakersfield, California to be with her on her special day. It turned out to be a family reunion, of sorts, as Morry had been their foster child as well. The Thompsons were a middle-aged couple who had loved all the children they'd fostered over the years, but Sarah and Morry had been their favorites, and they'd secretly hoped that the two of them would be wed. It had been something of a revelation when they discovered that Sarah was marrying someone else entirely. Of course, they would never know the truth, that Sarah's husband-to-be was actually Morry's father.

The week before their wedding day, Derek had been concerned about the weather, since the forecast was for possible thunderstorms. As it turned out, the day was hot and sunny, without a cloud in the sky.

Sarah had been breathtakingly beautiful in a strapless, navy blue sundress that matched her eyes, accessorized with white sandals and silver and lapis lazuli jewelry. Derek had worn a long-sleeved white dress shirt tucked into navy blue slacks to match Sarah's dress. When he remembered watching his wife-to-be walk toward him that day, her wavy, reddish-blond hair gleaming in the sun, he couldn't believe his good fortune.

Later, Sarah admitted thinking that she was the luckiest woman in the world, and Derek the handsomest man.

And as they stood before the pastor under the pine trees at the southeast corner of the park, they promised to love and to cherish each other forever. Remembering their vows still made Derek smile. They'd had to change ''til death do us part' to 'forever,' since he was immortal and Merlin had promised to make Sarah immortal, too.

Being married to Sarah was everything Derek had ever dreamed of, and more. Not only were they the best of friends, but they had a rich, fulfilling love life. The fact that they both had magic added a degree of intimacy and understanding few couples shared. And recently, they had even talked about having a baby.

Derek straightened in his seat and decided to appreciate the day. Wallowing in reminiscence was not his style these days and besides, it didn't accomplish a thing.

The air was warm, and there were still brightly hued wildflowers blooming profusely here in Salt Valley: globemallow, evening primrose, scorpionweed, and paintbrush. It appeared as if some cosmic painter had spilled orange, white, purple, and red across the otherwise barren expanse. And, of course, the ever-present greens of the various types of indigenous sage, and the dark green of Mormon tea, added to the palette.

As he drove slowly northwest along the washboarded dirt road he glanced around, reviewing what he knew about the area. Visitors were always quizzing him about various aspects of the park, and as a park employee, he liked to be prepared with information that was as accurate as possible.

Salt Valley was a geological feature called a salt-intruded anticline—a collapsed salt structure. Derek grimaced as he realized he needed a better explanation than that. He was no scholar, which was obvious, so he had to rely on reference material. He had a few good books on local geology in his own library at home (*A Traveler's Guide to the Geology of the Colorado Plateau* was one that he particularly liked), and there were books in the office that were available for Park Service employees to borrow. Perhaps he could just say that a salt anticline had to do with the arching of sedimentary layers associated with the movement or collapse of salt underground. He'd read that definition somewhere and hoped it would be sufficient. He decided he'd do a little more research the next chance he got.

He hadn't been paying attention to his driving, so when he hit a particularly rough stretch of road, taxing the vehicle's suspension, he figured he'd better focus on the task ahead of him.

Normally, Derek didn't come out this far, but a visitor had reported seeing graffiti and destruction of vegetation out at the parking area for Klondike Bluffs and Tower Arch, and he had been directed to check it out. He hadn't been to this location in months due to cutbacks in the budget, which resulted in limiting law enforcement patrols to the basic visitor favorites—Windows, Balanced Rock, Delicate Arch and Devils Garden. And he was heartily sick and tired of admonishing the tourists for the same old infractions: leaving the trail and thus destroying the fragile biological soil crust which held the sand together, parking in unauthorized areas, taking their dogs on the trails, and littering. It was hard to believe that people who professed to appreciate the park could be so unconscious and destructive, but it happened all the time.

Derek slowed his Park Service vehicle as he approached the parking area, and took a moment to admire the reddish-orange and off-white layers of sandstone in the blocky rock formation ahead of him.

He was forced to come to a dead stop at the end of the road, unable to enter the parking area. He counted more than a dozen vehicles, flabbergasted that so many visitors had decided to hike out here this particular morning. It wasn't normally a preferred destination.

Stopped behind a green Subaru Forester that was apparently one of the last to arrive, Derek decided to walk around the roughly circular parking area and see if he could find anything to back up the claim of vandalism. The lot was flat and had been graveled recently, and there were large rocks closely spaced around the perimeter to prevent a vehicle from passing between them. There was little vegetation anywhere near the edge of the parking area, which had a short but relatively steep slope, so that there was virtually no shoulder. Derek noted the positioning of the vehicles, and as they were all parked more or less legally, the only problem he could see was that the people parked closest to the toilet and the trailhead would have a hell of a time leaving, since they were totally blocked in. At least he didn't have to deal with any of the thoughtless destruction of vegetation that he saw every single day in other areas of the park. He checked all the signs, and then went around the outside of the small restroom, but he couldn't find any evidence of graffiti. He poked his head inside, and other than needing a thorough cleaning, an on-going issue due to shortage of park maintenance personnel, he couldn't find anything wrong with the building. Reluctantly, he admitted that perhaps the damage could be out at the arch itself.

Just freakin' wonderful, he thought.

Derek went back to his truck and leaned against the front fender as he debated his course of action. He finally decided that hiking all the way out to the arch, while enjoyable, wouldn't be a good use of his time. Who knew the extent of the damage these people could be doing to the arch right now?

If they were doing anything to it at all.

At this point, he was inclined to think that the person who had made the report might have a grudge against one of the visitors currently out at the arch. Or it might have been a local who resented all of the tourists overrunning the park. He glanced again at the vehicles and realized that more than half of them had California license plates. While it was true that people came from all over the country to visit Arches, it was still odd that so many from the same state were here at this particular arch at the same time.

Derek grabbed his water bottle and took a few long swallows, knowing that it was vital to keep hydrated in this dry, high desert climate. Then he laughed at himself—he used this spiel daily on the park visitors, but it really didn't apply to him—he was a magical being and could make adjustments to his body chemistry and metabolism. He had just recently mastered those abilities that had evaded him for so long, and he was proud of himself.

He decided that he'd better quit procrastinating and see what was going on out at the arch. He was wearing his bulletproof vest and his weapon was in its holster, ready to go. He then adjusted his flat-brimmed, summer weight hat to the Park Service-mandated angle and closed his eyes. He figured he'd teleport to a point below the arch that offered some cover, but he would also initiate an invisibility spell as he rematerialized, just to be on the safe side. He seldom got a chance to use magic on the job, so this was going to be kind of fun. Hopefully.

Derek cleared his mind and focused on teleporting. As if in slow motion, outside of normal time, he experienced each of his cells breaking apart and shifting through a golden haze, then suddenly coming back into focus. He was in human form again, but in the new location. He knew that someone watching him would only see him suddenly disappear, but it was different on his end. The process never ceased to amaze him.

He peered around the boulder behind which he had just re-formed. A large crowd of people were milling around a bonfire someone had built under the arch. A fire? Really? It was way too warm for a fire, not to mention that wood-gathering and ground fires were prohibited in the park.

He counted at least two dozen individuals, mostly men and a few women present. The normal hiking attire of T-shirts, shorts, hats and boots or Teva sandals prevailed, with a few odd clothing choices here and there. One woman had on a sexy sleeveless number with a very short skirt and no hat, which distracted Derek for a few moments. What the hell she was thinking?

Probably hadn't brought any water or sunscreen with her either. He snorted derisively, having seen this kind of oblivious behavior many times before, which often resulted in dehydration, severe sunburn and heat exhaustion.

Then, a familiar form caught his eye and he did a startled double take. *Ken? No, it can't be*, he thought. *There's no way he could've remembered who he was and come back here.* But it certainly appeared to be his old friend, lover, and fellow Park Service employee, Ken Wilson.

Suddenly, Derek sensed a surge of magical energy, and it was obvious that these were not the usual park visitors. All of them seemed to possess at least a modicum of magic.

But as far as he knew, Ken didn't have any magical abilities, and Derek couldn't imagine why he would be here. Then he looked again for his friend and saw no trace of him.

What the hell? He scanned the crowd of people again, more carefully this time, and though he did spot a few faces that he thought he recognized, Ken's wasn't one of them. He finally decided he'd been seeing things.

Derek sighed. How the hell should he handle this situation? Perhaps initially as a law enforcement officer, a representative of the National Park Service, since that was his job. If that didn't settle the issue, he could always use magic. As that thought entered his mind, however, he heard echoes of the many lectures he'd received from Merlin about not revealing his magical skills to anyone.

But his father's restriction didn't apply if the individuals in question also possessed a magical nature, did it? He decided to play it by ear. If things got out of hand, then he would undoubtedly have to employ his own considerable talents.

He stood tall and deliberately enhanced his apparent size and bulk, then cancelled the invisibility spell and stepped forward confidently.

"Excuse me, ladies and gentlemen! What's goin' on here?" he demanded in an authoritative voice.

"Well, look who's here. Smokey the Bear, all dressed up in his fine uniform." The man who had spoken was standing slightly in front of the group that had congregated on the ledge above Derek. He was tall and rangy and although Derek didn't remember his name, he recognized him as a proficient wizard who had helped Merlin battle Nimue in 2013. The man stood protectively in front of a statuesque woman who was dressed inappropriately in what appeared to be a costume from a Renaissance fair—a long flowing dress in forest green with a tight bodice of heavy gold fabric. The sleeves were tight and hung down in points at her wrists. Her long blond hair was pulled back in an elaborate braid which hung down almost to her waist. She was stunning.

Derek's first thought was that the woman must be too warm in such a garment. Then, he tore his attention away from her and replied calmly, "Sorry, sir, wrong branch of the government.

Smokey the Bear is the mascot of the Forest Service, Department of Agriculture. I work for the National Park Service, which is Department of the Interior."

He crossed his muscular arms over his equally impressive chest and waited for a response. He was afraid that he would have to force these people out of the park one way or another, and they all looked like they were itching to gang up on him.

Derek sensed that everyone but the tall woman was a wizard of varying degrees and no threat to him. She, however, was an enigma. She looked human, yet emanations of power revealed her as a sorcerer. But the most disturbing thing about her was an overwhelming aura of ancient evil that belied her appearance of humanity. And he felt sure he should know her. He just couldn't seem to figure out her identity.

Then the woman touched the man's arm and said something to him in a quiet voice. He looked at her intently and nodded. "Whatever you say, my lady," he said, obsequiously.

Suddenly, there was a brilliant flash of light and a surge of power, which completely incapacitated Derek, and in the short time until he could move and think and see again, the entire group had disappeared. He was stunned. He should have been immune to the effects of her magic. The evil he had sensed should have alerted him to her strength, but unfortunately, he'd been woefully unprepared for her actions.

Although he wanted to heap blame upon himself for underestimating her abilities, he didn't dare waste any more time. As he levitated up to the area where the wizards had started the bonfire, he gazed up at the underside of the arch, hoping that the smoke hadn't blackened the red sandstone surface. Fortunately, the light breeze that he'd barely perceived had dispersed it before any damage had been done.

It was a simple matter to magically extinguish the fire and dispose of the debris, after which he teleported back to the parking lot. He had spent only a couple of minutes at the arch after the group disappeared, but he was still too late. All the cars had departed.

Stifling his frustration, Derek cast out his senses in an effort to locate the wizards—and the sorcerer—but she had apparently covered their tracks with a spell that even he was unable to break. He was fairly certain that they would turn right once they reached the intersection and head back towards the park exit, rather than turn left to Devils Garden, where the park road ended.

He hurried to his truck and unlocked it with magic. It started immediately and he turned around and headed back up the dirt road, a cloud of dust rooster-tailing in his wake. He wasn't going to be able to catch up with them, so maybe someone else could help. There were no other law enforcement rangers working today, so there was only one other alternative. He steered the speeding vehicle with one hand as he grabbed the mike and keyed it.

"Arches Entrance, Arches Patrol. Please acknowledge." He hoped the staff in the entrance booth would be able to stop some of the cars to obtain contact information and inquire about the purpose of the visit. But if that didn't work, maybe they could write down a few license plates.

"Arches Patrol, Arches Entrance. What do you need, Derek?"

He described what he wanted them to do if they spotted a long line of cars from California all traveling together on their way out of the park. They promised to try and get the information he'd requested.

Once he was back on the paved road, he drove as fast as he dared past the turnoff to Delicate Arch and up the hill towards Balanced Rock. As he rocketed past the Balanced Rock parking area and down the hill toward Courthouse Wash, Derek thought about what had occurred out at Tower Arch. What could he have done differently? If he had somehow been able to anticipate his reaction to the woman's power and responded instantaneously, would he have been able to stop the group's departure? He had obviously been overconfident of his abilities and allowed himself to arrogantly assume he had the upper hand.

Who the hell could that woman be? He wracked his brain, feeling as if he should know the answer. And suddenly, as unlikely as it seemed, Derek realized who she was. He finally connected all the dots—indisputable facts that had accumulated since Merlin left Wales in 2013 combined with his knowledge of Merlin's life in Camelot—and came to a horrifying conclusion: It had to be Morgana, King Arthur's half sister.

Thirty minutes later, he pulled up at the entrance station. Unfortunately, he'd had to stop a visitor for speeding near Park Avenue, which was ironic since he himself had been driving way over the speed limit all the way from the Tower Arch parking lot. The stop had delayed him longer than he'd expected because the visitor had insisted on arguing with him. He probably should have written the man up, but instead let him off with a warning, anxious to get down the hill as soon as possible.

The park employees who staffed the fee booths were apologetic. They had spotted the line of cars Derek had mentioned, but due to the number of incoming vehicles, they hadn't been able to get the information he'd requested.

Fighting his disappointment, Derek quickly sent his senses out in all directions, but the cars were long gone, or at least magically camouflaged. He sighed, frustrated. Now what?

He hoped to God that Merlin would resurface before it was too late.

That night, Derek tossed and turned, unable to get comfortable. The day had been full of unresolved issues, all of which were weighing heavily on his mind. And one thought in particular was causing a tremendous amount of mental anguish.

Ken Wilson. He had once loved the man dearly, both physically and emotionally. His brief sighting of his friend earlier that day had brought all those suppressed memories to the forefront of his mind. First, the birthday party in 2014 out at Devils Garden when the dragon had grabbed them both and killed them, then, his own painful rebirth and Ken's resurrection by Merlin's intervention, and finally, Merlin's decision to send Ken away with his memories changed to preserve Ken's sanity and the family's secrets.

Out at Tower Arch, Derek had been baffled by Ken's presence among the wizards, and then figured he'd been seeing things when the man disappeared.

Unfortunately, he now understood.

"Ken, I'm so sorry," he whispered.

Not your fault. Ken's ghost appeared at Derek's bedside, looking as corporeal as he had in life. *Of course, I didn't remember you or Merlin at the time Morgana was coming after me, so I had no idea why she wanted to kill me until it was too late.*

"She must have known who you were and been aware of our connection."

Yes. The image of his friend wavered, as if he were having difficulty staying visible. *Sorry, I'm still trying to get used to this. I can't seem to—*

As Ken faded away, Derek sighed and turned over, staring sightlessly into the dark corners of his bedroom. Sometimes, being an immortal demigod sucked bigtime.

CHAPTER 30

Moab, June 1, 2018

SEVERAL WEEKS AFTER THE INCIDENT at Tower Arch, Derek and Sarah were just cleaning up after breakfast when Lumina came in the front door without knocking and stalked into the kitchen.

"We have to talk," she said peremptorily, addressing her brother and totally ignoring her sister-in-law.

Instead of taking offense at the slight, Sarah understood that Lumina hadn't meant to insult her. She smiled at Derek and said lightly, "Well, I guess I know when I'm not wanted. I'll go to the grocery store and let you two have some privacy." She hadn't yet put her makeup on, but she was confident that she looked acceptable anyway. And she had a travel-sized hairbrush and some tinted lip balm in the car, so she was good to go.

"Thanks, babe." Derek gave Sarah a peck on the cheek and thought how lucky he was to be married to her. Any other woman would have been hurt and angry at being treated that way, especially in her own home. He gave her a little wave as she grabbed her phone and her purse, and then he closed the door behind her with a flick of his wrist.

As Sarah unlocked her car door using one of the many spells she had learned since meeting the legend who was now her father-in-law, she fervently hoped that Lumina's abrupt invasion of their home indicated a breakthrough in finding Merlin. Derek was close to a major meltdown, and considering his level of power, that did not bode well for the family—or the town itself. And poor Emily, knowing how ineffectual her own powers were in this case, suffered from an erosion of her self-esteem, which in turn increased her despair.

Sarah realized she'd been brooding for the past few minutes and started the car. As she headed toward the grocery store, she grinned at how familiar she now was with the neighborhood, having moved into Derek's house only a few months after Merlin disappeared. Even though there had been major upheavals since then, she knew in her heart how fortunate she was to have married into such a family. Of course, she was concerned about everyone and hoped Merlin returned soon, but looking at it strictly from her own point of view, she was happier than she'd ever been in her life. She and Derek had even considered having a baby soon. She knew she wasn't *quite* ready to get pregnant, but maybe in another year or so.

Sarah pulled into the Town Market parking lot and found a space close to the entrance. As she stepped out of the car, she felt the buzz of her husband's presence in her mind, and she headed into the store with her grocery list in hand and a huge grin on her face. Magic was real and it was part of her life.

As soon as Sarah left, Derek turned to his sister impatiently. "I know what you're going to say—that it's time to get off our dead asses and bring Dad home. Especially now that we know who's really behind all the crap we've experienced the past five years. And to hell with Llyr and his restrictions."

Lumina winced at the forcefulness of his statement, knowing full well that Derek was still somewhat in awe of their grandfather and would normally not be so belligerent.

"Well, that isn't *exactly* what I was going to say, but yes, we need to get Dad home as soon as possible to deal with *her*. But I'm convinced that God arranged this whole thing with Dad and Beli so they could mend what was broken between them. I believe that we'll definitely need Beli's help in the near future." Lumina paused as she contemplated the newest developments in the complicated scenario that had been playing out for years now.

"Actually, I think that Grandfather Llyr has been waiting for us to decide to act despite the fact that he forbade it." She looked at her brother with one eyebrow raised.

"Yeah, that sounds about right." Derek chuckled dryly, then grabbed his coffee mug from the counter and drained the last of the liquid. It was cold and bitter. He shuddered and put the mug down hastily, then waited for his sister to continue.

Abruptly, Lumina reached out and took his hands and guided them to her temples.

"What're ya doin', Sis?" He looked questioningly at her as she closed her eyes and effortlessly entered his mind.

Derek, remember that I am a goddess. Her inner voice resonated as the ancient soul inside of her communicated with him. He'd heard that voice before, on occasion, but it stilled shocked him.

He inhaled sharply, assailed by images he could hardly fathom. He realized she was showing him a vision of herself and their father in the realm of the gods, in their natural forms of pure energy. Although Merlin had shown him the same thing years ago, the reality was so staggering he'd filed the knowledge away in his subconscious mind.

"Jesus," he whispered, "I'd forgotten how magnificent you both are." And he knelt in front of her, laying his head gently on her feet.

"You know there's no need to bow to me—I'm not in the same league as Myrddin Emrys," she said, affectionately stroking his shaggy, sandy-brown hair. "Besides, brother, you are a demigod. It's true I outrank you, but there's no need to be concerned about that right now. I merely wanted to remind you that between us we have more than sufficient power and status to accomplish our goal."

He looked up at that sweet young face, her hazel eyes so full of ancient wisdom.

"I've never really figured out *how* to be a demigod, Lumi."

She smiled, and Derek once again heard her voice in his mind. *It is your true nature. You just have to relax and accept that. But, don't worry, I'll help you. And then a plan will just naturally present itself.*

CHAPTER 31

Moab, June 3, 2018

EMILY SAT ON HER BACK porch step, a mug of coffee sitting forgotten next to her on the concrete. She looked around at the attractively landscaped back yard she and her family had created in the past few years. First, they had built a seven-foot-high concrete wall around the perimeter to ensure their privacy, using red sand so it would look natural. Then, Emily had planted flowering vines and trained them up that vertical surface.

In one corner of the yard, several young fruitless mulberry trees provided cooling shade in which a stone bench resided. The bench itself was carved with vines and flowers, among which were scattered various symbols she had seen in a book of Celtic mythology. A patch of green grass was nearby, flanked by a thick border of lavender, which then transitioned to the starkness of sandstone boulders and an area dedicated to strictly desert plants. A small kitchen garden with a few tomato and green pepper plants, interspersed with marigolds, basil, rosemary and sage completed the picture. The overall effect was pleasing, producing a low hum of earth magic that few humans could perceive. Emily shivered in delight when she walked through the space she had worked so hard to create, the magic caressing her with a refreshing breeze.

But now, with the source of her inspiration still missing, none of that seemed to matter.

By means of the magical and familial connections with her daughter and stepson, Emily was aware they had decided to ignore their grandfather's directive and put their formidable powers to work finding their father, to finally bring him back from whatever time or dimension he currently inhabited. She sensed from their thoughts that this would mean actually bending reality and creating a portal, then reaching through time and space, using a special spell to summon Merlin and then reversing the process. She frowned—that last part didn't seem right, so perhaps she'd misunderstood.

Not for the first time, she wished her magic was more powerful, more effective. Maybe she should have tried harder. And if wishes were horses, she'd have a full stable by now.

She sighed and tried to be more positive. After all, if everything went well, it was possible she could actually be with Merlin in a matter of hours. God, she vehemently hoped so. She was damned tired of being without him. At this point, she would give up centuries of her immortal existence just to see him again. To hold him in her arms would be priceless.

Emily glanced at her gold wedding ring with the special protection symbols Merlin had magically engraved on it the day they had gotten married, and sensed their bond. She hoped he still felt it too, even if he didn't remember her.

She closed her eyes and tried to meditate the way he had taught her the first year they were together, but she couldn't seem to calm her mind. So instead, she imagined what it would be like to feel his warm, soft lips on hers again, his intoxicating breath mingling with hers, his whispered words assuring her of his enduring love and devotion. He would caress her and hold her against him, then, impatient, he would magically remove their clothing and she would feel his tall, slender naked body covering hers. She would open herself to him, welcoming him home. Her breath started to come faster as she anticipated the moment his sleek hardness entered her and—

"Em? Where are you, darling?" Rae's plaintive voice came through the open window of the laundry room behind her.

Emily sighed quietly in frustration. "Out here, Mom." She turned to greet her mother as Rae Crandall came through the back door and joined her. She tried to conceal her irritation, but she knew she'd failed when the tentative look on her mother's face turned to chagrin.

"I'm so sorry. I've interrupted you at a bad time, haven't I?"

"It's okay, Mom, don't worry about it," Emily hastened to reassure her. Lately, her mother had been increasingly agitated, and Em sensed that it had something to do with her dad.

Years ago, just before Merlin disappeared, her father had

escalated the verbal and emotional abuse that had marred her parents' relationship for decades. Rae had moved to Moab to get away from him and had started divorce proceedings. Unfortunately, Jack Crandall had disappeared once he'd been released from jail, where he'd been incarcerated after Rae had had him arrested for assault, and the process servers she'd hired hadn't been able to locate him to serve him with the divorce papers. Em wondered if her mother had been receiving some kind of communication from Jack recently. Although she could read Rae's thoughts directly, she would never invade her privacy.

Em took her mother's hand in her own and gave it a gentle squeeze. "Mom, what's going on? You've been so unhappy lately. I'm really worried about you. Is this about Dad? Has he contacted you and threatened you again?"

Rae ducked her head and didn't answer, and Em noticed a tear tracing its way down her cheek.

"Oh, Mom, please tell me what's wrong. I want to help."

"I hate to burden you with my problems when you're so sad already."

Emily blinked back her own tears and straightened her spine. "I'll be fine. Merlin should be home soon if Lumina and Derek have anything to say about it."

"Alright, if you're sure." Rae wiped her eyes and took a restorative breath before she spoke. "I had a nightmare the other night."

Em's eyebrows shot up. Her mother never had nightmares. "Really? What was it about?"

"Well, uh…" Rae paused, glanced at her daughter and cleared her throat before continuing. "It was about Satan coming here to Moab. And he had your father's face."

"What?!" After everything Emily had experienced since she'd met and married a sorcerer who was also a god, she knew better than to doubt the veracity of a vision or a nightmare.

"He leered at me and told me that none of us would escape his wrath this time."

"*This* time? What in the hell does that mean?"

"I don't know! Oh, Em, I have a horrible feeling that Jack has been taken over by Satan, or Lucifer, or whatever you want to call the ultimate evil. Do you think that Satan may be the one who has been after Merlin all along?"

Emily just stared at her mother in silent horror.

CHAPTER 32

The Crystal Cave, July, 2007

WE TELEPORTED EFFORTLESSLY TO THE grassy area in front of the cave on Bryn Myrddin—Merlin's Hill in Welsh—and I gazed at the magically concealed entrance, then turned and looked out across the countryside. The view was partially blocked by trees and bushes that hadn't been there in my time. However, the little I could see triggered visions from my past: a horse pulling a barge laden with supplies along the River Tywi, the old Roman villas in Maridunum, partially derelict but still habitable, and myself as a young boy sitting at my mother's feet as she sewed. Overall, it had not been a happy time for me, as my burgeoning powers had made me a pariah. But I'd loved exploring the town and the outlying areas, even by myself.

I stood still for a few minutes as the memories washed over me like waves upon a beach, tumbling shells and sand before it. Beli stood quietly at my side, waiting patiently.

I emerged from my thoughts and glanced at Beli, who looked into my eyes and waited for me to speak. "My past self still sleeps in the cave, and will not awaken until the spring of 2013, so we cannot enter, and my caretakers mustn't know yet that I'm here. But I had to come, to see this place again."

"Yes, I know," he replied, gently.

I gazed at my companion speculatively. "I wonder if we could get away with walking around town without people recognizing us." I was feeling suddenly light-hearted and mischievous.

He shrugged. "Why would they? You, Merlin, are just a legend to them in this century. And the god of death hasn't been worshiped here for almost two thousand years, so who in this time would recognize *me*? I think we are both safe from discovery. People wouldn't believe us even if we told them who we are."

"You've convinced me, my friend. Let's go."

The road into town was still as narrow as it had been for centuries, though now it was paved with a thin layer of asphalt. There was no shoulder, so we walked along the edge of the road single file for awhile until a vehicle stopped alongside us. Although we were perfectly capable of walking the few miles into downtown Carmarthen, the weather was warm and humid and we were already sweating profusely, so we decided to accept the offer of a ride. The seats were small and worn and we were decidedly cramped, but the air conditioner worked, and the driver was outgoing and friendly. The engine coughed and sputtered and the car seemed ready to break down any minute, but we appreciated his gift and expressed our gratitude for his kindness. When he let us out a few minutes later in Nott Square, in front of the old castle gatehouse, I decided to magically do some repairs to his engine since the man seemed somewhat financially strapped. As he drove off, he had a confused look on his face, as if he couldn't believe that the car was running smoother than normal. And as he glanced back at me, he suddenly looked shocked, as if he had guessed who I was. I just smiled and gave him a "thumbs up" as he drove away.

Beli gave me a wry look. "I think you just gave him a reason to remember a certain sorcerer, maybe even the gods of old."

I raised one eyebrow. "Perhaps it has been too long since this god walked among his people."

Sometime later, Beli and I teleported back to the cave, aware that we would soon need to part. I would return to my "human" life in the future, and he would return to his incorporeal state in the realm of the gods. We faced each other, smiling as we examined each other's tattoos, colorful and bold even in the waning light. On a whim, we had stopped in a tattoo parlor and hired a team of artists to ink the designs we had chosen onto our skin. Since our time was limited, we had surreptitiously applied a bit of magic to help them work faster—and to later forget we had been there. Unfortunately, Beli's tattoos would cease to exist as soon as he became incorporeal again, but regardless, we had both enjoyed the hours of companionship while the distinctive markings were applied.

As the sun sank lower and the radiant hues of sunset spread across the sky in tendrils of orange and pink, we reminisced about our experiences of the past eight months. We had lived off the land in ancient Inverness, tangled with the Fae in their stronghold beneath Tomnahurich Hill, been executed and subsequently resurrected in sixteenth-century Edinburgh, teleported into the passage tomb at Newgrange, and caroused the pubs in Dublin in 2007. And we had returned to Wales and gotten tattoos in modern Carmarthen. Then, we were back at the Crystal Cave, having come full circle, to where it all began for me in this human realm.

I cleared my throat and debated whether I should rock the boat by discussing Adrestia with him. I finally decided the subject had to be addressed before he left, since it might be some time before we saw one another again.

"What is it, my friend? You have that look on your face." Beli crossed his arms over his chest and adjusted his stance.

I chuckled and shook my head. "You know me too well by now."

"Just say what you need to say."

I sighed, hesitant to disrupt our last few moments together. Then I blurted out, "Why did you send my daughter to Hell in the first place? I realize that later, after I killed Nimue and her essence took over Adrestia's body, she was able to handle the situation, but when Adrestia first arrived, the demons—there's no easy way to say this—*raped* her repeatedly." This had been troubling me since Nimue, housed in my daughter's body, had initiated my journey to Hell in February of 2014 and I needed an answer.

Beli stared at the ground, avoiding my gaze. "I am ashamed to admit it, but I made a mistake. I had only wanted to keep her safe during the battle between you and Nimue, so I decided to send her to the Underworld—*my* domain. I hadn't intended to send her to another pantheon's version of Hell, particularly the Christian one, and it definitely wasn't my intention to subject my own granddaughter to rape and torture. You have to believe that."

The god of death stood with his shoulders slumped, the picture of misery.

"I do believe you, and I forgive you. We may be gods, but it seems we're still capable of making mistakes. However, I'm not sure where we go from here. I keep Adrestia's body in stasis in a cavern accessed only by magic, where Nimue cannot awaken and cause more havoc. But we must address this issue, so that I can move on with my purpose here in the human realm."

Beli closed his eyes and was still for a moment, perhaps conferring with God. "Yes, you're right, and we will do so very soon." He paused and looked into my eyes. "I won't forget our time together, Myrddin Emrys. We have been friends, which has never happened since we were created millions of years ago. Perhaps this will be the dawning of a new era for us, eh?"

He reached out to clasp my hand. I gripped it, wishing I never had to let go. Then, he faded slowly from my sight as he returned to his natural state as pure energy in the realm of the gods.

My arm fell to my side. With Beli gone, it was time for me to leave as well. I really didn't belong here in this time, and it could be disastrous if my caretakers found me here.

When I originally moved into the Crystal Cave in the fifth century, I had arranged with a local family to assist me with my household needs and to oversee my property. I had eventually decided to sleep through the centuries when it became obvious that Arthur's return might take a millennium or more, and I instructed my original caretakers to pass along the knowledge of those responsibilities to their descendants. As it turned out, they had neglected to do so, and it had caused some problems when I awoke in 2013. If the current caretakers found me here too early, it could negatively affect the timeline, and I didn't want to have to untangle the resultant mess.

I took a long, slow breath and centered myself, letting go of my thoughts of the past. Then I allowed my 2007 attire to dissolve as I sank to the ground, manifesting a lightweight blanket around my shoulders. Despite the fact that I wanted my children to get the full impact of my tattoos at first glance, the air was turning cool—and I wanted to set the stage.

I had always had a flair for the dramatic—one of my weaknesses, I admit—and the runes and other ancient Celtic symbols inked on my body were impressive. And necessary, now that I knew who was ultimately responsible for all my tribulations since my awakening in the twenty-first century. I had every intention of keeping those tattoos until they had served their purpose.

As I bowed my head in silent gratitude for the experiences the one God had bestowed upon me, I acknowledged the insistent pull from the future, and allowed my children to bring me home.

CHAPTER 33

The Crystal Cave, June 4, 2018

Derek and Lumina stared at each other in disbelief as they realized that their plan had worked. They'd found Merlin and had summoned him back to the current time.

The siblings had worked tirelessly for several days straight to create a spell that would act in conjunction with opening a portal through time. They figured that it would be most effective if they performed the summoning spell in front of the Crystal Cave, so they'd teleported to Wales earlier in the day. The spell contained the most powerful of their combined magic, infused with the essence of Derek's singular ability to merge with their father's very soul.

And it had worked. They laughed excitedly as they turned to witness their father's reemergence. Merlin had been visible through the slight distortion of the portal they'd created as he started to fade out in that other time, and then slowly rematerialize in the flesh right in front of them.

Derek suspected that they had been *allowed* to find him, and *allowed* to bring him back because it suited Merlin and the one God to have them do so, but the bottom line was the same: he would be back with them after having been gone for four long years.

Both Derek and Lumina felt the intensity of Emily's emotions, even over the thousands of miles that separated them, as she sensed her husband's return to the present.

Derek nodded to his sister.

Despite her desire to run to her father right away, Lumina teleported back to Moab to get her mother, glittering particles of light floating in the air in the wake of her departure.

Derek noticed a thin blanket with bold designs on it partially covering Merlin, who was sitting quietly on the ground, facing away from him. He was puzzled, since the sun was still shining and the breeze was warm—and his father was adept at adjusting his body temperature. But he quickly realized that the ploy was deliberate.

The seated figure started to move.

Derek's eyes widened as he watched his father unfold his tall, slender body and rise gracefully to his feet, dropping the blanket dramatically to reveal an intricate red and black dragon tattoo covering his entire back and shoulders. Other ancient markings covered his arms and legs and Derek assumed that they were Celtic, maybe even druidic.

Merlin's hair was unbound, longer than Derek had ever seen it, hanging past his shoulders in a shining cascade of black silk. It was almost like looking at a stranger.

Derek watched in awe as his father slowly turned around, gazing at him in a detached manner, as if he was trying to remember who he was. The black runes tattooed on his chest contrasted starkly with his pale skin and he was supremely unconcerned about his nudity, a godlike response that reminded Derek just who and what Merlin really was. And he was…beautiful. He glowed from the inside out, *leakin' god Light*, Derek thought, dazed—only now it was obviously more of a flood than a mere leak.

I was back in the twenty-first century, and it was a privilege to know exactly who and what I was: a god living in the human realm in the guise of a mortal man.

For a moment, I forgot and looked for Beli, even though I knew that he had returned to the realm of the gods, his human body fading away as though it had never existed. I felt a pang of regret that the man I had spent all those weeks with, and loved like a brother, was no longer at my side in the mortal plane.

At least I knew that the next time we met it would be as friends. We had both learned that much from our trip into the past together, and from the understanding and camaraderie that had developed between us. We had spoken briefly regarding the situation with Adrestia, and while we had not entirely resolved the matter, at least we had made a start. Sometime back, God had directed me to control Beli through Adrestia, but I now knew that wasn't necessary. We would deal with it together when the time was right.

I emerged from my introspection and gazed at the young man standing near me who was waiting with barely contained impatience for me to acknowledge him. According to his thoughts, I had been gone for more than four years, and yet for me, it had only been eight months. Time was flexible, malleable, and now I was truly aware of all of its attributes.

I smiled at my son, thinking to myself that he resembled Arthur Pendragon to a startling degree. "Hello, Derek."

"*Dad.* Oh God, I've missed you. We all have, but Emily missed you the most. She'll be here soon; Lumina went to get her." Derek knew he was babbling, but then, he could hardly speak past the lump in his throat.

He watched me in mute fascination as I spread my arms in an almost negligent fashion and was instantly clothed, then glided towards him regally and clasped him hard to my chest. Gods, I loved my son. I ached with the strength of it.

Derek sighed and relaxed in my arms, finally relinquishing the strict self-control that I sensed he had held onto since I disappeared in May of 2014. Then he pulled away from me slightly and spoke.

"I wanted Morry to be here, too, but he said it didn't feel right to him since his magic wasn't sufficient to help bring you back, that it was supposed to be just me and Lumina here when you returned."

"I know."

Derek looked perturbed and his accent became more pronounced. "Did we have *anythin'* to do with bringin' ya back home?"

"Of course you did. The whole thing was a lesson for everyone. I'm just sorry that all of you suffered so." I truly did regret the pain and anguish everyone had felt while I was gone, but in some ways, I couldn't relate to it.

"Okay, I can't wait any longer to ask this—what's with the tattoos?"

I chuckled. "I was inspired to have them done, and I find I quite like them. The red dragon is an obvious choice, not only representing Wales, but also King Arthur, and the runes and Celtic symbols are all various magical devices that God has given me to complete my task, and my transition." I paused, aware of his concern that I would cause a stir in Moab with such symbols displayed prominently on my body. "The tattoos may be inked into my skin, but you know that I can conceal them magically at any time."

"Yeah, that's true. Sorry, I'm just in a state o' shock." Derek paused as my words registered. "Wait, what? Your *transition*? Holy shit, you're gonna fully manifest your god self now?"

"Relax," I said gently. "I'm getting prepared because the time is swiftly approaching. But it's not going to happen today." I decided to change the subject. "Bel chose biker tats, which was most amusing. He ended up with a skeleton riding a motorcycle and a flying skull, among other things."

It took a few seconds for Derek's mind to switch gears. "Bel? You mean, Beli?

"Yes, Beli. During our ordeal, he remembered nothing about himself, not even his full name, but then again, neither did I. I was just Emrys, an herbalist and healer. And I—"

There was a slight disturbance in the air and my wife and daughter were suddenly in front of me, their arms reaching for me with feminine exuberance. The sweet smell of their natural scents filled my nostrils and their excited, high-pitched voices sounded like the most melodious celestial chorus imaginable. Derek stepped forward into the embrace as well, and finally, my feeling of separation disappeared. My wife and family surrounded me and my heart was full.

Derek stepped back and disappeared for a few moments, reappearing with Morry, who grinned and threw himself at me excitedly. I laughed and enfolded my grandson in a bear hug. Gods, he was dear to me.

I was ecstatic to be reunited with all of them. They were mine, and I was theirs. I had been blessed with a human life, and a family with whom to share that life, and knowing what I knew now about the nature of the universe—and time—made that life even more precious to me.

And with that thought, my gaze was irresistibly drawn to the vision of loveliness that was my precious wife. As much as I adored my children and my grandson, all I wanted at this moment was to be alone with Emily. I excused myself and, reaching for her hand, we followed the path down the hill a short ways and found a comparatively secluded spot behind the broad trunk of a towering oak tree. A light breeze carried the fragrant, earthy scent of hay and horses from the small stable nearby, and the dappled shade in which we stood enhanced the color of Emily's hair to a rich medium brown with golden highlights. She stared at me as if she were drinking in the sight of me, quenching her terrible thirst. Then, she gave a heartfelt sigh. Tears welled in her wide hazel eyes and she began to weep.

"Oh, Merlin, I…" She swiped impatiently at the moisture on her cheeks and threw herself into my waiting arms.

I found myself at a loss for words as well, as her voluptuous body pressed against me, and I responded automatically by holding her tightly. As I blinked back my own tears and buried my face in her neck, inhaling her unique scent, I remembered why I couldn't live without this woman. She was everything that inspired me to be a better man.

Lumina watched as her parents held each other and caressed each other's faces. They were partially hidden behind a large, old oak tree, but still visible to her god sight. Emotion swelled in her chest and her own tears threatened to fall as she felt the enduring love they had for each other. It was almost shocking to witness her father, an ancient god, pressing his face against her mom's neck with a sigh of relief.

"It's heartwarmin' isn't it, Sis?" Derek whispered as he stepped closer to her and drew her against him affectionately.

She looked up in surprise, but then remembered that as a demigod he could see them as clearly as she could. She nodded, noting that he was surreptitiously wiping his own eyes.

"I hope I find a love like that someday." A tear escaped and she let it roll down her cheek in tribute.

Morry appeared at her other side, also a witness to the moving scene in front of them. "Me, too," he said quietly, but with an unusual intensity that had his father eyeing him questioningly.

Emily and I turned and walked hand in hand back up the hill to join the others, who all acted overly nonchalant, leading me to believe that the three of them had watched our reunion. I had been so focused on greeting my wife I hadn't even thought to create a shield to ensure our privacy.

My family began chattering happily all at once, content to stand here in front of my cave and socialize, but there were a few things to take care of before we could depart. I cleared my throat, effectively quieting everyone down.

"I want to return to Moab as soon as possible, but since we're here, we should pay a courtesy call on the Reese family. And Emily has informed me that our bank balance is perilously low, so we'll need to access my cache as well."

Throughout my extremely long life, during most of which I'd had no inkling of my status as one of the Welsh gods, I had put away gemstones and precious metals, storing them in a secret crevice at the back of my cave. I had surmised that I would require them as assets in the future to sustain myself. Coins and paper money may or may not have retained their value over the years, and while some from particular times may have ended up being worth more than their original face value, precious gems and metals like gold and silver would always be worth more than currency.

"Besides," I added, "I would like to say hello to my caretakers, since I haven't communicated with them in a very long time."

I glanced back and forth questioningly between Derek and Lumina. "Did you two stop in at the farm when you first arrived, to let the Reeses know your intentions?"

"Yeah, we did. Neither of us really know the family, and they don't know us, so it took some convincin' for them to let us up here, didn't it, Lumi?"

"Well, they don't have magic, so they couldn't have stopped us from coming to the cave anyway. But it seemed the polite thing to do to explain ourselves." She looked at me sheepishly. "We were a little off, uh, actually *a lot* off, on our coordinates of the Crystal Cave when we teleported here, and we ended up in their driveway. Your caretakers almost freaked out when we showed up out of thin air. We had to talk to them for some time to convince them that we meant no harm."

"Alright, then, let's go greet them, then we'll head home." I gestured to everyone to gather close to me and we disappeared.

We rematerialized in front of the old manor house, which was about a mile as the crow flies from my cave, and I noticed that only one of the original Reese family members was present, waiting in the yard to welcome me back. Even though I had expected this, I felt a slight pang of disappointment. The Reeses had kindly allowed me to use the name of their deceased son, Michael, and all of his identifying documentation, so that I could fit into this vastly changed world of the twenty-first century. Fortunately, I was close to the height, weight and hair color that Michael Reese had been just prior to his death. I would always be grateful to the family for their understanding and generosity.

"Lord Merlin! I almost didn't recognize you! It's wonderful to see you, sir." A brown-haired young man with a wide white smile came up to me and reached for my hand. I pulled him into a hug from which he emerged breathless and rather taken aback at my lack of decorum. I had changed since that day years ago when I had wakened in the spring of 2013, enthusiastic about finding my way back to Arthur Pendragon but reserved and formal with my caretakers. It was ironic that I behaved more like a human being now than I did then, when I wasn't even conscious of the fact that my humanity was only an illusion.

When I'd first awakened, I'd heard a voice commanding me to follow my heart and use my powers to create a new beginning for mankind. I would never have believed it had I been told then that I was destined to be the only fully manifested god on the planet.

I forced my mind back to the present, regretting that the rest of the family was no longer living in the manor. Change was inevitable, however. Tom and Sandy Reese, the caretakers who had been here when I arose from my centuries-long sleep, had moved into the nearby town of Pembry, relinquishing their duties to their youngest son Ben. I had sensed long ago that he would be the logical choice to continue in my service, and I had left instructions to that effect before I'd departed for America.

Tom and Sandy's oldest living son Rob had obtained employment in Cardiff, and had been more than willing to keep silent about his family's role in supporting my activities.

Ben had married a few months before my disappearance and started a family of his own. It was obvious that he had been diligent in keeping the farm going as well as fulfilling his duty to me. At first, his wife, Sharone, had a difficult time adjusting to working for an immortal sorcerer and I'd been concerned that she wouldn't be able to keep my secret, but my worries had proven groundless.

We spent a good hour at the farm, since I wanted Ben and his wife and children to become acquainted with my own family. The fact that every one of us except Lumina was an adult close to the same age confused them, but I didn't feel the need to explain, and they didn't ask for clarification.

Ben and Sharone graciously offered us a warm welcome any time we chose to visit, and I assured them that we would endeavor to give them adequate notice in the future.

In addition, I inquired as to Ben's financial status, and supplied him with ample funds to support his family—and the farm—for the next few years. I dealt with our own requirements as well.

Pleasantries and business matters concluded, I noted that it was growing late. I was eager to get home to Moab, so I thanked my young caretakers, assuring them that either one of my family members or I would stay in contact with them on a regular basis. I decided to make Lumina responsible for this task and would discuss it with her at the appropriate time.

Finally, we were ready to leave, and I transported everyone back home instantly, effortlessly. One moment we were in Wales, and the next we were standing in my living room in Moab, Utah, USA.

I looked into the faces of the people I loved. I saw their expressions as they realized that I was not the same person who had been torn away from them four years ago. I was more confident in my god powers and no longer entertained any fantasies about being human. I would forever incorporate the traits of humanity that I admired into my life—I still lived in this human body, after all—but I couldn't afford to ignore the fact that I was a being of spirit and energy whose reality spanned the realms of existence.

I looked forward to telling everyone about my travels with Beli and about our renewed relationship and commitment to each other, but I decided to wait until tomorrow, after we had all had some rest. There was an seven-hour time difference between Carmarthen and Moab, so it was only early afternoon here, but we all needed time to refresh ourselves, both physically and emotionally.

Derek and Morry were understandably reluctant to leave me, but I convinced them I was indeed home to stay and looked forward to seeing them in the morning at breakfast. As I hugged my son and grandson, I knew Derek would bring Sarah and Morry would bring Jim. In fact, I suspected that the whole group would appear, ostensibly for a meal, but in reality to hear about my adventures. And that was fine with me.

Alone in our bedroom, I stood in front of my wife and felt an overpowering wave of love engulf me. I was stunned by the force of it and how it meshed with Emily's love for me. Our wedding rings warmed and tingled on our fingers, as they had done on our wedding day, and I supposed that this homecoming was very similar to the day we had officially joined our lives, mated by the gods and married in the human way as well. It was an affirmation of our commitment.

I was so grateful for these human emotions, and for all the myriad experiences I'd had that could never have happened in my natural form. Having a human life was worth everything to me, but without the love of my wife and family, that life would truly be without meaning.

I surfaced from my introspection as Emily spoke.

"I think that Derek, Lumina and Morry were disappointed that you didn't spend more time with them," Emily said quietly, gazing raptly into my eyes and rubbing my back in long gentle strokes that were rapidly stimulating my entire body.

I was glad that we were alone. Lumina had disappeared into her room after hugging me tightly, a knowing look on her face. In many ways, she had become a woman while I'd been gone.

"I'm positive that they understand, my love," I whispered as I held her in my arms, the evidence of my desire pressed firmly against her abdomen.

We clung together, stroking each other's hair and fervently kissing one another's lips. I was fiercely aroused and I had no patience for removing our clothing in the mundane way, so I simply made it disappear. My wife had apparently been anticipating such an action, as she gave me a sultry smile and sensuously pressed her bare breasts against my chest. Combined with the feeling of her soft, warm, naked skin under my hands, such a consuming desire sparked inside me that I flashed us to a horizontal position on our bed and promptly buried myself in her welcoming heat.

"Oh, my God, Merlin, you feel so good inside me," Em murmured as we moved together, our bodies synchronized to the beating of our hearts and the blending of our magic.

After our initial joining and tumultuous, simultaneous climax, we separated, but lay with our arms wrapped around each other, legs intertwined, kissing and touching as we uttered endearments and promises for the future.

"It feels like a decade since we made love. I truly thought I'd never *see* you again," Em said, her voice quavering with emotion. She ran her fingers through my long, thick hair and then reached to trace the Celtic designs tattooed on my arms.

I grasped her fingers and kissed each one, then the center of her palm, before I pressed her hand against my chest, where the beat of my heart was still rapid from our lovemaking.

"I'm so sorry that I wasn't here for you all those years, but I'm back now, my love," I whispered. "Please believe me that I never intended to leave you."

I reached down and stroked her intimately, then inched down on the bed and replaced my fingers with my mouth and tongue, rekindling her desire as well as my own. Effortlessly, my magic surrounded her and her breath caught at the wave of passion she experienced. She moaned and caressed my face as I pleasured her, causing me to harden even more than the first time.

As we both approached a peak of arousal, I rose up and covered her, entering her slowly and deliberately. As she writhed ecstatically beneath me and tightened her inner muscles, the sensation was so intense that I immediately climaxed inside her, triggering her own orgasm. I caught myself wanting to disregard her request and impregnate her—my body was practically trembling with the need to do so. However, years ago I had given her my solemn promise not to impregnate her again until she was ready, so I had to stifle that compelling urge—for now. The time would come very soon when it would be appropriate, and indeed destined, to plant another seed in her belly.

As we gazed into one another's eyes afterwards, we wordlessly renewed our commitment to each other, and I knew I was truly home.

Later, after a short nap and an extended shower, we wandered out into the kitchen, looking for sustenance. Emily rummaged through the refrigerator for meat, bread and condiments and began assembling our meal. She wouldn't let me help her, so I leaned on the counter as she worked, and we talked and laughed. Then, we voraciously consumed the thick roast beef sandwiches she had made, complete with juicy slices of red, ripe early tomatoes from the garden, and drank tall glasses of ice-cold milk. Replete, we went back to bed, this time to sleep.

Long after Em had turned over and fitted her backside against me in our traditional sleeping pose, I stared at the ceiling, thinking about gods and human nature and the complexity of life. And how to finally put an end to my nemesis.

CHAPTER 34

The Dream

THAT NIGHT, THOROUGHLY SATED AND loved, Emily fell asleep knowing that all was well in her world. Her husband was home and her family safe. And she dreamed…

She was in an ancient forest, with immense oaks, maples and sycamores towering overhead, their luxuriant foliage blocking all but a few rays of sunlight. The breeze was cool and she shivered, chilled and excited at the same time. Deep leaf mold, damp and fecund, cushioned her footsteps as she walked purposefully towards a patch of sunlight. She was searching for the little black cat that used to visit Merlin and had been instrumental in organizing the shapeshifters to fight on his behalf against Nimue all those years ago.

As she approached that open glade, resplendent as faceted gemstones in the dazzling sunlight, she thought she saw it—a small black shape squatting next to a log, intent upon stalking its prey, which could have been a mouse or a small rabbit. She couldn't tell exactly which it was.

As she neared the cat, it looked around and made eye contact with her, stopping her in her tracks. The awareness in its eyes jolted her, that bright green gaze reminding her of someone she knew.

Time seemed to slow, the sound of the wind became a song, and the sunlight turned a lustrous golden hue. She closed her eyes for just a moment, and when she opened them again, a sleek black panther stood where the small domesticated feline had been. And then, as she watched in wonder, the panther seemed to stretch upward until fur became skin, paws became elegant hands and feet, and a tall slender man stood before her.

His long ebony hair shone like obsidian, and his slanted green eyes were reminiscent of the wild creature that had been crouched before her moments ago. Naked, his body sleek and sculpted, the man was magnificent, a lambent glow surrounding him as he stood silently observing her.

She inhaled sharply, recognizing him. She strode swiftly to his side, bowing down to gently kiss his feet, her love for him expanding until it reached the heavens and...

"Emily, my love."

"Mmph?"

"Wake up, sweetheart."

"Hmmm...What?" Eyes squinted against the early morning light streaming through a narrow gap in the drapes, she blinked and sat up abruptly at the foot of the bed. Her dream had felt so real that she had pulled the covers from me and had been caressing and kissing my feet. I held my hand out to her.

"Come here, love," I said, quietly.

Emily smiled and crawled up to her accustomed spot next to me in our king-sized bed, putting her hand in mine. I pulled the sheet up to cover us both, and then turned onto my side to face my wife, running my fingers through her tangled golden-brown mane. Her large, luminous eyes stared back at me with a look of such utter love, devotion and trust that it brought tears to mine.

Her eyelids slowly drifted down and I knew she had gone back to sleep. I rested my head against my plush pillow and then turned to stare at the ceiling, deep in thought. Waking up to Emily's adoration at my feet had reminded me that the time was drawing near when I would irrevocably reveal my god self to the entire world.

As Myrddin Emrys, god of magic and healing, having devotees went with the territory. Thousands of human beings across the globe would soon be drawn to me, most of them not knowing why, and I would have to get used to it. God had assigned me this task and I would fulfill it to the best of my ability. But it certainly begged the question—logistically, how would I deal with the sheer numbers? Moab would be overrun by people who wouldn't necessarily be able to pay for their food and lodging. And this small community could not handle such an invasion on a long term basis.

I started to devise a plan which would take into consideration that, when I revealed myself as a god, Arthur would be back and ready to lead the world. As I set my subconscious mind to these preparations, I brought my conscious thoughts back to things closer to home.

I smiled as I remembered the day the knights had finally come to me, *en mass*, and had declared their devotion to my god self. They had long been loyal and staunch supporters of me as Arthur's Sorcerer of the Realm, but now they were mine in a deeper sense.

I blinked. Wait, that hadn't happened yet. It was imperative that my memories of future events be channeled into a different compartment in my mind before I inadvertently revealed certain information prematurely.

I turned to look at Em once more as she slept, and thought about how she and Derek, Lumina, Sarah, Rae, and Morry had all seen and accepted my true self, pledging their devotion to me, unconditionally, and I loved them all for it. But my darling wife was the first and most beloved of my devotees.

I still hadn't totally reconciled myself to the bowing and the foot-kissing, however. I'd finally accepted the fact that I wasn't human, but there were still some aspects of my godhood that weren't easy to incorporate into my daily existence.

A lot had changed in the time that I'd been gone. One of the things I truly regretted was that I'd missed a crucial time in my daughter's life. Lumina was now driving Em's Xterra, and working full-time at my shop. She was, to all intents and purposes, an adult. But I was reluctant to let go of my perception of her as the child she had been four years ago. I'd sworn when she was just a week old that I wouldn't miss any of her childhood or her teenage years, but that is exactly what I'd done. I could say that my absence was through no fault of my own, but perhaps my previous actions *had* led up to the event that had taken me from this life for the past four years.

Unaware of his existence, I'd missed Derek's life before we met here in Moab in 2013, and I'd been adamant that I wouldn't miss any of Lumina's formative years. *So much for my good intentions*, I thought.

I contemplated going back to sleep, but my guilty conscience reared its ugly head regarding another pressing issue, and I sighed, resigned to revealing the truth as soon as my wife awoke.

Last night, as we were sitting at our dining table finishing up the late snack we'd had in lieu of dinner, Em had expressed a burning desire for details of my adventures, and for the most part, I had been looking forward to sharing them with her. However, I'd given her an edited version of my adventures in the realm of the Fae until I could figure out how to tell her about my unintended sexual liaison. I prayed that I wouldn't break her heart. I would never have compromised my marital vows under normal circumstances, but the truth was I couldn't undo it, especially now that I was aware that I'd fathered a child with the Fae female.

It wasn't fair to keep that information from her, since the living, breathing evidence of my infidelity would be showing up here in Moab in just over a month.

Emily awoke slowly, returning to full awareness in the soft morning light. She blinked lazily and stretched, looking around at the sand-colored walls and the spectacular painting of Fisher Towers by a talented local artist that she had recently acquired. In the past few years, she had filled her free time with projects around the house and yard. One of those projects had been to redecorate the bedroom with the colors and artwork of the southwest. At some point, she also wanted to replace the carpet in the whole house, when she had the funds to do so.

Oh, that's right, Emily thought. *I do have the money now because*...And her entire being was abruptly suffused with joy when she remembered that Merlin was really home. Tears of happiness welled in her eyes and she blinked, the drops running down her cheeks. A long slender finger carefully brushed away her tears and she glanced over at the face of the one she adored. She cupped his cheek, thrilled to be able to touch him again.

"I love you, Merlin."

"I love you, too, darling Em," he replied in the lightly accented baritone that was music to her ears. "I'm very glad to be home."

"God, I missed you. And when I felt you die…" Her voice faltered, and it was difficult for her to continue. "I wanted to die, too. Lumina knew better, and she tried hard to convince all of us that it was just temporary. I feel so ashamed that I didn't have faith that you'd come back to life. After all, you've died before. I should have known better."

"Yes, you should have," he admonished her gently. "Love is a marvelous thing, but it is a human emotion that can cause immortals great distress if we get too caught up in it."

But she felt that same love motivate him to reach out and touch her. He stroked her hair and kissed her lips, her eyelids, her cheeks and her chin. He tenderly framed her face with his large hands, and spoke softly.

"I dreamed about you while I was gone. I didn't remember you, not really, but I knew I had a wife somewhere whom I loved beyond all reason."

Emily smiled joyfully and smoothed his long dark hair. His green cat-eyes glowed with that otherworldly light she had come to recognize as the Light of the gods, and she was caught up that mesmerizing gaze. Humming her magic, she reached around his long, slender, naked body and stroked lightly down his back to his muscular buttocks and squeezed.

He inhaled sharply and pulled her hips tightly against his burgeoning erection, causing her inner muscles to clench with desire for him. Her breasts tingled as they flattened on his chest and her nipples hardened to sensitive points. Her entire body quivered with sexual awareness.

His mouth captured hers, their tongues mating. He rolled over on top of her and she groaned, anxious for him to take her. She felt his hand cup her, long fingers stroking deep, and she spread her legs in invitation. He positioned himself and pushed inside until he was entirely embedded in her body. She sighed rapturously at the welcome fullness and pressure inside her and gripped his hardness, clamping her legs up around his waist.

Em gazed up at her husband and they locked eyes as he slowly withdrew. Then she felt his hips flexing as he drove into her once more, and withdrew and thrust again, the rhythm bringing her ever closer to a monumental climax. Distractedly, she thought she saw a hint of sadness in his eyes. It quickly changed to a look of rapt pleasure, so perhaps she had imagined it.

I realized that she had seen the look on my face as I remembered betraying her, and I immediately banished it. Explanations could wait until after we had finished. I was soon caught up again, not only in the physical and emotional sensations of our lovemaking, but in our spiritual connection as well, until a powerful orgasm slammed through me and I was lost to all conscious thought.

We must have slept after that, because the persistent and annoyingly cheerful tone of Em's cell phone, which was sitting on her bedside table, roused us sometime later.

She reached out a hand and touched the screen, and without lifting the phone to her ear, said in a lazy voice, "'Morning, Derek."

"Oops, did I interrupt somethin' important? Sorry about that." He didn't sound sorry; in fact, he sounded very pleased with himself. "By the way, it's ten o'clock. Time to rise and shine…*Stepmom*." For years, they had teased each other about their relationship, first one then the other feigning annoyance at the use of that term.

"I'm so happy and relaxed this morning that even you calling me the hated 'S' word can't ruin my mood. Hold on—did you say *ten*?" Em threw back the covers and leaped out of bed in a panic. "Oh, my God, I forgot about the big shipment of herbs coming in this morning and—"

Derek relented. "Hey, it's okay, Em, really. Sarah and Lumina have it covered, and your mom is handlin' the customers."

She flopped back down on the mattress. "I never even heard them leave this morning."

Derek laughed. "Well, I guess you had other things on your mind. Hi, Dad, I presume you're listenin' in?"

What do you think? Besides, you're on speaker. I projected to both of them telepathically with a hint of a smile included.

"Sarah went in early just to make sure everythin' was ready in the back room. She really loves her job so she didn't mind and she…"

I tuned out their conversation and stared up at the freshly painted ceiling, pondering how in the world to tell my wife what I'd done.

"Merlin, what's wrong?"

I had been so absorbed in my thoughts that I hadn't even realized that Em and Derek had ended their call and she was up on one elbow, watching me with a slightly put-out look on her face.

"You're blocking me, and you know I hate it when you do that. What is it that you're not telling me?"

I dreaded her reaction, but decided I'd better just jump in with both feet. Waiting wasn't going to help.

I cleared my throat and swallowed nervously. "Em, I mentioned that while I was lost in time…I, uh, didn't remember you, and…when I was in the Fae realm, I…I had sex with a Fae female. I must have been affected by some kind of binding scent she secreted. It seemed like a dream at the time, but afterwards, I knew it had actually happened, and that I had been unfaithful to you."

Emily's face went white and I was afraid she was going to faint. I reached out to touch her and she turned away, her shoulders shaking as she began to sob.

"Em, I'm *so* sorry, my love," I said, wishing that I'd never had to tell her. The knowledge that she would soon forgive me suddenly filled my mind, and for once, I was thankful for my awareness of the future. But frankly, I was amazed, as I was seldom aware of future events that affected my immediate family.

"Please, just leave me alone for a few minutes, will you?" Her voice was thick from crying and she wouldn't look at me.

"Of course." I got out of bed hurriedly and teleported into the bathroom, where I busied myself with showering. Despite the fact that I knew I hadn't deliberately cheated on my wife, I still suffered from a tremendous sense of guilt, and I would never forget the haunted look on her pale face.

I used magic to dress in my usual T-shirt and an old pair of cutoffs so I wouldn't have to go back into the bedroom and disturb her, then transported myself directly to the kitchen to make the coffee I craved. Unfortunately, there was one more thing I had to tell her.

CHAPTER 35

Moab, June 5, 2018

THE PAIN IN HER HEART was so severe it felt like it was going to explode. How could he have done such a despicable thing? Her magic man, her one true love had actually given to someone else what rightfully belonged only to her. She almost wailed out loud in despair, but managed to control herself.

Take a step back and try to look at this from his point of view, the voice of reason whispered. *He didn't remember who he was, and he was lost in time with someone who was a stranger. And who knows what kinds of magical influence the Fae had exerted on him in that realm beneath the mountain? It could have been exactly as he said, that the female released a scent that had beguiled him. Let's face it, even though he's a god, he's still in a man's body, right?* She smiled a little, recognizing that he was a virile man who had been without a woman for many weeks prior to that encounter, and with the Fae magic affecting him, it would have been difficult for him to fight that purely male response. She recalled the time she and Merlin had inadvertently switched bodies while making love, and how that experience had helped her understand how thoroughly a man's hormones affected his behavior.

Emily sighed deeply and decided to get out of bed and get on with her day, and let her husband know that she forgave him. As she consciously let go of the hurt and the feeling of betrayal, a tremendous weight lifted from her spirit. After all, he had returned to *her*, not to that Fae bitch.

I felt my wife let go of her anguish and knew she had forgiven me, and despite the fact that I'd already known this would happen, a profound sense of relief rushed through me. Hopefully, she would retain that feeling of forgiveness when I informed her she had a new stepson.

I waited until Em came into the kitchen and I had handed her a steaming mug of French Roast. We stood facing each other as we sipped our hot, strong coffee and I could see she suspected I had more to say. There was determination etched into her face as she initiated the conversation.

"First of all, I want you to know I forgive you."

"Thank you, Emily. You have a truly generous soul, my love," I said in my humblest tone of voice.

"Well, that remains to be seen, doesn't it?" She pursed her lips and cleared her throat, I suspect to give herself a little extra time. "I thought about what you said, and I came to the conclusion that you told me for a reason. You got her pregnant, didn't you? So you have another child." She stopped and took a calculated breath, obviously determined to keep calm.

"Yes, and he will be coming here to Moab before long." It was hard to watch the hurt flicker across her face, but I was proud of the way she handled it. I'm not sure I would have been so gracious had I been in her position.

"And you think we should keep it quiet for now. Not tell anyone until your, uh, son, arrives."

Em had gleaned that sensitive information directly from my mind. I had decided no good would come of me withholding anything further.

"I think it would be best."

She looked perplexed. "He's older than you? How can that be?"

"He was born several years before I was, but remember that time anomaly. His existence was inserted into the timeline due to my presence in the early fifth century prior to my own birth."

She considered that confusing information for a few moments, drinking her coffee.

"Do you know his name?" she asked, hesitantly.

"It's Seth. Seth MacAdam."

"That's sounds kind of biblical, doesn't it? His first name, I mean."

"Well, that's what he calls himself, anyway. His Fae name is difficult to pronounce and there's no point in going into that until he arrives. Even then, he may not wish to tell us his true name."

And that's when everyone showed up expecting a meal and to hear my story. Derek walked through the front door, laughing and talking with Morry and Jim and the three knights, who had followed him in. Shortly after that, Lumina, Sarah and Rae entered, having successfully received and processed the herb shipment, and then closed the shop for the rest of the day in honor of my return.

I was surrounded by friends and family who showered me with such an abundance of love and goodwill that I was most gratified, and I reminded myself of my previous decision, that I would not lose my connection to humanity. It was too important to me, and to my goals in saving mankind. If I lost that crucial understanding, I could no longer relate to the human condition. I needed to reflect upon this further, but I realized that my guests were all staring at me—some in puzzlement and some with outright concern when they saw the serious look on my face.

Deciding that I'd better lighten up, I smiled. "Thank you all for coming. I'm glad to see you again. And I am most grateful that you didn't give up on me during my long absence."

As I looked from one individual to another, I perceived their thoughts, their desires and their most embarrassing moments—everyone's secrets, even my family's. I knew their past lives and their ultimate destinies. Inside, I sighed. This god business was not for the weak.

I noticed that my wife had started meal preparations and I exhorted everyone to pitch in, which they did with alacrity.

"I hope pancakes and sausages are okay, 'cause that's what we're having," she said as she hauled our extra large griddles out of the cupboard.

"Whatever you've got is fine, Em, thanks," Derek responded, and everyone nodded in agreement and got busy.

I was reminded of so many other times we had all convened for one reason or another. At one point, Emily had confessed that she was tired of hosting large meals for everyone and had decided our future meetings would not include anything more than drinks and snacks. Apparently, she had let go of her objections to the events we'd hosted in the past, which made sense, since I was the reason we were all here to begin with.

A while later, just as we were preparing to sit down to our meal, the one person I hadn't seen yet, and certainly hadn't expected to see at such a large gathering, popped in.

"Is there room for one more?" asked the memorable voice.

There was dead silence in the room as Llyr appeared out of thin air and walked toward the table, dressed in T-shirt and shorts and looking more like my brother then my father. In reality, he was both, and neither. But that was a fact that I would reveal at a later time. His arms and legs bulged with well-toned muscle and he looked like he had been working out at the gym. I wondered if anyone realized that he could appear any way he chose. There were obviously no gyms in the realm of the gods.

"You bet, 'Dad.'" I conjured another chair. And pretended I didn't notice the astonished looks on everyone's faces.

CHAPTER 36

Moab Rim, June 6, 2018

As I hiked up the Rim Trail early the next morning, I thought about the previous day's gathering and laughed out loud. Having Llyr show up unannounced looking like my buff elder brother had been a shock even to the people who had seen him before. Although I'd entreated him to stay for a while, he'd taken his leave as abruptly as he had arrived as soon as the meal was over. But I was pleased that he had stopped by, since he normally avoided interacting with anyone other than our immediate family. Thinking of immediate family, I knew I would need to meet with Derek after he arrived home from work. He'd already told me his news and expressed his concerns about the mysterious woman he'd encountered out in the park; however, he'd been very insistent that we meet in person to discuss the situation. This wasn't a hardship, as I desired his company in any case.

I glanced around as I heard the low-pitched growl of several four-wheel drive vehicles making their way up the slope, and realized that I'd better pay attention and step off to the side unless I intended to get run over. I waited until the Jeeps had lumbered past and then continued hiking up the rocky surface, breathing a sigh of relief when the noxious odor of the exhaust fumes had dissipated. Thankfully, the annual Jeep Safari event had occurred before my return, or the number of vehicles on the Rim Trail would be even higher.

Just for a moment, I questioned my decision to hike up to the Rim, rather than teleport. But I wanted to enjoy the sensation of the muscles in my legs working hard as I trekked up the steep sandstone trail, and of my lungs laboring at the change in elevation.

Finally, I reached the top of the ridge, then walked over to the edge and found a large boulder to sit on. As I gazed down upon the city I had come to call my own, I could not help but see how it had changed in the four years I'd been gone. Nearly a dozen new hotels and countless expensive summer homes had been built or were in the process, and I knew that the impact on the year-round residents would be severe. Affordable housing was in short supply for both residents and new employees of all the hotels, and there were too few restaurants to feed the anticipated influx of visitors.

Even on my own street, the changes were evident. At least a dozen new homes and duplexes, some of them two-story, had been built in the time I was gone.

The pleasure I'd felt initially at being back in red rock country was tempered by these changes, and by the information that Derek had conveyed to me yesterday after the details of my journey had been shared and marveled over by one and all. And the fact that my Fae son would be arriving near the end of July unquestionably complicated the situation.

Derek's experience at Tower Arch with the woman he had described as human, but with powers no human could possibly have, was the first thing that needed my attention. He told me he thought it was Morgana and I agreed, despite the fact that her presence in Moab was literally impossible without major supernatural and temporal intervention.

Also, the fact that he'd seen Ken Wilson was something else that I had not anticipated. Although I had expected that young man's eventual return to Moab, I had not foreseen the sad truth, perhaps because his close association with Derek in the past prevented my awareness of it. Poor Ken, he hadn't deserved such a fate.

My simultaneous knowledge of past, present and future was already becoming a burden. Many times since I'd awakened in this century, I'd encountered people who wished for the ability to know the future. What they didn't understand was that part of the excitement of living a human life was *not* knowing what would happen.

And the most significant piece of information I now possessed, I could not share with anyone at present. It was ironic that the location of the new portal connecting this human realm to the mythical land of Avalon, which I'd searched for so assiduously since my arrival in Moab in 2013, was not where I, or anyone else, expected it to be. And to take advantage of that knowledge and pursue it would have me breaking an oath I had made years ago.

CHAPTER 37

Moab, July 27, 2018

Seth MacAdam had been hitchhiking for weeks, intent upon looking and acting like a typical tourist. But since he had never been a tourist before, he might or might not be behaving properly. He had flown in a commercial jet to the United States from Scotland rather than try to transport himself by magic to a place he had never been before. It was uncomfortable to say the least, since the airline seat didn't conform to the shape of his body. Being only half Fae, he didn't have the full complement of powers he would normally have been blessed with, which would have made it possible to bypass all human forms of transportation. By rights, since his father was a god, other remarkable abilities should have been bestowed upon him at birth. But those abilities had never manifested. He assumed that they would have to be activated by his sire, Myrddin Emrys, god of magic and healing, who was currently living in human form in the United States. He'd always thought it strange that his father was a Welsh god, while he considered himself Scottish, but one doesn't choose one's parents. He'd waited impatiently, century after century, knowing intuitively that it was his destiny to meet his father in America in the twenty-first century.

Sensing that his destination was near, Seth surfaced from his reverie. He stretched and yawned, still groggy from having dozed off earlier in the back of the truck he'd been riding in for hours, reclining against several large sacks of dried beans. The old man had picked him up just north of Dove Creek, Colorado, with the condition that he ride in the back; the man's ancient black Labrador retriever was sleeping on the bench seat inside the truck cab.

Although it was now quite late in the afternoon, early evening really, the sun was still high in the sky. Between the intense heat and the dry wind, Seth was uncomfortable to say the least. He could certainly use a pint of ale or two, to quench his raging thirst.

Och, and I could use a bath, as weel, he thought, as he caught a whiff of himself.

The truck slowed as they entered downtown Moab, finally pulling over in front of a place called Moody's Tavern. The driver slapped the roof, indicating that his passenger should get out. Seth grabbed his backpack and vaulted over the side of the vehicle, taking care to lift his pristine white wings so they didn't drag. He could feel the tension in his upper back and knew he'd have to fly soon to relieve the stiffness. As he looked around, he realized he'd have to wait until nightfall for that. There were too many mortals about.

As he drove off, the old man waved briefly, and then continued on his journey. Seth raised his hand in acknowledgement. He was finally in Moab, a place that was as different from his native Scotland as night and day. It was blistering hot here, and he could see the heat waves dancing above the road's surface. There were many strange plants and relatively few trees, all of which seemed to be thriving despite the harsh conditions. He thought about the cool, green, lush vegetation that abounded in Inverness and missed his home acutely. But he felt his father's presence in this town, and that of several other people with magic who seemed to be related to him, and he allowed a burst of optimism and excitement to stir him. First things first, though. He hoisted his pack and entered the pub.

He paused just inside the door to let his inhuman eyes adjust to the low light. A few people glanced at him disinterestedly and then went back to their conversations, thanks to the glamour he used to hide the physical aspects of his Fae self that he couldn't allow humans to see. He stepped up to the bar, making sure his wings were tucked close to his body and off the floor, which wasn't particularly clean, then slid sinuously onto the tall stool and placed his order. He pulled his wallet out of a back pocket and sorted through the currency to find an American ten dollar bill amidst the Scottish five, ten and twenty pound notes. That ought to be more than adequate to buy a few drinks. He had just paid the bartender and taken a sip of his ale when he realized who was sitting next to him.

The two sorcerers had just finished a challenging game of pool and were debating whether to have another beer or something stronger. They discussed having a few shots of Scotch and then playing one more game before heading home.

Doesn't really matter what we drink since we can't get drunk anyway, Derek thought ironically.

Then let's just stick with beer—it's less expensive. Besides, we both like it, Morry rationalized. They grinned at each other, pleased to acknowledge their connection yet again. They had started making this a weekly ritual, a father-son thing, and they enjoyed the hell out of spending quality time with each other. Derek currently had Fridays off and Morry got off at five o'clock, so it worked well for them. And now that Merlin was home, they didn't feel guilty about taking time for themselves.

The men grabbed vacant stools at the end of the bar, placed their order and started to discuss a nature film they both wanted to see, which would be presented at the MIC—the Moab Information Center—in a couple of weeks. Then someone sat down next to Derek, and they both became keenly aware of a heavily-accented male voice. Something disturbingly familiar about the voice drew them both to look closely at the stranger. When they did, they almost fell off of their stools. They couldn't help staring at him, stunned by his resemblance to Merlin. And when he casually scratched his head and then tucked a long strand of ink-black hair behind a very pointed ear, both men's jaws dropped in astonishment. Then, to make matters even more bizarre, they realized they could see the outline of another physical attribute that seemed to be under a powerful glamour—wings.

Aware that he was the object of attention, Seth turned towards the two men on his left.

"Dinna ye ken 'tis rude tae stare, lads?" Seth's Scottish brogue was thick and his voice was a pleasant baritone, similar to Merlin's.

"Sorry, it's just that you remind us of someone we know." *Hey, Dad, there's a man here that looks an awful lot like you. And he's definitely not human—he's got wings. How's that possible? What the hell is goin' on?*

As Derek communicated with me telepathically, I felt his confusion. I hadn't shared my sexual experience in the realm of the Fae with anyone except Emily, and perhaps I should have.

I had actually sensed my Fae son as soon as he came into town, and I was both dreading and anxiously anticipating our meeting. Thank God, I had already talked to Em about what happened to me in the Fae realm beneath Tomnahurich Hill. She had been extremely hurt but had forgiven me when she realized that there was something otherworldly at work, reconciling herself to welcoming another adult son of mine into our lives.

I breathed in carefully and let it out slowly. I guess I was a little nervous after all, especially since I hadn't warned Derek, or my grandson, about Seth.

Wings, huh? Well, it's a long story. Don't let him leave, alright? I'll be there momentarily. Oh, and by the way, he's your brother.

Derek choked on a pretzel and his "brother" reached over and whacked him on the back, a potent current of magic flowing between them. "Are ye alright?"

"Yep, just fine, thanks," Derek gasped hoarsely. The shocks just kept on comin' didn't they? He was curious whether the guy felt that telltale magical buzz when he touched him. What the hell, he might as well introduce himself to this…*brother.* Christ, what next?

"I'm Derek Colburn and this is my so—uh, my cousin, Morry. You're new in town?"

His brother stuck out his hand, and first Derek and then Morry shook it, feeling powerful magic sizzling on their palms. "Seth MacAdam, from Inverness, nice tae meet ye. Aye, I've just arrived in town the day, looking for a man who looks a lot like me." He stared into the two men's faces and waited. He'd felt the magic in their handshakes and suspected they'd sensed the family connection as well.

"And you've found him," I said quietly, as I stepped through the tavern door and approached my Fae son.

Seth turned around slowly and his eyes widened in recognition. Like Derek and Morry, I could see past the glamour he maintained that prevented mortals from seeing the strangeness of his eyes, the shape of his ears and the impressive set of wings sprouting from his upper back. In some ways, it was like looking at myself in the mirror, but with a few obvious differences between us. His slanted eyes were an unusual color, mostly yellow with only a hint of green, and the shape of his pupils reminded me of a reptile. His hair, black like mine, but wavy like Llyr's, was thick and long, through which ears even more pointed than Lumina's protruded. I didn't remember that his mother had had ears like that, but then again, I'd been under a powerful enchantment at the time, and I'd been intently focused on other parts of her body.

And I certainly hadn't anticipated that Seth would have wings. His mother must not have been a simple handmaiden after all, since only royalty could produce offspring with wings—although the likelihood of a half-breed Fae having them, royalty or not, seemed remote. But with that thought, I realized there could very well have been a conspiracy to get me into that Fae realm in the first place, and then to impregnate a Fae princess. Interesting.

"I've been waiting to make yer acquaintance for over a thousand years, Father." It was obvious from his jovial tone of voice that he wasn't making an accusation, just stating a simple fact. But, between his thick accent, his inflammatory statement and the fact that he called me father, the effect on the occupants of the bar was galvanizing: the background noise suddenly fell to zero and an identical look of horror on Derek's and Morry's faces echoed the shock I felt.

"*Oblitus!*" The three of us simultaneously cried the spell aloud, enchanting everyone in the bar to forget what they had just heard, which would most effectively have revealed the truth about our family. Any one of us could have initiated the spell, but it was fascinating how seamlessly the three of us had reacted together.

"Ye're no going to acknowledge me as yer son, Myrddin Emrys?" Seth exclaimed loudly, incredulously, his features stiff with outrage, as he rose from the bar stool in a distinctly inhuman way to face me. Instantly, I reinforced the forgetting spell to encompass this last damning statement as well.

Without taking my gaze off of my Scottish offspring, I telepathically instructed both Derek and Morry to let me handle this situation. They had leaped to their feet defensively as Seth seemed to tower over me threateningly. This was a Fae illusion since he was only about an inch taller than my six two.

I decided that we should take this confrontation away from Moody's, so I teleported the four of us to the back room of The Moab Herbalist. Fortunately, the shop had closed for the day and everyone had already gone home.

Seth took the change of venue in stride, barely glancing around. His power was evident—his body was glowing with it—but he couldn't seem to utilize it fully. I knew he should have inherited a number of magical abilities from me, and it occurred to me that I would have to activate those abilities for him. I wasn't sure what Fae powers he might have gotten from his mother, but it seemed that one of them was a formidable ability to block my telepathic inquiries. As my son, he was a demigod, and he was unquestionably aware of it; he was, in fact, almost arrogant. But the bottom line was that *I* was the god here, and he would do well to remember that.

"I will gladly acknowledge you as my son, Seth, but not to the population of Moab in general. We have all gone to great lengths, for many years, to establish a credible history for our family here, and I have no intention of allowing you to destroy everything we have built, merely to satisfy your need for reassurance.

"It's obvious that you know who I really am, since you announced my god name to everyone in Moody's Tavern. What is it you want from me? You seem to have prospered for many centuries without my presence in your life, so what do you expect me to do for you now?" I was purposely being cold and imperious to provoke him into responding truthfully.

"*Do* for me? Christ, ye're ma father, so it might have behooved ye tae have been present for a wee bit o' time as I was growing up! The Fae do things differently than humans, I admit it, but I still wished to ken ma father! But then, as ye're a god I guess ye had better things to do than to help raise yer son." He crossed his arms defensively and scowled at me, daring me to respond.

I sensed the deep hurt behind the anger in his statement. I had felt the same way when I hadn't remembered Llyr's presence during my own childhood. I hadn't even known of Seth's existence until I had returned to Moab from my adventure and was able to tap in to my god knowledge again. But I would have had no doubt that he was mine, even if he hadn't looked so much like me.

I reached out to Seth and wrapped my arms around his almost too-slender body, pulling him against me. "I'm sorry, truly sorry, that I wasn't able to be there for you."

Seth's defensive shell cracked within seconds and he returned my embrace, crying on my shoulder as Derek and Morry looked on, distinctly uncomfortable watching a stranger lay claim to what had so recently been theirs alone.

As Seth and I stepped back a little from each other, I sensed that Derek and Morry were feeling left out and resentful.

"Seth, this is your brother, Derek Colburn, and his son, your nephew, Mordred Colburn."

Instead of expressing doubt, as most people would have done since they looked to be a similar age, Seth accepted my words without question and proceeded to wipe his streaming eyes with his shirt.

He gave a wry chuckle. "Aye, weel, we introduced ourselves in the pub shortly before I opened ma big mouth, right, lads? Derek, I'm glad to ken ye, Brother. And Morry—no Derek's cousin after all, but his son—ye got King Arthur's nephew's name, then, did ye? Well, be assured 'tis an honorable one. I met him once when the Royal Family journeyed to Edinburgh. I was young, and ma mother and I'd gone through the portal that linked Tomnahurich Hill in Inverness with the hill in Edinburgh where Arthur's keep stood. Mordred was protecting Arthur at the time, and…."

Seth kept talking about his experiences with the Pendragon family, and I wondered how he had gotten off on that subject before we'd even remarked on Derek's and Morry's connection to Arthur. Apparently, he had sensed that and more by means of his Fae abilities. I glanced at Morry, who had a glazed look on his face as he stared at his uncle, and I hoped that Seth had an off switch. I turned to Derek and looked into his eyes.

Would you mind cutting in? I'm afraid he'll talk all night. I had no idea that the Fae could be so garrulous. He surely didn't get that from me.

Derek nodded, then interrupted Seth's narrative to mention that his own mother had been Arthur Pendragon's half sister.

"Och, I thought I sensed Pendragon blood in ye, Brother. Well, Father, ye certainly produced some interesting bloodlines with all the women ye've bedded."

I felt my face flush as both Derek and Morry responded to my newest son's indelicate statement with identical looks of outrage and disbelief, and I sensed how angry they were: first, with Seth for insulting me, and second, with me for bringing Seth into the picture. I needed to nip that anger in the bud.

"Seth, can you give us a few minutes, please?"

"Aye, Father, I can do that. Just summon me telepathically when ye're done, will ye?" And he slowly faded out, using his own version of teleporting.

Derek and Morry stood in stony silence, waiting for me to explain myself. I loved these two young men and I hated to create hard feelings between us, but I needed some time alone with Seth, and I didn't particularly appreciate having my son and my grandson criticizing me for my actions.

"Derek, do you remember when you were under an enchantment and impregnated your sister?" I paused for a moment, my head cocked to the side. "I can see that you do. When I was in the Fae realm, I didn't remember who I was, and I was lonesome and in need of a woman. Seth's mother offered herself to me and I took her willingly, without a thought to the consequences. I realized later that she had beguiled me with a sexual binding scent, but by then it was too late. Sound familiar?"

Derek managed to look embarrassed and glanced briefly at Morry, who was silently looking back and forth between the two of us speculatively, gray eyes troubled.

"Look, you know I love you both. And I'm sorry for not warning you ahead of time of Seth's arrival. But I'd appreciate it if you'd give us some time to get to know each other."

Seemingly resigned to the inevitable, Derek nodded. "Okay, Dad, I'll catch up with you later. Let's go, Morry." He touched his son's arm and the two of them disappeared.

Seth, come to me now, my son, I summoned him.

Coming, Father. I heard his response mere seconds before he slowly materialized in front of me.

I smiled at him warmly and he smiled back, his teeth perfect and white. "I believe I have something you need."

"Aye, that ye do, and as I've been but half a man for centuries I appreciate ye making those powers awaken, finally. I can transport maself, as ye've seen, and I can fly—ye ken how I can do *that*, surely—but the rest, the sorcery, 'tis that I've truly needed all these years. And—" As he noticed my impatience at his wordiness he winced, then stopped talking and looked expectantly into my eyes. I met his gaze and made the connection so that we Saw each other's inner selves. It was an unusual experience for me, as I had never merged with a Fae being other than Emily, and the alien feel of his spirit caught me off guard. But it turned out to be a simple matter for me to release the powers he had inherited from me, as they shone with the white Light of the gods within his very soul.

"Dad, why are you so jealous of Uncle Seth?" Morry asked curiously, having felt the raw emotion his father had exuded in response to Seth's claim on Merlin. They were both seated casually in Derek's living room, beers and burgers in hand. Sarah was visiting a friend in Provo and was not expected back until late the next day, so it was just the two of them.

Derek put his food and his beer down on the coffee table, then got up and started pacing back and forth, rage and hurt overpowering his common sense. He knew that he shouldn't let the situation affect him like this, but it did. The similarity to his own enchantment when Morry was conceived didn't stop him from feeling betrayed and slighted. After all, Merlin had been gone for years, not taking any responsibility for his family. Derek deliberately ignored the fact that his father's absence had been due to divine intervention and not by his own choice.

Okay, that's enough of that, Morry thought to himself, and stepped in front of Derek. He grabbed his father in a bear hug and silently transmitted all of the love and friendship that he now felt for him. "Dad, it'll be okay, you know it will. Have some faith."

Derek sighed and clung to his son, grateful for his presence and his level-headedness. "Thanks, I needed that."

Later, at home, Morry sat on the edge of his bed and let his thoughts roam. He was tired and confused. Comforting his father earlier had felt right, but now, alone, he was having second thoughts. Perhaps Derek had the right idea. How in the world had his grandfather, the legendary Merlin, allowed himself to be seduced by a Fae woman to the point that he had no choice but to have sex with her? Could the mere fact that he didn't remember his life have caused it? He didn't think so, but maybe it was meant to be. Perhaps the Fae were following orders from God? Hard to believe. He doubted the Fae had any relationship with the Supreme Being.

He had to admit that his Uncle Seth was impressive. Morry had been fascinated right from the start by those incredible wings and by Seth's Fae powers.

But despite that, he agreed with Derek. There was something about Seth that just didn't ring true. Maybe it was his boyish, "aw, shucks" demeanor.

Oh well, maybe Morry just needed a good night's sleep and his outlook would be better in the morning. He truly hoped that's all it was.

After Derek and Morry had left the shop, Seth and I talked about our experiences. I gave a detailed account of my time in the past, and he described his life growing up with the Fae and later living on his own for centuries in the Highlands of Scotland. After we'd had a cup of coffee, I made a decision and broached an idea to my son.

"I have plenty of room at my home and want you to know you're welcome to stay with me while you're in Moab. I'd like you to meet and get to know my wife and daughter. I hope you'll accept my offer of hospitality, Seth. Unless, of course, you've made other arrangements?"

"Now, when did I have the time tae do that, Father? 'Tis kind of ye tae offer and I accept gladly. Besides, I would like tae meet ma stepmother and ma wee sister—Lumina, is it? And she's a goddess, is she? A lovely one, I'll wager, and—"

"Seth, stop talking," I admonished him firmly.

He looked sheepishly at me, his wings drooping a little. "Och, sorry, I talk overmuch when I'm nervous, ye ken?"

I gave him a wry grin and silently instructed him to follow me as I disappeared.

CHAPTER 38

Moab, July 27, 2018, Evening

EMILY WAS ON EDGE. WHEN Merlin had let her know Seth was in town, and that he intended to invite him to stay with them, she'd been too busy preparing for his arrival to think about it. Now, she wasn't sure she was ready to face this man Merlin had sired during his sojourn in early fifth-century Scotland. Or was it called Caledonia then? She knew that the country had also been called "Scotia" and "Alba," but she wasn't certain when those names had been used, or by whom.

It scarcely mattered now, anyway. The country had been part of the United Kingdom for many years now.

Irritated at herself for letting her nerves affect her focus, she took a breath and continued working.

She hummed her magic to facilitate cleaning the office and setting up the inflatable bed for Seth. After she'd finished putting the sheets on it, she stopped to wonder if it would be suitable for Fae royalty. Well, if not, he had magic, so he would just have to make adjustments if necessary.

She moved on to cleaning the guest bathroom, now to be shared by Rae, Lumina *and* Seth. When she was finished, she used magic to give the fixtures and the mirror an extra sparkle, then stared at her reflection. She was glowing, and her eyes gleamed silver, a natural response to using her magic.

Em realized that, except for what she'd done tonight, it had been awhile since she'd used her magical abilities at home. She usually cleaned house like a normal person. Perhaps she needed to rethink that since she hadn't been normal for many years, and it was a waste of her time and energy to do her chores the mundane way.

As she turned to leave the good-sized bathroom, she remembered, ironically, that when they had purchased this house, both she and Merlin had considered it extravagant to have four bedrooms and two bathrooms. Now she wished they had more. For one thing, she'd never anticipated having her mother living with them full time. She tapped her upper lip as she contemplated the possibility of Merlin conjuring up a new bathroom. It could be a small one with just a toilet and a washbowl if they utilized the linen closet space in the hallway…

She shook off her ruminations—she had things to think about at the moment that took priority over a new bathroom.

Thankfully, Rae and Lumina were busy putting together a late dinner for the two men, so Em walked into the master bedroom, sat on the bed and claimed a moment for herself before Merlin and Seth arrived. She closed her eyes and took several measured, cleansing breaths, willing herself to relax. It worked. She felt rejuvenated and energized and her nervousness had disappeared. She could do this.

When she heard the sound of male voices in the living room she thought, *Okay, it's show time.* Exuding confidence, Emily left the bedroom and walked down the hallway with her back straight, her head high, and her hair tucked behind her ears so that the pointed tips showed.

She came to an abrupt halt in the doorway and stared at the sight of what appeared to be Merlin with wings, realizing right away that it had to be her stepson, Seth. He looked about the same age as Merlin, but that made sense, since he was immortal and probably stopped ageing around his thirty-second birthday, like his father had.

Holy crap, he was breathtaking, and those wings, my God! He almost looked liked an angel, and it occurred to her that the supposed sightings of angels could be people seeing the Fae who had allowed their wings to be visible.

Seth felt her gaze and heard her thoughts, and turned to her with a smile.

"Son, I'd like you to meet my wife, Emily. Em, this is Seth MacAdam, my son from Inverness." Merlin beseeched her on their private wavelength to make Seth feel welcome.

"Stepmother, I thank ye kindly for allowing me tae stay in yer home. And ye're correct. Sightings of ma kind have occurred many times over the centuries for just that reason, but we Fae are no angels—far from it."

"Of course you're welcome here, Seth. I love your father to the depths of my soul, and you came from him, so how can I not love you, too?" Emily said sincerely, looking into his eyes briefly, then into Merlin's.

Thank you, Em. She heard a silent, grateful sigh of relief.

Later on, as he struggled to get comfortable on the inflatable bed that didn't really accommodate his wings, Seth thought about meeting all of his relatives that day.

Poor Emily. He could tell that she wasn't thrilled that her husband had mated with another female and had a child with her. But it was obvious that she was not only irrevocably in love with Merlin, she was also devoted to his god self, so she made the best of an awkward situation. Emily, his sister Lumina, and Em's mother, Rae, made him feel welcome, serving him and Merlin dinner, despite the fact that the three of them had eaten hours ago.

And his wee sister, och, she was a sweet one. But her unwavering fascination with his anatomy was disconcerting, bordering on annoying. First of all, she wanted to compare ears, and it turned out that though her ears and Emily's were pointed, the general shape wasn't the same as his. He explained that while Elves were a type of Fae being, he himself was not an Elf. Then, Lumina became obsessed with his wings and had begged him to spread them all the way out. He'd stood in the middle of the living room and carefully unfurled his feathered appendages—and they had almost reached from one side of the room to the other. Sometimes he forgot what a magnificent set of wings he'd been born with, and sometimes he even forgot the reason he had them. He was a prince of the Seelie Court, and a descendant of the Tuatha Dé Danann, the mysterious beings who had lived in pre-Celtic times in the lands that had eventually become the countries of Ireland and Scotland.

He really didn't want the responsibility that royalty conferred, but what could he do? He'd been born into the position. The other princes weren't pleased to have a half-breed amongst them and continually persecuted him for it, but there was no point in dwelling on that right now.

How wonderful and yet how strange it had been to gaze upon his father for the first time and see a slightly distorted but recognizable version of his own face. There were differences between them, of course, such as in their eyes and the shapes of their ears. Merlin's brilliant green eyes were slanted but human, and didn't have the vertical slit pupils of the Fae. Seth's body shape and size were similar to his father's, although he had wings and Merlin did not.

How amazingly human his father looked and acted, but at the same time he couldn't hide that blindingly bright aura of his god self. Seth had had to adjust his Fae eyesight to even see Merlin's features. It was obvious his kin couldn't perceive the extent of the Light that illuminated Merlin, although Derek was clearly aware of it when he referred to "leakin' god Light." It was a surprisingly apt description.

Seth sighed and decided to get up, since he couldn't sleep. Maybe he'd fly a wee bit to help him relax. It was late now, and there shouldn't be too many humans around to see him. The ones that did would assume the sighting was due to intoxication.

When he came back from his flight, he would magically adjust the bed to his liking and to the needs and shape of his body.

He slipped quietly out of bed and pulled his jeans on. No shirt or shoes—the night air was warm and he had no intention of walking anywhere. He transported himself outside, rematerializing on the sidewalk in front of the house. He was so distracted by his thoughts that he never reactivated the glamour that hid his Fae attributes.

He flexed his shoulder muscles, spreading his wings out and back in anticipation of his imminent flight. He looked up and used not only his physical senses, but also his preternatural ones, to make sure there were no electrical lines—or anything else—in the way that might be hazardous. Getting tangled in a high voltage power line would be dreadfully painful and might damage his wings, possibly even kill him, although, being immortal he would come back to life as good as new. But why risk it?

Seth let his breath out slowly, then crouched and leapt into the air, his mighty wings pumping steadily as he rose into the night sky, which was illuminated by the light of a full moon. The first thing he noticed was how stiff he was. He hadn't taken the time to fly for several weeks and now he was feeling it. He went straight up until he was high enough to avoid being seen, and then began riding the air currents over Moab.

Chris Colburn berated herself for being an irresponsible fool. Why had she thought that it was okay to hike by herself at night, even if the moonlit landscape did seem as bright as day? She and several friends had made plans weeks ago to hike up to Delicate Arch by moonlight. They'd all done it before, many times, but always in a group, never by themselves. However, every single one of them had backed out this time, for one reason or another, until Chris was the only one left. So she'd decided to do it by herself. After all, she knew the trail well, and there were bound to be other hikers out there, so what could possibly go wrong? Famous last words.

She'd never anticipated falling and twisting her ankle so badly that she couldn't walk, never thought that she would break her flashlight or drop her water bottle, which promptly rolled off the sharp decline and disappeared. And the last straw was when she'd reached for her phone to call for help and discovered she'd left it at home.

Chris began to cry, not only from the pain in her ankle, but also from sheer frustration. But all *that* had done was make her sinuses congested. God, she was a mess. She dozed for a while, until she was awakened by the cry of a wild animal not far away. Fear made her heart beat fast and hard in her chest, and she dared to hope that Derek or Morry might hear her if she called for help in her mind. It was worth a try anyway. She closed her eyes and concentrated, doing her utmost to send a message. Nothing. No response. Oh, God, she was in trouble.

Seth was having an enjoyable flight, letting his mind drift and his body relax, when he sensed a human in distress. The female was alone and in danger, and he headed in the direction of her piercing mental cry for help. He had always been susceptible to damsels in distress, despite the fact that his Fae family thought he was ridiculous to get so involved with the weak and often pathetic human race. But what could he do? He truly liked humans.

It didn't take him long to fly out over the moon-drenched landscape, unerringly homing in on the frightened female.

Chris heard the rustle of wings and glanced up to see a huge shape hovering over her. She was amazed at the size of the bird. Only, it wasn't a bird—it was a man with wings, surrounded by an aura of white light. She wasn't a particularly religious individual, but the sight of such a magnificent being was awe-inspiring. Had God heard her cry for help and sent an angel to rescue her?

"No hardly, lass," came the response in a thick brogue. Seth landed next to her and held his hand up. He conjured a small orb of light, which flared brightly for a moment then suddenly disappeared.

"Weel, shite, I guess I need more practice."

"Mer..Merlin?" Chris stammered, having seen a familiar face while the light had lasted.

"Och, nay, lass, but I'm flattered tae be mistaken for him. I'm Seth, Merlin's son, just in from Scotland the day. And ye're Derek's wife—Chris, is it?"

"Uh, yeah, ex-wife actually. How did you know that? What are you? I know that Merlin flies, but he doesn't have *wings*."

"Aye, weel, I'm of the Light Court of the Seelie. Fae, that is, if ye're acquainted with the term?"

"Seelie? You're Fae royalty?" Chris had been thoroughly introduced to the world of the Fae, the Tuatha Dé Danann and numerous other myths and legends during her marriage to Derek, never dreaming that they could possibly be real. "My God, what are you doing here in Moab?"

"Come tae meet ma father and ma kin…" His words tapered off as his preternatural hearing picked up the stealthy approach of a mountain lion. "Lass, we need tae go now. A large wild animal is approaching, and it wants tae make a meal of ye."

Seth leaned over and picked up Chris as if she weighed next to nothing. Holding her tightly in his arms, he spread his wings and ascended easily into the warm, bright night. He was uncomfortably aware of the fact that he hadn't showered that evening and hoped his body odor didn't offend her.

Unaware of his concern, Chris looped her arms tightly around Seth's neck and closed her eyes, terrified that he might drop her.

"I have ye, lassie, and I willna drop ye!" Seth exclaimed indignantly. When she didn't answer, he realized that she was incoherent with fear, and decided to stop somewhere and let her rest for a moment, perhaps find her some water.

He flew over exotic formations of stone and absently wondered what they were called, especially the ones he had just passed, which looked almost like windows, or eyeglasses. He was heading roughly in the direction of the lights of Moab, but he had no idea where to land.

"Lass, ye'll have tae help me out here for a moment. I dinna ken this area. Is there some safe place tae stop for a wee bit?"

Chris stirred reluctantly in his arms. Glancing quickly around, she noticed a lighted building ahead and several hundred feet below them. "There, that's the visitor center coming up. Please stop there." She gulped and closed her eyes again, fighting nausea.

The visitor center was long closed for the night—it had to be at least two o'clock in the morning—but Seth checked to make sure there was no one around before he landed. He gently seated the small woman on a bench in a courtyard full of displays outlining the park features. He noticed that there were vending machines offering bottles of water in an alcove near the restrooms.

"*Rest*rooms," he snorted contemptuously as he walked towards the alcove. "Och, ye're not going to rest in there are ye, ye're going tae use the toilet, aye?" He shook his head at the strange way Americans phrased such things. In Europe, it was toilet, not *rest*room, not *bath*room.

He dug into the pockets of his jeans and realized that he had no money with him—his wallet was on the desk in his makeshift bedroom at Merlin's house and the coins were there as well.

“Weel, ’tis a good thing I have magic then, aye?” Seth focused on a bottle of water, it rolled down into the tray below, and then, as he reached out for it, the bottle flew into his hand.

He walked back over to where she sat rubbing her injured ankle, and thought that he might have made a mistake by revealing his Fae nature to this woman, even if she was a relation of sorts. Of course, if he hadn’t, she’d still be sitting out in the park, at the mercy of the wild animal that had been stalking her.

As he handed her the water bottle their fingers touched, and there was definitely a strong spark of sexual attraction between them. He had already thought about it as he held her firm little female body against his naked chest during the flight, although having sex with a human wasn’t really in his plans, despite the stirring in his loins. But perhaps, if she was willing…after all, it had been over a hundred years since he had bedded a woman, and Chris was adorable.

Chris reached up to accept the bottle of water from Seth and couldn’t help the wave of sexual desire that flooded her senses as their fingers brushed. She had been so afraid during the flight that she hadn’t considered the fact that a very sexy male held her in his arms. Even so, she had been affected by his strong, but by no means offensive, male scent. He wasn’t human, that was obvious, but her own ex-husband wasn’t completely human either (to her everlasting amazement) and that hadn’t stopped her from being attracted to him again. And then she remembered all the stories that Derek had related to her years ago, about the Fae being a blatantly sexual race, able to draw an unsuspecting woman into their thrall if they chose. As she stared into Seth’s strange eyes that were shaped just like Merlin’s, she felt herself blushing as she realized he knew exactly what she was thinking. She tore her eyes away from his intense gaze and found herself staring directly at the large, distinctive bulge in the front of his jeans. Well, that answered her unspoken question about whether Fae males responded like human males.

“Dinna make the mistake of thinking we are like human men, lass,” he said in a gruff voice, seeing her obvious interest in his crotch.

But, despite what sounded like a warning, he still held her protectively against his bare chest as he flew back towards town, both of them feeling decidedly aroused.

By the time Seth neared her apartment complex—and she realized she couldn't see his wings or his unusual pupils anymore—Chris had already decided to ask him if he would come in with her. She was captivated by this winged son of Merlin and ached to be held against his naked body. But then she remembered when she had first moved back to Moab and had met Derek's son Morry, who had shapeshifted right in front of her from a huge wolf into a very naked, well-endowed man. She'd ended up having a short but passionate affair with Morry since she was so attracted to him. Ultimately, her feelings of guilt for having seduced her ex-husband's son overcame the attraction she'd felt, and she had ended the relationship. Morry had been disappointed and a little hurt, but he'd met someone else soon after that and had quickly gotten over her.

She surfaced from her reminiscing and realized that Seth was grinning at her, having obviously seen a glimpse of her with Morry. Great, now he'd think she was a slut.

"Dinna worry, Chris, I willna say a word tae my nephew, or tae my brother for that matter, if ye dinna wish me to."

She was mortified, as she somehow hadn't connected the fact that if Seth was Merlin's son, he was also Derek's half brother and Morry's uncle. Well, too late now, she thought to herself as she unlocked the front door and invited the Fae prince into her home.

She had hardly closed the door and locked it when strong arms picked her up and deposited her on the couch.

"I dinna think ye should be walking with that injury, Chris. Here, I'll just fix it for ye." Seth sat down next to her, his wings tucked snugly up against his body, and covered her ankle with his large hands. A surge of heat and a flash of light and it was completely healed.

"How'd you do that, Seth?" Chris whispered.

"Did ye truly just ask the son of the god of magic and *healing* that question?"

"Well, Derek is Merlin's son too, and he's never been able to heal anyone."

"Ma brother is half human and I'm no human at all, and that is the difference, ye ken, lass? Derek is powerful, but in an entirely different way than I am, so dinna ever underestimate him."

Chris mutely agreed with him as she stared into his hooded eyes.

Seth stood before her in the candlelit bedroom, naked and more alien-looking than ever as his eyes turned dark and mysterious. His body, while obviously humanoid in shape and proportion, seemed too perfect, and his wings made him appear to be some kind of mythical creature.

Her eyes widened as she noticed his genitals; it was obvious that he was hugely aroused and ready for her, and she certainly felt aroused herself just by looking at him. He reached out for her and pulled her unresisting body against his, and the first thing she noticed—other than his erection pressing heavily against her—was that his body was smoothly muscular and entirely hairless. And—

Chris realized she was still sitting on the couch. That scene with both of them naked had played out entirely in her mind. Seth was silently watching her with a brooding, hungry look on his face and it was obvious he had been an active participant in that vision. Her face flaming in embarrassment, she still couldn't seem to look away from him.

Seth was torn. Chris was a bonnie wee lass, who would normally make a fine temporary bed partner for him. And having participated in that scene in her mind, he was certain they would be more than compatible despite the difference in their heights. He was sorely tempted—she aroused him like no other female had in over one hundred years.

However, the fact that both his brother and his nephew had carnal knowledge of her could cause untold problems, and he didn't want to encroach upon his newfound family's territory, even though it was apparent that their sexual relationships with her were over.

His body wasn't being very cooperative with his decision to back off. His erection had a mind of its own and he ended up having to use magic to make it subside. It was a shame, to be sure, to let such a fine, hard cockstand go to waste, but in this instance he would have to ignore his Fae nature, which had few scruples when it came to sex.

Seth would be the first to admit that his Fae half warred with his more human-oriented demigod half. Prince or not, he had never completely fit in with the Fae. His mother loved him, but it was a very distracted, inattentive type of love, and had been ever since he was born. It was as if by doing her duty and seducing Myrddin Emrys she had fulfilled her responsibility, and had nothing left to give her son.

Seth reached up absentmindedly to scratch his right ear. According to his stepmother, whose ears had only recently attained their current shape, pointed ears itched more than human-shaped ears. Perhaps she was right about that.

Chris could almost read Seth's thoughts as she watched his expressions and saw his final decision to withdraw from her. She was very disappointed and felt no small amount of shame at his rejection, particularly when he had clearly desired her. At the same time, she was relieved that he hadn't taken her up on her offer. Having sex with Seth would definitely have complicated her life, perhaps even changed it forever.

"I'd better go, lass," Seth said quietly, hoping she wasn't going to make a scene. He'd felt her reaction to his rejection and he was sorry to have shamed her. Then he wondered why he cared. After all, he hardly knew her.

"Okay." She tried to smile but it didn't reach her eyes. "Well, I'll see you soon, I'm sure."

"Oh?"

"Everyone associated with the family is getting together for brunch tomorrow…" She looked at her watch and shrugged. "I guess I should say today. We normally get together on Sundays, so this is kind of unusual, but maybe it's because you're here. Merlin undoubtedly knew you were coming."

“It wouldna surprise me if he did,” Seth muttered.

Chris continued as if he hadn’t spoken, “Emily always includes me and I’m grateful, since I don’t have any other family here in Moab.

“And Seth, thanks for healing my ankle—and for saving my life!”

“Ye’re welcome, lass, ‘twas my pleasure, tae be sure.” He paused for a moment too long, during which she was certain he was going to change his mind, but then he said, “Alright, then, I’ll be going. Sleep well, Chris.”

And with that, the Fae prince faded out and left her to her thoughts and regrets.

CHAPTER 39

Moab, July 28, 2018

By the time Seth re-formed in his makeshift bedroom it was after three, and he realized that he was physically and emotionally exhausted. His wings drooped with fatigue. He rolled his shoulders and stretched his back muscles, trying to release the tightness. Utilizing his wings as he had tonight, without stretching beforehand, was like running a marathon without warming up first. Plus, the strain of carrying a hundred-pound woman in his arms had made his upper body ache. He was normally much stronger than a human male of similar weight and height, but apparently he was out of shape, and that was irksome.

He looked at the inflatable bed and sighed, but decided it would have to do for what remained of the night. He'd just have to sleep on his stomach. He pulled off his dirty jeans and tossed them on the floor, then magically increased the temperature of the air-conditioned room so that he would be comfortable without any covers—he disliked having sheets and blankets touching his wings, because they invariably messed up his feathers. He settled on the bed with his face in the pillow and his wings folded down, covering his back, and before long sank into unconsciousness.

I lay awake next to my sleeping wife and replayed Seth's nocturnal adventure in my mind. When Emily had mentioned that Chris was back in town and had joined the family, my curiosity was piqued. What vagary of fate had decided that a mortal with no special abilities should be a part of my retinue?

The answer came to me swiftly, in a vision that spanned centuries—she was meant for Seth. Unbeknownst to her, Chris's roots were in the Scottish Highlands, and my magical Scottish son was her destiny.

Reassured, I smiled and closed my eyes. I heard Seth fussing about his wings and was glad I could fly without them. I snuggled closer to Emily and finally drifted off to sleep.

A few hours later, Seth reluctantly opened his eyes in time to see Lumina reaching out to touch his feathers.

"What are ye doing there, lass?" he snapped, not pleased to be awakened so early, and uncomfortably aware that he was bare-arsed naked.

Lumina let out a shriek. "Oh, you startled me! Uh, nothing…"

"Nothing, wee sister? Ye were merely going tae stroke me, as if I was some big bird, admit it. I'm a Seelie prince, no someone's pet!" He shouldn't really be angry with her; she appeared to be sixteen or seventeen years old but he knew that she'd been born only four years ago, so in many ways she was an inexperienced innocent.

Not to be outdone, Lumina bristled. "And I'm an ancient Roman goddess," she said haughtily, as she stomped out of Seth's room with her nose in the air, slamming the door behind her.

"Lumina, what in the world were you doing in your brother's room?" Emily asked as her daughter flounced into the kitchen. "Let him sleep, for Pete's sake. He was up really late rescuing Chris from being eaten by a mountain lion. Hmmm, I can see the handwriting on the wall—you and Seth are going to be at each other's throats, aren't you? Well, sorry to put a damper on your little snit, Miss Roman Goddess. Just cut it out, right now!"

Seth allowed himself to listen to the whole thing with his preternatural hearing, enjoying every word, until it was directed at him.

Don't think I'm unaware that you're listening, Seth. You should know better than to get into an argument with your sister, particularly when you're under Merlin's roof! Since you're awake, you might as well get up and help us get ready for our get-together.

Aye, Stepmother, I'll be there shortly, he thought, calmly. Actually, he was seething with resentment. She was treating him like a child, instead of the ancient exalted royalty he really was. He was usually an easygoing fellow. After all, what did he have to worry about? But, to be honest, he really didn't give a shite about being royal. For some reason, though, he felt irritated and put-upon. It couldn't be because he was sexually frustrated, could it?

More than a little out of sorts, he transported himself into the bathroom. He considered himself fortunate that he wasn't competing with his sister or Merlin's mother-in-law for the privilege of taking a shower. As he stood naked in front of the large mirror and carefully straightened a few feathers that were out of place, admiring the subtle, thin black line around each individual white feather, he suddenly had a shift of perspective. He lifted and spread his wings slightly, and as he did so, he realized that he actually *did* look like a big bird. He'd never really looked at himself in such a large mirror before. He started to chuckle, then erupted into deep belly laughs.

"Do you hear that, Mom? He's laughing at himself. I guess he's not as pissed off as he seemed."

"No, I guess not," Emily said, smiling at her daughter.

Before I made an appearance this morning, I listened to the familial squabbling going on both vocally and telepathically, and smiled to myself. While still in the realm of the gods, when I had yearned for a body and a human life, I had never imagined the pleasure I would derive from these simple interactions and altercations.

Despite her apparent maturity, Lumina often displayed a younger girl's temperament, evident in her argument with her newest brother, who happened to possess an attribute she coveted—wings. This realization diverted me momentarily, and I made a mental note to revisit this issue later.

Back on track, I thought about Seth, another son whose childhood I had missed. My child and yet so alien, I loved him already in a way that surprised me. Was it because he looked like me? Derek was as much my son as Seth, and I adored him, yet outwardly he resembled me very little. We shared only a few minor physical traits: our feet were the same size and shape and our faces were both somewhat narrow. Derek's eyes were slightly slanted, like mine, but he swore he couldn't see it. Despite the lack of similarity, however, I knew that Derek was completely devoted to me. Seth was, so far, an unknown factor.

It was evident that while Seth could be good-natured, he also had a hair-trigger temper. Then I remembered how Derek had behaved when he was initially exploring his powers. He'd been very temperamental and prone to explosions of wrath. Maybe they were more alike than I realized.

I blinked, and found there were tears in my eyes. I was experiencing what I'd always wanted—a human life and all its attendant ups and downs. But by far the most valuable, I was experiencing love. In my incorporeal state in the realm of the gods, I could never have experienced the intensity of emotion that was part and parcel of being human.

Seth stood underneath the spray of hot water and felt his father's emotions. He marveled that a god, even in human form, could be so *human*. It was actually refreshing. Although he had lived among mortals off and on for over a thousand years, there was still a part of him that couldn't understand many of their emotions. Thanks to his father's influence, Seth looked more human than many of the Fae. But he wasn't human. Though he sometimes wished he was, he'd never willingly give up his immortality, his wings, or his unique lifestyle. He was quite vain about his wings, but he wished now that he hadn't been so hard on his little sister. His sudden feelings of regret took him off guard. Would he be able to maintain his objectivity while he was here?

He rinsed off and stepped out of the shower, carefully folding his wings so as not to scrape them against the metal frame of the shower doors, and wistfully thought of his custom shower at home.

He hadn't gotten his wings wet since it took a long time for them to dry, so it was a simple matter to quickly towel off his hair and body. He needed to get out to the kitchen; he could sense his stepmother's annoyance.

How did human families *deal* with each other on a daily basis? He sighed and hoped he could handle it.

He grinned. He could always go visit his ancestors, the Tuatha Dé Danann, in Tír na nÓg. You couldn't get any farther from the human realm than that.

Em and Lumina were assembling the ingredients to start preparing the meal when Seth, sans glamour, appeared in the kitchen wearing a kilt. The incongruous sight startled Rae so much that she dropped the silverware she'd been sorting.

All three women had a hard time keeping their eyes off his muscular legs.

He cleared his throat carefully, then adjusted his facial expression to one of contrition and said, "Ladies, please forgive me for being insensitive and rude earlier. Allow me tae take everyone out tae eat so ye dinna have tae cook this morning." He figured that should constitute an adequate apology.

"Oh…well…that would be nice, thank you. Are you sure you can afford to do that?" Em began returning the food to the refrigerator.

Seth pulled his wallet out of his sporran and extracted an American Express Centurion Card.

"Aye, I'm sure. I've been saving money for a thousand years. 'Tis time I spent some of it."

"Oh, my goodness! The AmEx Black Cards are hard to come by. I actually worked for AmEx in a big call center for a time, and those cards are normally available by invitation only." Rae was extremely impressed.

"I dinna know aboot that. I—"

"What's going on?" I asked mildly as I entered the kitchen. Being able to discern the future certainly wreaked havoc with trying to act surprised.

"Seth has generously offered to treat all of us to brunch." *As if you didn't know, magic man.*

I smiled genially, and telepathically informed everyone who had planned to attend our gathering to meet at the Red Rock Grill in an hour rather than come here to the house.

"Thank you, Seth. That is very kind of you, considering there are so many of us."

"Father, I've a $120,000 limit on ma AmEx card. I think I can handle it."

"Why would you, a Fae being, even need a credit card?" Rae asked curiously.

"Weel, I live in this human realm, aye? So, 'tis easier to hide in plain sight when I look and act human, which includes using a credit card tae purchase things."

We all stared dubiously at his obviously inhuman form until he reactivated his glamour, hiding all of his Fae attributes, even from us. Seth sighed. "Better?"

"I don't know about 'better,' because your wings are really awesome, but maybe 'necessary' is the right word," Lumina stated with the candor of youth.

Seth realized then that she desperately wished for the ability to fly. Assuming that it was impossible, and being the practical lass she was, she had accepted it. He speculated whether it would be appropriate to discuss the subject with his father, because it would be a shame that, with all the magical powers in the family, she could not somehow be granted her fondest wish.

When it was time to leave, it was decided that Seth and I would take my old black pickup, while Emily, Rae and Derek would ride in the Xterra with Lumina driving. Everyone else would meet us at the restaurant. I had called in a reservation, and fortunately the back dining room, which was meant for large groups, was available, along with our favorite server, Sydne.

When I walked in the front door of the Red Rock Grill with Seth at my side, it caused a stir, as he could easily pass for my twin brother. Such was the story we would tell if asked, but fortunately no one questioned us. The fact that I was Welsh and he was Scottish didn't seem to matter, since most people didn't recognize the origin of my accent anyway. It was a good thing that I had convinced him to wear jeans instead of his kilt, which would have drawn even more unwanted attention to the two of us.

The three knights had already arrived and were chatting in a desultory fashion over coffee, until the two of us entered the room. Then I heard gasps of surprise and one quiet utterance of "What the hell?" as they saw Seth.

The remainder of our party arrived soon thereafter, and when they had taken their seats, I closed the door between the two rooms.

"Ladies and gentlemen, meet Seth MacAdam, my son from Inverness, Scotland."

Jim Singleton gazed raptly at my Fae son and then turned to his roommate. "Damn, Morry, I didn't believe you when you told me how closely he resembles Merlin!"

Seth didn't comment and I realized he wasn't paying any attention. He was staring intently at Chris, who was staring hungrily back at him. Their silence fairly sizzled with sexual tension and I cleared my throat. They both glanced at me, startled, as if they'd forgotten anyone else was present.

Perhaps the two of you could tone it down until you're alone together? I directed this request to Seth, who held my gaze for a few moments and then nodded briefly.

Derek, who was just now sensing the not-so-subtle clues between his ex-wife and his brother, scowled as he looked back and forth between the two of them.

Dad, what the hell is going on? Did they have sex?

I glanced at Derek and debated how much to reveal. It was obvious that Seth was not allowing him access to his thoughts, so I decided to make it brief. I informed Derek of Chris's rescue last night, and then sent him one last thought: *They haven't had sex yet, but to make a long story short, it's their destiny.*

"What!?" Derek sputtered aloud, drawing attention to himself. He'd forgotten he had been communicating with me telepathically.

I covered for him by explaining that Derek had been thinking about something unrelated to our gathering and hadn't meant to express his frustration aloud.

Calm down and we'll talk later, I thought sternly.

He struggled to suppress his annoyance and nodded curtly. His reaction seemed extreme and once again, I chafed at my occasional inability to discern my family members' thoughts, feelings and intentions. It was apparent, however, that there was a growing antagonism between my two sons.

The noise level continued to increase as a half dozen different conversations escalated in volume. Finally, I stood up and broadcast a telepathic request for silence before I spoke.

"I just wanted to say that Seth is buying this morning." Whistles and cheers followed my announcement.

"Ye're most welcome," Seth interjected, his response practically drowned out as everyone spoke at once.

I raised my hand and the noise level instantly dropped. "Okay, decide what you want and we'll get Sydne back in here to take our orders." She had distributed menus, and then gone to fetch coffee for those of us who were caffeine-deprived, as well as other beverages for those who didn't want coffee.

The door opened and Sarah slipped in, excitement and anticipation lighting up her pretty, heart-shaped face.

"Hi, sorry I'm late," she said breathlessly.

"You're fine, Sarah. We were just about to order," I reassured her.

She sat down in the chair next to her husband and then glanced curiously at Seth. After Derek had spoken to her the previous night, filling her in on his brother's arrival, she'd decided to cut the visit to her friend in Provo short, saying that she wouldn't miss this event for the world. But it was clear that Derek hadn't given her all the details.

At that point, Sydne entered the room with a large tray containing our drinks, which she quickly distributed before taking out her order pad. We limited our conversations to mundane chitchat until she left.

Sydne's departure triggered a deluge of questions, to Seth's dismay.

"So, Seth, how come you're just now coming to visit? Merlin never mentioned he had another son. Can you tell us where you've been all this time?" As Jim lapsed into reporter mode, his typical modus operandi, Morry rolled his eyes and Percival frowned in annoyance.

"I've lived in Scotland all of ma life," Seth said, his tone indicating he was already irritated at being questioned. "I didna come afore this as it wasna time, ye ken?"

"How old are you? What year were you born?" Sarah was aware that his youthful appearance was no indication of his true age, but didn't think about how rude it was to ask until it was too late.

I cringed imperceptibly at her faux pas.

Seth gritted his teeth as he answered. "I was born in the fifth century, in the year 415, so I'm 1603 years old." This information caused a few confused looks, since everyone knew that I had been born after that, in 420.

"I don't understand—how can you be older than your father?" Gawain asked, legitimately mystified by the obvious inconsistency.

"'Tis the nature of time, ye see." Seth shared a look with me at that, and I smiled.

Jim, Rae and the knights looked mystified; they had no idea what he was talking about. Emily had a slight frown on her face as she struggled with the concept.

I chuckled. "A man named Huston Smith once said, 'Yesterday and today and tomorrow are not an arrow that shoots from past to present to future; rather all tenses, and sleeping and waking, mix and cohabit in a temporal duration beyond clocks and calendars.' Does that help explain it?"

From the looks I received, I could see that it didn't. "Okay, how about this: Time isn't linear." I raised my eyebrows questioningly, glancing around at numerous blank faces, and then sighed in exasperation. "Come talk to me later, alright?"

Jim, who had recently become a fan of urban fantasy novels, piped up with another question for Seth. "Are you really Seelie Court Fae? I thought that the Seelie and Unseelie were just characters in those fantasy books that take place in Dublin, Ireland. You know, the ones in which the walls between our worlds came down, releasing the dark Fae, who decimate the world's population."

"Aye, I am Fae, a prince of the Light Court of the Seelie. Seelie and Unseelie are actually the Scottish terms, not Irish, but many of the myths of Ireland and Scotland are interconnected. The author who wrote the books ye mentioned is actually a friend of mine. She's one of the few humans I've ever spoken tae aboot ma race, and she has kept her promise *not* tae use all of the information I gave her. I insisted that I needed tae read each manuscript through afore 'twas published, tae make sure she hadna betrayed us. She came close tae the truth a couple of times, but most 'tis fiction. I mean, we Fae are already in yer world, aye? No walls had tae fall tae make it so, since we can move magically between dimensions. But we *are* descended from the Tuatha Dé Danann, and—Och, thank the gods." Seth breathed that last sentence quietly, grateful for the reprieve as Sydne and several other servers carried in large trays of food. He took a few moments to slug down his coffee, wishing it had a shot of Scotch whisky in it.

That was brutal. I thought they'd never give me a moment's peace. And I can sense all of the questions that they're saving up tae ask me later. Seth directed his thought to me, so we could have a private conversation.

Son, you're a part of this group now, so they feel that you're fair game. And you're not just part of the group, but part of our family.

Seth recalled his earlier thoughts about human families. Being part of a family was something new to him, as the Fae generally didn't separate into family units. But he had to admit, it felt surprisingly pleasant to know he belonged to and with these people, despite the fact that he wasn't human.

Then he laughed to himself as he remembered that his father was a god as old as the universe, and as far from being human as anyone could be.

The more he thought about it, the more amused he became. The only human beings at the table were Chris (who was aware of everyone's magical secrets) and the three knights, and two of those men were reincarnated souls of ancient warriors. That left Percival, who had been born in the past and transplanted here by the god Llyr. And then there was Jim, Morry's friend, who was human but had the soul of Queen Guinevere Pendragon. Derek's wife Sarah was human but possessed a little magic. So, in other words, no one here was normal in any way.

I fit right in, Seth thought.

Merlin glanced at him with an ironic look. *You know, they might not be so persistent for answers if you didn't look so much like me. On a slightly different topic, what's going on with you and Chris?*

Seth suspected that his father was baiting him and responded impatiently, *Ye have been around for how long, Father? Sired four children, at least, and ye dinna recognize sexual attraction between a male and a female? Come on.* He nonchalantly salt and peppered his rare steak and over-easy eggs, then raised his eyebrows.

Merlin laughed at the look on Seth's face and the entire group focused on them with curiosity. Apparently, his father had seen that expression many times in the mirror.

Seth watched the people around him light up with pleasure as Merlin literally shone like a miniature sun. He made an admirable human being for someone who never had been, and never would be, human. He was the being they revolved around, like planets around a white-hot star.

I knew that Seth was starting to understand my role here, and that he had never expected to fit in as he did. I could see his glamour of normalcy start to fade as he relaxed, and I magically locked the door to the main dining room and the side door to the bathrooms so that no one from the restaurant staff could inadvertently come in and see what he really looked like.

The moment his magnificent wings, pointed ears and reptilian eyes became entirely visible, I heard various gasps and other sounds of surprise as everyone saw his true Fae appearance. Of course, half of us had already seen his real form, but it was still somewhat shocking to see the undeniable evidence of his alien nature so blatantly displayed.

Seth was prepared for a strong reaction when he allowed his glamour to drop. He never would have considered doing such a thing in the past, but he trusted his father implicitly and his father trusted these people. He felt strangely naked, baring his secrets for all to see. Not that he was embarrassed—he was a prince, for Christ's sake. In fact, he found that he enjoyed revealing himself. His brother and his nephew were only partly human, although there was no outward sign of it in either of them, and no one thought anything of it.

He smiled tentatively at the people gathered around the table and they smiled back at him. Perhaps this visit would go smoothly after all.

For a time all was quiet, as the attendees applied themselves to their repast.

As Seth consumed his very rare steak, the bloody meat seemed to enhance his lust, and the intensity of the looks he and Chris exchanged increased until he realized that their coupling was inevitable. Their attraction to each other was extremely powerful, possibly even destined, and he could barely tolerate waiting until this gathering concluded. He had to have her in his arms soon, her body beneath his, as he possessed her fully.

CHAPTER 40

Moab, July 28, 2018

As we pushed our empty plates aside and conversations turned to plans for the rest of the day, Derek stood up and came around the table to stand next to me.

"I need to speak with ya privately, Dad."

"Why don't we meet up on the Rim in our usual spot, in say, twenty minutes?"

"Yeah, that'll work since I took the day off. See ya soon." He turned and left the room, trailing Sarah, Morry and Jim. In my mind, I could hear my grandson saying goodbye outside of the restaurant as he and Jim headed back home.

"What was that all about?" Em asked, grabbing her purse and settling the strap on her shoulder.

"Derek has some things he wants to discuss, and while I'm already aware of most of them, I'm having a hard time reading him right now."

"Not a good time for your god powers to be on the fritz, honey."

"Tell me about it." I turned to the knights as they started out the door. "See you later. Thanks for coming. I'll be in touch soon."

Ryan nodded and waved in acknowledgement. He turned to thank Seth for breakfast, but couldn't catch his eye. He just shrugged and winked at me.

Seth and Chris stood facing each other, chatting and holding hands, so caught up in their mutual attraction that they were oblivious to everything going on around them. I was just about to ask Seth what he planned to do this afternoon when the two of them turned abruptly, threaded their way through the crowded restaurant and walked out the front door. I grinned wryly. It was obvious that they were going directly to Chris's apartment to have sex. I could literally see the pheromones trailing behind them.

I leaned over and grabbed the check off the table, sighing as I saw the total.

"Seth didn't pay the bill, did he?"

"No, and I'm tempted to take it out of his hide."

"It's a good thing you replenished our bank account then, isn't it?" Em grinned at me. We both recalled how many times I had paid for food the summer Derek had accompanied us when we'd gone to Las Vegas to get married.

As we walked through the restaurant and stopped at the cash register, I pulled my wallet out of my pocket and examined the contents.

"Have you got enough cash? If not, I can use my credit card."

"No, I'll get it." As we waited for someone to take our money, I reached out and put my arm around my wife, drawing her against me. She looked up at me in surprise—I wasn't normally so demonstrative in public. I looked down into her hazel eyes and just smiled.

"Hasn't anyone helped you yet, Mr. and Mrs. Reese? Sorry about that." Sydne put the tray of drinks she was carrying down and came over to the register.

"It's alright, I know all of you are busy." As she finalized our ticket, I handed her two crisp hundreds plus a fifty dollar bill and told her to keep the change.

"Oh, my goodness, thank you so much!" Her eyes widened and I could tell she was very pleased. She reminded me of the young woman in Dublin who was able to pay her rent because of the extra gratuity I had given her. Sydne deserved the large tip for all the hard work that she'd done. Waiting tables was not necessarily an easy way to earn a living.

Since I had plenty of money, I didn't regret paying for our meal, but I was rather irritated that Seth had forgotten his promise. The Fae had their own code of ethics, but my son was living in the human realm and needed to understand the concept of honoring an agreement.

As I held the door open for my wife and we headed towards our vehicles, I asked where Rae and Lumina had gone. My god powers were acting up today. I hadn't even noticed when they'd left the restaurant.

"Home, of course. They decided to walk, so I guess we each get to drive a vehicle." Emily unlocked her Xterra using magic and climbed in. "Were you and Derek going to meet somewhere, or is he coming over to our place?"

"We're going to meet up on the Rim." I leaned in the window, capturing her mouth in a kiss that raised my blood pressure. She responded by grabbing my T-shirt and pulling me closer.

"I can never get enough of you, magic man," she murmured, deepening our already provocative kiss.

I released her mouth reluctantly. "I'm glad, because I can never get enough of you either." I framed her pretty face with my hands and looked into those bewitching eyes. "I love you."

Emily smiled widely. "I love you, too."

"See you soon." I waved as I walked towards my old pickup, got in and started it, then pulled out of the parking lot and drove towards home.

Seth and Chris headed back to her apartment, which was only a few blocks from the restaurant. They walked hand in hand, so self-involved that nothing existed outside of their desire for each other. They crossed Kane Creek Boulevard, dodging traffic, and then cut across the lawn at the apartment complex to get to her particular unit.

Chris dug the key out of her purse and smoothly unlocked the front door. Inside, with the lock re-engaged, they barely made it down the hall and into her bedroom before they launched themselves at each other, frantic to caress bare skin. And when the two of them were finally divested of their clothing and were wrapped in each other arms, sighs of relief and moans of desire were uttered by them both.

"I shouldna want ye so much, lass—ye're human, and ye have no magic," Seth admitted as he caressed her petite, lithe body, feasting on her succulent lips and nibbling on her small but perfectly shaped breasts. He pressed his burgeoning erection against her belly and she gasped, desperate to feel that velvet-covered steel moving inside her.

"And you're *not* human, but I really don't care. You're simply the hottest man I've ever seen in my life and I want you also,"

Chris said breathlessly as she stroked his slender, hairless torso and marveled at his unusual scent. Her skin felt especially sensitized as she lay on her side against him, becoming increasingly aroused.

Seth wondered if he should tell her that the Fae had the ability to release a scent that attracted the opposite sex whether they were interested or not. It was the reason Merlin had been attracted to his mother, which had resulted in his conception. This ability was not something he normally shared with anyone since it gave his kind an unfair advantage. He suspected he was the only one of his race who thought it unfair, however, and he was sure he was the only one who had learned to control it completely. Chris was already attracted to him, thank the gods, so he only released a small amount of scent, just to pleasure her. He had to release some of it anyway. Sexual arousal caused his body to manufacture a surplus, and a build-up in the scent glands could be extremely painful. He'd learned that from previous experience and had no desire to repeat it. It was infinitely more enjoyable—for him at least—to have sex with someone who was attracted to him from the start, as she had been.

He inhaled her unique scent, of spices and warm, willing woman, and knew he couldn't wait much longer. He reached down and inserted two long fingers into her wet heat, testing her readiness, then pulled her beneath him. As he settled on top of her sweet, soft body, she opened for him and he slid his considerable length inside her.

Chris gasped as he impaled her, his tall, winged form covering her completely. She was such a small person that he filled her and stretched her to exquisite capacity. He was gentle, yet he took her with focused determination and skill, bringing her to one climax after another by adding a touch of Fae magic to his lovemaking.

She knew she was caught up in his sexual thrall, and she wasn't at all sorry about it. He was masterful as he touched her as no one else had ever done, stirring more than just her body. He stirred her emotions, her heart. She suspected that part of the attraction was his species' way of binding a sexual partner, but she really didn't care.

After they were thoroughly sated and relaxed, legs entwined, Chris asked if she could touch his wings. She had been very careful not to come in contact with them as they made love, just because it seemed as if they were off limits.

At first, Seth was reluctant to grant her wish, but she had been so respectful of his graceful appendages that he relented. "I suppose ye can, just be careful not to ruffle the feathers—it feels verra strange."

"I'm fascinated by how the wings attach to your back, Seth."

He reluctantly disentangled himself, then turned over onto his stomach to allow her to get close to his upper back. "I've never let anyone do this afore," he said, his voice muffled as he pressed his face against the pillow, his long black hair a stark contrast to the white pillowcase.

She ran her hand over smooth skin and onto one of the thick bones that protruded from his back between his shoulder blades and his spine.

"It's like another limb. There's skin up a little ways and muscle attached underneath."

He chuckled quietly. "Lass, they *are* limbs. I was born with them, so I should know. I take them as much for granted as ye do yer arms and legs."

As Chris continued to caress his back and shoulders, examining his wings, she thought of something that baffled her. "I don't understand how you can wear normal clothing. How in the world do you put your shirts on?"

"Weel, lass, how do ye think I put ma shirts on? Do ye suppose there's a shop that makes shirts especially for the Fae?"

She flushed in embarrassment as she realized how naïve her question was, and dropped her eyes.

"Ah, lass, I didna mean to make ye feel bad. I use magic, of course."

"Of course, how else?" she murmured. Then she leaned closer, in fascination.

"The feathers are amazing. They look pure white from a distance, but when you look closely, each one has a narrow line of black around the edge."

Seth turned his head and watched her as she delicately traced several feathers, and he shivered. The sensation made him want to bury himself inside her again. His cock swelled and his breath came faster. Who knew that his feathers would prove to be an erogenous zone?

Then, to his surprise and dismay, he felt his lateral incisors lengthening. He started to panic, knowing that he couldn't let them descend fully. No one here knew he had fangs; in fact, he'd almost forgotten about them. And he didn't want anyone calling him a vampire. He was unsure why he had them—was he a throwback to earlier times? It was unusual for a Light Court prince to have fangs; usually it was only Dark Court Fae who exhibited that trait. He concentrated on making them retreat into his gums. He wished he could just have them removed. In this day and age, Fae didn't use them to feed anymore; blood hadn't been on the menu for thousands of years. Maybe the rare steak he'd consumed earlier had triggered the fangs to drop.

It amused him to imagine walking into a human dental office and requesting a fang extraction. Wouldn't that just confuse the hell out of the dentist?

"Enough." He turned on his side and pulled her against him, her back to his front, and he thrust himself inside her again.

Sometime later he stirred as a memory surfaced. He had told Chris that he had been born with wings, but that wasn't precisely true. When he was very young, perhaps two or three years old, his wings had erupted out of his back suddenly and unexpectedly. His mother had not prepared him for the event, so it was possible that she hadn't known it would happen. Fortunately, the centuries had softened the memory of that excruciating pain and the suffering he had endured until his body had fully adjusted to having extra limbs.

Of course, since no other Fae that he knew of had white wings, he had been teased and ridiculed for centuries by his peers, who had black or gray wings, if they had wings at all. For years he had suspected that his wings were white due to his mixed heritage. Perhaps he would discover the answer here in Moab.

Seth folded one of his wings so that he could stroke the feathers. He shivered in delight as his cock responded. Gods, it was almost like masturbating. He could have sworn that he never had this type of response before when he'd touched his feathers. Perhaps being with Chris had something to do with it.

He reached out for her again.

As I parked the truck in the driveway next to Em's SUV, I felt a wave of sexual energy and magic so potent that my own body started to react. I determinedly blocked the sensations and teleported to the spot up on the Rim where the old chairlift had terminated. It had been dismantled and removed years ago, but the location itself had an exceptional view of the valley and Derek and I had been up here many times to enjoy it. Occasionally there were hikers and jeepers passing by as they explored the Rim Trail, but we had the place to ourselves at the moment.

Derek was waiting for me as I rematerialized, his normally pleasant features distorted by anger and disgust.

"Dad, do you feel that—"

I cut him off impatiently. "Yes, and you know who and what it is, Derek, so just block it." Were they going to have sex all afternoon?

My son gritted his teeth and took a quick breath. "I have to tell ya somethin'. I think Seth has been sent here by the Fae to spy on us."

"I already know that," I snapped. "I sensed a trap when I was in the Fae realm, oblivious to my true identity, after I'd been seduced by Seth's mother."

"Well, as long as you're aware of it." He was silent for a moment, still worried about Seth and his intentions, and struggling to control his response to their passion.

We eyed each other warily as we both took a few seconds to cool off. Normally, Derek and I did not get on each other's nerves, and since I had been gone for so long, there was no reason he and I should be so irritated with each other. It appeared that my newest son had the ability to push both of our buttons.

I took a calming breath then gave him a wry grin. "Look, it's okay, there's a plan at work here greater than you can ever imagine. Remember—with a few exceptions—I know the past, the present and the future of every single creature on this earth, in all dimensions and universes, and that includes the Fae. It's daunting, I have to admit." I closed my eyes for a moment and sighed, all levity gone.

"Damn it, sometimes I sure as hell wish I was just a bloke with a few magic tricks up his sleeve, instead of a god who was created when the universe itself was born, almost fourteen billion years ago." I slowly opened my eyes and looked at my son, who was staring at me aghast, his face drained of color.

"What's wrong?" I frowned, perplexed by the expression on his face.

"Someone else was speakin' out of your mouth. Do ya know what ya just said?"

"I believe the last thing I said was, 'It's daunting, I have to admit,'" I recited. "Why?"

"No. Look at my memories, Dad."

When I saw myself through his eyes, and heard words coming out of my mouth that I didn't remember uttering, in a strangely accented voice I didn't recognize, I was stunned. I wondered if my two selves—Merlin and Myrddin Emrys—were separating, and other Merlins in an untold number of times and dimensions were somehow starting to overlap. But that theory didn't seem right. There was something I wasn't seeing…

Then, abruptly, I knew the truth. Since I was the original Merlin, all the others were but *reflections* of me, copies if you will, split off at the beginning of time to inhabit other dimensions, for a reason only the Creator knew. Perhaps events were transpiring to merge my various selves together again.

I surfaced from my musings and carefully tucked away the realization that I'd had. This shift in my perception could very well be happening in conjunction with my transition. As a fully manifested god, I would be connected in every way to the energy that powered the universe.

"Dad, why did you sound like someone else? I don't understand." Derek said.

"I barely understand it myself. I think one of my other selves, from a different timeline or dimension, somehow overlapped into this one just for a second. Needless to say, I'm going to need to meditate on it and figure out what to do."

"But, Dad, what—"

"Not now, Derek," I said sharply. I took a moment to remember that Derek was being affected as well. "Sorry. Let's get back to our original topic of conversation. Please, try to get along with Seth. I know that he is being difficult, but I honestly think he is happy to have found all of us. Apparently, he is being used by the Fae to create discord between us, perhaps as a diversion. Unfortunately, here is another instance where my connection to a family member blinds me to certain details of future events. And there *is* something momentous in the works, which explains why Morgana is here in Moab."

"But it doesn't make sense—how can she be here? Didn't she die back in the fifth century?"

"Yes, she did, in *our* reality, but this is a Morgana from another timeline in which she didn't die."

"How did she get here, though? And if someone brought her here, who was it, and for what purpose?"

"Those are all very good questions, Derek. Obviously, we have some work to do." Work we should have already started on weeks ago when she appeared out at Arches.

He wasn't satisfied by my response, but when I declined to say more, he finally relaxed and stood quietly by my side. In silent contemplation, we gazed across the valley, watching the heat waves shimmer across the landscape and hearing the low hum of hundreds of cars as visitors and residents drove through town. It was a typical hot, dry summer day in red rock country.

I turned back to my son, reluctant to bring up the next subject. "By the way, you mentioned when I first returned that you saw Ken out at Arches with Morgana and her group of wizards, and then he disappeared. You haven't said anything more about him."

Derek remained silent, staring blankly across the valley.

"You do realize he's dead?" I asked, gently.

He closed his eyes and sighed. "Yeah, I know. He came to me one night, in spirit form, but I was still hopin' I'd dreamed it. Shit." A tear welled and ran down his cheek.

I reached out and gripped his shoulder in silent sympathy.

"He said that 'she' killed him, but didn't say who it was. But since he appeared out at Tower Arch with Morgana and the wizards, it's clear who he meant."

"I think she killed him deliberately to cause just this reaction. But she's not the brains behind this whole bloody scenario."

Derek cut his eyes at me in surprise. "Then who is?"

"Satan."

CHAPTER 41

Moab, July 28, 2018, Late Afternoon

"ARE YOU KIDDING ME? GRANDPA actually said that?" Morry whistled through his teeth and starting pacing back and forth across his small living room. "And what's his plan to deal with Morgana—and Satan?"

Derek shrugged. "He didn't say. He just got that look on his face we all get when we're listenin' to someone telepathically, and then he disappeared. He must've been communicatin' with Emily." He leaned back in the chair and folded his arms over his chest, engrossed in his thoughts.

"Dad, I wouldn't try to second-guess him, if I were you, especially since he obviously knows more about it than we do." Morry wandered restlessly over to the window and watched a car drive by the house. He turned to Derek speculatively.

"Hey, feel like getting a beer? We just went out yesterday, but what the hell."

"Sure, why not? I'll just let Sarah know I won't be home for a few more hours." He pulled the phone out of his pocket and sent her a text message.

"What's it like, having a wife at home, someone to share things with, especially one who also has magic?"

Derek looked up at Morry and smiled contentedly. "It's better than I ever dreamed it would be. We really love each other, but it's way more than that. We're partners and friends, too. It's great bein' married to her."

"That's wonderful, Dad. I'm happy for you," Morry said softly. "You know, at first, I hated you for taking Sarah from me. But I finally realized that she was never mine, other than as a friend. She was always meant to be with you. So, I'm still waiting for someone to come along…" He paused introspectively. "I'm getting worried, though, that it's not going to happen for me. I've been dating—and sleeping with—a lot of different women off and on for years, and frankly, it gets old after a while."

"What does Merlin say? Have ya discussed it with him?"

"Well, yes, several times, and he just grins knowingly and tells me to be patient."

"Yep, that's my dad. Just trust him, okay? He never lies." *Unless it suits his purpose,* Derek thought, as he remembered how Merlin had lied to him repeatedly about his identity in the first few months he had known him.

CHAPTER 42

Moab, August 4, 2018, Early Morning

I WOKE UP WITH A start and felt the powerful presence of another god standing next to the bed.

What are you doing here?

It's time, Myrddin Emrys. There is a great disturbance in the Force.

I glanced over at my sleeping wife, and not wanting to wake her, teleported directly into the kitchen, clothing myself in jeans and a gray T-shirt as I rematerialized. Llyr was already leaning nonchalantly against the counter, mimicking my style of dress, although his shirt had Obi-Wan Kenobi on the front.

"You've been watching Star Wars again."

Llyr looked inscrutable and didn't answer.

"It really wasn't necessary to show up before dawn, in my bedroom." I glanced at him as I filled the carafe with water, poured it in the coffee maker, and scooped coffee into the filter. I flipped the switch and raised one eyebrow.

Llyr just shrugged.

"Alright, what's going on? Did God send you?"

"Yes and no. I took it upon myself to deliver the message in person."

"Now? You couldn't have waited a few more hours?"

"No, and the hour is irrelevant. Furthermore, you're so close to transitioning that you don't really need to sleep anymore. And you know it." Llyr turned and watched me shrewdly as I walked over to the cupboard and chose a coffee mug. I didn't offer him coffee because he normally turned it down.

"Myrddin Emrys, Satan has escalated his plans and God is… concerned. Time to get your family and friends headed down the paths they are destined to travel."

I folded my arms across my chest and frowned. I thought back to the last week and realized that I hadn't seen this coming. What was happening with my god powers? When I had returned to Moab from Wales my knowledge of past, present and future had been overwhelming me, and I had started to compartmentalize that knowledge to keep my sanity. But since then, there had been periods of time when my awareness of various close family members had been, as Emily put it, "on the fritz."

A week ago, after our group breakfast, Derek and I had met on the Rim to talk privately. I had experienced a brief blackout when one of my clones from another timeline had attempted to merge with my consciousness. I had then departed abruptly when Emily summoned me to discuss Rae's prophetic dream about Jack being Satan.

I now realized that I didn't remember anything about that discussion, except that it had happened. Since then, I had been caught up in business matters at The Moab Herbalist.

"Now do you understand, Son?"

I sighed impatiently. "Llyr, it's just the two of us standing here, so there's no need to keep up the pretense."

"I thought you liked the fact that I impregnated your mother."

"You didn't impregnate her. You were there only in her dreams, my friend, using the face and form God wanted her to see. I implanted myself in her womb."

Llyr chuckled. "I wasn't sure if you had remembered that yet."

"Yes. I regained several key memories as I was showering last night."

We eyed each other solemnly for a few moments and then we both laughed and allowed our physical forms to dissolve into pure energy. We merged into a dazzling globe of Light that swirled, danced and sang, then separated again into our two human forms.

Just like old times, Bro. Now, get to work, chop, chop.

As Llyr disappeared from the kitchen, I shook my head in exasperation, and poured myself a large coffee, liberally adding cream and sugar. I lifted the mug to my lips, tasted the creamy sweetness and frowned. One of my clones had snuck through for a few seconds. I dumped the coffee in the sink, rinsed the cup and poured another, black.

I took a careful sip, found it acceptable and thought about the revelation I had experienced the previous night.

I had just turned the water off and picked up a towel when the real truth about my human life slammed into my consciousness. The elaborate story of my conception that I had narrated the night we banished the evil from Mordred's body was just that—a story. For a moment, I had been taken aback. Then I'd had a good laugh.

As I finished my coffee, I contemplated the immediate future. The tasks I still had to accomplish in this realm were legion. Llyr was correct—I had work to do. For one thing, it was time for my grandson to meet his mate and for me to gain a new devotee.

CHAPTER 43

Moab, August 4, 2018, Late Afternoon

IT WAS A HOT, CLEAR day, the sky a color that Lainie had always loved and that many residents of Moab called "Utah Blue." But this particular afternoon, she was oblivious to the weather, so completely was she mired in her thoughts.

I can't believe it! The bastard—how could he do this to me? she fumed silently. She was a thirty-six-year-old, twice-divorced woman who had recently been involved in a brief affair with a married man. She'd known it wasn't the smartest thing to do, but she'd done it anyway.

The angry diatribe in her head soon turned into an internal accusation. *Oh, God, it's all my fault, I should never have said the "L" word so soon. Idiot!* She'd been warned long ago by a therapist not to engage in such destructive self-talk, but since it seemed to be the unvarnished truth, she figured her self-castigation was valid.

Lainie had planned on doing some window shopping, maybe even some purchasing if she found something she really wanted, so she was strolling, lost in thought, along the sidewalk on the west side of Main Street, across from the bank and a T-shirt store. Unfortunately, all those thoughts and emotions racing through her at the speed of light had distracted her, so she never noticed that someone had stepped through the doorway of one of the shops, right in front of her, until she collided with him. One minute she was minding her own business, cussing herself out thoroughly for yet another failed relationship, when she slammed into a warm, solid male body.

"Oof," popped inelegantly from between her lips, which hadn't seen a tube of lipstick for over a week, ever since her lover had called it quits. She was also aware that she hadn't washed her hair that morning.

"Whoa, watch it!" A masculine voice sounded not far from her eye level. At five feet ten, Lainie was a tall woman, but the man she had just run into was at least a six-footer. He grabbed her arms to steady her, which set her back from him just enough to allow her to take in his features. She stared at his chin, which was lightly dusted with a hint of brown stubble, then noticed the sensuous lips twisted into a smirk. When her gaze made contact with his eyes, which were silver-gray flecked with blue, green and brown, her breath caught. She'd never seen such unusual eyes, slanted, with a feral quality to them, and he was currently looking at her curiously, waiting for her to speak.

"Uh, s-sorry, I wasn't watching where I was g-going." Lainie stammered. *You complete idiot! Here you run into a hot man with gorgeous eyes and you start stammering. Seriously?* She blushed hotly, utterly embarrassed.

Morry dropped his hands and stepped back from the woman who had collided with him as he'd stepped out of The Moab Herbalist. "No problem, just look where you're going, okay?" Having uttered that sage advice he started to walk away, but then paused and turned back to her. "I think you're being too hard on yourself. I don't think you're a complete idiot. Just distracted, that's all."

He gazed into her eyes for a moment. "So, you think I'm hot, huh?"

At her surprised look he winked, then strode quickly up the sidewalk to the intersection with Center Street, where he crossed against the light in complete disregard for traffic. Distracted, Morry continued east past the bank and entered the front door of the newspaper office, intending to finish the article he'd started before he left work the day before. But all he could think about was the woman with the violet eyes, and the fact that his hands still tingled with the magic that had arced between them.

He wouldn't put it past Merlin to have set up this whole scenario, since the reason his grandfather had asked him to stop by the shop was pretty flimsy. Merlin said he wanted to invite him to a reading next week, but he could have extended that invitation telepathically, or by phone or text message.

Morry shook his head and his lips curved up in a wry smile. Yeah, it was definitely a setup.

As the man disappeared from view, Lainie stared after him with her mouth hanging open. Holy crap, he'd heard her thoughts! What a way to take her mind off of her problems. Of course, she could be imagining things. He was young, perhaps ten years younger than she was, and extremely attractive. He had a nice body: slender, yet muscular, with wide shoulders and a fine ass, straight brown hair cut conservatively, slightly crooked but sparkling white teeth, and oh, God, those eyes….

Although such a chance encounter shouldn't have made that much of an impression on her, it did, and not just because of his eyes and the fact that he might have read her mind, but because long after he'd let go of her upper arms, the skin tingled as if his hands were still there. And that deep voice echoed hauntingly in her mind.

"Excuse me, young lady, are you ill? May I assist you in some way?" An elderly male voice interrupted her thoughts, and she realized that she had been standing in a daze, blocking the flow of foot traffic for who knows how long while she indulged in a nearly sexual fantasy.

"No, no, I'm fine. Gosh, I'm so sorry." She leaped back against the plate glass window of the storefront, effectively relieving the bottleneck on the sidewalk and allowing the shoppers to proceed.

The old gentleman who had inquired about her well-being gave her a nod and his green eyes twinkled. "Why don't you take a look in this shop? You might find a nice potion to relax you, or perhaps something that will relieve that tingling sensation in your arms." He winked at her and shuffled off.

With a slight frown, she watched him go. *Who the hell was that*? He seemed vaguely familiar but she knew she'd never met him before. His suggestion was a good one, however, so she decided to check out The Moab Herbalist since she was right outside the shop. She grabbed the handle and opened the door, which activated a tinkling bell meant to alert the proprietor when a customer entered his domain. As soon as she stepped inside, Lainie felt surrounded by a welcoming sensation of warmth that had nothing to do with the air temperature in the room. It was a cozy shop, and the scents of the herbs and spices, as well as something incredibly enticing that she couldn't identify, caused her to stop in the middle of the polished oak floor and inhale sharply. *Good God, what was that scent?*

She blinked, and became conscious of the fact that everyone in the small shop, staff and clientele alike, had stopped what they were doing and were staring at her curiously. She stared back, wondering what in the world had possessed her to come in here. She'd never purchased an herbal potion in her life.

Then, a tall, handsome man in his early thirties, whom she guessed was the owner, approached her. He was dressed in typical Moab style, jeans and a T-shirt, but there was something so uniquely different about him that she couldn't put her finger on it. He was slender, with wide shoulders, and he moved with the grace of a big cat. He had long, glossy black hair and the greenest eyes she'd ever seen. He was magnificent.

"Hello, I'm Michael. Can I help you find something?" His lightly accented baritone voice was melodic and…well, it sounded like heaven. *What the heck?* She found herself gazing longingly into those captivating eyes, and she realized at the same time that the mesmerizing scent was actually emanating from the man. He calmly returned her gaze and she felt like she could lose herself forever in those startling depths.

Then, she did something unexpected and totally foreign to her temperament, religion and lifestyle: she got down on her knees in front of him and placed her forehead on his sandaled feet. Part of her was freaking out, thinking that she had finally lost her mind, but in her heart and soul, she knew this was where she belonged. She had come home.

Lainie felt as if she was under the influence of a potent hallucinatory drug when she heard the man whose feet she was kissing (*what the fuck?*) say in a kind, amused voice, "Em, I think we have another one." And then she lost consciousness altogether.

I smiled as I watched the tall woman enter my shop. I was already aware of her identity and I knew why she had come here. I therefore wasn't surprised when she gazed yearningly into my eyes and sank to her knees, gently kissing my feet and laying her head on them with a sigh. I knew that her inner being had recognized my true nature, my god self. This was the first time that a total stranger had offered me her devotion, but it would not be the last.

Through the bond I had with my grandson, I had experienced the encounter the two young people had had on the sidewalk a few minutes ago, and I had felt the tingle of magic when Morry gripped her upper arms to keep from knocking her over. Although she had decent magical potential, she had blocked her powers for so long that it was uncertain whether she could access them without some training. She thought of herself as a witch, a freak of nature, and therefore would need some help with her self-image as well.

Rae, who had been on the phone and had not seen the woman enter, turned to Emily.

"I told the person who just called that lavender, peppermint, comfrey and mustard seed are all useful herbs for tinctures and compresses. Is that correct?"

"Yes, that's fine, Mom. And lavender is also good for purification," Emily responded to her automatically, her attention on the woman at my feet.

Then she remembered the customers who were watching the proceedings with avid curiosity. She quickly uttered a forgetting spell and then ushered them swiftly out of the shop, locking the door behind them. She flipped the sign on the door around to "Closed," lowered the blinds in the front window, and then turned to me.

"Do you know who she is, magic man?" Em stepped beside the still form of the kneeling woman, and then knelt down to smooth the unruly mop of natural blond curls back from her face in an effort to see her features. The woman was lovely, with a sculpted nose, sensuous lips and clear skin, and for just a moment, I could sense that Emily was experiencing a faint twinge of jealousy, which she swiftly banished. I was proud of her, especially since she'd made such a valiant effort recently to subdue that poisonous emotion after I had informed her of my unintentional infidelity.

"Yes, but I've never met her. She has an intriguing magical background and will make an appropriate mate for Morry."

"I'm sure Morry will be pleased. She's gorgeous." Em eyed me thoughtfully. "She recognized you as a god."

"Yes."

Em stood up and looked searchingly into my eyes. "It has started, hasn't it? You set this up."

I smiled. "You heard me talking to Llyr this morning."

She nodded.

I thought it prudent to switch to telepathic communication at this point, since I didn't want anyone but Em to be privy to the information I was about to impart. *So now you know that Llyr isn't really my father, he's my brother. God is my father.*

She seemed surprised by my sudden use of our private mental wavelength but responded the same way. *I don't understand. You've* always *said that the gods were more or less the children of the Creator.*

That's true, but I actually am a son of God.

Her eyes widened. *What? So you're...an angel?*

I shrugged. *I suppose you could say that. I've just always considered myself a god, not an angel.*

Em looked shocked as another thought occurred to her. *So...if you're literally a son of God, does that mean* Jesus *is your brother?*

It was the one thing I was never supposed to reveal, to anyone, ever. I paused to consider what response would result in the least amount of damage. *Well, yes, but please don't mention it to anyone else.*

My lips are sealed. Besides, who would believe me?

We smiled conspiratorially at each other. I knew that I could trust Em with that sensitive information.

I roused myself. Time to get back to the matter at hand.

As I looked down upon my newest devotee, I sensed that despite her heart's acceptance, her unconscious mind was already in a state of denial, so I decided to block her memories of this moment until she'd had some time with Morry. My grandson had a habit of over-sharing information about his heritage, so I'd let him give her some of my background during their time together in the near future. I chuckled as I imagined her reaction. He would even find a way to help her reconnect to her magic. And they would establish a bond, as I knew they would.

Lainie shook her head and blinked a couple of times, feeling as if she'd been in a trance. She looked around and realized that she was standing on the sidewalk outside the herb shop with her purchases in hand, but she didn't remember what had transpired since she entered the store. She frowned and opened the bag to see exactly what items she'd purchased. She normally wasn't this absentminded. Maybe she needed to go back inside and get an herbal potion for her memory. She checked her watch and noted with dismay that it was already five forty-five, and she still had chores to do before she was done for the day, so she decided to pass on the memory potion. She sighed and headed for her car.

That night, Lainie slept soundly and didn't remember her dreams. She woke up the next morning refreshed and alert, her strange experience the day before relegated to the recesses of her mind. It was Sunday, and she had plans to have lunch with her mother. She cleaned the house as usual and got her laundry done, all the while feeling that she had forgotten something vital. She had a pleasant visit with her mom and thoroughly enjoyed the food and the ambiance at the new Mediterranean restaurant at the north end of town.

Hours later, Lainie hummed as she got ready for bed, and realized that she hadn't thought about her ex-boyfriend all day. She was relieved that she had gotten over the affair so quickly and resolved never to date a married man again. As she slipped under the covers and then rested her head on her down pillow, she felt happy for the first time in weeks.

When she drifted off to sleep, her last coherent thought was that she was ready to find someone new.

She was lying naked in a grassy meadow, on a soft quilt under a bright, warm sun, a light breeze stirring her riotous curls with its gentle touch.

Stretching luxuriously, she turned to her companion and smiled. He smiled back, then leaned forward and kissed her slowly, deliberately, his soft, sensuous lips and tongue making sweet love to her. He traced the curve of her cheek, then starting at her neck, he stroked her with his large palms, fondling and teasing her generous breasts. She closed her eyes and gasped with pleasure as she felt her nipples harden, and a wave of heat raced through her. He continued to work his way down her body, across the slight roundness of her abdomen until he reached the golden curls at the apex of her thighs. He parted her intimate folds, found her to be moist and ready for him, and gently pushed two fingers inside her.

"Look at me, Lainie," he whispered. She opened her eyes slowly, gazing into beautiful slanted eyes that were surrounded by long dark lashes, and felt a jolt of love so potent that she could hardly contain it.

She sighed rapturously and opened herself to him, pulling his naked body down on top of her. She felt his weight settle onto her, and her breath caught as he started to enter her. She arched her back and grabbed his magnificent ass, wanting him to bury his substantial erection as far into her body as possible.

He kissed her again, pushing slowly inside her. She met his thrust, enjoying the complete surrender to his possession. Then he withdrew, turned her over and pulled her up onto her knees. He draped himself over her backside, nudged her legs further apart, and eased his thick cock into her heat again. As he began rocking in and out, he picked up the pace until he was taking her almost inhumanly fast, as a canine might service a bitch in heat.

Lainie panted as the pace increased and realized that it was not a man penetrating her. It was a large gray and brown wolf. And she herself was no longer human. She was also a wolf, with white fur and a tail that was thrown up over her back as the male impaled her until he ejaculated, triggering her orgasm. She heard herself howl in satisfaction. She knew she was now officially mated to this male, for life, and that he had just impregnated her.

A buzzing sound intruded and she automatically reached out to silence it. Lainie surfaced from her dream drenched in perspiration and breathing hard, with a distinct ache between her legs, and the sensation of just having had the best sex of her life with a man who could turn into a wolf. Holy cow, that was very cool, but do wolves actually have orgasms? It was an interesting thing to ponder as she got ready for work. She grinned as she threw back the covers and stretched, trying to remember whom she had met recently with eyes that shape and color. She sat up, preparing to get out of bed, and then paused as she recalled exactly who it was.

She had dreamed about the cute young guy with the brown hair and the exceptionally fine ass that she had bumped into on Saturday. And she had dreamed he was a werewolf and she was mated to him. That was intense, but for some reason, strange as it seemed, it felt right.

As she headed for the shower, Lainie felt optimistic about her life for the first time in years.

CHAPTER 44

Moab, August 6, 2018

MORRY STARED UNSEEING AT THE ceiling of his small bedroom, his heart pounding and his cock in his hand. He'd had the most realistic dream he'd ever experienced and had ejaculated all over the sheets. He was no stranger to wet dreams, having been a virgin before coming to Moab, but this was different. It had felt real, being buried in her to the hilt in his wolf form, knowing that the wolf with the violet-colored eyes was his mate, and that he had impregnated her. Damn.

His alarm clock went off, and the dream was all but forgotten as the reality of workday rituals intruded. He leaped out of bed, pulled the sheets off to wash later, and then headed for the bathroom, hoping his roommate wasn't in there. Since they worked the same schedule at the newspaper, they usually vied for the shower every morning. This time it seemed he'd lucked out. Jim had already finished and had returned to his room to get dressed.

Morry really didn't want Jim to see him naked this morning in his semi-aroused state, and he didn't own a robe. While he was reasonably sure that his friend and roommate wasn't gay, he still felt kind of funny about walking around bare-assed. Jim always seemed disturbed by Morry's nudity when he watched him shift into wolf form, perhaps because he had been his great-aunt Guinevere in his past life.

Morry still couldn't relate to the fact that he himself been born in the Dark Ages. His father and his grandfather had been hurled back in time to the fifth century by an unknown force, taking refuge in Merlin's old quarters in Camelot. Derek's half sister Adrestia had seduced him by enchantment and Mordred had been conceived, an unwitting pawn in a plan to destroy everything Merlin had worked towards in the twenty-first century. During their sojourn in Camelot, Merlin had remembered that Derek's mother Cara was King Arthur's illegitimate half sister, and therefore Morry was Arthur's grand-nephew.

Knowing that he shared a house with King Arthur's wife in her present incarnation as a man sometimes seemed way too bizarre. He and Jim had discussed their connection numerous times, but had finally let the subject drop.

He breathed a sigh of relief as he climbed into the narrow tub shower and turned the water on. As the spray of warm water erupted from the showerhead and cascaded over his scalp and down his torso, he grabbed the bar of herbal soap and lathered up, thankful that the layer of fat was gone from his body, courtesy of the magic involved in shapeshifting.

As he rinsed off, he thought about the blond woman in his dreams and remembered where he had seen those violet eyes before. It was the sexy goofball who had walked right into him in front of his grandfather's shop yesterday. She had thought he was hot, which was good to know, even if he shouldn't have been tuning in to her mind in the first place. And then he'd made matters worse by letting her know he'd heard her thoughts. He'd been unashamedly flirting with her. She was a good ten years his senior, but that didn't matter to him. She was an alluring woman, and tall as well, which was a real turn-on. He was definitely attracted to her, even if she was kind of ditzy. His cock jerked and his breath caught as he remembered having sex with her in his dream. But did he honestly think she could be his future mate? His life partner? Seriously? She *did* have magic. That was an absolute must for him. Of course, just because she had magic didn't make her immortal. And he didn't want to think about that right now.

He had stepped out of the shower and dried off when all of a sudden, he knew he had to find her. He decided to ask Jim if he knew any tall, blond, curly-haired, violet-eyed goofballs in town. He smiled, deciding he'd better get out of the habit of calling her that, just in case he found her and they hooked up.

He dressed quickly but carefully in a white long-sleeved button down shirt tucked neatly into a pair of tan chinos, then tied the laces of a pair of lightweight hikers he'd just bought. He didn't like going in to work looking like a slob, particularly if there was the slightest chance he'd run into *her* today. When he'd slimmed down, he'd had to buy a whole new wardrobe. Twenty pounds was a considerable amount of bulk to lose, and the old stuff had been way too baggy. Not that he was complaining. Since his transformation in 2014, he'd gone on more dates than he could count. He no longer had to wear glasses, and when women got a look at his eyes, and his tall slender body, they tended to pursue him.

His thoughts went off on that tangent. Only a few of the women he'd gone out with had let him do more than kiss, but the ones that he'd actually had sex with had been smoking hot. Like Chris, his father's ex-wife. That connection could actually have developed into a relationship, but Chris had backed out before it had gotten too far.

Morry shook his head in disbelief as he remembered all of those past encounters. The women had happily shared their bodies with him and many of them wanted more. But he'd deliberately steered clear of women who were looking for something permanent. He enjoyed being single.

He remembered the time Derek had insisted on having what he called "The Talk."

"This is serious, Morry, so listen up," Derek had said as he looked intently into his son's eyes. "As soon as Merlin released your powers, your life changed, permanently. You'll never again be that person who felt unworthy and ashamed of his background. You're an immortal demigod, so your love life won't be the same as if you were human. You have to realize that if you decide on a long-term relationship with a mortal woman, it'll most likely end in heartache, 'cause she'll age and you won't."

Morry remembered how he'd felt at the time. "I guess I didn't realize what it really meant to be immortal."

"You're Merlin's grandson on both sides, so how could you be anythin' but a magical immortal bein'?" Derek thought for a moment, and then continued. "All I'm sayin' is, have fun, but don't be in a hurry to get serious with anyone, okay?"

"Okay, Dad."

"Oh, and by the way, I'm damn proud of ya, Son."

They had grinned at each other and merged their minds, enjoying their remarkable relationship. It wasn't until they had initially Seen each other that their present bond had taken root. Now they were so close, neither could imagine life without the other.

But his attitude about being single changed in June, when he'd witnessed Merlin and Emily's reunion after four years of being apart. The outpouring of their love for each other had made Morry realize that he wanted to find someone to love, someone with whom he could share his immortal existence.

Emerging from the deep well of his thoughts, Morry glanced at the clock on the bedside table and realized that he'd better get moving. He made a quick breakfast of cold cereal, then after brushing his teeth, he headed to work. Since the newspaper office was only three blocks away, he usually walked. He owned a vehicle, but why waste the fuel?

He still planned on asking Jim about the blond, but that would have to wait until he got to work. His roommate had apparently left for the office while Morry was in the shower. He wasn't aware of any special deadlines, so he was curious why Jim would take off without at least wishing him "good morning." Well, he'd find out soon enough.

God, she really needed to find that guy, Lainie thought longingly as she dressed for work. She knew exactly what she wanted to do to him, and that was to jump his bones, preferably today. But whether he'd be willing was another story. Some men were all too conscious of a ten-year age difference, but on top of that, she knew the fact that she was a witch, albeit a nonpracticing one, could be a deal-breaker. It had been so long since she'd cast a spell, or used her erratic powers at all, that she wasn't even sure she could access them anymore. She'd never felt comfortable with that part of her life, and usually kept it well hidden.

Lainie glanced at her watch as she drove south on 4th East to the intersection with Highway 191, then turned left at the traffic light by the Maverick gas station. Her initial optimism flagged as she realized she was running late and she didn't want to get fired.

She exceeded the speed limit as she raced out of town on 191 for several miles, and then turned left onto Resource Boulevard, taking the ninety-degree turns faster than safety dictated.

She finally pulled into the gravel driveway leading to the Call Center. She parked, grabbed her purse, and ran into the office, knowing that the next few hours would be so busy she wouldn't be able to think straight. She'd have to contemplate her next steps to find the brown-haired hottie at lunch time.

CHAPTER 45

Moab, Monday, August 6, 2018

"WHAT'S GOING ON, MORRY?" JIM asked as he poured two cups of coffee in the break room around ten o'clock. His roommate had come to work this morning acting as if he had a lot on his mind, and had gotten more and more antsy as time went by. Jim had kept an eye on him, wondering what the hell the kid's problem was. He'd left for work early this morning just to give Morry some space, which obviously hadn't helped.

Morry took a swallow of coffee before he spoke. "I ran into someone Saturday when I was leaving the herb shop, and I almost knocked her down. I think that she…" he paused to glance stealthily around the room to make sure no one was listening, before he continued quietly, "…has magic. I've never felt that kind of tingling before, except when I touch, you know, my family."

Jim knew exactly what his friend meant, even though he himself had no magical abilities. He'd heard Derek describe the tingling sensation he'd felt when he first touched Sarah.

As for the magic itself, he had several times observed Morry transform into an animal. It was extremely disconcerting to see the younger man's feet and hands turn into paws, his legs and arms change shape and his body become covered with fur. The first time he'd changed back from wolf to human, Morry confessed that even though he could become any animal, he seemed to resonate with wolves the most. Jim couldn't begin to imagine what it was like to change form at all, let alone to transform into a large, hairy predator.

Morry ran as a wolf several nights a week, and Jim always spent the entire time his friend was gone praying that he wouldn't be seen, or if he was, that someone would think he was just a big dog, like a Malamute, or a Husky. The one time he'd taken Morry, in wolf form, out to run at Sand Flats it hadn't worked out too well, since Morry's wolf was considerably larger than most domestic canines. A hiker had threatened to call the sheriff and report Jim for keeping a wolf as a pet. Fortunately, Morry had been able to transform back into his human shape and place a forgetting spell on the man and his friends.

And Jim was always afraid someone would find out about Morry's supernatural abilities and think he was a werewolf. Since sorcerers, dragons, vampires, ghosts and shapeshifters existed, werewolves probably existed as well. And *he* had been the Queen of Camelot, so anything was possible.

With an effort, Jim dragged his thoughts back to the present and cleared his throat. "So, you want to go out with her, or what?"

"I, uh, dreamed about her last night, and uh, well…" Morry said, clumsily.

"And?" Jim put his cup down and crossed his arms, waiting for an explanation.

Morry looked around again, not wanting anyone to hear what he was going to say next. "We were both wolves, and we…*mated.* It felt so real that when I woke up, I, uh…needless to say, I'll have to change the sheets when I get home."

Jim chuckled. "Oh, that kind of dream." He correctly interpreted the source of Morry's unease and decided to be frank with him.

"Look, I'm not your great-aunt Guinevere any more, so there's no need to tip-toe around about a morning hard-on or a wet dream. And just because you've never seen me with a woman doesn't mean I'm gay." *I hope*, he thought. "Even if I was, you think gay guys don't need to jerk off occasionally?"

"Okay, man, that's just way too much information!" Morry's face was flaming red. "Break's over and I'm going back to my desk. Talk to you later." He stalked out of the break room, coffee cup still in hand, and headed to his cubicle.

Jim grinned wryly. He used to love to get the kid flustered; in fact, he was often cruel about it. But now, he could only go so far before Guinevere's innate kindness and compassion surfaced in his being and rained on his parade. Or his growing emotional attachment to Morry wouldn't allow him to hurt the younger man's feelings. Besides, most of Morry's former moodiness and belligerent attitude had evaporated once his transformation had removed the evil from his cells, so he didn't react in quite the same way that he used to. And Jim had to admit, albeit reluctantly, that was a good thing.

He rinsed out his coffee cup and put it in the rack to dry, then returned to his desk. It was aggravating that he didn't even have his own office, despite his more than ten years in the newspaper business.

Jim shrugged it off. *At least I have a job.* He sat down to peruse his next assignment, but his mind kept drifting to the irrefutable fact that he finally had a higher purpose, to help Merlin and his family bring King Arthur back. He could focus on that.

Though he wasn't sure what would happen once the king was resurrected. For some time now, he found himself yearning with every breath to be reunited with Arthur Pendragon. He knew that it was mostly his soul's and not his body's desire, since he was—at least physically—a heterosexual man in this life. He was no longer the famous ruler's wife. He was just a single male in his late thirties in twenty-first-century Utah. Except there were those erotic dreams he had about Arthur, who had been a very passionate man. And most embarrassing of all, the way he felt when he saw Morry unclothed. He shook his head to dispel those exceedingly inappropriate thoughts, and tried to concentrate on his work.

He glanced down as a message popped up in the lower right corner of his monitor screen. Morry asked if he knew any women in town with blond, curly, shoulder-length hair, violet eyes, about five ten in height. Jim chuckled. His friend was hooked.

He replied in a flurry of clacking keys that he did indeed know her. She was an acquaintance of his, and her name was Elaine Ogilvie, nicknamed "Lainie."

Morry replied a few seconds later, thanking him for the info. Jim figured that it was Merlin who'd arranged their meeting, so it was obviously meant to be. He'd suspected the first time he'd met Lainie that she might be a witch, so she'd be a good match for his roommate, even if she was a few years older. He was happy for them. At one time, he had thought about asking Lainie out, but he was so apprehensive about the difference in their heights that he had gotten drunk and ended up going home with Patty, the petite, young Goth girl in the office. Jim was her supervisor and way too old for her, but he'd slept with her anyway. Not the best decision he'd ever made, and the sex had been disappointing. She didn't really want him either. She was completely infatuated with Morry, who wasn't interested in her.

Jim's mind refused to focus on the work in front of him, instead returning to his sexual dilemma. He sighed and contemplated undergoing gender reassignment to satisfy his soul's destiny. He'd been thinking about it all morning and suspected that it was a good possibility. He glanced dispassionately at his crotch—ironically, it seemed that he'd been looking at it a lot lately—and thought about all the times he'd had an unsatisfying sexual encounter.

Ah, well, he'd never felt entirely at home in this male body anyway.

CHAPTER 46

Moab, August 6, 2018

LAINIE WATCHED THE TIME DISPLAYED on her computer until it finally showed twelve o'clock and she was able to leave for lunch. She turned her phone off and hung up her headset, then clocked out with a sigh of relief. She liked her job, but she was tired of the same old routine day in and day out.

Earlier, she had almost fainted with excitement when she remembered that she knew someone working for the newspaper, someone who undoubtedly was acquainted with the cute guy she had her eye on. Maybe if she went by there, ostensibly to see Jim, she might run into her dream man again. She started her blue, ten-year-old Ford Escape and drove as quickly as possible into town, pulling into the only open parking spot in front of the newspaper office.

All of a sudden, she felt anxious. Glancing around for the possible cause of her edginess, she realized that her purse was floating at dashboard level. She groaned. *No, not now! Fucking hell!* She had been perfectly happy without her abilities for years, and now they decided to show up?

Feeling a headache coming on, she was rubbing her forehead to ease the tension when she heard a tap at her window and sighed. *It's probably a cop wanting to give me a ticket for practicing witchcraft in a spell-free zone*, she thought sarcastically. She turned her head and gasped. It was the guy, the hottie, and she could see him eyeing her purse as it floated serenely above the passenger seat. *Oh, crap.*

He stood at her car door and waited until she pressed the button to lower the window. She looked up at him mutely, wondering what he would say. God, he really was good-looking. And then she realized that he was smiling at her and giving her a thumbs-up for the floating purse. What the hell?

He leaned in the open window and said in a deep, sexy voice, "Watch this." He made a slight hand gesture, and the purse slowly dropped back down to the seat and stayed there.

Lainie's eyes widened and then she grinned, her face radiant. "My God, I thought I was the only person in town with magic, although I should have gotten a clue when you heard my thoughts Saturday. I wondered if I was hallucinating."

"You weren't hallucinating." He held out his hand. "I'm Morry Colburn. Nice to meet you."

She smiled. "I'm Elaine Ogilvie, but most people call me Lainie." She reached for his hand. "Nice to meet you, too. Whoa!"

"Yeah, that's how I knew about your magic when I touched your arms yesterday." He held her hand securely in his and felt the tingling increase until they were both breathless, the sensation almost sexual.

"Oh my God," she gasped. She blinked, then looked up at him shyly and blurted out, "Did you happen to have an unusual dream last night?"

He looked startled. "Yes, did you?"

She looked relieved and nodded her head, remembering just what he had done to her in that dream and desperately wanting him to do it to her while she was awake.

He looked intently into her eyes, and then quickly looked away, and she could tell he was breathing hard. Then he leaned forward and whispered in her ear, "Me, too, Lainie," and she realized that he was answering her thoughts.

"Can you take this afternoon off?" he asked with a gleam in his eyes.

"I think so, what about you?" Her heart was pounding hard in anticipation.

Instead of answering, he got his phone out and made a call. "Jim, I'm taking the rest of the day off, okay? Make sure to knock when you get home, in case we're, I mean *I'm*, busy. Thanks, buddy, I owe you one." He grinned at her and raised his eyebrows questioningly.

She nodded. "I texted my supervisor that I'm staying home sick this afternoon, so I'm all set, too." She felt faint. She'd never been so brazen before. Holy hell, she was actually going to have sex with the guy this afternoon.

He winked. "Oh, yes, we most definitely are going to have sex." He walked around to the passenger door, made a slight gesture, and the lock disengaged. He got in the car, moving her purse so he wouldn't sit on it. Then he glanced at her, a hint of a smile on his lips. "Kind of nice not to have to hide the magic, isn't it?"

She nodded and backed the car out of the parking space, then drove west on Center Street, stopping at the traffic light at Main Street. She glanced at him wordlessly, waiting for directions.

"Just keep going straight to The Rio, then make that little jog onto the extension of Center Street, okay?"

As the light turned green, she accelerated with a jerk.

"Are you nervous?" He reached out and gently squeezed her shoulder.

"Yes," she squeaked, and cleared her throat. "Uh, what are you, anyway? I mean, I know you have magic, but what level? I'm a witch, but it's been a long time since I actually did anything with my powers."

He paused, considering his response. "Actually, I'm a sorcerer, but that's not all. There are other things that I am, and can do, and I'm not sure I should tell you everything until we know each other better."

She turned to stare at him, and then quickly returned her eyes to the road. *Christ, what am I getting myself into*, she asked herself, then hoped he hadn't heard her silent comment or sensed her fear.

Oh, shit, now she's afraid of me, he thought glumly. *How much power does a witch have anyway? Can't be much compared to a sorcerer. Is that why she's afraid?*

He pointed out his house, and she pulled up to the curb. They sat there for a few minutes, eyeing each other warily. Finally, she gathered her courage and said, "Let's go in. I feel this connection with you that doesn't make sense, but I really want to be with you."

"Then let's go do this, because I feel the same way." He got out of the car and walked around so he could open her door, then took her hand. She stood up next to him and he felt the attraction as their bodies touched briefly. They walked up to the door hand in hand and he unlocked it with a simple spell. As they entered the house, they rocketed into each other's arms, kissing and touching each other's bodies feverishly. Morry flicked his hand at the door and it closed and locked itself.

"Wow, that's handy," Lainie breathed, and then pulled his hips against her so that she could feel his hardness. She was only a couple of inches shorter than he was, and their bodies lined up as if they were made for each other.

He looked a little startled at her bold move, then groaned and steered her into his bedroom, where he remembered that he hadn't made up his bed after ripping the sodden sheets off that morning.

"Sorry about the bed," he murmured as he nuzzled her neck.

"No worries," she breathed, pulling out of his embrace to remove her shoes. Then she hurriedly unzipped her jeans and tugged them off along with her lacy black bikini panties. Her purple blouse and matching bra came off next. Finally, she stood naked in front of him, feeling a little uneasy, but very aroused. This man turned her on without even touching her.

Morry stood perfectly still for a moment, staring at her perfect form. Her breasts were large and full, her waist tiny and hips wide, and her oval face was smooth and unlined. He had never seen such a gorgeous woman. He inhaled with a groan and his body tightened with need. He swiftly removed his hikers, threw his clothes off and backed her up to the bed, gently pushing her down. He reached for a foil packet on the night table, opened it quickly, and rolled the condom onto his erection. He might want to have sex with her, desperately as a matter of fact, but he didn't want to be a father anytime soon. In their shared dream, he had mated with her and gotten her pregnant, but this was real life and he wasn't ready for that.

As she watched him cover himself, disappointment stirred as she realized that this wasn't going to be exactly like her dream, but she resolutely shook off that notion. She didn't want to be pregnant and "mated" to a stranger.

More than ready for him to take her, Lainie reached up and pulled Morry down on top of her. She gasped as she felt his weight settle onto her, and her breath caught as he slowly entered her. He was even bigger than she'd imagined and he felt incredible inside her, despite the lack of intimate foreplay.

He agreed with her, he thought, as he thrust even further into her body until he was buried to the hilt, just like in the dream. They both started moving, slowly at first, their bodies adjusting to each other. The sensation was exquisite. He stilled for a moment and took each of her nipples in turn into his mouth, and as he suckled, he looked up at her through a curtain of straight shiny hair.

Lainie had thought it was plain medium brown, but this close to him, she could see streaks of blond, red, black and gray alternating with his basic brown color. She had never seen anything like it.

She grabbed his ass and pulled him even deeper inside her.

Lainie moaned, more intensely aroused than she'd ever been before. He filled her perfectly, completely, his cock thick and long, and she felt like she was already on the verge of a massive orgasm. She had never felt so alive.

As she gazed into his eyes, she just had time to admire their exotic slant before he closed them and stiffened, and they both came.

After what felt like an eternity of pleasure, they finally pulled apart and collapsed, panting. They turned to smile giddily at each other, sharing their enjoyment. Then they reached out at the same time and caressed each other's bodies, skin slick with perspiration from their exertions.

"That was...*awesome*." Lainie laced her fingers through his and kissed his knuckles.

Morry agreed, but his natural reticence wouldn't let him do more than to nod and kiss her hand as well.

"I noticed that you won't look me in the eye for very long. Do you regret making love with me?"

"Hell, no!" Morry wasn't sure how much he should tell her, but she should be able to understand his motivation better than any of the other women with whom he'd had sex. "God, how do I say this? Because I'm a sorcerer, I can't look directly into your eyes for more than a few seconds, or it will activate what my grandfather calls the 'Seeing,' and I'm way too new at this to be able to navigate my way through your being with any amount of skill."

Lainie's eyes widened. "Navigate your way through my *being*? What does that mean, anyway? And who's your grandfather? Is he a sorcerer too?"

Morry frowned as he realized he'd once again spoken out loud without thinking of the consequences. But suddenly in his mind, he heard a well-known, accented voice say, *Go ahead and tell her about me, Mordred, it's alright.*

His lips twitched as he suppressed a grin. "You might say that he's the *original* sorcerer. His name is Merlin Ambrosius."

She stared at him in disbelief, and then scoffed, "As in *King Arthur* and Merlin? You're kidding me, right?"

He shook his head, realizing too late that he had opened a rather large can of worms, even if it was with his grandfather's permission. "No, I'm not kidding. In fact, I was born in Camelot in the fifth century, just like Merlin and my dad."

"No fucking way, that's impossible!"

"You and I have magical powers, and most people would think *that's* impossible," he said in a reasonable tone of voice. He turned on his back and stretched his hand out. As a baseball-sized orb of light appeared in his hand, Lainie gasped. She'd never been able to conjure anything so effortlessly.

Morry turned his head and looked intently into her violet eyes. "If you shared that dream with me, then you must remember the last part."

"You mean, when we were both *wolves*?" she whispered.

He nodded and tossed the ball of light back and forth from one hand to the other. "I'm a shapeshifter, and I'd be willing to bet that you are, too."

Lainie sat up and wrapped her arms around her knees. "I've never shifted into another form except in my dream, but I suppose it's possible. I've never wanted to use or explore my powers before. Uh, are you *really* a werewolf?" she asked hesitantly.

He frowned and clenched his fist, obliterating the light orb instantly. "What? No, I'm not a freaking werewolf, I'm a man. I can take the shape of *any* animal I choose, but I prefer my wolf form. I told you that I'm a sorcerer and a shapeshifter, but I'm also, uh, something else. I'm...." He swallowed nervously. "I'm not really human, I mean...uh..." Shit, now he was babbling, and the look on his lover's face was not reassuring.

"I don't understand," Lainie said in a low voice that quavered a little with uncertainty.

"Sorry, this is still fairly new to me. I'm an immortal demi-god," Morry said, worried about her reaction. He waited nervously, watching her face.

As she started giggling uncontrollably, he stared at her in startled disbelief and then scowled. "Well, I never expected that reaction. What the fuck?" He bounded up off the bed and hurriedly pulled his pants on. "Maybe you'd better leave, if you think I'm that hilarious. Shit, I practically bare my soul to you and you *laugh* at me!" He stood with his arms crossed defensively against his chest, which made the silky brown hair arrowing down towards his groin all the more evident beneath his partially zipped trousers.

Lainie hastily got up off the bed and touched his arm. She again felt the tingle of their magic interacting and was abruptly unsure of herself.

"Wait, Morry, are you serious? I thought you were messing with me. I'm so sorry. I didn't mean to hurt your feelings." She reached out and caressed his face, kissing his pursed lips as he continued to glower at her.

"Oh, come on, you have to admit that everything you just told me is mind-boggling. How can I just accept that you're Merlin's grandson? That you were born in the fifth century, in Camelot? And how do I know you can really do what we dreamed about? I mean, it's such a cliché: 'Man with magic powers turns into wolf.' Have you ever read Sharon Shinn's novels about shapeshifters? Or Sherrilyn Kenyon's Dark-Hunter and Were-Hunter books? They're fantasies!"

"Sorry, I'm new to that genre and haven't read them yet," he replied stiffly.

She sighed, then took his hand and pulled him down next to her on the edge of the bed.

He wouldn't look at her but held her hand tightly. She was beginning to wonder if she'd made a mistake. Maybe he was too young and inexperienced for the two of them to have a meaningful relationship.

And again, he responded to her thoughts. "Look, Lainie, I'm not a child, I'm twenty-six," Morry said forcefully. "That's plenty old enough for us to have a meaningful relationship. What are you, thirty-five? Thirty-six? Listen, Merlin is almost sixteen hundred years old and his wife is only thirty-three. My dad is also thirty-three years old, believe it or not, and his wife is my age. We're an unusual family and I'm lucky to be a part of it." Morry ran out of steam and breathed slowly in and out a couple of times, calming himself. He really wanted this woman in his life, despite the fact that she still didn't believe him.

Resolutely, he looked directly into her eyes and made a decision. "The only way you're going to believe me is if you See my inner being, my true self, my *soul*, and in turn I'll See yours. As I said, I'm not very experienced at it, but I'll try. Would you trust me to do that?"

Lainie was in a state of shock as the truth finally sunk in. His grandfather—Merlin the sorcerer!—was sixteen hundred years old, and his father was a mere seven years older than his son. And Morry had the ability to "See" inside her very soul. My God. She realized that she had one hand in his and the other one clenched so tightly that her fingernails were gouging holes in the palm of her hand.

She looked thoughtful. "You said your last name is Colburn. Is your father Derek Colburn, the ranger out at Arches National Park? I know who he is. And Merlin is his *father*?" Lainie's heart was pounding as she finally started putting the facts together.

Morry's patience failed him at that point. "Look at me, Lainie," he commanded. "See me, See inside my soul and let me See inside yours." The power in his voice was undeniable and mesmerizing.

She hesitated for a fraction of a second, and then felt compelled to turn her frightened gaze to his piercing gray eyes, and they Saw each other.

She felt his consciousness merge with hers as slickly and

intimately as their bodies had come together earlier. They explored each other's hopes and desires, memories and experiences, constantly diving deeper, until they passed beyond their current lives and into their past incarnations. It felt like they were traveling in time within their own beings. Finally, Morry was able to guide them, by trial and error, back to their conscious minds.

"That was unbelievable," Lainie said faintly, blinking as she realized she was still sitting on the bed in Morry's—*Mordred's*—bedroom. She saw him now from an entirely different perspective. She had seen glimpses of his mother and father (who were actually sister and brother) in an ancient village with the ramparts of a castle in the background, with his grandfather, Merlin—holy shit, it was Michael from The Moab Herbalist!

Morry smiled crookedly when he saw the dawning realization on her lovely face.

"Oh! I just remembered something. I went into the herb shop Saturday after we collided on the sidewalk, and Michael—your grandfather Merlin—smelled so good, that I, I, uh, kissed his *feet*."

"Join the club," Morry murmured as he recalled doing the same thing not so long ago.

Lainie gaped at him and he felt compelled to explain. "Merlin's a god, and you must have sensed it. He's the Welsh god of magic and healing, here on earth in human form, and no one but a devotee—or a future devotee—can detect that irresistible scent he gives off. Personally, I think it's the scent of divinity. And the main reason he's here is to resurrect King Arthur."

Lainie blinked. "What? How…?"

"I don't think he's figured that out yet."

Making a decision, Morry took his pants off and stood in front of her, in all his naked glory.

"I definitely admire the view, but can I ask what you're doing?" Lainie looked at him curiously.

He didn't answer but smiled at her mysteriously, closed his eyes and *changed*, faster than Lainie's senses could process it.

There before her stood a huge gray-brown wolf with her lover's slanted eyes and a very dog-like grin on his face.

"Oh, you're gorgeous," she breathed, reaching out to stroke his head. He licked her face in response and she giggled. "Morry, this is weird."

So, join me, she heard in her mind.

"I have no idea how to do that," she said, feeling close to panic.

Just close your eyes, connect to the magic inside you, and picture what you want to become. Then make it happen. You have magic. Use it.

She stood up next to the large animal that was Morry, and called upon powers she had ignored for too long. She wanted to be a wolf, to be with her lover in wolf form. She desired it with every fiber of her being.

Suddenly, she felt as if the earth moved and she opened her eyes. She was down on the floor on the same level as the male wolf, and he was sniffing her muzzle. She rolled over submissively as she acknowledged that he was the alpha animal. He nudged her to get up, and when she obeyed, he mounted her, his front legs gripping her tightly. Without thought, she responded as nature intended and swung her plumy tail aside to give him access. He entered her, thrusting deeply and repeatedly as he claimed her for his own. And she found out that a wolf, or to be more accurate, a shapeshifter in wolf form, could indeed have an orgasm. She howled her pleasure, and felt as if she soared to the stars and beyond.

A short time later, they regained consciousness on the floor of the bedroom, back in human form, with him still inside her as he clutched her against him. Morry opened his eyes and realized that he had done what he had sworn he wouldn't do—he had taken her for his mate in wolf form, which was tantamount to marrying her. *Oh, shit*, he thought as he rested his forehead against her back. *What have I done?*

Lainie stirred, blinking as she gradually came back to her human thoughts. She felt Morry still inside her, sans condom, as they lay sprawled inelegantly on the bedroom floor. And she recalled what they had done and how absolutely amazing it had felt. But then she remembered what it meant, at least according to the dream she'd had, and she moaned, covering her eyes with her hands.

"Are you okay? Did I hurt you?" Morry asked, concerned and feeling guilty. He pulled out of her and helped her up off the floor. They stood close, facing each other, and Morry knew, without a doubt, that in the eyes of the gods they were now mated for life.

He swallowed hard as he looked into her troubled eyes. "I don't know how to tell you this, but what we did, as wolves, bound us together. We became mates. I'm so sorry, Lainie. I didn't even give you any choice in the matter; I just took you."

The reality of the situation slammed into her, dislodging the romantic nature of the dream. She had submissively allowed a male to mate with her, and if the look on his face was any indication, Morry apparently understood the significance of their actions.

She looked up into his exotic, slanted eyes and saw that they were shaped just like his grandfather's. She had just mated with someone who wasn't totally human, someone who was immortal, the grandson of a god.

She paled. "Does this mean we're married? We hardly even know each other." But as soon as she said that, she knew that wasn't true. She did know him, better than anyone, having Seen his soul and experienced their many shared past lives.

Morry nodded. "Yes, it does. But we'll also need to get married in the regular way, though, to be official in this realm."

"Realm? You really are from another century."

"I may have been born in the past, but I grew up here, as an orphan. I didn't know about my magic or my family until four years ago. It was miserable, to be honest, but I really was raised in the present time."

Lainie swallowed hard, feeling as if she had a huge lump in her throat. "Uh, Morry, I'm really not ready to be married to you. Can we just be engaged for awhile? This feels so unreal, and I'm overwhelmed."

He frowned slightly. He knew what he'd Seen and felt in her soul. They had been together in the past, many times, and although it sounded trite, they really were soul mates. They were bound together by the gods through a dozen lifetimes, yet she denied the truth because of her fear of commitment.

Morry reached out and caressed her dear, familiar face, his frown smoothing out as he let go of his irritation. He remembered that this happened every time—her fear, then her capitulation and eventually her acceptance. In one of these incarnations perhaps she would learn to let go of the fear altogether.

"I'm scared," Lainie whispered, shivering, and wrapped her arms around her naked torso as if to protect herself.

"I know, sweetheart," Morry said softly, holding her against him and kissing her cheek. "Welcome to the family, Elaine Ogilvie. Again."

That evening, Lainie sat at her kitchen table staring at the simple engagement ring on her finger. Late in the afternoon, she and Morry had walked to the jewelers, found the perfect gold ring with a tiny diamond in it, and he had ceremoniously placed it on her finger in front of everyone in the store. They had then returned to his home and made love again, slowly and deliberately, reaffirming their commitment. And they hadn't used a condom. What was the point after what they'd already done?

Her cell phone suddenly emitted her mother's ring tone and she panicked. How was she going to explain that she had just bonded with a virtual stranger, who expected her to marry him in the next few weeks?

She took a long, fortifying breath before she reluctantly picked up the phone and accepted the call. "Hi, Mama, how are you?" she asked brightly, trying to sound upbeat and carefree.

"Elaine Marie, what's wrong?"

Lainie sighed, closed her eyes and shook her head. Her mother could sense her emotions even on the phone. "Mama, something rather momentous happened to me today."

"What do you mean?" Ann Ogilvie asked sharply.

"This afternoon I had sex with a man I just met, and, well, we're getting married. We have to because I think I'm pregnant," she blurted, and then promptly burst into tears.

"Elaine, stop crying and talk to me!" Her no-nonsense tone got through to Lainie as nothing else could. "Sometimes women get pregnant right away and sometimes they don't. So, you go out and buy one of those pregnancy tests and use it before you do anything rash, you hear me?"

"Yes, Mama, I hear you. I'll get the test and let you know what I find out," Lainie murmured, feeling relieved, even though she knew she'd be marrying Morry, pregnant or not. It was inevitable—they were mated for life. She felt as if she had been branded in some invisible way by their physical joining in their wolf forms. It was obvious they were soul mates. She'd Seen it in their inner journey, so she wasn't sure why she was fighting it so hard. She'd felt an undeniable connection with him all along.

However, the fact that she wasn't immortal like her fiancé seemed to be an insurmountable issue. They both had magic and were shapeshifters, but still, she didn't see how the relationship could possibly work. She had sensed Morry's uncertainty about that also, but he hadn't said a word.

"Okay then, I'll talk to you tomorrow, honey. I love you," Ann said.

"I love you too, Mama. Oh, wait, I have a question. Do you remember that old story about your great-grandmother Deborah?" Lainie asked abruptly.

"Well, of course I remember. Why do you ask?" Ann said guardedly.

"Is it true what they said about her? That she was not only a witch but a shapeshifter?"

Ann Ogilvie's sudden intake of breath answered her question.

"I thought so. I'm coming over. I have something to show you," Lainie said.

When Lainie arrived at her childhood home on Rosetree Lane, she had a serious case of déjà vu, remembering all the times she had run up the front steps and into the house crying for the comfort of her mother's arms when something in her young life had hurt or scared her. And then she had the disconcerting sensation of standing in the same doorway in a long, old-fashioned dress, watching a young girl run to *her* arms for comfort.

Lainie opened the sturdy oak front door and stepped into the foyer of the old Victorian house. Her mother was waiting for her and Lainie walked into the shelter of her loving embrace.

"We'll figure it out, okay?" Ann stated without hesitation as she gave her daughter a good squeeze and released her.

"I'm not sure you'll feel so optimistic once I show you what I can do," Lainie said as she led her mom into the guest bedroom.

"What are you doing?" Ann exclaimed, as Lainie started to remove her clothing.

She didn't answer, since what she was doing was obvious. As her clothes weren't coming off quickly enough, Lainie ripped the rest off and stood before her mother stark naked. She closed her eyes and focused on becoming the animal she now knew intimately. As she felt the tingling, rushing sensation of magical transformation she shivered, then sat down on her furry behind. She wrapped her tail around her paws and stared up into her mother's horrified eyes.

"Oh, dear God! So that's what you meant about my great-grandmother Deborah." Ann took a deep breath and continued. "There's an old story, a folktale really, about her being a shapeshifter, and that every hundred years a girl is born into our family with the power to change forms. I never imagined that it could be real."

The wolf cocked her head and grinned. Ann's eyes widened as she realized there was more to the story.

"But that's just part of it, isn't it? You're Deborah reincarnated. There is only one shapeshifter in the family, and it's always you. Your soul comes back time after time." Ann sank down to her knees on the floor in front of her wolf daughter and plunged her fingers into the soft ruff of fur around the animal's neck. "Oh, Lainie, I'm so sorry, darling. I didn't know."

The wolf licked Ann's cheek and whimpered, then pulled away. She reared up on her hind legs and at the same time morphed back into her human body.

"It isn't your fault, Mama. And there's a part of the story you don't know." As she got dressed again, regretting that she'd pulled the buttons off her favorite blouse, she told her mother how she'd met Morry and who he really was, and that he had reincarnated with her through time.

Ann Ogilvie looked perplexed. "But that makes no sense. If he was born in 460 and was brought directly here to grow up, how could he have been with you throughout all those centuries?"

"I don't have a clue, but it could have something to do with the fact that he's the grandson of Merlin, the god of magic," Lainie said dryly. "Think about it, Mama. If he has come with me throughout time and has been my husband and the father of my children, our family is descended from Merlin as well. That's why we have magic in the family. Not to mention that I am my own ancestor. And you are my great-granddaughter. Hard to fathom, isn't it?"

Her mother was speechless.

CHAPTER 47

Moab, August 6, 2018

WE WERE RUNNING LATE AT The Moab Herbalist, having had a well-attended storytelling session, and I decided to let Lumina and Rae go home and start dinner while Em and I finished up. I was thinking about my new devotee as I caught up with some paperwork when I heard the conversation between Lainie and Ann in my mind. I chuckled. Oh, this human life seemed so convoluted, but it really was quite simple: There were no coincidences, just a plan God came up with to amuse himself and the gods.

Emily, who had been restocking the bulk herbs, turned to me and smiled. "I love hearing you laugh, magic man. I really missed it when you were gone. What's going on?"

"My newest devotee has already figured a few things out. What a mind that woman has! It will be a pleasure to have her on our side when we confront my nemesis."

"Does Morry know?"

"Oh, he knows some of the story. After they made love today—in both human and animal form—he realized that they were mated. He Looked into her being, and they both Saw their entwined pasts. Lainie was upset and fearful at first, and even after Mordred bought an engagement ring for her, she held onto her fear until she finally figured it out. Then she shared her conclusions with her mother." I gave Em a more detailed accounting telepathically.

Emily looked at me quizzically. "But if Morry is immortal, how could he have died and been reincarnated in all those past lives with her? I don't understand."

"It only makes sense if you truly understand the nature of time and the structure of reality. I tried to explain it to everyone a couple of weeks ago at lunch, but didn't have any luck. Those concepts are difficult to grasp, I grant you." I paused for a moment while I thought about the best way to explain it to her.

"Remember when I mentioned all those time anomalies, and that time isn't linear? Well, there are an infinite number of realities existing concurrently. Those of us who can travel through time or perceive the shape of it may remember more than one of our realities. That's the case with Morry and Lainie."

"My *God*, Merlin." Emily was awestruck as she finally understood, and I could see her eyes traveling down towards my feet.

I knew that look. "Em, remember what we talked about."

She sighed. "You are determined to be a buzz-kill about that, aren't you, god man? No kissing of feet in the shop. Got it." She pulled my head down and kissed me thoroughly. "But I can kiss these lips any time I want."

"Yes, you can," I murmured, and snaked my arm around her waist, teleporting the two of us to the small bedroom upstairs. I willed our clothes gone and held her soft, voluptuous body against my lean one. We lay down on the bed, reveling in the feeling of our naked bodies touching, and I manifested a light blanket to cover us in the chill of the new air conditioner. We were already highly aroused from being around each other all day and I pulled her under me, entering her in one long thrust. My breath caught, she felt so exquisite: hot, wet and tight. I had missed the wondrous feeling of our sexual connection during the time I had been gone.

Em moaned and wrapped her long legs around me, holding me inside her body. "Merlin, my love, I—"

"Hey, Grandpa, can I talk to you for a minute?" Morry yelled from the bottom of the stairs.

Can't it wait? I'm a little busy right now, I thought impatiently. I gritted my teeth as my erection throbbed and Emily used her inner muscles to keep me tightly inside her. She kneaded my buttocks and stroked the small of my back and I groaned.

"Well, it's kind of urgent," Morry said.

I must have had a rather desperate look on my face, because Em smiled sympathetically and said silently, *It's okay, we can finish this later at home. Better talk to him. He needs you now.*

I sighed as we separated, then we both got up and dressed hurriedly. My jeans were so tight in the crotch it was almost painful. I could have taken care of my now superfluous erection using magic, but I wanted to teach Morry a lesson.

"I'll see you in a little while, Em, and tonight we'll finish what we started," I said quietly, then waved my hand, sending her home.

"What do you need, Grandson?" I asked brusquely, as I materialized next to him at the base of the stairs in the back room of the shop. I already knew, but I wanted to give him a hard time for disturbing us.

Morry jumped as I startled him, and then he noticed the bulge in my pants. He quickly glanced away in embarrassment.

"Uh, sorry, I didn't mean to interrupt. I didn't realize that you and Emily were, uh, busy."

"Yes, we were. And if you had been paying attention telepathically as I taught you to, you should have been able to sense that we were unavailable," I said, as I surreptitiously adjusted myself to ease the bite of my jeans into my swollen body parts. "So tell me what's on your mind, Mordred."

He just stood there staring at me, and it was obvious that he now sensed my impatience and sexual frustration.

My grandson had not yet reconciled my appearance of youth and my desire for sex with the fact of my true age, or for that matter, that my skills as a sorcerer stemmed directly from the power of my god self. Intellectually, he understood that my spirit, which was as old as the universe itself, kept my body from ageing, and that despite my appearance of humanity, I *wasn't* human, but emotionally, he hadn't accepted it at all. Ironic, really, since he wasn't entirely human himself.

Morry cleared his throat nervously. "Uh, Grandpa, I'm getting married to Lainie in a few weeks. You know, the woman I bumped into the other day?"

"Yes, of course," I said. "It's fine, Mordred, it's meant to be. I've known about that for some time now." I grinned wickedly as his eyes widened and he looked shaken to his very core.

"Oh, come on, Grandson, you know I'm a god. I just usually don't flaunt the fact that I know the future. And I am aware of your past lives in all those other timelines."

Morry grimaced. “Yes, of course you know about that. What am I thinking? Uh, I’m just afraid to tell my dad. He told me I shouldn’t marry a human. But I kind of have to. We mated in wolf form and I think she’s pregnant.”

“Morry, she’s a shapeshifter so she’s not totally human. Besides, I chose her for you, so there’s no need to worry. You’re doing the right thing,” I said kindly, and placed my right arm across his shoulders. I looked at him intently, considering the best course of action. “I think we need to shift and go flying together. In fact, I’ll contact your Uncle Seth telepathically to join us. What do you say?”

His face lit up, his expression making him look ten years younger. “Really? Now?”

“Yes, now.” And I willed my clothes gone.

Quickly he turned his head away and covered his eyes, but not soon enough. He had glimpsed my groin area. “My God, I think I’m going to go blind!”

“Oh, stop it, Morry. We’re both male. And you’re built just as I am in that department, so it shouldn’t be a surprise. Now, take your clothes off,” I said irritably.

He reluctantly complied and we both stood there, naked. He was forcing himself to keep his eyes above my waist, and I couldn’t help laughing out loud.

“Let’s go. It’s dark enough out that no one will see us.” I touched his arm and teleported us to the top of the Rim, where we stood for a moment, admiring the view. There was a light, warm breeze, bringing with it the sounds and scents of a summer evening in Moab: the muted roar of cars and trucks traveling through town, the aroma of fresh-ground coffee, the mouth-watering scent of barbecued pork, and underlying those, the dusty dryness of red sand and sagebrush.

“Well?” I said, raising an eyebrow.

He responded by shifting into the form of a huge owl. Spreading his wings, he dropped over the edge of the cliff and soared majestically over the town. I swiftly changed as well, and followed him, the wind and our magic keeping us both aloft. I could fly without shapeshifting, but this night, flying in the form of an owl alongside my grandson seemed like great fun.

"Well, fuck me sideways," Colin Campbell said breathlessly, as he watched the two naked men turn into giant owls and fly away. Then he realized that there was another form soaring in to join them, and—hot damn, it was a man with wings who could be Michael's twin brother! He'd heard that there was a new guy in town but he hadn't seen him yet. Colin continued to watch through his night-vision binoculars as the three of them glided back and forth above the lights of downtown Moab. He was right, by God, he was right! Not only was Michael Reese some kind of a magician, maybe even a sorcerer, but so was the kid who worked at the newspaper, whose eyes just happened to have the same slant to them that Reese's did. And the other one—Colin had no idea what that guy was. He actually had *wings* sprouting out of his upper back. Jesus. Could the whole bunch of them who worked and hung out at The Moab Herbalist be one big magical family? Had to be, right? And he'd be willing to bet that the potions were magical, too. No wonder they worked so well. Now he just had to prove it. He couldn't wait to arrest Reese. Colin wasn't sure exactly what he would arrest him *for*, since as far as he knew sorcery wasn't against the law, but he'd think of something.

He knew exactly what he needed to do, and even though he was aware that what he planned was illegal, he rationalized that it was necessary for the greater good.

He'd stayed in the city building after he'd gotten off work, enjoying the peace and quiet of a few hours alone up on the roof. He wasn't really supposed to be up there, but he had found an access hatch through the attic of the old building and used it frequently. The roof wasn't flat, but the slope wasn't that steep either, so he just sat on a folded blanket, enjoying the solitude. The only thing that he didn't enjoy was the heat that radiated off the roof, so he normally didn't spend a lot of time there in the summer. But this particular night he'd worked later than usual and most of the heat had already dissipated by the time he'd climbed through the hatch.

He always had his special binoculars with him, along with his cell phone, ever since Josh's four-wheeler had broken down on the Rim and he'd had to rescue him. Damn kid, always getting into trouble. But having his binocs along tonight had sure paid off when he'd spied the two men morphing into birds.

When he finally lost sight of the trio, he figured they'd called it quits for the night. Time to implement his plan to break into the herb shop. Whether magic was involved or not, he still hoped to find evidence that Reese was using illegal substances in his potions. Once Colin found the stuff, he wouldn't touch it—he'd get a warrant to arrest the man. He conveniently forgot that to obtain a warrant based on his findings he would have to submit an affidavit showing probable cause. And how would he explain his knowledge of the "illegal" substances without revealing that he had burglarized Reese's shop? He immediately buried this errant thought under several layers of mental trivia.

He quickly gathered up his gear, climbed back down through the access hatch and stealthily exited the building.

He hurried home and changed into a long-sleeved black turtleneck pullover, black jeans and athletic shoes. He considered blackening his face and the backs of his hands with some soot from the woodstove, but finally decided that the soot would be overkill, as his natural olive skin tone was dark anyway. And his hair was still as black as it had been in his twenties. He grabbed his small, high-intensity flashlight and his tools and stuffed them into a pack, then left the house. It was fortunate that his family had gone to the movies; otherwise, he never would have gotten out of the house without explaining his garb or his intentions.

As he walked down Center Street past the library and the City Center offices and realized how many tourists were out and about, he was very grateful for his own sense of self-preservation. If he'd walked down the street with his face blackened, he would have attracted attention, which would not have been in his best interest. As it was, people eyed his long-sleeved turtleneck as if he'd lost his mind. And no wonder, it had to be eighty degrees and he was sweating profusely.

"Good flight, you two. It was most enjoyable," I said after we had all teleported back to the shop, Morry and I having shifted back to human form up on the cliff.

"It was incredible, thanks, Grandpa!" Morry grinned as we put our clothes back on. He knew how to will his clothing off, but the habit of dressing in the human way was so ingrained that he sometimes still forgot that he could do it differently. He gave me a quick, enthusiastic hug before going out the door, and mentioned how happy he was that I was back. What a difference there was between this confident and happy young man, and the repressed and angry boy he had been four years ago. I loved him with all of my heart. I waved, and then turned to my Fae son as he also prepared to take his leave.

"I need tae go as well, Da. Chris is waiting for me. *Oidhche mhath.*" As Seth wished me a good night in Scottish Gaelic, he faded out, transporting himself to Chris's apartment. The two of them had been inseparable since our lunch at the Red Rock Grill. He had moved in with her that day and I had to admit that I was glad of it. He and Lumina had been bickering the morning of our get-together, and I suspected that the situation would have escalated had he continued to stay in my home. Whether they were the offspring of a god, possessing magic and immortality, or the children of a normal human couple, siblings—even adult ones—quarreled and competed for the attention and affection of their parents. And I had no patience for that kind of behavior from either one of them.

When I was alone again, I started thinking about everything that had happened since Beli and I had been transported to ancient Caledonia, and how Derek had stepped up and worked with Lumina to learn the secret of using the time portals. I was exceptionally proud of his abilities. Yes, he was my son, so he came by those abilities honestly, but he was still part human.

A sudden noise outside in the alley riveted my attention to the back door of the shop, and I sensed that I would soon have a visitor. The only light currently on was the overhead one in the back room, dimmed to the night setting, and I extinguished it with a glance. As I stood waiting in the dark, contemplating exactly how to deal with the intruder, I heard the unmistakable sound of the lock being picked. If I had reset the protective wards around the building, picking the lock alone wouldn't have enabled him to break in, but I hadn't done so yet.

I smiled as the knob rattled yet again and then slowly turned. Could he be any more obvious?

As the door swung quietly inward, I watched the dark-clothed figure enter the shop and tentatively train a small flashlight at the worktable. I wondered how he could stand wearing a turtleneck in this heat.

I moved silently into the doorway leading to the front room and crossed my arms over my chest, allowing a small amount of god Light to emanate from my body.

I heard a gasp from the man who had entered my shop unbidden, and I willed the overhead lights on full.

"Well, Detective Campbell, how interesting to find you entering my shop at this hour, especially through the back door, when clearly we are not open for business," I said in a soft yet deadly voice, my accent returning with a vengeance.

He straightened and cleared his throat, dismayed to be caught breaking and entering. He blinked his dark eyes, striving to adjust to the brightness. I could hear his heart pounding rapidly, yet he stood his ground at the sight of me. Brave man. Foolish, but brave.

"What are you, Mr. Reese?" he rasped fearfully.

"And what gives you the right to question me?" I carefully kept my anger in check, even though my god self was highly insulted by his disrespect.

My entire family sensed what was going on and asked if I needed assistance. *No, thanks, I'm fine, he can't hurt me. He doesn't even have any kryptonite with him.* The family, unused to me displaying a sense of humor, did not respond. *That was a joke—oh, never mind.* Even Derek didn't get it, despite all his past suggestions that I get a Superman cape.

I returned my attention to my uninvited guest.

Campbell didn't answer me at first, knowing that he had no

rights at all in this situation. He had entered my private property illegally.

I stared pointedly into his eyes, preventing the Seeing that would normally result from such a gaze, yet holding his attention with my will. At some point in the future, it would be appropriate for him to See into his inner self, but it was not yet time for that.

"I don't have that right and we both know it." He finally let go of his bravado and sighed. "To be honest, you fascinate me, Mr. Reese. I've been watching you for years, buying your products, looking for an excuse to arrest you. I know that you're different, so you must be some kind of wizard, or even an alien. There's no other explanation."

"Are you sure about that?" I chuckled, though I still had my guard up. "So you watched as we changed into birds and flew above the town. And you saw a man with wings join us as well."

He jerked, dismayed that I knew of his covert observation of our activities. "Ah, yeah, I did, how did you know?" He paused, waiting for me to reply. When I remained silent, he continued. "That's when I figured it all out."

"And what conclusion did you come to, pray tell?" I was actually just leading him on, as I knew more than I was telling him. I had not only read his mind, but was aware of all of his secrets.

"That you and the kid are related and are both shapeshifters. But the guy with wings who looks like you—who the hell is he? Your brother? *What* the hell is he?" he blurted out. He became increasingly unsettled as it dawned on him that he could be in danger.

I let him worry about it for a few minutes by refusing to answer, and then relented. "Relax, Colin, I'm not going to hurt you," I said in a wry tone.

His eyes widened as I used his first name, and he was worried that I had somehow read his thoughts.

"Of course I read your thoughts, Detective, and I also know everything about you, including a surprising fact about your heritage."

He frowned. "My heritage? I'm Irish, although my ancestors were originally from Scotland. They traveled to what's now Northern Ireland in the early 1700s. What does that have to do with anything?"

"Oh, I was referring to something more…unusual."

"What do you mean?"

"In fifth-century Inverness, your many times removed great-grandmother had sex with the Welsh god of death, and now, here you are," I said. I remembered when Beli and I were in Inverness, trapped in the past, neither of us aware of our real identities. Bel, as he had called himself, had spent a good deal of time, and what little money he had earned, with a woman he called Molly, and I knew that he was very fond of her. He had apparently impregnated her before we left town. Colin's ancestor had proudly born a dark-haired, dark-eyed son, whose descendant also sported those same characteristics.

"I—what did you say?" He looked at me, uncomprehendingly.

"You are descended from the Welsh god of death, who happened to be in human form at the time."

He just stared at me. He was so overwhelmed that he never questioned how I came by that information. I stared back at him, seeing a man in his early forties, about an inch shorter than my own six two, a little overweight and out of shape, but smart, brave and persistent, and I valued those qualities. He didn't have an evil bone in his body, but it was possible that his connection with the god of death, however distant, could be problematic. Although, now that Beli and I were on good terms with each other, perhaps it wouldn't be an issue. Maybe Colin could be of use to me after all.

"Who the fuck *are* you?" Colin whispered, his eyes wide and frightened.

"Who do you think I am?"

"Are…are *you* the god of death?" he asked tentatively, noticing that we both had straight black hair and were of a similar height.

"No, I'm not your ancestor, Colin." I spoke in a normal, matter-of-fact tone, answering the question he was really asking.

However, I couldn't resist adding, "I can introduce you to him the next time he decides to drop by."

"Jesus, Mary and Joseph!" He crossed himself, and then acted as if he was going to collapse, so I grabbed a chair and indicated that he should sit down.

"I happen to know that Jesus wasn't present, and I'm quite certain that Mary and Joseph weren't there either." I paused and looked at him thoughtfully. "I'll tell you what. If you will agree to assist me when I need help from law enforcement, I'll give you a hint as to who I am."

When he nodded, mystified at my request, I continued. "Alright, Detective, here it is: I put a sword in a stone, so that a young man could pull it out and use it to become the greatest king the world has ever known."

"King Arthur pulled a sword called Excaliber out of a stone, if you believe that fable."

I sighed and conjured up my robe and pointed sorcerer's hat, the props I used to convince Ben, my present caretaker, of my identity many years ago. My hair was longer now than it was when I first came to Moab, so it was appropriate for the image I wanted to project.

The look on Colin's face was priceless. I got rid of the hat and the robe and grinned at him.

"No, it can't be. You're not real…are you?" His eyes widened. "Are you Merlin? Merlin, the Enchanter?"

Excellent. "Yes, Colin, I am Merlin. Who else could I possibly be?"

"I…I don't know. Maybe King Arthur?"

"Oh, for God's sake, I look nothing like Arthur!" I shook my head in disbelief. "Don't you read or watch television? There have been hundreds of stories written and numerous TV shows and movies created about me. Look, if you can't handle it, I'll just make you forget the whole thing and send you home. Is that what you want?" I leaned nonchalantly on the counter and waited for him to answer.

He stared at me intently for several minutes, and then he sighed. "No, I don't want that. I want to help you, with whatever you need. I may be over forty and out of shape, but I have a few good years left in me."

"Great, I was hoping you'd say that." Actually, I already knew he would respond that way. Once again, I felt the burden of knowing what was going to happen at any given time and I was sick of it. I had to figure out a way to suppress that knowledge unless it was absolutely necessary to have the information at my fingertips.

"Uh, Merlin, I'm curious. Who were you flying with tonight? If you don't mind telling me, that is," he hastened to add.

"I think you've met Morry—he's my grandson, who is a shapeshifter, as you surmised. And the other man, the one with the wings, is my son, Seth."

A puzzled look flickered across his face. "You don't have wings. Why does he?"

"On his mother's side, he is Seelie Court Fae royalty, a prince."

"Fae? You mean he's a *fairy*? Seriously?"

"Yes, but they prefer the term 'Fae.'"

"What about the other man I've seen with you sometimes, with the light brown hair—Derek—the one who works out at Arches National Park?"

"He's also my son, and happens to be Morry's father."

"But you're all the same age! How in the hell…?"

"I think that's plenty for now, Colin, and to answer the question you haven't asked yet, no, you don't have magic, I'm sorry to say."

The look of disappointment on his face was almost too much to bear, and I wished that I could remedy the situation. But I couldn't do that—shouldn't do that. However, I decided to amp up some of his natural abilities, the ones that made him such a good detective. I looked into his eyes, straight into the center of his being, and made a few adjustments. There. That should do it. A brief jolt of power and a flash of joy deep inside of me seemed to indicate that I had done the right thing.

I smiled as Colin shook his head slightly and got an introspective look on his face. Interestingly, he'd sensed what I'd done. He was way more intuitive than I'd expected.

"What did you do, Merlin? I feel different." Then his face brightened, a look of wonder flashed across his swarthy countenance, and in that moment, he actually resembled Beli, moustache and all. "Thank you for whatever you did. I feel like I could live forever."

"You are most welcome." I hadn't actually made him immortal, but I had enhanced his health and healing abilities, and he would live far longer than had been his original destiny. That would work out splendidly, because he would be serving Arthur Pendragon for many years. I began to think about the day that Arthur would arrive…

Colin cleared his throat, which brought me out of those distracting thoughts, and I realized that I had been staring blankly at him for several minutes.

"I guess I should go, unless you have some task for me tonight."

I had to stifle my amusement at his eagerness to please me. What a difference there was in his attitude. He had broken into my shop, intent upon finding evidence of something illegal so that he could arrest me, and yet now he was ready to assist me in my magical endeavors.

"Well, there is something you can do for me, Colin."

"Sure, whatever you need, Merlin."

"Stop sending your son here to spy on me and my family. You're more than welcome to come in yourself to purchase anything that you require, but do not send Josh. I dislike the way he leers at my daughter."

His eyes widened and his jaw dropped. "How did you know about that? You were gone for four years. And how do you know my son's name?"

"I know everything about you and your family. *Everything*. And by the way, you no longer need the potion for your gout. I cured it for you."

He gaped at me for a moment longer, then pulled himself together and bowed to me solemnly. He departed through the front door, which I had opened magically for him.

As Colin Campbell walked hastily down the sidewalk then turned east on Center Street, he paused a moment to glance back at the shop. His normally dark, middle-aged countenance now radiated an aura of youth and vitality. He waved and then continued on towards his home, only a few blocks away.

As it turned out, I was actually pleased that Colin had stopped by, even though he did break into my shop. Soon, I would need his assistance with an incident involving the wizards who had infiltrated the area recently. I couldn't help but feel betrayed, since most of those practitioners of the magical arts had sided with me in the battle against Nimue in 2013. Morgana must have used her own potent magic to influence them against me.

I sighed. Enough of that. I made sure the shop was secure for the night and teleported home, looking forward to a late dinner, a shower and a few hours alone with my wife to finish what we'd started earlier.

CHAPTER 48

Moab, Monday, August 6, 2018,10:30 PM

As I rematerialized in my familiar living room, with its heather-green drapes, soft carpet and comfortable overstuffed chairs, all the tensions and concerns of the day dropped away and I relaxed. I could smell dinner cooking and my empty stomach rumbled.

I turned as my daughter walked into the room and saw her eyes light up with pleasure to see me. Her long, dark brown hair shone and her hazel eyes glowed with love. I noticed that she was wearing the headband that Emily had given to me when I first moved in with her, before we were married. I hadn't seen it in years, in fact I'd forgotten about it until now. It looked better on Lumina, as a hair band, than it ever did on me.

What a beautiful woman she is becoming, I thought as I smiled fondly at her. And I made an executive decision to give her what she wanted so badly. I had already broken the rules today, several times, so what was another infraction? I was a god, and if I chose to use my powers to improve the lives of others, so be it.

"Hi, Dad."

"Hello, sweetling, come here and give me a hug."

She grinned and launched herself at me as she had done when she was just a little girl, the difference being that now she weighed a hundred and thirty pounds. I caught her in my arms and held her close as I enveloped her in my Light and made an adjustment to her magical nature.

As I kissed her cheek and released her, she kneeled humbly at my feet.

"Oh, thank you, Dad! Thank you," she whispered.

"Lumina, my dear daughter, you don't have to kneel to me." I helped her stand as she stared up into my face, tears of joy welling in her eyes. She was now as tall as her mother was, but it felt like I was towering over her.

"You just gave me my heart's desire, my lord, and I am grateful for your kindness," she said formally.

"You are most welcome. It was my pleasure." I responded just as formally.

Then, as I watched, she arched her back slightly and a perfect pair of wings appeared. They were similar in shape to Seth's but sized in proportion to my daughter's smaller frame. The feathers were lovely, the soft gray color of a dove, with a narrow white edge.

She carefully moved her new wings up and down, experimenting with the feel of them. Then, with a determined look on her face, she folded them up and retracted them magically into her body, something Seth could not do. I had wanted her to be able to hide her wings from mortal view without using a glamour. And not only that, wings were unwieldy things to have to deal with on a daily basis.

Lumina looked at me curiously. "Dad, why don't you ever use your wings when you fly?"

For a moment, I was nonplussed. Then, I laughed. "Because I had forgotten that I had them." It was true. They had been there all along, waiting for me to call them forth.

"Can I see them?"

"Alright, but give me a moment. It has been thousands of years since I last used them." I closed my eyes, envisioned those ancient appendages, and then slowly manifested massive, iridescent black wings that unfurled majestically.

In the kitchen, Emily and Rae stood riveted, watching the scene between Lumina and Merlin evolve into a magical revelation. Initially, they had anticipated observing a sweet, poignant greeting between father and daughter and had wanted to share it. But neither of them had any idea what was about to transpire.

"Oh, my *God*!" Rae breathed, as first Lumina and then Merlin sprouted wings.

Emily was astonished. It was evident that he had just gifted their daughter with wings. But *Merlin* had wings? No wonder Seth had them, being Fae notwithstanding. She felt lightheaded with awe and had an overpowering desire to fling herself down at her husband's feet.

And then, as he seemed to grow taller and his tattoos began to glow, she knew without a doubt exactly what had happened.

"*Merlin...*"

I turned around and watched my wife walk slowly toward us, her facial expression one of awestruck devotion.

"You've done it. You've made the final transition."

CHAPTER 49

A frisson of awareness shot down my spine and I realized that she was correct. I had, without fanfare, made that final step. I recalled that moment of power and joy pervading my being when I had given Colin his enhancements and knew them for the portents of my transition.

I closed my eyes and saw the universe expanding around me, and ecstasy arced through my being. My true home, the realm of the gods—also known as Heaven—beckoned, Llyr and Beli applauded, and my father evinced his approval with an unexpected meteor shower.

And when I opened my eyes to find my wife, my daughter and my mother-in-law all kneeling at my feet, I finally understood that this was the way it was supposed to be. It was not about lesser beings humbling themselves before me, but about my being humbled by their unwavering love and devotion. My Light flared blindingly in response to my epiphany, and I carefully dimmed it to a manageable level before the rest of the family appeared. I knew they would, since my transition had caused a cascading awareness to surge through the bonds I had with each individual.

I looked up with a welcoming smile as both of my sons, my daughter-in-law and my grandson appeared in the room and instantly went down on their knees to me, their heads bowed. Seth's wings were pulled tightly against his body in obeisance.

The room was getting very crowded, so I magically moved the walls out and willed the furniture out of the way. The house itself remained the same size on the outside; I merely increased the space inside by expanding into another dimension.

Next, I summoned my brothers. Llyr and Beli appeared in their human forms, tall and regal in robes of gold and silver, their own dark wings unfurled. We were all the same height now.

"You did it, Bro," Llyr said. "I was beginning to think you'd never remember."

"I'm glad you summoned us, Myrddin Emrys. I haven't seen

you in your full glory for millennia. And you've managed to keep your human body, I see, even if it's a bit altered." Beli grinned widely and clapped my shoulder with his large hand.

All of my family members were clambering back to their feet and staring at the three of us in fascination.

Emily came forward to stand humbly at my side. As she put her hand in mine, I held it close to my heart and sent her a wordless message of appreciation for her selfless devotion.

And when I noticed that Rae and Lumina had tears in their eyes and their arms around each other, I sent them reassurance of my love and respect for them.

"So that's why I have ma wings. As a half-breed Fae, even though I'm a prince, ye ken, I shouldna have them." Seth's Scottish brogue was so thick that, prior to my transition, it would have been difficult to understand him. Now, I could easily understand any and all languages, dialects and inflections.

Derek and Morry glanced at each other and then turned to me questioningly.

I waited, already aware of what they wished to know.

"So, do we have wings also?" Derek asked hesitantly.

"Actually, you don't, although I'm not sure why." Before Derek could respond, his hopes crushed once again, I hastened to add, "However, if you want to fly badly enough, I can manifest them for you."

Derek's relief was tangible.

Morry looked thoughtful. "You know, I can fly in bird form, so I really don't need them. Thanks anyway, but I'll pass."

Seth looked scandalized. "What? Wings are a blessing, to be sure, Nephew."

Morry just smiled and shrugged, then turned to his father. "Well, Dad, do you have your heart set on flying?"

Derek beseeched me with a look, and I remembered his anguished expression in 2014 when I had not been able to find any trace of the ability to fly in his magical repertoire. I could hardly grant Lumina her greatest desire and not Derek, so I motioned him to come closer. I enfolded him in my wings, surrounded him with my Light, and granted his wish. Then I stepped back and again dampened that radiant evidence of my celestial nature.

His brows furrowed in concentration until wings the color of his hair sprang from his back. Then he turned to me with an ecstatic look on his face.

"Now we can truly fly together, Son," I said softly.

Thanks, Dad. I can't tell ya how happy this makes me. Before I could respond, he disappeared from the room, anxious to soar into the night sky. Lumina smiled at me, manifested her wings and teleported out of the room as well, so she and her brother could fly together.

As the last sparkles subsided after their departure, I glanced around to find Sarah staring at my wings.

I smiled. "Are you alright? Is there some gift I can give you?"

She dragged her attention away from my back and nodded. "Yes, please. Can you fix it so I won't get sick every time Derek and I teleport somewhere?"

"Yes, of course, that's easy. Come here, Sarah." I held out my hand to her and she grasped it trustingly.

"This won't hurt at all, my dear," I murmured.

She gasped as I put my other hand on top of hers and manifested a quick burst of energy, making a minute adjustment to her body chemistry.

She thanked me and then looked skeptically. "I don't feel any different."

"Don't worry, it's done. You won't notice a change until the next time the two of you teleport together.

"Now, I think we all need to get some rest." I winked at Llyr conspiratorially, since some of us had no need for it, and continued. "So I release you to your own homes and realms. Thank you for your support and good wishes. Obviously, my transition is just one more step towards my goal—our goal—to restore Arthur to his rightful place in this human realm. This is only the beginning."

Beli and Llyr bowed deferentially. *Later, Bro.* I could hear Llyr's voice in my head, and Beli winked as the two of them vanished.

Seth looked directly into my eyes for a moment and then slowly lowered his head obsequiously. He faded away and was gone, leaving Morry, Rae, Sarah and of course Emily, still standing close, as if reluctant to abandon me as I came to terms with my new status.

I eyed my grandson, knowing that he had teleported for the first time to be at my side. "How do you like your newly-discovered ability?"

His eyebrows shot up. "You did that?"

"No, you always had the ability to teleport. You just needed a good reason to finally use it."

"I guess you're right, Grandpa. And I like it a whole lot. Now I need to get home and calm Jim down. He was really upset when I disappeared without an explanation." And then Morry dematerialized.

"It's time for me to go as well, so I can be there for Derek when he comes home." Sarah started toward the front door, and then paused and turned back to me with a respectful nod and a wide smile. "Thank you again, Merlin."

As the door closed behind Sarah, I glanced enquiringly at my mother-in-law. "Rae? What gift can I give you?"

"You have been so kind and generous, giving me shelter, food, protection and employment, for which I can never repay you. So I have only one small request: may I touch your wings?"

I unhesitatingly folded them forward again, around my body, so that she could easily touch them. "You may."

Her face lit up and she reached out, gently stroking a few feathers. "Oh, my, they're just like satin." She boldly looked into my eyes, which she seldom did, and said softly, "Thank you, Merlin. I'll always remember this, even if I never see them again."

Oh, I'll make sure you see them again, Mom.

She beamed with pleasure and bowed her head. Then, without another word, she turned and walked calmly down the hallway toward her bedroom.

Silence reigned and I released a breath. I retracted my wings and allowed my height to return to normal.

I gazed at my wife, searching for signs of stress. "How are you holding up?"

She squeezed my hand and smiled crookedly. "I think I'm okay. I was just about to ask you the same question. But I'm dying to know—earlier tonight, when you sent me home from the shop so that you could talk to Morry, were you aware this was going to happen?"

"No, I wasn't, believe it or not." I paused as my stomach growled insistently. "Em, do you mind if we have something to eat now? I'm starving. Then we can talk about everything."

She gasped. "Oh my God, I forgot all about dinner!"

"It's fine, I'm sure. I suspended the passage of time inside the house when my wings appeared."

"Ah. Okay then, I'll just check to make sure the casserole is still edible."

I followed Em to the kitchen. "It really doesn't matter what state it's in, I can fix it."

I was practically giddy with the bliss of having all my restored god powers coursing through me. I felt—and was—invincible.

However, since it was obvious that my wife, despite her claim to the contrary, was shaken up by the evening's startling occurrences, I decided to restrain myself. For now.

She stood facing the stove, preparing to take the casserole out of the oven, tension evident in the set of her shoulders. I gently turned her around, and then pulled her into my arms, cradling her head against me.

"Everything will be fine, my love."

She blurted out, "I'm afraid you'll leave me now that your god self has fully manifested."

"I will never leave you, wife," I reassured her.

"How can you promise that?"

"Because this transition isn't at all what I expected. It didn't happen in a blaze of glory in front of the population of Moab, nor did I have to leave my human body behind to achieve it, thank God. The process apparently started after Colin Campbell broke into the shop and confronted me."

"Oh? I knew that he'd showed up unexpectedly, but I didn't realize that's what triggered your transition. And what was that about kryptonite?"

"Remember, Superman was vulnerable to kryptonite?"

"Yes, and what does that have to do with Colin?"

"Never mind, it doesn't matter. Anyway, back to my story: Morry and I had gone flying after our discussion, and Seth joined us. After we returned to the shop, Morry left, and Seth departed a few minutes later. Then Colin showed up, and long story short, he is now part of our group. When I told him he was descended from the god of death, but that he didn't possess any magic, he was so disappointed that I felt sorry for him. So I enhanced his existing mundane abilities and his health, so he'll live hundreds of years longer. I healed his gout, by the way, so he shouldn't need to buy that potion again." I touched Em's face and showed her everything that had transpired.

"Colin Campbell is descended from *Beli*? I didn't see that coming. He's going to be your liaison with human law enforcement until Arthur returns, and then he'll be the king's assistant. Holy shit." She had retrieved the casserole dish from the oven, but she froze in the act of putting it on the table as she tried to process what she had just learned.

I reached for the dish. "Here, let me take that. It seems to be alright, so let's eat." I instantly conjured up a hot pad to put it on, as well as two place settings, a carafe of water and a vase of roses.

Emily folded her arms over her chest and watched me, her eyes twinkling with amusement. "I guess there's no point in doing most of our mundane household chores anymore, god man. You've got it covered."

"Oh, this is just regular magic, Em, and you can do most of this yourself. You know that. It's not that impressive."

She gave me a loving look. "It is to me, god man."

We sat down and Emily started dishing out the casserole, which included pasta, vegetables, chicken, cheese and a savory herb mixture I had put together the other day. Simple yet filling, the food was somewhat dried out from being in the oven too long, but at this point, I didn't care. Fully manifested god or not, my body insisted on being nourished, even if it was midnight.

Em picked up her fork and speared a chunk of chicken. "Wait

a minute. How can you be back to your regular height? I thought becoming your god self meant that your whole body transformed."

"Oh, it did. But remember that when Llyr visits us he can actually appear any way he chooses. Maybe he likes being six eight. Our form in Heaven is pure energy after all."

Emily stared at me. "*Heaven?*"

I paused. "We can still call it the realm of the gods if you'd rather. Heaven is the Christian term for it. Other cultures and religions call it Nirvana, Valhalla, Paradise, the Other World, et cetera, but it's all the same."

"I thought it was just for the gods. I didn't realize that's where human souls go after death."

I smiled. "Em, it's a big place, practically infinite. And remember, the truly evil souls don't go there."

"And speaking of Heaven, I'm totaling confused about your… wings."

"The other day you asked me if I was an angel, and angels traditionally have wings, correct?

"Well yes, but you've never used them to fly before. And I don't understand why I've never *felt* them before. We've been together since 2013, been as intimate as two people can be, slept in the same bed—how can I not have touched them?"

"It's hard to explain, Em. I know you're aware of some of it, but just bear with me." I thought how best to describe something that defied description in human terms.

"Originally, long before I was born into this human body, I existed as pure energy. No body, no wings, just Light. But in that Light existed the intelligence of the universe, of God. No verbal communication, but a kind of *thought* and *knowledge* and *intention*. And when God decided to populate the earth with human beings, the form that he created was perfect for living on the physical plane. So after that, when God sent his children to check on humans, we took the form of those humans, but with wings so we could get around on the planet easily." I stopped to take a drink of water, and realized that Em was wide-eyed with wonder, hanging on my every word.

"Don't stop now! This is fascinating," she said.

I nodded and continued. "When humans began to be more aware of their surroundings and started questioning the purpose of life, they noticed us observing them and assumed we were gods. This was fine when the world was primitive; in fact, it suited our purposes admirably. We could actually go among them occasionally, and the awe humans felt kept them from interfering with our work.

"And then a strange thing happened to me. I felt an increasing desire to live among humans, to be one of them, until it became an obsession of mine. And sometime near the end of the Roman occupation of Britain, in anticipation of a new king arising who had the potential to lead the Britons to an enlightened age, my father decided to send me to earth to assist this new king—Arthur. So I was born to a human woman, and well, you know the story after that."

"Yes, but what happened to your wings?"

"When I was born into this human body, I couldn't very well bring my wings with me, could I? And even if I had, it would have been physically impossible to retract such enormous appendages into my body. The reality is that they are in another dimension, one that exists between one breath and the next, and when I call them forth, I'm using magic to manifest them in *this* dimension, visibly and tangibly attached to my body."

"But when you gave Lumina and Derek their wings, you didn't tell them any of that, so how did they know what to do?"

"Em, part of my gift was the magic involved in manifesting their wings in this human realm." I tilted my head and raised my eyebrows in a silent question.

She smiled and reached out to stroke my face. "No, I don't want to fly, Merlin, but thank you for thinking of it."

We leaned forward to kiss each other gently, and then returned to our meal.

My wife looked thoughtful as she ate a few florets of broccoli. "You know, the knights will be very unhappy that they missed your big event." She raised her eyebrows as if to say, 'And what are you going to do about it?'

"I thought about that, and I'll meet with them tomorrow. They'll forgive me."

"Well, that's kind of arrogant of you."

I chuckled softly. "I already know that they will. But you're right. I have to watch that, don't I?"

She nodded. "And by the way, Ryan may take exception to you making Colin Arthur's assistant. Didn't Sir Lancelot have that job?"

"In a way. First and foremost, he was head of the Knights of the Round Table. Colin will be Arthur's administrative assistant and legal advisor since he went to law school before he switched to law enforcement." I took another sip of water before continuing. "I was expecting more of the knights to show up before this, by means of reincarnation. Perhaps they still might." I paused for a moment and thought about all the worthy knights I had known. "I would like to have Sir Leon here. He was dependable and trustworthy…*and* a good friend." I stabbed a curl of pasta with my fork. "That gives me an idea, though. I could bring him here from the past."

We were quiet for a few minutes while we finished our meal. Emily got up and started clearing the table, but I just shook my head and used magic to clean up. We had something more important to do.

We didn't bother showering. It was very late and we didn't want to disturb Rae. We just threw off our clothing and tumbled into bed. I was already hard, and frantic to make love to my wife. Emily's precious face glowed with an inner light that drew me like a moth to a flame, and as she opened to me, I slid inside her. I was instantly scorched—pleasantly so—by her heat and overwhelmed by her loving embrace.

She was my soul mate, my other half, and I loved her with a passion so intense that there was no separation; we were one body, one soul, one mind. I had never experienced such an expansion of my consciousness, despite my magic and my divine origins. We made love that night with such fervor that I should have known that neither of us was truly in charge of the experience.

As I reached a peak that surpassed all others and I emptied myself into her, unconsciousness claimed me.

A small boy stood before me, reaching out for me to pick him up. His hair was sandy blond and his eyes were green and slanted like mine.

He resembled Derek, but it couldn't be he, for Derek was a grown man and I had not known him when he was a child. Puzzled, I picked the boy up. As I held him in my arms and kissed his baby-soft cheek, a feeling of love and protectiveness swelled in my heart.

The boy looked directly into my eyes with innocence and trust and said, "I love you, Merlin."

And I responded softly, "I love you, too. I've always loved you. I came here for you, and I will be here for you until eternity passes away."

I came to with a start as my vision of the future faded. I glanced at Emily, who was sleeping soundly, sprawled inelegantly with her arms and legs draped over mine. I kissed her gently and eased out of bed without disturbing her.

It was five o'clock in the morning, but I wasn't weary in the slightest. Apparently, I really *didn't* need to sleep anymore.

I dressed and teleported to the Rim. As I gazed out across the lights of Moab, the night still holding the area in thrall, I realized what I had done during our tumultuous lovemaking: I had impregnated my wife without her consent. However, I knew that it was time for the child to be conceived, irrespective of my wife's desires. A power greater than I was had determined the course of events, and it was time to begin.

CHAPTER 50

Moab, August 7, 2018

I WAS FIXING A LATE breakfast when Emily came into the kitchen, stretching luxuriously. She was still in her robe and slippers and it was obvious she didn't know what time it was.

"Good morning, wife. Would you like some herbal tea?"

She walked up behind me as I was turning the bacon and looped her arms around me. "I'd rather have a cup of coffee." She got a puzzled look on her face and looked around. "I wonder where Mom and Lumina are."

"They've gone to work, I believe."

She glanced at the clock on the stove. "Oh, no, I was supposed to inventory the fantasy books this morning and place an order. Why did you let me sleep so late?" It was eleven o'clock.

"Because I kept you awake until almost five. I couldn't sleep, so I teleported up to the Rim, then out to Arches National Park for awhile. I sat on top of Balanced Rock, invisibly of course, contemplating what to do about Adrestia and her infernal inhabitant."

Years ago, just before I was transported to the past, I'd had to rescue Derek from the clutches of my oldest daughter, who had been possessed by her mother, my original nemesis, Nimue. She had badly underestimated me, and I had been able to put her in a suspended state until I could decide what to do with her. She was still there, entombed in a cavern deep in the earth below Balanced Rock.

Now, I had determined a course of action, but needed some time to plan the details and to enlist my son's assistance.

I realized that Emily was staring at me, a frown creasing her brow.

"You're holding something back again, Merlin, and it's not about Adrestia. You know I hate it when you do that."

I looked back at her stoically, knowing that she would come to the right conclusion any moment. I handed her the mug of raspberry leaf tea I had already prepared.

She looked at it and grimaced, then huffed in annoyance. "Oh, for Pete's sake, you got me pregnant didn't you? I thought you were going to wait until I told you I was ready?"

"I was," I said apologetically, "but it was time for the child to be conceived. It was destined to happen as soon as I transitioned. I'm sorry, darling Em, but I really wasn't in control last night."

"I somehow doubt that. But we did screw like bunnies all night long, which was unusual to say the least, so it shouldn't surprise me that I got pregnant."

I grinned wryly at her crudeness. "We could have *made love* twenty-four hours a day for a week and you wouldn't have gotten pregnant unless God willed it, my love."

"So you're saying it's your *father's* fault that I'm pregnant?"

"In a way. But it was imperative that the child be conceived *last night*. He needs to be born six months from now so that he can grow to an adult and be ready when the world needs him the most." The gestation period for immortals and most non-humans was shorter than for humans.

She looked at me suspiciously. "What do you mean, 'he?' He, who?"

"Why, Arthur, of course."

Emily's eyes rolled back in her head and she crumpled to the floor in a dead faint.

When she came to, I was sitting on the couch, holding her in my arms. She finally stirred and looked into my eyes questioningly.

"I'm really going to be the mother of the King of Camelot reborn? Oh, God help me."

"I'm sure he will," I said to reassure her. "He did ask me if it was alright and I said yes. I thought you'd be thrilled, Em."

"What? *God* asked *you*?"

My eyebrows shot up in surprise. "Well, of course. Why not?"

"Oh, Merlin, you're a powerful god, and my husband, and I love you, but sometimes you are so clueless."

I was trying to decide whether to be amused or insulted by her comment when I was distracted by the smell of burning meat.

After we breakfasted on overdone bacon and a couple of fried eggs, Emily dressed and left for work, and I decided to linger over a last mug of coffee. I was just taking the final swallow and considering my next step when Morry materialized in the kitchen looking frantic.

"Grandpa, Jim's gone, and I'm afraid something's happened to him!"

"Why would you think that?"

"He was supposed to meet me at the Red Rock Grill for lunch and he never showed up. I tried to call him on his cell and when he didn't answer, I went by the house. His car was in the driveway so I figured he'd stopped there before meeting me. But then I noticed that the front door was ajar, and his wallet was on the floor in the hallway. And, oh, God, there was a smear of blood on the door knob." Morry's face was lined with fear and concern for his friend.

I, too, was concerned for Jim. In his former incarnation as Guinevere Pendragon, he had been my friend and my queen in that long-ago time in Camelot. I was frustrated as well, since I hadn't seen the abduction happen, hadn't known anything about it. With my god powers now at their peak, I should have known beforehand, but I hadn't. However, I knew who had to be responsible for taking him: Morgana and the renegade wizards. Damn them for their treachery. They would be very sorry for their actions once I caught up with them. An avenging angel—or god—could do a lot of damage.

I grabbed my phone and quickly entered a number. As I waited impatiently for him to answer, I thought, *I hope you're available, Detective, because I need your help.*

CHAPTER 51

Moab, August 7, 2018, 12:45 PM

COLIN WAS BURIED IN PAPERWORK, an unfortunate by-product of his job, when his cell phone rang. Technically, he wasn't supposed to take personal calls at work, but in his position, he occasionally needed to be in touch with people who wouldn't necessarily be willing to call in on the official department phone line. He didn't recognize the number, but that wasn't unusual.

"Colin Campbell."

"Detective, I need you. Meet me at The Moab Herbalist at your earliest convenience." The call disconnected.

Colin was astonished. That accent was unmistakable—*Merlin* had actually called him. His experience the night before seemed unreal, a dream, and he had chalked it up to too many beers before he went to bed, combined with his overactive imagination.

He gazed at the mess on his desk and thought, *would I rather finish up this paperwork or go help King Arthur's sorcerer?*

Colin grabbed his crime scene kit, just in case, and was out the door so fast that several stray documents, disturbed by his passage, floated to the floor.

When he walked through the front door of the herb shop a few minutes later, the entire family turned to him curiously. He couldn't help but notice that Merlin's look-alike son, Seth, was present, wings, pointed ears and all. Even Merlin's wife and daughter were there, along with two other women, but he guessed that wasn't unusual, since all of them ran the store. He did a double take, though, when he caught a glimpse of pointed ears on two of them. Holy God, they weren't human either! He felt panicky being the only non-magical person in the room until he noticed the three men in the corner who seemed as left out of the circle as he was.

As if Merlin's family had all been privy to his thoughts, everyone smiled briefly at him.

“Detective, thanks for coming,” Merlin said. “You may already be aware of who they are, but let me introduce you to my wife, Emily, my daughter, Lumina, my mother-in-law, Rae, and my daughter-in-law, Sarah.” He indicated in quick succession the woman with golden-brown hair, a young woman with dark brown hair, then an older woman with red hair and another young woman, this one with reddish-blond hair. They were all lovely, and Colin murmured that he was pleased to meet them. They responded in kind.

“And these two are my sons, Derek and Seth, and the three gentlemen over there in the corner are—“

The man with multicolored hair interrupted heatedly, “Grandpa, I don’t see why we need help from *human* law enforcement. Why can’t you use your god powers to find Jim?”

Merlin frowned at his grandson, apparently wanting to reprimand him for his rudeness, but Colin could see how upset the young man was about his friend’s disappearance and didn’t take offense. However, the way he emphasized the word “human” made Colin suspect that the fellow *wasn’t.* He guessed he shouldn’t be surprised since Merlin probably wasn’t human either. And what did he mean about Merlin’s ‘god powers?’

“Morry, calm down. I promise we’ll find him. We need to utilize all avenues open to us in order to solve this. I don’t always see the obvious when someone close to the family is involved. If absolutely necessary, I can slow down or reverse time temporarily. And I should be able to heal Jim’s injuries as well, once we find him.”

Colin, already feeling both privileged and overwhelmed to be included in this unusual group of people, felt light-headed when he heard Merlin talk about manipulating time and using his powers to heal. But this paled in comparison to what Merlin revealed next.

“Besides, Colin isn’t totally human. He’s descended from Beli, and I magically enhanced his natural abilities last night. So he’s one of us now.” I glanced around and noticed that everyone besides Morry was willing to submit to my wishes and accept the detective into our midst whether they agreed with me or not, which was the way it should be.

I turned to Colin and saw his eyes widen at my statement. Apparently, it had not occurred to him what it meant to be the descendant of a god.

I nodded to my son to make the first overture. Although he had harbored negative thoughts about the detective in the past, Derek nodded back and reached out to shake Colin's hand.

Colin met Derek's grip. "It's good to finally meet you, Mr. Colburn, although I wish it had been under different circumstances."

"Good to meet you, too, Cousin."

Colin gaped. "What did you call me?"

"Cousin. Merlin is my father, so if you're descended from Merlin's brother Beli, that means we're related, right?"

"I…yeah, I guess so." Colin looked at me in confusion. "But if they're brothers, and Beli is the god of death, then—"

"I am the god of magic and healing," I broke in, giving Derek a quick, exasperated look. I hadn't wanted to overwhelm poor Colin anymore than he already was, but perhaps it was best to get it out in the open now.

As Colin stared into my eyes, aghast, I decided to go ahead and initiate the Seeing. This experience would generate a connection between the two of us that would come in handy as we searched for Jim.

"Colin, I am now going to show you your true self and all you have been before. Trust me, for you are my relation, my kin." My voice and tone both relaxed and mesmerized him, and we went swiftly into the depths of his being, into the past, back, and further back. Colin absorbed it all without question, completely fascinated.

Ironically, among his many incarnations, one in particular stood out: he had been one of the soldiers who had killed Beli and me in Edinburgh Castle on March 10, 1566.

That particular revelation shook me. Being executed was one of my least favorite experiences of all time, and I was tempted to confront him about it. But he had only been following orders, and had thrown the weapon down in disgust and regret afterwards. I realized that there would be no point in saying anything to him about the incident.

I continued to journey back with him until we reached his ancestor's beginning in ancient Inverness. Colin was able to witness his many times removed great-grandfather, Beli, and Molly, the woman Beli had loved, looking passionately into each other's eyes. Then I brought Colin back to the present, where he saw my family and me from an altered perspective.

"That was truly the most uplifting experience I've ever had! I don't know what to say." Colin looked at all of us in turn, really seeing us this time, as the magical, yet imperfect, beings we all were. Gods, demigods, Fae, reincarnated humans—it didn't matter. And then he surprised me. He knelt at my feet and took my hand in his.

"Merlin, I'm so sorry for what I did to you, and to Beli, in Edinburgh in the sixteenth century. I was ashamed then and I feel ashamed now. I was acting under orders from my superior, but that didn't make it right."

I smiled and pulled him to his feet. "I forgive you, Nephew."

Colin's face, which had been strained and troubled from the recollection of killing me, cleared. He sighed in relief.

"*Now* can we go?" Morry's impatience broke the spell that had been woven during the Seeing and Colin's subsequent apology, and I began giving instructions to everyone, including the knights. Ryan, Gary and Percival, who obviously had ties to Jim in his previous incarnation as Guinevere, were longing to get out and start searching for him.

"I need to see the scene, ASAP," Colin cut in. His ability to take charge when appropriate was one of the reasons I had desired his assistance.

Leaving the rest to get organized, Morry and I accompanied Colin to the house. We listened while he ranted and raved about the scene being tampered with. Apparently, Morry had picked up the wallet and then disturbed the blood smear when he closed the door.

"How the hell do you expect me to do my job? Your fingerprints are all over the wallet and the doorknob. You probably obliterated the ones the abductors left!"

"Well, it's *my* house, so my prints are everywhere anyway,

Cousin." Morry was practically frothing at the mouth as he spat out that last word.

Grandson, I know your concern for Jim is making you angry with the detective, but I'm asking you to cooperate and not make matters worse.

Morry took a calming breath and ran a hand across his eyes. *I'm sorry, Grandpa.*

You should be apologizing to him, not to me.

He nodded and turned to Colin, who had been looking back and forth between the two of us with a perplexed frown.

"I'm sorry I've been rude to you, Detective. Please tell me what you need me to do at this point."

While Colin talked to Morry, I reviewed the instructions I had given my sons before we left the shop. I had sent both Derek and Seth out to scour the area from the air, admonishing them to use their invisibility spells and any other magic necessary to keep others from detecting them. It certainly wouldn't do to have the entire population of Moab and innumerable tourists witnessing two men with wings, one in a National Park Service uniform, soaring above their heads. Neither would it be a good idea to alert the perpetrators that we were searching for them. After my sons had departed, I sent a silent prayer to my father that the two of them would refrain from attacking each other.

I mentally gave myself a shake and focused on the current moment. Colin had finished collecting forensic evidence, so I gave him a brief description of the people I suspected of abducting Jim. When Colin indicated that he had done as much as he could do at the scene and had slung his kit over his shoulder, I teleported him back to his office to evaluate the meager evidence. The Moab City Police Department had a very small crime scene investigation unit, so Colin usually did the majority of the work himself.

As I released the detective from my grip on his forearm, he groaned and took a shallow breath. "Holy cow, Merlin. Do you travel that way all the time?"

"No, not all the time. Quite often I walk. Sometimes I fly," I reminded him. I noticed that Colin was clutching his stomach, and

I realized that he was experiencing the same nausea that Sarah had until I'd fixed it for her.

"Here, let me take care of that." I touched him lightly and a small burst of god Light took care of the problem.

He glanced into my eyes then down at his stomach, and he looked startled.

"What did you do?"

"I fixed the problem, of course."

"Oh. Well, thanks. Okay, I need to get to work. I'll call you when I find out anything. It's usually nowhere near as fast as it seems on TV, I'm sorry to say. If whoever grabbed your friend wasn't wearing gloves, we can always hope his fingerprints are in the system. I'm also going to call in a favor with the Grand County Sheriff's Department. Hopefully they'll be able to locate the group you mentioned."

"Thank you for your help, Colin."

"My pleasure, Uncle," the detective said shyly, his swarthy face glowing with my gift of youthful vigor.

I nodded solemnly and teleported out of his office.

CHAPTER 52

Moab, August 7, 2018, Midafternoon

Derek had to admit that Seth was helpful when he had experienced some difficulties during the flight. He'd been so excited about flying the night before that he'd never thought that there might be a learning curve involved. He and Lumina hadn't attempted anything particularly complicated, so he had just assumed that it would be easy to leap into the sky and flap his wings like a bird as he followed Seth.

No that easy tae fly, is it, Brother? Seth's accented voice in his mind reminded Derek that his brother could hear his thoughts. *Yer lucky ye didna have to feel the pain as yer wings burst through the skin of yer back.*

Derek glanced over at his Fae sibling as they glided on warm air currents over the Sand Flats area. He couldn't help but notice the trace of envy he heard in Seth's voice. He *had* been very lucky. He couldn't imagine his wings, which were definitely attached to his back next to his shoulder blades, erupting out of his body. He shivered slightly in horror at the thought.

Seth looked over at Derek impatiently. *Ye needna feel sorry for me. I was a small child at the time and ma wings werena fully formed.*

But his own situation was different, Derek realized. He sensed that his wings existed in another dimension, so when he retracted them or called them forth, it wasn't into, or out of, his body at all, even though it appeared that way. So they never would affect the skin of his back. And he suspected that Seth would never be able to retract his wings, because they existed only in *this* dimension. Of course, Seth could choose to hide his wings using magic, but they were still *there*, so if you knew where to touch him, you'd feel them.

Derek took another quick look at his brother, who frowned at him questioningly, and he decided he'd better focus on flying.

They were circling around, planning to skirt the edge of the La Sal Mountains and fly over Castle Valley toward the Colorado River, when he heard a faint voice in his head.

Hurry, Derek. Jim Singleton is dying.

Ken?

Yes. An indistinct image of his dead lover hovered off to his right. *It's really hard for me manifest up in the air, for some reason. And since when do you have wings?*

Since last night. But we can talk about that later. Right now, we need to find Jim before it's too late. Do ya know where he is?

You passed him a ways back. He's somewhere near that sandstone ridge called The Lion's Back. You know, the one they closed to off-road vehicles years ago because it's so dangerous.

Ken started to fade out entirely.

Wait, buddy, don't leave yet—you need to show us exactly where Jim is! Derek silently implored the ghost of his friend.

It's really difficult…to stay visible…but I'll try.

Then don't. Just talk to me, okay?

Who are ye talking tae, lad? Seth's bewildered voice was clearer in Derek's mind than Ken's had been.

Never mind, I know where Jim is. Derek banked sharply to the left and flew swiftly back the way they had come. He was so intent upon listening to Ken's spectral voice that he didn't notice Seth following him.

I was out at Arches with Lumina, soaring over Ham Rock on the way to Delicate Arch, when I heard Derek's telepathic conversation with Ken.

Lumina.

Heard it, Dad. Let's go.

We changed course and headed southeast, bound for the rock formation called The Lions Back, which was located westerly of the hairpin turn near the entrance to the Sand Flats Recreation Area. But I realized that flying the entire way would take too long, so I made sure Lumina was on the same page and we teleported, wings and all.

Derek and Seth had just arrived at the east end of The Lion's Back, when they witnessed above them a truly remarkable sight:

Merlin and Lumina appearing with wings spread, backlit by the dazzling afternoon sun.

Derek's heart skipped a beat at the sight, faced as he was with the indisputable evidence of their divinity.

"An awe-inspiring sight, tae be sure," Seth said quietly. "But, Brother, ye are like them, aye? Angels, gods, demigods. There's no a lot of difference, ye ken?"

"Seth, you're Merlin's son too, so you're the same."

"Och, nay, Derek, I'm afraid ma Fae half is so dark that it overshadows the part of me I inherited from Da."

Derek stared at Seth's familiar face and wanted to agree with him, but when he saw resigned acceptance and a hint of sadness in his sibling's expression, he said something that surprised them both. "I don't care, you're still my brother."

Seth was dumbfounded. He hadn't expected Derek's response, since there had been such antagonism between them ever since they met. And Seth knew that he had deserved Derek's initial distrust.

They might have said more to each other, but by that time Merlin and Lumina had joined them on the ground, their wings retracted and out of sight.

"Let's find Jim, and leave the soul-searching for later," I said firmly, having heard their discussion in my mind. I was glad to have my sons finally bonding but this was not the time. "Use your magic to locate him."

It didn't take long with all of us searching. Jim's battered body was crumpled at the boulder-strewn base of the huge sandstone structure on the south side, partially hidden by a clump of sagebrush.

I gently lifted him into my arms and transported him instantaneously to The Moab Herbalist. Taking him to the hospital was obviously out of the question. First of all, there wasn't time, and second, I could do far more for him than any hospital could.

Jim and I appeared in the back room of the shop just as Emily, Rae and Sarah rushed in with blankets and bandages. Very thoughtful of them, but there was no time to utilize such things. I carefully placed Jim on the long table we used to blend the herbs and create the potions.

Morry teleported in right after that, clutching Colin's forearm, and Seth, Derek and Lumina appeared shortly thereafter. I sensed that Derek had already sent an urgent text to the knights to head back to the shop. But I knew they wouldn't arrive in time to see Jim again.

Everyone crowded around as I laid my hands on Jim's still body. He was very close to death; his heart had almost stopped and his lips were turning blue. He was covered with blood from head to toe from deep lacerations, many of which had been caused by the fall from the top of The Lion's Back. I magically removed most of the blood covering his face and body so that I could visually confirm what I had already sensed.

Morry's eyes swam with tears as he begged me to save him.

I intended to do so. But despite my knowledge and abilities as the god of healing, I knew that there was only one option open to me considering the extent and severity of Jim's injuries—and his ultimate destiny.

"Stand back," I commanded.

I lifted Jim into my arms, transformed into a brilliant, whirling globe of healing Light, and disappeared.

CHAPTER 53

Moab, August 7, 2018, 5:00PM

EVEN AFTER HIS RECENT MIND-BLOWING experiences, Colin couldn't believe his eyes. With the mortally injured man in his arms, Merlin became a large, pulsing ball of energy and then winked out of existence.

It seemed to Colin that only a few seconds passed before Merlin was abruptly standing in front of them again, holding a slim woman with curly brown hair in his arms, her clothes torn and bloodstained. Merlin carefully set her on her feet and she smiled reassuringly at Morry, who stood gaping at her in disbelief.

Colin looked around and realized that the gaze of every individual in the room was riveted on the woman standing next to Merlin. He didn't understand what had happened—who was she and where was Jim?

His attention was momentarily diverted when the front door opened and the three knights raced into the shop, the burly blond man in the lead. The blond halted abruptly at the connecting door as he caught sight of the woman, then rushed up and pulled her tenderly into his arms, tears streaming down his face.

"Gwen, oh my God, *Gwen.*"

"Lancelot, my dear, calm down, I'm all right," Guinevere said softly, as she smoothed her hand over Ryan's back. She looked up into my face as she comforted her ex-lover and beamed. "My old friend Merlin saved me, in more ways than one."

I returned her smile. "I've known how you felt for some time now, and given the need to perform major healing work on Jim's body and brain, I decided to give your female body back to you."

"I'm so grateful. I don't know how to thank you."

"You can thank me by taking good care of yourself so that when Arthur returns, you two can be reunited."

She nodded her head regally in assent.

Ryan Jones, also known as Sir Lancelot, cognizant that everyone present knew about his tumultuous history with Guinevere, backed carefully out of her arms and got down on one knee before her. Sir Gawain and Sir Percival followed suit.

"All hail, Queen Guinevere Pendragon of Camelot!" I proclaimed.

Colin's jawed dropped in complete and utter astonishment.

The assembled group stared mutely at the tableau in front of them. The young woman in the stained, ragged, men's clothes, her curls tangled and dirty, could not have appeared less regal, except for her bearing. She stood proudly before them, the three men still kneeling at her feet in obeisance.

"Okay, everyone can relax. Please, there's no need to treat me any differently now than you would if I was still a man." She glanced wryly at Morry, who hadn't moved any closer to her.

Guinevere insisted that the knights stand so that she could give each a hug, embarrassing all three of them.

"Your turn, Morry. Get over here, will you? I'm still Jim inside," she insisted. She even held her hand out to him and still Morry balked.

Guinevere pursed her lips in frustration and said quietly, "Merlin, what should I do? What if he doesn't accept me?"

"Give him a few minutes, Gwen. He'll come around." I could see that the two of them, who had been so close, needed a little privacy, so I herded everyone else into the front room of the shop, including the shell-shocked knights, and shut the connecting door.

Morry glanced over his shoulder to make sure they were really alone, then reluctantly stepped to the woman's side. Admittedly, she did look like a feminine version of his roommate, right down to the mannerisms and speech pattern, but…

"Uh, I really don't know how to behave around you now, Ji… uh, Aunt Guinevere." In his nervousness, he deliberately held back, not touching her.

Guinevere, emotionally overwrought by the trauma she had already suffered this day, burst into tears at his rejection, which promptly threw Morry into a panic.

"Oh, God, please don't cry, Jim, I mean, Guinevere!" Morry relented and took her into his arms as he would Emily, or his Aunt Lumina, holding her gently and patting her back.

Guinevere sighed and relaxed into his embrace. "I know it's highly inappropriate to say so, but do you realize how many times I've wanted you to hold me—and more—since we became roommates?"

Morry's cheeks turned red and he cleared his throat. "Yes, actually, I do. I was beginning to think you were gay." He gave her a quick squeeze and kissed her cheek, then carefully disentangled himself and took a step back.

"I wasn't really gay, but I kept dreaming about having sex with Arthur. It was very confusing." Guinevere wiped her eyes, then looked down at her breasts and briefly touched herself at the apex of her thighs. "This is the body, more or less, that I remember from my previous life, but I'd been born a man in this lifetime. I never really had any decent sexual experiences in my male body, which didn't exactly help my dilemma."

She looked up at Morry and grinned, her expression very much like Jim's at that moment. "Living with you, and watching you take your clothes off whenever you changed form, didn't help at all. Do you have any idea how well-built you are?"

Morry had already been feeling very uncomfortable and her comment was the last straw. His face flushed to an even darker red and he deflected her question by asking one of his own. "I don't know if we're going to be able to keep living together, do you?"

"No, but you're getting married soon, correct?"

"I almost forgot about that." Morry looked guilty. "I need to call Lainie and ask her what she wants to do. I guess you can stay until we work out the details."

Guinevere nodded. "Okay, that's fine with me. In the meantime, I'll start looking through the classified ads for an apartment."

Morry frowned. "Hey, what happens now with your job at the newspaper?"

"What do you mean? *Oh.*" She looked stricken. "Oh, no, you're going to have to tell everyone Jim is…gone."

Morry grimaced and said sadly, "I know. I'll talk to Merlin about it. Maybe he and Detective Campbell, who investigated your kidnapping, have already come up with a plan. And I could write an article, leaving out the supernatural details, of course, detailing your abduction and your death…" His voice faded out as he started assembling the facts into a coherent story in his mind.

My death. Oh, God, I actually died. Guinevere closed her eyes, shivering as she recalled the horrific pain and fear Jim had suffered prior to his fall and subsequent unconsciousness, and later the visceral knowledge that his mortal body had expired. After Merlin had healed and transformed her, and before he had rematerialized in the shop with her in his arms, he had merged his mind with hers to let her know everything that had happened during the search and after Jim's rescue. And in that quick joining of their minds, Merlin had seen the details of her abduction. Her face twisted with anguish as she recalled those details.

"Are you alright?" A concerned voice interrupted her thoughts.

She opened her eyes to see Morry's handsome face close to her own and she couldn't resist the temptation.

Reaching out, she drew him closer and kissed him thoroughly. The opportunity would never arise again, as he now belonged with Lainie, and she herself was still Arthur's queen, not to mention Lancelot's ex-lover, so she took full advantage of it.

At first Morry tried to pull away, but he finally accepted the inevitable and enjoyed the way her soft warm lips slanted across his. Eventually, they both came up for air.

"Is it wrong to say that my aunt is a fantastic kisser?" Morry thought his voice sounded rather husky, so he cleared his throat and tried to control the red flush that continued to bloom across his cheeks.

"Hmmm, maybe I should have just given in and kissed you before," Guinevere commented with a jaunty tilt of her head.

Morry looked horrified. "Before? But you were a man, and I don't kiss men on the lips!"

"I'm kidding. I would never, I mean, *Jim* would never have done that," she said. "On a different note, I am desperately in need of a shower and a change of clothes. And I've got to go shopping for something more feminine. Can you teleport me home?"

Morry nodded and got that familiar faraway look on his face as he communicated silently with his dad and his grandfather. "Sure, I'd be happy to take you home, Guinevere. Then I need to come back here. We're having a meeting."

"Okay, thanks." She paused and gazed into Morry's eyes for a second before glancing away. "Can you please call me Gwen?"

Morry smiled. "Yes, I can do that…Gwen."

He put his arms around her and took her home.

Morry set her down in Jim's bedroom—her bedroom—and gave her a quick kiss on the cheek before disappearing.

Gwen closed her eyes for a moment and sighed, weary to the bone from everything that had happened to her this day. She knew that there was a mess in the hallway that would have to be cleaned up sooner or later, but what she really needed first was a nice, rejuvenating shower and some clean clothes. She stripped off the blood-stained remnants of her clothing, and stuffed them into the wastebasket next to the nightstand. She had no idea what had happened to her loafers.

Naked, she slowly walked into the bathroom, looked at herself in the mirror and started to shake. It was real. She was no longer Jim Singleton. Her height was still five-six, she still had curly brown hair and brown eyes, and her features were similar to Jim's. But even though she still had all of Jim's memories, she wasn't Jim any more.

Now that she was back in Guinevere's body, she also remembered everything from Guinevere's life. She remembered her marriage to Arthur, and how she had betrayed him with Lancelot, not once but many times. And then, when both of the men she loved had perished at Camlann, she had done her duty and become Camelot's ruler. It had been a busy, difficult time, learning to rule the kingdom alone, although Merlin was constantly by her side, guiding and supporting her. And then even he had forsaken her when he decided to retreat to the Crystal Cave. Decades later, when she was an old woman, she had finally died quietly in her sleep, putting an end to her exalted, but achingly lonely, existence.

Letting go of her ancient memories, she turned her back on her reflection and grabbed a clean towel. She pulled the shower curtain aside, made sure she had everything she needed to clean herself head to toe, and then turned on the faucets. She pulled thc pin and warm water sprayed from the showerhead. As the blood and grime sluiced from her hair and her slender young body, she realized what else Merlin had bestowed upon her: time. Before Jim died, he had been thirty-nine years old. Now, restored to Guinevere's body, she looked about twenty. Merlin had given back to her almost twenty years.

Stunned, she realized he'd done it to give Arthur a chance to be born again and grow to adulthood. Merlin had promised that it wouldn't take more than five years of accelerated growth. After all, as Merlin's son, he'd be immortal and a demigod, and the rules of humanity wouldn't apply to him.

At the thought of seeing Arthur again, vibrantly alive in the current time, she felt her spirits lift. Enthusiastically shampooing her hair, she started singing an old Three Dog Night song, "Joy to the World," at the top of her lungs.

CHAPTER 54

Moab, August 7, 2018, 6:00 PM

As Morry regained his physical form in the front room of the herb shop, Colin had just begun to describe the forensic evidence he'd analyzed.

"I collected numerous fingerprints at the scene, and as I expected, most of them turned out to belong to the victim, Jim Singleton, and to his roommate, Mordred Colburn. We lucked out, however, and found a single fingerprint on the doorknob that belonged to someone who didn't live in the house. The name came up much faster than I expected, as did the results of the background check we did on the individual." Detective Campbell paused, apparently ruminating on the fact that I had magically enhanced the process which would normally take days rather than mere hours. He glanced at me questioningly, as if he was uncertain whether he should divulge the information.

I gave him the go-ahead with a brief nod. Of course, I knew what he was going to say, and I also knew that this knowledge would, unfortunately, cause my wife and mother-in-law considerable distress.

"The print we found belongs to a Mr. Jack Crandall, the father of Emily Crandall Reese and the estranged husband of Rae Crandall."

"*What*? You're saying my *dad* kidnapped and hurt Jim?" Em's voice was laced with scornful disbelief.

"No, Mrs. Reese, I'm not saying that at all," Colin stated patiently. "The presence of his fingerprint at the scene of the crime, overlaying the prints of the residents, proves that he was one of the last individuals in the house. Therefore, he's a strong suspect in the case. If nothing else, he participated in Jim's abduction and may have been involved in his murder."

Emily and Rae turned to look at each other, speechless with horror as they realized that Jim Singleton *was*, in fact, dead. He had been tortured and flung off a cliff to his eventual death, possibly by the person they both still loved.

Jim's re-created body was back now, with his soul—Guinevere's soul—intact, but the man they had known was never coming back, and Jack was somehow involved.

I knew something they did not, and wondered how I would ever tell them. Jack Crandall was gone forever as well. His mind, body and soul had been completely taken over by a very powerful god. And that god's name was Satan. He was also known as Samael, the angel of death, Hades, Lucifer and many other names. He was my brother whom I had always called Sam back in the early days of our creation. He had been the only one of us, ironically, that had golden blond hair when he took human form, and was indisputably the most resplendently beautiful of all the gods.

The most discontented of all of us, he had left the realm of the gods eons ago to wreak havoc in other realms. I sighed and returned my attention to Colin's report.

We somehow got through the rest of the meeting. Colin was careful to present all the details of his search for the missing group of wizards, who seemed to have dropped off the face of the earth. I suspected that their leader—and I didn't mean Morgana, who, despite her powers, was most likely just a figurehead—had a lair somewhere here in Grand County, or possibly in neighboring San Juan County, protected from discovery by god powers that rivaled, if not surpassed, my own.

After he had concluded the meeting, Colin approached me and apologized.

"What for, Detective? You've done your best on all levels of this investigation. It is obvious to me that my brother is behind this entire affair, and that being the case, there is no way you will be able to solve it without my help. I may even need to send for Beli and Llyr to assist us."

"I thought you said Satan is behind this mess?"

"That's right, I did."

"Satan is your *brother*?"

"Yes, unfortunately. And that makes him a relative of yours, as well."

"Jesus H. Christ!"

I cringed inwardly at Colin's use of that name. I really didn't want J.C. showing up here as well. He tended to keep a low profile, so it was doubtful he'd appear in Moab. I did suspect his ears were constantly burning at the inappropriate use of his name in this day and age. If he decided to come here, I hoped he would do so incognito. He was rather easy to recognize, with his golden aura and gold-edged white wings.

I glanced over at Emily, who was staring at me wide-eyed, having also seen that unmistakable image in her mind. She was the only one with whom I'd ever shared that monumental secret.

Derek and Seth had walked in on my conversation with Colin and heard my comments about Satan. I hadn't allowed my thoughts about my other brother to leak to anyone but Emily.

"Are you fuckin' kiddin' me? Satan is our *uncle*? Well, that's just swell," Derek said sarcastically, glancing at Seth and then at me, shaking his head in disbelief.

"Derek, some of ma Fae relatives make Satan look like a boy scout. We can handle this, *mo bràthair*."

I raised my eyebrows at Seth's declaration. My sons were apparently thick as thieves now if Seth was calling Derek "my brother" in Scottish Gaelic. "Don't underestimate him, you two. He's been a powerful force for evil for millennia, and even I don't make light of his abilities."

Derek narrowed his eyes at me. "And why have ya never mentioned this before, Dad?"

His tone of voice was extremely disrespectful and I narrowed my eyes right back at him. "I'm the god here, so I'll be the judge of what I need to tell you and what I don't. *Do you understand*?"

My temper was escalating and I wasn't sure why. I had never spoken to Derek this way before. I glanced at Seth out of the corner of my eye and caught a brief look of satisfaction on his face. The Fae took pride in manipulating others, and it appeared that my son's powers had been at work.

I took a deliberate breath and calmed myself, which effectively negated the spell's effect on me, then turned to Seth. "Well, congratulations."

"For what, Da?" The look of confusion on his face did not appear to be feigned but it had to be.

"For causing a rift between Derek and me. You can now report back to the Fae elders that you succeeded in your task."

For just a moment, he looked surprised, and then ashamed.

"I'm verra sorry," he muttered before he abruptly faded from view.

Derek clenched his fists and glared at me. "What the hell did ya mean by that, damn you?"

He was still under the manipulation spell. We would have come to blows if I hadn't clapped my hand against his forehead, countering Seth's magical influence. Derek, remembering every angry look, thought and word, stared at me in horror. "Dad? What just happened? And where'd Seth go?"

"I suspect he's made a quick trip to Inverness to report in with the Fae." I was disappointed beyond measure in Seth. "I hope he plans on coming back here, but I wouldn't count on it."

The pain and betrayal on Derek's face cut me to the quick, and I felt like reaching into the Fae realm with my god powers and yanking Seth back here to explain himself.

So I did.

CHAPTER 55

In the Fae Realm beneath Tomnahurich Hill

Seth MacAdam appeared in the midst of a meeting of the High Council, which included the Elven lords. Even though he had been summoned and belonged there by right of royal birth, he felt extremely uncomfortable surrounded by so many elders of the Light Court, especially after he had just betrayed his father and his brother by bringing dissension to their normally easy-going relationship.

"So, the son of Emrys has returned. What say you?"

"Aye, I have returned, but I refuse tae participate in this scheme any longer. The truth must be revealed. Myrddin Emrys is not the being ye have always claimed him tae be. He is no evil. He is the fully manifested god of magic and healing and a genuinely good man. 'Tis his brother Satan, or Hades, who is the evil one. Satan is on the verge of a major strike against ma father, so I request permission tae return tae the human realm. As ye ken, the child has been conceived and will need protection while in the womb. I need tae be there tae—"

Before Seth could finish his sentence, he found himself not in the jeweled hall of the High Council, but back in The Moab Herbalist, standing in front of an angry god, huge black wings spread wide.

Seth immediately prostrated himself before his father, his own wings flattened against his back in submission.

As soon as I decided to retrieve my son from the Fae realm, I quickly sent everyone home with instructions to wait for my call. Derek wanted to stay, but I didn't want him to witness his brother's chastisement at my hands.

With my god powers flowing completely unrestrained through my being, bringing Seth back to Moab was as easy as a thought. Then my son was on the floor at my feet, shaking in fear, and my first reaction was regret. The second was resolve. He could not continue on his current path; he would have to bend to my will to make amends.

And then the truth of the situation flashed through my mind in a burst of clarity. During his audience with the Fae High Council Seth had not betrayed me. He had stood up for me. And it was apparent that the Elven Fae who had been protecting Arthur's soul all along had sent Seth to investigate me, to make sure I would protect and nurture the young king.

Somehow, my brother had infiltrated the Fae realm and had planted the seeds of suspicion and fear about my worthiness to bring King Arthur back. And while they were not able to prevent the destined conception of the new king, they sent Seth in as a spy, and as a protector, in case I proved to be the evil god my brother had claimed.

"Seth, get up."

He slowly rose to his feet, his gaze on the floor and his shoulders hunched in shame and sorrow. "I'm so sorry, Da," he said hoarsely. "It was inexcusable of me tae deceive ye that way and I deserve tae be punished."

I didn't respond and he looked beseechingly into my eyes for the first time since I had called him back.

"Da, can ye forgive me?"

I sighed and retracted my wings. I looked down at my son from my god height of six feet eight and decided that I'd rather interact with him from my normal height, even if I had to look up at him.

Seth watched me let go of all of my godly attributes and become Merlin again. He smiled at me tentatively. "Sometimes I wish I could retract ma wings. They can be a pain in the arse."

I returned his smile, but withheld its usual warmth. "To answer your question, yes, I forgive you, but if you ever use that manipulation spell of yours again in this realm without my permission, I will not be so lenient."

"I understand, my lord," Seth replied formally, and went down on one knee in front of me, then gently took my hand in his and kissed it.

I felt his sincerity, but I couldn't help but wonder what the future would bring. Although I had attained that one moment of clarity with regard to Seth's interaction with the High Council and his honest intentions to safeguard Arthur, I could see nothing more.

I was aggravated beyond measure that my ability to sense my family's thoughts and futures was even more limited than usual, so I did something I would normally not consider doing. I sent a thought directly to God.

Seriously, Father? What in the world are you thinking?

In response, I heard a rumble of thunder that sounded suspiciously like laughter.

EPILOGUE

Moab, October 30, 2018 6:30 PM

Emily and I sat alone on the stone bench in our garden, holding hands and watching night fall around us. We were dressed warmly in jeans and sweatshirts, but the air was a chilly forty-nine degrees now that the sun had set. The crickets had given up their nightly serenade weeks ago. Across town, off of Bittle Lane, the flock of peacocks living in the vicinity still made their disconcerting cries. Emily said she couldn't hear them, but since my god powers had fully manifested, my senses were spectacularly enhanced and I heard *everything*. It was overwhelming and inconvenient, to say the least, and I'd had to make numerous adjustments in order to keep my sanity.

At the moment, however, I was experiencing a feeling of peace and tranquility. I knew it wouldn't last, but I could revel in it while it did.

Emily was watching the play of emotions on my face and leaned over to kiss my cheek. "I love you, god man."

I turned to her and smiled. "I love you too, Em. And I shall love you for all of eternity."

She leaned into me with a sigh of contentment, and I put my arm around her. We sat there a while longer as the sky darkened and lights came on in the house. I heard the clatter of pots and pans and the clink of utensils as Rae and Lumina started dinner and set the table.

Em shifted restlessly and I knew what was on her mind.

I waited for her to speak.

"I was just remembering when Jim was abducted and you arrived back at the shop with him in your arms. When you put him on the table, I was sure you were going to heal him right there, but then you picked him up, turned into a ball of Light and disappeared. When you came back, it was with Guinevere, not Jim, and that really upset me. What prompted you to do such a thing? I know you had to heal him, but why not just make him male again?"

I noted my wife's troubled expression and decided to tell her the details that I hadn't wanted to mention that day. "Jim had been cruelly tortured. He had been cut repeatedly, in a ritualistic fashion, so that every inch of him had sustained severe injuries. Not to mention that falling several hundred feet had caused numerous severe lacerations and broken his back. He had suffered massive blood loss. I literally had to re-create his body. And since he had been agonizing over his sexuality ever since he discovered he had the soul of Guinevere, I decided to re-create his body as a female. It's what he wanted."

"Oh, Merlin. My God, poor Jim."

"He died in my arms as I transformed into the Light. Since it was destined for Guinevere to return for Arthur anyway, I just stepped up the time frame. It was meant to be this way, Em."

"Well, he's, I mean, *she's* clearly happy now, and she even got her old job back, posing as Jim's 'sister,' Gwen Singleton."

I chuckled. I thoroughly enjoyed having my old friend back in my life, and looked forward to the time when Arthur was born and grown to adulthood so they could be together again. Emily was skeptical that Gwen would want to wait that long, assuming that it would be decades before Arthur was ready to resume his worldly responsibilities. Em was wrong—it would only take a few years—but I didn't need to tell her that yet. She'd had a hard time accepting Lumina's growth from newborn to adult in only a few years, so she wouldn't be pleased when it happened to Arthur as well.

I reached out and caressed Emily's baby bump, which at three months was larger than normal for a human, but just the perfect size for the growing immortal demigod inside of her.

Emily smiled when I left my hand splayed out on her belly. She could already feel Arthur moving in her womb, responding to my touch.

I sensed that she was getting cold and I conjured a warm, blue fleece jacket with a hood for her.

"Oh, thanks! It's a little chilly." She paused for a moment to admire the feel and fit of the jacket and then continued shyly. "Do you suppose we could fly up to the Rim for a few minutes? I'm still amazed that you have wings."

"Say no more, my dear." I stood up and moved away from the trees to give my wings room to expand, then called them forth. The sudden weight on my upper back always gave me a start, but manifesting my wings made me feel more complete, my transition more of a reality. I beckoned to Emily and she stood up, then stepped into my embrace. I lifted her effortlessly and leaped into the sky, mindful of the various power lines overhead.

It was thrilling to feel the movement of my wings as they pumped up and down, and to hear the quiet whoosh of air through the feathers. I'd forgotten how much I loved to fly this way, to soar without limits. I threw my head back and laughed for the sheer joy of it.

Emily felt safe in Merlin's arms, held against his warm chest as he winged his way towards the spot on the Rim where he always liked to watch over the city. His city.

She could sense the Light of the gods sustaining his body, and the power in him almost overwhelmed her. And seeing the joy and serenity on his face as his enormous black wings carried them higher in the sky, she finally believed that he really was a son of God.

As I landed at our destination and gently set my wife on her feet, I knew she was reconciled to the truth at last. Admittedly, the story of my life was an outrageous tale that most people would never believe. But Emily was not most people. She had been born to be with me, and she had experienced things during our lives together that most partners would never have understood, tolerated or accepted.

It was colder on the Rim than it had been in our backyard, so I carefully wrapped my wings around Em to keep her warm. I wasn't cold and hadn't bothered with a jacket. Years ago, I realized that I could regulate my body temperature, but with my transition, I no longer had to think about it at all. It was entirely automatic.

As I stood gazing down on the lights of Moab, my pregnant wife snuggled against me, I thought about the momentous events our family had experienced in the past few months.

First and foremost, I had made that final transition to being the only fully manifested god on this planet, easily and without fanfare.

And secondly, the quest to find the portal through which Arthur would come into this modern world had officially come to an end. The portal was Emily. And Arthur would be my son this time, as well as my king.

Jim's abduction and subsequent murder had triggered several events that also related directly to Arthur's return. Guinevere was with us now instead of Jim. She was ecstatic to have her body back and soon, her husband. We were saddened at Jim's loss, but at the same time pleased to have Gwen with us. In addition, our ranks now officially included a local law enforcement officer, Detective Colin Campbell, who had wholeheartedly dedicated himself to my service, and who would eventually become Arthur's assistant. That he had also recently become my devotee warmed my heart and vindicated my decision to include him in our ranks.

Several things continued to trouble me deeply. The fact that Morgana and her gang of renegade wizards were still unaccounted for, not to mention the knowledge that Satan was their true leader, was the first thing. The second was that I still had not been able to resolve the situation with Adrestia. How was I to banish Nimue forever without destroying what was left of my daughter's soul, when the two seemed to be irrevocably interconnected? It seemed that I would have to maintain the status quo, at least until after Arthur was born, though it went against the grain to put off the resolution of this issue yet again. I had previously come up with a plan that seemed to be the most logical course of action, but then I realized that I was missing some key parts to the puzzle. I hoped for clarity on resolving both of these issues in the near future.

There were several happy occasions as well. In mid-August, Morry and Lainie decided to go to Reno to get married and forego the traditional religious ceremony. As Morry pointed out to his fiancée, why would the great-grandson of God need a church wedding to make their relationship official? When Morry had introduced Lainie to the family, and those of us with wings had displayed them to her, that overwhelming proof of our divine origins had convinced her.

When the newlyweds returned, Derek and Sarah helped to organize a reception for all four of them. During the festivities, Derek confessed to me that he and Sarah had delayed their wedding for years, wanting to wait for my return. But in light of my continued absence, they had finally married in a simple ceremony witnessed by family and friends. He felt guilty that they had not held out for my presence, but I assured him that he had done the right thing.

"Merlin?" Em's voice jarred me from my thoughts.

"Yes, my love?"

"It's time to go home."

I kissed her cheek, picked her up, and glided serenely with her down to our back yard. I set Emily down carefully, retracted my wings and opened the door for her.

"Dad, guess who's here?" Lumina met us in the kitchen with a wide smile on her face. I already knew but didn't want to spoil my daughter's enjoyment of the surprise.

My brother was standing in the living room with a man that I knew very well. Llyr gave me a wink and disappeared.

I walked up to the man, we grasped each other's forearms, and I said in Old British, "Welcome to the twenty-first century, Sir Leon."

AUTHOR'S NOTE

It is always a bit of a challenge when an author places fictitious characters based on legendary figures into real, historical locations or situations. Historical references are many times disputed, found to be based on assumptions, or have been determined to be pseudo-historical—in other words, pure fantasy. This seems to be the case with Geoffrey of Monmouth's *History of the Kings of Britain,* which was written around 1136.

In writing the Merlin in Moab series, I have taken the liberty of creating a new approach to a legend that has persisted for many centuries.

I have always loved the legend(s) of Merlin and King Arthur, but there are aspects and much-debated details that always bothered me, and I decided to change them to suit myself. My characters are now full-fledged and real and live in my head, often directing, changing and vehemently opposing the plans I'd originally made regarding the direction the stories should go. Honestly, it's hard to get a word in edgewise sometimes.

When I went to Glastonbury in 2013, I saw a sign in the ruins of the old abbey, which indicated that King Arthur and Guinevere were buried there. This was posted at the direction of King Edward I (my 22nd great-grandfather, by the way) because he was a fan of the Arthurian legend. So I come by my interest quite naturally!

The modern countries of Scotland, Wales and England obviously did not exist in the fifth century, but for clarity, I use the modern terms for some cities and areas and hope that those of you who are students of history will forgive me—artistic license, and all that. Merlin, coming from the old Roman town of Maridunum, would have been from the Kingdom of Dyfed; in fact, he was descended from the King of Dyfed in my story.

Trying to imagine what it would have been like to be dumped in Edinburgh at the time of Mary, Queen of Scots, was quite a challenge. But having climbed to the top of Arthur's Seat (in a very cold, stiff breeze, I might add), and having toured through the Palace of Holyroodhouse and its grounds, I could put myself in Emrys's shoes. And Edinburgh Castle, although quite different now than it would have been in the sixteenth century, is extremely impressive. The view from its southern ramparts is fabulous.

Regarding my use of a few Irish Gaelic (pronounced GAY-lick) and Scottish Gaelic (pronounced GAH-lick) words and phrases, the source of my information was mostly the internet, although I do thank my friend Seamus Hannigan for his help—and his patience. I studied Irish Gaelic for a few years on my own, using the website www.bitesizeirish.com (based in Limerick, Republic of Ireland), but I am nowhere near fluent and haven't had time to pursue it recently. I am fascinated with the language, and some day, I hope to attend classes in Dublin.

In response to questions regarding spells Merlin and his family have been known to utilize, I have listed a few common ones below and how *I* pronounce the words. I never studied Latin, so the correct pronunciation may be different. Since this is fantasy and not a language lesson, please feel free to pronounce the words any way you like.

Oblitus (oh-BLEE-toos). This spell comes from the Latin word meaning "(you) forget." Our English word, obliterate, means to remove from recognition or memory, so it seems appropriate.

Adolebit (ah-doh-LEE-bit). This spell comes from the Latin word for "burn."

Extinguo (ehx-TING-gwoh). This one comes from the Latin word meaning "to extinguish" or "to put out" (like a fire).

Desino (deh-SEE-noh). This spell causes the subject to be frozen in place. Our English word desist means "to cease to proceed or act."

I've had many requests for a genealogy, as Merlin's family connections can be rather confusing. You can find Merlin's family tree here: **http://carylsay.com/genealogy/**

And one last comment. I have cited various sources of the

information I used in my books, but the bottom line is that any errors are mine alone.

Caryl Say

CARYL SAY is a writer living in Moab, Utah. She is an avid reader of several different genres, including fantasy, science fiction, mystery and paranormal fiction. She enjoys working on her family tree and travels regularly to Ireland, Scotland and Wales. She is currently working on the fourth book in the Merlin in Moab series. You may contact Caryl by email at carylsay.author@gmail.com, on her website: www.carylsay.com, or on Facebook: www.facebook.com/AuthorCarylSay.

THANK YOU for reading *The Shape of Time*.
As a special bonus for Merlin in Moab fans, I
have a short story available on my website.

You can get it here: **http://carylsay.com/tsot-bonus/**

A SPECIAL REQUEST…

Would you be so kind as to leave an honest review of this book on Amazon? Reviews help authors gain more visibility online and more importantly, your review helps other readers like you find books they will enjoy.

Many thanks,

Caryl

Made in the USA
Columbia, SC
09 May 2022

60033673R00193